THE LAST MASTERPIECE

THE LAST MASTERPIECE

THE MASTER'S PROTÉGÉ TRILOGY BOOK III

ELEANOR CHANCE

Barlington
Publishing

Published by Darlington Publishing

eBook ISBN: 978-1-951870-19-5

Paperback ISBN: 978-1-951870-20-1

Hardcover ISBN: 978-1-951870-21-8

Cover Design by Dissect Designs, London

❀ Created with Vellum

FROM THE AUTHOR

Historical Information

Naming Conventions: Italian women during the Renaissance did not take their husband's surname when they married. The father's surname was passed on to his children. This continues to be the convention in Italy today.

The Guilds: The majority of artists during the Renaissance belonged to the merchant class, and in the fifteenth century, were considered more craftsmen than inspired artisans. Master artists owned workshops and operated as businessmen as well as creators. They usually employed several people, including apprentices. Just as other merchants and craftsmen, these artists were required to belong to one of a number of guilds in order to secure commissions and sell their artwork. These guilds were powerful and had their own system of laws and regulations. They governed all aspects of merchant business and also religious aspects of artists lives.

CAST OF CHARACTERS

Celeste Gabriele, Duchessa: (41) Wife of Luciano Vicente, Mother, Revered Master Artist

Luciano Vicente, Duca: (51) Husband of Celeste Gabriele, Father, Revered Master Artist

Mateo Vicente: (20) Adopted son of Luciano and Celeste, Luciano's heir

Angela Vicente: (15) Daughter of Luciano and Celeste

Cristina Vicente: (15) Daughter of Luciano and Celeste

Luca Vicente: (13) Son of Luciano and Celeste

Elena Vicente: (11) Adopted Daughter of Luciano and Celeste, Birth daughter of Veronica Gabriele (Celeste's Sister)

Livia: (42) Beloved handmaid and friend to Celeste Gabriele

Prior Girolamo Savonarola: (44) Historical Figure, Fifteenth century friar and one-time religious and political leader of Florence

Messer Mancini: (40) Leader of the *Arrabbiati*

Portia Gabriele: (62) Beloved Aunt of Celeste Gabriele (Father's Sister), Mother of Tomaso Gabriele

Marco Gabriele: (37) Brother to Celeste Gabriele

Adrianna di Calis: (28) Wife of Marco Gabriele

Jacopo Gabriele: (35) Brother of Celeste Gabriele

Gisella Carbone: (29) Estranged wife of Jacopo Gabriele

Veronica Gabriele: (34) Sister of Celeste Gabriele

Bianca Gabriele: (28) Sister of Celeste Gabriele

Enrico de Fazio: (35) Husband of Bianca Gabriele

Sandro Gabriele: (26) Brother of Celeste Gabriele

Tomaso Gabriele: (17) Son of Portia Gabriele

Elisabetta Vicente: (45) Sister to Luciano Vicente

Giulio Ferretti: (50) Husband of Elisabetta Vicente

Angelica Vicente: (42) Sister to Luciano Vicente

Silvio de Santis: (49) Husband to Angelica Vicente

Diana Vicente: (39) Sister to Luciano Vicente

Umberto Donato: (47) Husband to Diana Vicente

Michelangelo Buonarroti: (22) Actual Historical Figure: Master painter and sculptor

Leonardo da Vinci: (44) Actual Historical Figure: Italian Polymath

Sandro Botticelli: (51) Actual Historical Figure: Florentine master painter

Piero Leoni, Duca: (42) Longtime friend to Celeste Gabriele

Giuseppe Leoni: (9) Piero Leoni's son and heir

Serena Leoni: 7 – Piero Leoni's daughter

Rosabella (Rosa) Leoni: (31) Piero's sister, longtime friend to Celeste Gabriele

Salvatore Fasciano: (45) Art patron and collector

Carlo Riva: (47) Trusted manservant to Celeste Gabriele

Filippo: (52) Trusted Valet to Luciano Vicente

Bardo: (25) Loyal Footman to Luciano

PART I

VENICE, FLORENCE & ROME: 1496-1497

CHAPTER ONE

VENICE 1496

CELESTE GABRIELE PULLED her cloak tighter against the chill as the gondola glided along the canal. The only sounds rising from the mist over the water were the shrieks of gulls and the rhythmic splash of the gondolier's oar. The previous days had been unseasonably bright and clear for Venice in winter, but that morning the weather had turned gray and dismal to match Celeste's mood. The dampness made her forty-year-old joints ache and her mind drifted to her younger days.

The bleak weather reminded her of the day ten years earlier when she and her brother, Marco, delivered their disgraced sister to the only convent near Venice willing to accept her. The two of them were now on their way to take Veronica home. After another week in Venice, Celeste would take her sister back to Florence. Celeste doubted that allowing Veronica out of her sequestered life was wise, but she'd left them with no other choice.

"You're quiet this morning, sister," Marco said, startling her out of her musing.

Celeste sat straighter and turned to face him. "Please, tell me again what our sister wrote in her letter."

"Veronica insists she's ready to leave the cloistered life and do her part to make the wicked world a holier place. She refuses to live another day behind walls and threatened to escape if we refused to come for her. The Reverend Mother wrote that she wouldn't have stopped Veronica from going as she has 'become a constant source of vexation in recent days,' as she put it."

"I'm sure all the Sisters will miss of her is the generous monthly stipend we've paid for her support all these years," Celeste muttered. "Marco, do you believe what we're doing today is best for Veronica in the long run? Shouldn't we have tried harder to discourage her leaving?"

Marco's look told her all she needed to know of his feelings on the matter.

"I'm not sure removing Veronica from the convent is right for any of us, but she's forced our hand. What else can we do, Celeste?"

She pondered his question for a moment, wondering if ten years had been long enough to calm Veronica's reckless spirit. Celeste wasn't sure an eternity would have been enough for her proud, obstinate sister to change. Not once since the early days after Veronica entered the convent had she ever expressed a desire to leave, so the sudden insistence to go had caught them all off guard. Celeste assumed her sister would spend the rest of her life sequestered and never expected to lay eyes on her again. This was the customary way of dealing with women from respectable families who caused shame and humiliation, so she'd felt no need to question it. As much as she'd missed Veronica, she believed the convent was the best place for her.

Buried memories of those turbulent days a decade earlier surfaced unbidden in Celeste's mind. Veronica had been married to Duccio Zani, a decent nobleman with a modest country estate. They had only recently welcomed their daughter, Elena, to the family, but Veronica was restless, immature, and dissatisfied with her life. She longed for the nightly dinner parties and glittering galas she'd enjoyed in Florence before becoming with child. Celeste had been away on an extended art exhibition tour, so her poor husband, Luciano, had been left to deal with her rebellious sister.

One fateful night, Veronica abandoned her husband and infant daughter to run off with an unscrupulous man who impregnated her, then discarded her in a country public house, many days' ride from Florence. After working as a serving wench to earn money for her survival, she landed with a band of highwaymen who used her nightly to satisfy their lustful desires.

It was nothing short of a miracle Veronica managed to escape and make her way to Venice. Celeste and Marco nursed her to health but were left with no other choice than to exile Veronica to a convent. She'd given birth to a son there, and the Sisters graciously placed the baby with a childless Venetian couple. Celeste's family had no knowledge of the boy's whereabouts.

After learning of these scandalous and tragic events, Duccio vowed to kill Veronica if he ever again laid eyes on her. It was a despicable threat, but in the eyes of the law, he would have been well within his rights to carry it out. He managed to persuade the Church to grant him an annulment, thus erasing his marriage to Veronica in the eyes of God and man. With the stroke of a quill, Veronica became a person without inheritance or a family name. She was just one of hundreds of other disgraced women, hidden away in convents to do penance and live their remaining days in solitary service to God.

Once his petition was granted, Duccio promptly disowned their daughter Elena as well. Luciano willingly adopted her, and Celeste and Luciano had raised their niece as their own daughter. In the intervening years, Duccio had married a hearty but docile woman who had borne him three robust sons. Reports were she was content to live a placid life in the Florence countryside, something Veronica had been unwilling to do.

Celeste prayed Duccio had abandoned his plans to retaliate against Veronica. If not, her life could be in danger once she left the safety of the convent. Men never seemed to forget acts of infidelity committed against them, though they saw no shame with participating in those acts themselves. Celeste shook her head to banish such thoughts as they neared the convent. No point in inviting trouble where there was none.

"We can't allow Veronica to take charge of her own fate," she finally said. "We all remember how disastrous that was the last time. Is there no way to persuade your dear wife to let our sister live with you in Venice?"

Marco removed his cap, and a chill breeze lifted his dark curls as he shook his head. "The decision is ultimately mine, but I won't ignore Adrianna's wishes. She would be the one forced to cope with Veronica daily while I work long hours in the workshop. I'm seldom home before late evening, which I know you understand."

"Perfectly," Celeste said, smiling.

"My wife is tasked with management of a large household staff and our four young children. Our marriage has been less than blissful these past years. I'd hate to do anything that might drive a further wedge between us. I'm convinced that living in Florence under your watchful care is the best place for our sister."

"I pray you're right, Marco. Though many years have passed since she lived in Florence, I fear she'll seek out acquaintances who will draw her into that old reckless life."

"Let us not get ahead of ourselves. We must see Veronica before we judge her. I am still hopeful these many years of religious influence have changed our poor sister for the better.

Have you forgotten her letter that stated she plans to devote herself to aiding the poor and downtrodden? She professes to have no interest in the extravagant and wanton ways of the aristocratic class in Florence. Besides, Veronica's former friends will want nothing to do with her after the scandal she caused."

Celeste gave a sarcastic laugh. "Veronica has never been one to resist the lure of the *wanton rich*, as she calls them. Only time will show if her transformation is true and lasting. If Veronica truly means to live a humble, devout life, our zealous leader, Prior Savonarola, will find an enthusiastic new disciple in her, but my primary fear is that if she becomes embroiled in another scandal, she won't just face the cloister. She may end up paying with her life." Celeste gave a backhanded wave. "But enough of this talk. I'm already gloomy this morning, brother. Let's speak of our favorite subjects, art, and our families. How is the opening of your workshop progressing?"

Marco stroked his beard. "Your Luciano makes running a workshop look effortless. I'm finding it more of the struggle."

Celeste shook her head. "Don't compare yourself to my husband. By the time you entered his workshop, he'd been managing it for many years. He's told me of similar struggles he suffered in those early days. Competition among artists is fierce in Venice."

"You know better than most that's true everywhere. We artists tend to be sensitive and driven. That's a challenging combination."

Celeste chuckled at that. "Truer words were never spoken. You're an exceptional master painter, Marco, and I couldn't be prouder. Be patient with yourself. I have no doubt of your future success."

"Only because I'm following in the trail you blazed. It's a blessing that artistic talent runs in families, like with the Bellini brothers who mentored me. Speaking of artistic families, how is Angela's apprenticeship coming along?"

Celeste smiled fondly as she thought of the eldest of her twin daughters. Angela had shown a talent and interest for painting from an early age. Luciano had taken her on as an apprentice two years earlier. At fifteen, she was on pace to soon pass both her parents' abilities.

Her eyes glistened as she said, "She's a remarkable artist, far more talented than I. There's no limit to the heights she'll attain."

"I find it difficult to imagine anyone with talents greater than yours, sister. You've always undervalued your abilities, but I'm delighted to hear of Angela's progress. Is Cristina dealing with the situation any better?"

Celeste shrugged. "Perhaps marginally. She's always envied the closeness between Luciano and Angela from their mutual love of art, but she's finally coming to understand the love her father has for her. She's also becoming a beautiful and accomplished young woman in her own right. I'm working to help her understand she doesn't have to aspire to be an artist to have value. She'll make an exceptional wife someday if Luciano can ever bear to part with her."

Marco laughed, and said, "As the father of two daughters, I understand perfectly."

"How are you finding it being the father of four darling children since the baby's birth?"

Celeste's anxiety lessened as Marco proudly chattered on about his two sons and two daughters. She was pleased he'd taken to fatherhood so effortlessly and hadn't followed in the footsteps of their worthless drunkard of a papa. Hearing the contentment in his voice made her long to return to her own darlings in Florence. No matter how the world may be darkening around her, she'd always found her solace waiting to welcome her home.

When the gondola finally pulled up to the landing, Marco said, "Here we are," then stood to help Celeste from the boat.

The coach that would carry them the rest of the way to the convent waited just beyond the landing. They settled in for the ride, but Celeste's anxiety returned the instant the convent came into view. At the convent gate, the Sister who had answered the bell asked them to wait outside while she went to fetch their sister. Since Marco had written to inform her that Veronica wished to leave the cloister, Celeste had imagined what their reunion would be like, but she had no idea what to expect. She'd hoped to remain calm, but instead, fiddled nervously with a tassel on her belt. Veronica was thirty-four, and Celeste wondered if her appearance had altered much and how her sister would react when she saw them.

"Calm yourself, sister," Marco said with a laugh. "It's just Veronica."

As she gave him a weak smile and took three long breaths, the iron gate swung inward, and the Sister stepped into the opening beside a woman Celeste hardly recognized. There was a trace of Veronica in her facial features, but beyond that, she was a stranger. Short, cropped ends of her once long and lush brown hair peeked out from beneath her coarse cap. She wore a heavy but simple light brown dress and worn black shoes. Veronica had always been the most beautiful of the two of them and their youngest sister, Bianca, and this had not changed despite her years of menial labor.

The most astounding change was in her demeanor. She gazed at Celeste and Marco in an attitude of piety and peace. Who was this woman that had replaced their haughty, defiant, and taciturn sister?

They stood staring at each other without speaking until Marco broke the silence by retrieving her canvas satchel from the Sister at the gate.

Veronica approached Celeste with her head bowed and sank to her knees on the damp ground. "I am so sorry for the pain I have caused over the years. I am eternally indebted to you and your good husband for agreeing to take me into your home, Signora. It is a kindness I will never deserve nor be able to repay. Consider me your servant from this day forth."

Celeste continued to stare at her in stunned silence, unsure if Veronica's behavior was pretense or if she was in earnest. She reached down and took her hands to help her to her feet. "Nonsense," she said as she embraced her. "You are a Gabriele and my sister. You must never again speak of being my servant."

Veronica pulled away and studied her with a look Celeste couldn't decipher. "If that is your wish, sister."

Marco dropped her satchel and threw his arms around Veronica. "Enough of this acting so formal and serious. It's just us."

Veronica nodded, then gave him a hint of a smile. Celeste noticed the Sister watching them from the gate. As they locked eyes, Celeste gave her a smile of thanks, then handed her a small bag of silver coins. "This is for your continued and devote service to the poor."

The Sister accepted her gift and bowed solemnly before closing the gate on Veronica's former life.

Celeste linked her arm in Veronica's and urged her toward their carriage. "It's freezing out here. Let's get to the warmth of the carriage."

As they walked, Veronica gazed in wonder at the world she hadn't seen for more than ten years. Celeste tried to imagine how she felt as she experienced these sensations for the first time in so long, and hoped she'd soon adjust to her new life.

Celeste also wondered why Veronica was so sedate and emotionless when she was brimming with love and joy at reuniting with her sister. She did her best to draw Veronica into conversation as the carriage carried them to the waiting gondola but gave up after all she gave were one or two-word answers. It finally occurred to Celeste that her sister had likely rarely spoken while in the convent, so she left her in peace. The three of them traveled the remainder of their journey in uneasy silence.

Celeste noticed Veronica tense when the palazzo came into view, but she was glad to have arrived back at her second home. It would be a relief to have help from Marco's family in dealing with Veronica's transition. If Adrianna wouldn't assist her, Celeste had an entire clan of Gabrieles to rely on.

Florence

In the pre-dawn darkness, Luciano reached for Celeste, but her side of the bed was empty and cold. Remembering she'd left for Venice ten days earlier, he frowned and rolled onto his back. After twenty years of marriage, he found it more difficult to sleep without her at his side. He was glad their separations had become far less frequent in recent years.

"Hurry back to me, my love," he whispered as his manservant came into the room. "Morning, Filippo. What time is it?"

"Half past eight, sir," Filippo said as he held a sealed note out to Luciano. "Messer Mancini's page has just arrived with a letter for you."

Luciano groaned as he reached for the letter. "Why can't that man leave me in peace?"

"I wouldn't know, sir. Should I bring your breakfast?"

Luciano nodded and waved him off before reluctantly unfolding the letter. Just as he expected, Mancini was requesting a meeting. Luciano's answer to the invitation wasn't a simple matter of replying yes or no. Messer Mancini was a leading member of the *Arrabbiati*, the faction most capable of removing Prior Girolamo Savonarola from power in Florence.

Luciano's thoughts turned to the time two years earlier

when Savonarola rose to become the de facto leader of their city. Most Florentines favored Savonarola with his fiery sermons and his charismatic manner. Many had been overjoyed to see him put an end to Medici rule and hoped the rise of Savonarola would usher in new golden age for their city. It didn't take long to realize that wouldn't be the case. He began as a pious leader, devoted to the Church, but sadly, soon transformed into a fanatical ruler. He'd formed a cadre of spies from among his young followers to root out what he deemed evil acts committed by the citizenry. The resultant political unrest had forced Luciano into a precarious position.

Forming an alliance with the Arrabbiati could put him and his family in danger of reprisals from Savonarola, but Luciano feared he'd soon have no choice. He was a god-fearing man but didn't hold with clerics running the government. All he desired was to protect his family and reputation, manage his prosperous workshop, and paint works of beauty and truth. As a prominent Florentine nobleman, however, he couldn't hide in his workshop forever from the growing political strife now consuming the city. The time would soon come when he would have to choose sides.

He climbed out of bed and went to his writing desk to reply to Mancini's letter. He would meet with the man to hear what he had to say, but he'd make it clear he wasn't committing to the Arrabbiati just yet. He hoped to be able to bide his time to see the forces play out more.

When Filippo came in with his tray, Luciano handed him the sealed note. "Is Mancini's page waiting for a response?" When Filippo gave a quick nod, Luciano said, "Give that to the boy and tell him to deliver it directly into his master's hand. He's not to hand it to anyone else."

Luciano's gut tightened as he watched Filippo go. He'd made no promises to Mancini, but even meeting with the man was a risk. He realized he'd started down a road that could determine the course of his future. He prayed he would choose the path best for his family and the people of Florence.

Venice

Celeste held the door open to her sister's chamber but couldn't persuade her to cross the threshold. Veronica stood frozen, her eyes wide with terror and bewilderment. She'd been calm and gracious when she greeted Adrianna and her parents in the sala earlier and had thanked them stoically for allowing her temporary refuge. She hadn't resisted when Celeste took her arm and led her upstairs. It was only when Celeste opened the door that she became overwhelmed by fear.

Celeste held Veronica's cold hands in hers, and said, "What is it, sister? Nothing here will harm you. It's perfectly safe. You are home, my dearest."

Veronica pulled her hands free and backed away from the doorway. "No, Celeste. You're wrong. Evil lurks in that place. I sense a malevolent presence. I cannot enter."

Celeste stepped through the doorway and surveyed the room with her hands on her hips. She didn't see or feel anything amiss. She was exhausted, hungry, and had no patience for whatever game Veronica was playing. "There's nothing here. Come inside and see for yourself."

When Veronica raised her chin and crossed her arms, Celeste saw a flash of the sister she remembered. It did not reassure her.

"I'll not set foot in that room until you remove the vile paintings and proud adornments and remove the bed. I will sleep on the floor. I cannot countenance this vain finery." She leaned forward and peeked around Celeste. "Where is my satchel? I wish to hang my crucifix above the bed. And please, have Marco call Father Domenico to come exorcise the room and bless it."

Celeste gave an exasperated sigh, then marched into the hallway, nearly knocking Veronica over as she did. After calling for her longtime faithful maid, Livia, she said, "If you wanted the life of the convent, why were you so eager to leave? You know what our lives are. You can't expect us to completely change our ways."

Veronica stepped closer to Celeste and laid her hand on her shoulder. "I have no expectations from the rest of you. I only ask this for myself. I've made a vow of poverty, which I intend to honor."

Livia appeared from around the corner and joined them in the hallway. She curtsied to Veronica, and said, "I never expected to see you again, Signora. Welcome home."

"Please address me as Sister Veronica, and never curtsy to me. You should only bow to God."

Livia raised an eyebrow at Celeste who just rolled her eyes. "My Mistress told me you never took your Holy Orders. Why would you wish me to call you Sister?"

"You're correct, Livia. I am not a nun, but that was how the Sisters addressed me. I desire to continue to be addressed thus."

Livia stared at her for a moment, clearly unsure what to say. She glanced at Celeste who gave a slight nod. *This will make for an interesting conversation in my chambers tonight*, she thought.

"Livia, please fetch the housekeeper and my brother Marco, then find Father Domenico."

Livia curtsied and shot Veronica a sideways glance before hurrying off.

"It's comforting to see somethings never change," Veronica said as she watched Livia go. "I appreciate you taking my desires into account, Celeste. My requests appear strange to you, but I'm not the person I was. That woman is long dead. I am reborn in the image of my Lord and Master, Jesus. For that, you should be thankful, sister. It was the purpose for sequestering me after all, was it not?"

Celeste was more concerned than thankful, but she nodded to satisfy her sister and avoid an argument on her first day home. Veronica had only just arrived but was already turning their lives on their heads. *What more is there to come?* she wondered. She consoled herself by believing Veronica would change with the passage of time. For now, she would do her best to placate her.

"I'll write to Luciano in the morning asking him to have your quarters prepared to your liking. Make a list of instructions."

Veronica folded her hands and nodded. "I'll begin as soon as I'm settled."

Once Veronica's room was arranged, exorcised, and blessed to her satisfaction, Celeste said, "Adrianna's mother, Florina, is a skilled seamstress. I've asked her to design some simple gowns for you. She's finished one. It's hanging in the wardrobe. She'll have two more finished before we leave for Florence in two days. Given your vow of poverty, I fear the gowns may be too extravagant, but I had not understood the depths of your commitment to your vows."

Celeste opened the wardrobe, then stepped away for Veronica to inspect the gown. Veronica spread it on the bed and studied it intently for several moments before turning to face Celeste.

"This will have to suffice for now, but I only need this gown and the one I'm wearing. Have Florina give the other two to someone with a greater need than I."

Celeste had to restrain herself from taking her sister by the shoulders and shaking her until she stopped her ridiculous charade. Her only hope was that Veronica would soon tire of the game. Until then, Celeste would be patient and play along.

"I'll see to it," she said softly.

Veronica gave her most pious smile. "Thank you, sister. I'll say my prayers now before I wash for dinner."

"Would you like me to call Livia to assist you?"

Veronica looked at Celeste as if those were the most ridiculous words she'd ever heard. "I'm perfectly capable of tending to my own needs, sister. I won't be needing a maid in Florence, so please inform Luciano not to bother with one."

Celeste couldn't prevent the frustrated sigh from escaping her lips. "If that's your wish. Dinner is in an hour."

She hurried out, closing the door behind her before Veronica could infuriate her further. She stepped around a corner and stopped to massage her temples.

Marco spotted her in the hallway and strode toward her. "What is it now? Is our sister asking to convert a room into a monastic holy abode?"

Celeste gave a small laugh. "Not yet, but I'm sure that will happen soon after arriving in Florence. I think I prefer the old Veronica."

Marco rested his hand on Celeste's shoulder. "Give her time. Remember the life she's been living. This is a challenging transition for her."

She gave him a weary smile. "For me too, but I'm comforted that I can always count on your good heart and voice of reason. I couldn't possibly persuade you to travel with us to help get her settled?"

It was Marco's turn to sigh. "Adrianna would never forgive me, and I have too many obligations at the workshop. I'll bring my family to Florence as soon as possible."

Celeste kissed his cheek. "I'll hold you to your word. Now, I must go change into my luxuriously vain and overly extravagant gown for dinner."

She heard Marco's laughter until she reached her

chambers. Her comment had been meant as a joke, but she feared her troubles with Veronica were only beginning.

CELESTE EXCUSED herself immediately after dinner on their final night in Venice, saying she'd need rest since they were getting an early start. The true reasons for needing to get away had nothing to do with sleep. She couldn't tolerate another minute of Veronica's overzealous lecturing, her adopted son, Mateo, behaving like Lord of all Venice, or the marital tension radiating off Marco and Adrianna. The strain had been building for the past two days and had reached a crescendo during the meal.

As she was rushing to her quarters, Mateo called out to her. She was tempted to pretend she hadn't heard but knew he'd only follow her to her chambers. Luciano had insisted on Mateo traveling to Venice with her as her escort. Celeste hadn't spent time alone with him since he was a child and hadn't looked forward to the journey with him. Since his coming of age, she'd seen little of Mateo in Florence, which was fine with her. He was an arrogant, taciturn young man who only seemed to enjoy carousing with the sons of other Florentine nobles. Celeste had warned Luciano that if he didn't rein the boy in, they could all face serious trouble.

Luciano had written to Marco, asking him to acquaint Mateo with the Venetian estates while they were in the city since he would one day inherit them. Marco had been patient, but Mateo treated him as no more than a servant. Celeste had scolded Mateo more than once to no avail. Marco had assured Celeste, he could handle him, but Celeste was dismayed and ashamed of her son.

She stopped in the hallway and took a deep breath before

turning to face him. Feigning a smile, she said, "What is it, son?"

Mateo straightened his shoulders and crossed his arms. "I'm here to inform you I won't be leaving with you tomorrow. I'm going to remain in Venice indefinitely."

Celeste did her best to hide her irritation as she studied his face. Mateo's pronouncement came as no surprise to her. He'd been hinting that he belonged in Venice, country of his birth. She had no doubt what Luciano would have to say to Mateo, but she had no authority over him beyond being his adopted mother.

She stretched to her full stature to make herself more imposing, but Mateo still towered over her. "Have you written to your father of this plan?"

"Why would I bother with that? I'm old enough to make my own choice, and he wouldn't have received my letter in time to reply before you left."

"I see," she said evenly. "In that case, you must return to Florence with me and seek his permission in person."

His facade of dominance slipped for an instant, but he didn't back down. "I'm no child, Mamma. I don't need Papa's seal of approval for every action I take."

"This is true but moving to an entirely different country isn't just any action. It's a momentous decision that requires thought and preparation. And your father's permission. The mature thing would be to return to Florence and discuss it with him."

The color rose in Mateo's cheeks. "I won't. I'm sure he'd approve, and what can he do from so far away if he doesn't?"

Celeste held his gaze before deliberately saying, "Remove you as his heir."

Her words had the desired effect. Mateo lowered his arms and backed away from her. "He wouldn't dare."

"Wouldn't dare? He would be well within his rights for such

a belligerent act of defiance. Fathers have disinherited their sons for far less. Your papa may do as he pleases on the slightest whim. He's still your Master and controls your fate."

He stared at her in stunned silence as he carefully considered her words. Luciano would never disinherit Mateo, but he wouldn't allow such disobedience to go unpunished. For good measure, she added, "And you haven't forgotten you promised to travel with us as chaperon for our journey. You wouldn't allow your mother and aunt to travel alone and at the mercy of bandits, would you?"

His shoulders slumped in defeat. "Fine, Mamma, I'll travel with you to Florence, but I'll only stay long enough to speak with Papa."

Celeste wrapped his hands in hers and gazed up with a loving smile. "You've made the correct choice, son. I'm proud of you."

He pulled his hands free, then turned on his heel and stormed down the hallway. She'd become accustomed to his tantrums over the years and was unaffected by this latest one. For all his insisting he was a grown man, he'd yet to behave like one.

"This will be a long trip home," she whispered as she hurried toward the blessed solitude of her chambers.

CHAPTER TWO

FLORENCE 1496

CELESTE SPRANG from the carriage the instant the driver pulled the horses to a stop in the drive. Veronica remained rooted to the seat, expecting Celeste to coax her out. She'd noticed Veronica's fidgeting increase the closer they got to home, but Celeste had lost her patience for catering to her sister's every mood over the past six days. One moment, she'd affect a posture of pious, almost regal reserve, and the next, that of a lost and neglected child. Veronica behaved her age no more than Mateo.

Celeste's only aim was to greet Luciano and the children, then leave Mateo and Veronica to their own devices. Bardo, the footman, swung the door wide for her to enter, then bowed as she passed. *How wonderful to be home,* she thought as she brushed by him. Bardo must have announced her arrival because her three daughters were rushing down the stairs as she reached the foyer.

Angela embraced her first, nearly bowling her over as she did. *How typical,* Celeste thought, as she pulled her daughter closer. Cristina approached next in her reserved, almost regal manner. She was a sweet, lighthearted girl who never failed to raise Celeste's spirits. Luciano was ever going on about how the twins were exact replicas of her, but she was pleased to see signs of their father's dark good looks appearing in their features as they grew. Elena stood apart, quietly waiting her turn to greet her adopted mother. Celeste pulled her tightly to her heart and whispered how much she'd missed her sweet girl. Elena's face beamed when she stepped free of her arms.

Once the reunions were out of the way, Angela and Elena babbled on about everything that had happened while she was gone, but Cristina stood back, quietly listening. It did Celeste's heart good to see nothing had changed in her absence. Angela told Celeste she'd completed the wood panel of the Ascension she'd been painting for the past few months. She tugged on Celeste's hand to get her to go to the studio and see it that very moment.

Celeste held up her free hand to quiet Angela. "Tomorrow will be soon enough, dear. I'm weary from traveling, and I need to get your aunt Veronica settled. I'll join you in the workshop first thing after breakfast."

"Yes, Mamma," Angela said, clearly disappointed.

Elena started chatting again the moment Angela finished. She excitedly described her new governess, Violetta, who had joined the household in Celeste's absence. When Elena left the nursery, the family's longtime nanny, Lapa, had temporarily stepped into the role of governess. Elena had since moved beyond what Lapa could teach her, so Celeste had persuaded Luciano to hire a trained governess since the one who had taught Cristina and Angela had left when the twins turned thirteen. Celeste hadn't met Violetta, but she trusted Luciano's judgment in such matters.

Celeste interrupted Elena by saying, "She sounds wonderful, darling. I look forward to meeting her after dinner." She put her arm around Elena's waist and turned to face

Cristina. "And what of you, sweetheart? What have you to tell me?"

Cristina stepped closer to her mother with a demur smile. She opened her mouth to answer but froze when she saw something over Celeste's shoulder. Celeste raised her eyebrows before turning to see what had startled her. Veronica stood still as a statue, framed in the evening light of the doorway. Her gaze was locked on Elena, who was her exact replica in miniature.

Elena glanced up to see what Celeste and her sisters were staring at and gasped when she saw Veronica. She leaned closer to Angela, and whispered, "Is that her?"

Celeste wondered what Angela had been telling Elena about their Aunt Veronica. One day two years earlier, Celeste came upon Elena in the front hall studying a portrait of Veronica. When Elena asked who the woman was, Celeste led Elena to her sitting room, and said, "She's the woman who brought you into the world. She's your first mother."

Celeste went on to explain that her mother had suffered from an illness of the mind and had gone to a convent far away to recover. At that time, Celeste never expected to see Veronica again and had told Elena as much. She had bent the facts slightly by telling Elena that her mother loved her dearly but wasn't able to care for her. The truth was that Veronica had felt little affection for her infant daughter and rarely paid her the least bit of attention. Celeste intended to take those truths to her grave.

Before Celeste left for Venice, she'd had a private conversation with Elena to prepare her for Veronica's arrival. She encouraged her to treat her as Aunt Veronica like the rest of the family. Elena agreed but Celeste sensed her confusion. She did her best to reassure her adopted daughter as she struggled with her own apprehensions.

Celeste had informed her sister of that conversation while

they were in Venice, which surprised Veronica. "I have no daughter, or son for that matter," she'd said. "Elena is yours now, as much as if she had come from your body and not mine."

Her response had both comforted and disturbed Celeste, but she did her best to put it from her mind. If those were Veronica's true feelings, she had no need to go searching for trouble where there was none. But as she stood there studying her sister's reaction to seeing her daughter for the first time in years, she began to doubt Veronica's lack of attachment to the girl.

Angela and Cristina broke the tension by running to their aunt and throwing their arms around her. As opposed to her feelings for her daughter, Veronica had adored and doted on her nieces from the moment they were born. The girls were five when Veronica went away, so they'd been old enough to remember her.

Veronica tore her gaze from Elena and smiled warmly at Angela and Cristina. Cupping her hand under Angela's chin, she said, "I didn't expect to find such beautiful and graceful women. So like your beautiful mother, you two are."

Angela stepped back with her hands on her hips and studied her aunt up and down. "You haven't changed at all, Aunt Veronica, except your hair is so short and you never would have worn such a plain gown back then. Welcome home."

Cristina kissed her cheeks. "Yes, Aunt, welcome home. We've missed you." She stepped away and turned toward Elena. "Come, greet our dear younger sister Elena."

Elena had been silently watching the touching reunion, but Celeste saw her muscles tighten as the three of them approached her. When Veronica stopped in front of her, Elena gave a formal curtsy, then stared as she waited for her to speak.

Tears formed in Veronica's eyes as she studied Elena's face.

"How truly lovely you are, Elena," she whispered. "Are you content living here?"

Elena bowed her head before saying, "Yes, thank you, aunt. I'm very happy here with my family."

Celeste saw Veronica cringe at Elena's use of the word *aunt*, but she quickly recovered her composure. "I'm overjoyed to hear that, niece."

Celeste let out her breath in relief that Veronica and Elena had crossed their first barrier without incident. She took it as a promising omen. When Celeste wrapped her arm around Elena's waist, she felt the tension flow out of her, and she smiled up at her in gratitude.

Bardo, who had wandered off somewhere after announcing their arrival, cleared his throat behind her. When she turned to face him, he said, "Mistress, my Master wishes me to tell you that he and Master Luca are dressing for dinner and will greet you soon."

"Thank you, Bardo. You're dismissed." As he scurried off, she said, "Your aunt and I must wash off the dust of the road, so we'll see you at dinner." She stopped and gazed fondly at her daughters surrounding her. "I'm so delighted to be home."

AFTER ESCORTING Veronica to her quarters and hearing her pronounce them satisfactory, Celeste rushed to her own chambers, eager for a moment to catch her breath and gather her thoughts. As she entered, Livia was pouring hot water into the basin on her washstand. After she'd replaced the water pot on its hook over the fire, she went to help Celeste undress.

The devoted Livia had become Celeste's confidant and true friend over the years. She could always count on her steadiness and for her to look out for her interests. She was Celeste's loyal servant, but in Celeste's private quarters, they were equals.

She untied the laces on her bodice before moving to her skirt. "So, how did the reunion go, Celeste?" she asked, using her Mistress' given name, which she only did when the two of them were alone.

Celeste blew out her breath in relief. "Better than I could have hoped. Elena and Veronica both seemed to have accepted the arrangement, though I can't imagine what Elena's feeling. I'll speak with her in private after dinner."

"She loves you as her one true mother," Livia said. "Veronica is no threat to you in that regard. She knowingly forfeited her right to be Elena's mother. She has no claim to her."

"Yes, I know, Livia. I'm just relieved to have that first meeting behind us." She ran the clean, wet cloth over her face and neck, savoring the comforting warmth. "Once we return to our normal routines, I'm sure none of us will give the past another thought."

"I pray that's true."

As Livia was about to lower a clean shift over Celeste's head, the door swung open, and Luciano burst in. "Allow me to do that," he said as he took the shift from Livia. "You may go. I'll help your beautiful Mistress dress for dinner."

Livia gave him a knowing smile as she went out, leaving them alone. As the door closed behind her, Luciano lifted Celeste onto the bed and climbed up beside her. As he brushed his lips and hands over her body, her hunger rose to equal his. As always, she was surprised and delighted that their desire for each other hadn't dimmed over the years.

When their passion was sated, Luciano rolled onto his back with a contented sigh. "Never leave me again, my love. I can't bear to be without you for even a day."

"Nonsense," she said as she got up and handed him his dressing robe. "You leave me all the time and survive it somehow."

"That doesn't mean I'm happy about it." He got up and wrapped himself in the robe as Celeste rang for Livia. The smile slid from his face as he grew serious. "I have questions about Venice and much to tell you."

"There will be time for that later tonight." Livia returned, so Celeste pushed Luciano toward the door. "Go dress for dinner. I don't want to keep the children waiting, and I haven't seen Luca yet."

He gave her one more lingering kiss before going.

Livia stared at the closed door for a moment before saying, "You are a most fortunate woman. If I had ever married, I would have prayed for a man like the Master. I never would have found one though. Men like him are scarce."

"He is a rare jewel indeed, Livia. I am truly blessed."

CELESTE PACED in the dining room, waiting for Luciano to join the family. Their five children were at the table behind her. Mateo was seated at one end, with thirteen-year-old Luca seated on his right. Her fifteen-year-old daughters sat across from Luca, with eleven-year-old Elena at Luca's left.

"Sit down, Mamma. You're making me anxious," Angela said.

Celeste spun around to face her. "It's been a trying day. I'm too distressed to sit."

Cristina got to her feet and wrapped her arm in Celeste's. "Then, I will pace with you," she said as she got into step with her mother.

Celeste kissed her cheek. "Thank you, sweetheart I feel calmer already."

Mateo huffed at that. "Why would Cristina pacing next to you make the least difference?"

Cristina's eyes narrowed as she faced him. "Kindness is powerful medicine, brother. You should try it sometime."

Mateo leaned forward with his elbows on the table. "Are you insinuating I never show kindness?"

Luca chuckled. "She's not insinuating. She's stating it outright. She's not wrong."

"No one asked your opinion," Mateo snapped. "And what would you know? You're barely out of the nursery."

Luca frowned as he slumped in his chair and crossed his arms.

Angela sat taller and stared Mateo down. "Leave Luca alone. You know he left the nursery years ago."

"Why must we always bicker at dinner?" Elena mumbled.

"Excellent question," Luciano asked as he strode into the dining room.

The children rose in unison, and Cristina turned to face him. Luciano gave a quick wave for them to return to their seats as he dropped into his chair. As her siblings sat down, Cristina let go of Celeste's arm and joined them at the table. Celeste hesitated for a second before taking her place beside Luciano.

"Good evening, Papa," the children said in chorus.

He answered with a nod as he stabbed his knife into a chunk of roast pig. While the others began filling their plates, he said, "What is the squabble about tonight?"

"We were debating whether or not Mateo understands what it means to show kindness," Angela said before stuffing a piece of fish in her mouth.

"You came in before we reached a consensus," Celeste said.

Luciano swallowed his pork before turning to face her. "And what is your feeling on this weighty matter, my dear?"

She paused to consider her words before saying, "Mateo is capable of showing great kindness. He just needs to put that ability into practice more often."

Mateo eyed her, clearly not entirely pleased with her backhanded compliment.

Luciano let out a laugh. "You take your mother's words to heart, son. Follow Cristina's example. She's the kindest person I know."

"Thank you, Papa," Cristina said, then turned and smirked at Mateo.

The color rose in Mateo's face as he opened his mouth to speak, but Celeste cut him off by saying, "Your aunt Veronica was weary and decided to take her dinner in her room. Since she's not here, I wanted to thank you for welcoming her so kindly earlier."

"It's better than she deserves,' Mateo said. "Why would any of you want to share a table with her? I'm still disappointed that you've agreed to allow that wanton whore under your roof, Papa," Mateo said.

Celeste slowly rose to her feet and clenched her fists. It took great restraint to refrain from slapping his foul mouth.

Luciano saved her from having to by saying, "Leave this table at once, son. Go to your chambers and wait for me there."

Mateo stood with his head bowed and shuffled from the room. Celeste noticed the other children struggling to keep from laughing. Nothing gave them more satisfaction than seeing their headstrong brother set in his place.

"Please give no heed to Mateo's words," Luciano said. "We will welcome Veronica into our home and give her the love and care she needs. Is that understood?"

"Yes, Papa," they answered in turn.

Celeste wrapped her arm around his waist. "When it comes to showing kindness, no one surpasses your papa."

Luciano kissed the top of her head. "We all know you hold the top honor for kindness, my dear, but I appreciate the compliment." He gestured for the children to finish their meal.

"Excuse us. Your Mamma and I have other matters to attend to."

Celeste waved to the children as Luciano escorted her from the room. As they mounted the stairs, she said, "I meant what I said. Allowing Veronica to live under your roof is a tremendous act of kindness. I would have accepted your decision if you refused."

"If ten years of sequestration in a convent haven't set your sister straight, nothing will. I hope she will find the peace that has always eluded her."

"That is my greatest hope for her." When they reached Mateo's chamber door, Celeste rose up on her tiptoes and kissed his cheek. "I wish you luck with him. Mateo grows more of a challenge every day. He's a man now. Such behavior is inexcusable." She stared at his door and gave a weary sigh. "He is too much like the parents that gave him life."

"I agree, but the difference is that I will curb his actions and guide him on the correct path. I'm determined to make a decent man of him yet."

"I trust you will. I must go to my aunt now. Neither of us has a pleasant task ahead."

Luciano winked and raised his arm as if he held a sword while he reached for the latch. "To battle, my dear!"

Celeste laughed softly as she headed for Aunt Portia's chambers. She was grateful to Luciano for easing the tension and reminding her that she could conquer whatever she faced with him by her side.

~

CELESTE SLOWED her pace as she headed for Aunt Portia's chambers. She loved her dearly but just wanted to climb into bed and forget the world. She decided to have a brief visit to let her know she, Veronica and Mateo had returned safely, then promise a longer visit in the morning.

Portia had lived with them in Florence since the death of her beloved Paulo seven years earlier. Once a robust woman, her aunt had grown frail during the intervening years and now rarely left her room. Celeste gave her a warm smile as she entered. She was propped on pillows looking weaker than Celeste had ever seen her. Portia had always been a force to be reckoned with, but it was time for Celeste to accept that her life was drawing to a close. Celeste loved Portia like a mother. Aunt Portia had rescued her from a life of poverty and degradation. If not for Aunt Portia, Celeste never would have met Luciano or become an artist. She owed everything good in her life to her. Over time, she had also become her closest confidant and greatest champion. Celeste dreaded the day when she'd no longer have her sage advice to rely on.

Celeste didn't look forward to telling her about Veronica's return to Florence. Portia had seen Veronica for what she was from an early age and didn't trust her ability to reform. Portia had warned Celeste against going to Venice. Celeste loved her sister but couldn't deny she'd been a perpetual thorn in her side. Sadly, Veronica took after their worthless father, just as their brother, Jacopo, did. An undeniable streak of devilry ran through certain branches of the family tree. Unfortunately, Veronica was perched firmly on one of those limbs.

Celeste kissed her aunt's cheek, then took the chair beside her bed.

"Stop looking at me like I'm already dead," Portia said, then gave Celeste a mischievous grin.

She chuckled, and said, "That's not what I was doing. I was just thinking how grateful I am for you. I'd be nothing without you."

Portia waved off her comment. "Nonsense. I simply got the

wheels turning. You took it from there and soared higher than anyone could have imagined. You are a marvel, my dear."

Celeste brushed a tear from her cheek. "Thank you, aunt."

Portia dabbed at her own cheeks with a handkerchief. "Having you home is the best medicine for my old bones. Is your sister with you?"

Celeste took a deep breath and squared her shoulders. "She's resting in her chambers."

As Portia studied her intently, Celeste squirmed under her scrutiny, unsure of what else to say.

Seemingly sensing her niece's discomfort, Portia lowered her gaze. After taking time to deliberately smooth her quilt, she folded her hands, and said, "I see. I still believe Luciano will rue the day he allowed Veronica under this roof. But who am I to question the will of my Lord and Master," she said, her words dripping with sarcasm.

Celeste rolled her eyes. "When have you ever held your tongue with Luciano?"

Portia smiled. "I'll grant you that, but I don't seem to have the strength these days. I disagree wholeheartedly with his decision, but I won't cross him. What state did you find your sister in?"

"I hardly know how to answer that. I believe she'll need time to transition to her new situation. The Sisters say Veronica is prepared to reenter the world. I want to trust them, but I'd be lying to say I'm not concerned. As glad as I am to have my sister close, I dread a repeat of her past mistakes."

Portia squeezed her hand. "I'm choosing to trust the judgment of the Sisters as well and give my niece the chance to prove herself. Isn't that the consideration we all deserve?"

"I suppose so. Ten years is a long time. I hope I've grown into a better woman since then."

"You've had much less improving to do than Veronica."

"Have you forgotten at that time I was refusing to leave

Rome after my art tour and return to my husband and children? I might still be there if you hadn't persuaded me that my place was with my family."

Portia patted her hand. "You'd have reached that conclusion on your own in time. Plus, you couldn't have stayed away from me forever. No one can resist my charms for long."

"Truer words were never spoken," Celeste said with a laugh.

Portia gave a weak smile. "Enough of Veronica. How was Venice? I would have loved to see my beloved city once more."

"I missed having you by my side every moment I was there." Celeste slowly got to her feet and kissed her aunt's cheeks. "I'm weary and must be off to bed."

Her aunt pressed her into promising to bring Veronica to visit her first thing in the morning. Celeste assured her they'd come immediately after breakfast. She kissed her aunt and wished her goodnight before leaving her to rest.

CELESTE'S LEGS felt like lead as she walked the hallway to her chambers. She could hardly wait to climb under the covers and drift off to sleep in her husband's arms. When she pushed the door open, she found Luciano propped on the bed, still fully dressed. His lighthearted manner had faded, and his face was serious as he stared into the fire.

She climbed onto the bed beside him and reached for his hand. "What is it, Luci? I've sensed you've been keeping something from me." Livia came in from the antechamber before he could answer. "I'm not ready to undress yet, Livia. I'll ring for you when I'm ready."

Before leaving, Livia said, "Should I bring you some spiced wine?"

Luciano answered for Celeste. "Bring something stronger. She'll need it."

Livia eyed him in confusion, but said, "And for you sir?" In answer, he held up his wine goblet. Livia gave a quick curtsy before going out to fulfill his request.

As soon as Livia closed the door, Celeste rolled onto her side facing Luciano. "You're worrying me. What's the matter, my love?"

He ran his paint-stained fingers through his hair before answering. "I didn't want to bother you with this since you had enough on your hands, but it's time you knew. You must promise to keep what I'm about to tell you between us."

Luciano had never asked such a thing of her, and her gut tightened. She'd always kept his confidences without question in the past, so she couldn't imagine why he felt the warning was necessary. "I've gone from being worried to scared."

"You should be. A few days after you left, Mancini wrote asking to meet with me."

She sat up and stared down at him, "You didn't go, did you?"

"I did but only to hear him out and made no promises. When I heard what he had to say, my reservations vanished. Savonarola has his spies but so do the Arrabbiati. They've long been sending reports to Rome and Milan. The situation is far worse than we imagined. There are rumors from Rome of Savonarola's excommunication, but the Holy Father doesn't have sufficient evidence to support that action yet. The Prior is stepping up his reprisals against ordinary Florentines. He's a threat to us and our work, Celeste. Rumors are emerging that he's planning to send his followers out to search houses for anything he deems worldly or sinful. Can you imagine what would happen if they searched the palazzo or my workshop? Savonarola would have us all living like pauper monks."

Celeste's heartbeat quickened. Savonarola had long

preached against possessions such as jewelry, face paints, and non-religious books and art. Most of her paintings were of religious subjects, but not all. Her jewels or gowns had never meant as much to her as they did most women, but she believed it should be her choice if she chose to own or wear them, not Savonarola's and his followers. He had also been quite vocal about the wealth and ostentation of the Church and her leaders.

"These are only rumors?" she finally asked. "How much stock do you put in them?"

"A great deal. You should know, I've officially aligned with the Arrabbiati, Celeste."

"No, Luciano! How could you risk putting us all in such danger?"

"We were already in danger, my love. Savonarola must be removed from power. The Arrabbiati have the backing of Rome and Milan. They can make that happen. Trust me. I'm convinced this is what's best for us and Florence."

She embraced him, then rested her head on his broad chest, and felt his strength flow into her. Luciano was a brilliant man, and she had always relied on his judgment in matters of politics and men. "As always, I place my life in your hands, but please tread carefully. How would I live if anything were to happen to you or our little ones?"

"I'm proceeding with the utmost caution. We understand the risks, but at this point, Savonarola claims to abhor violence. The most he can do is harm us materially and damage our reputation, if he is so inclined. Watch what you say to others, even Livia, and my sisters and their families. They know nothing of my involvement with the Arrabbiati. I wish it to stay that way. Like most Florentines, my sisters appear to support the Prior publicly, but I have no way of knowing their private beliefs. That said, I cannot imagine for one instant that Elisabetta supports that man."

Celeste smiled at that. Luciano's eldest sister cared for nothing as much as material wealth and her place in the patrician class, not even her children. She'd been incensed when Luciano adopted Mateo, then sired a son, pushing her eldest out of contention for the family title. Humility and frugality were not characteristics Celeste had ever seen her exhibit.

"Maybe I'll use underhanded tactics of my own to find out where she stands on the matter," she said with a laugh.

"I pray you're teasing, my love. For now, we must go on with our lives as before. We can't afford to arouse suspicion."

As Livia walked into the room, Celeste said, "You have my solemn word."

She caught the slight raising of Livia's eyebrow and wondered what she'd heard. Celeste had never withheld anything from her maid, much to Luciano's and Portia's dismay. They'd shared much together over the years, but this was one time she'd have to keep a secret from her. She trusted Livia, but it wasn't fair to put her in danger, too. For the time being, only she and Luciano would know the truth about their alliance with the Arrabbiati.

Once they had changed into their night clothes and were settled in bed, Celeste said, "This hasn't been the homecoming I'd hoped for. At times, I long for those simpler days when we only had each other and not a houseful of family vying for our attention and energies." Luciano brushed a lock of hair from her face, and she looked into his eyes. "Our lives have become so complicated. What if you've aligned with the wrong political faction. We could lose everything. The thought of that is overwhelming."

"I'm sorry for that. I'd shield you from the strain and toil if it were in my power. I fear our lives will only grow more complicated, but that doesn't mean we won't have our share of happiness." He kissed the end of her nose before arranging her pillows around her head. "You're weary from the road and the stress of dealing with Veronica. Rest now, my love. The world will look brighter come morning."

She closed her eyes with a sigh as she felt the tension draining out of her. "Have I told you how grateful I am for having you in my life, Luci? I feel I can conquer the world with you at my side."

"We'll conquer it together," he said as he moved closer to her and rested his arm across her. "I will always be here for you."

She smiled in the darkness and drifted off, doing her best to put aside the turmoil swirling around her.

CHAPTER THREE

FLORENCE 1497

Two Months Later

Celeste frowned as she stepped back to study her painting. She was working on a wood panel of the Annunciation for a local nobleman named Domenico Riva. He owned a quaint country estate outside of Florence. Celeste had begged Luciano to turn the commission down, but he hadn't wanted to offend Signore Riva. Her heart hadn't been in the project from the beginning, and it showed. Luciano told her to finish quickly and move on to commissions she was more passionate about, but she refused to put her name to mediocre work.

"Dinnertime, madam," Livia said as she came into the room. "My Master charged me with making you put down your brush and come with me to your chambers. He says I must deliver you on time to a meal for once."

Celeste gave her a backhanded wave, and without turning to face her, said, "What's your opinion of this painting, Livia?"

Livia sighed in exasperation. "Please, madam, I've asked you not to do that. I'm just an uneducated servant. What do I know of great art?"

Celeste shook her head. "We both know that's not true, and

you've spent enough time around art to recognize quality work when you see it." Turning back to the easel, she said, "Close your eyes and clear your mind."

Livia chuckled at that. "If I close my eyes, I can't see to give you a considered opinion, my dear."

"Just do as I asked." Celeste glanced at Livia over her shoulder to make sure she'd obeyed. "Take some deep breaths and relax." She waited several moments, then said, "Now, open your eyes and tell me what you think."

Celeste watched her as she studied the painting. She didn't need to hear Livia's opinion to know her answer. She could read the disappointment on her face.

"It's too early to say. Ask me again when you're finished."

"Tell me the truth. I promise not to be offended."

Livia peeked at her from the corner of her eye before saying, "It's not your finest work. Your paintings usually evoke emotions in me. Melancholy, joy, wonder, love. This painting is fine, but I feel nothing when I look at it. If I saw this somewhere, I'd forget it the minute I passed by."

Celeste met her maid's eye for a moment before moving past her to the worktable. After retrieving a large paintbrush and her palette, she walked back to the easel. As she stroked a line of white paint across the panel, she said, "I appreciate your honesty, Livia."

"Stop, Celeste!" Livia cried when she realized what Celeste was doing. "The painting was fine. Don't listen to me. I don't know what I was saying."

Celeste paused with her brush in midair before turning to face her. "You spoke from your heart, friend. If my paintings evoke no emotion or response in you, they're worthless. Isn't this the purpose of art?"

"I suppose it is, but truly, I know nothing about art," Livia said softly.

"You know enough. I shall start again. This project is my

fourth Annunciation in a row. I can't express enough how much I long to create a non-religious work, but with everyone living in fear of reprisals from Savonarola, it would be foolish of me to attempt it." She turned back to the easel and finished painting over her weeks of work. "How I miss the days when I could paint whatever I conceived in my heart instead of what was dictated to me."

When the panel was covered in dull white paint, she returned her tools and materials to the worktable and quickly removed her smock before heading to the door.

As she and Livia left the studio, Livia said, "Now I feel melancholy, as if I've lost a friend."

"Cheer up, my friend. The painting was only an arrangement of pigments on wood, it's not a living thing," Celeste said with feigned enthusiasm. "This isn't the first time I've covered over my work, and I wager it won't be the last."

Celeste was lost in thought as she and Livia headed to her chambers to change for dinner. Luciano wouldn't be pleased to hear that she was starting over on Riva's project. The man could be unreasonable and was already pestering Luciano about the painting. But even if he was a lesser patron, he deserved her best work. Luciano would have to make Riva understand.

When she and Livia reached the hallway leading to her daughters' quarters, she was roused from her musings by the sound of Veronica's voice coming from Elena's room. She looked at Livia and raised her eyebrows in confusion, but her maid just shrugged.

Celeste quickened her step. "My sister is not supposed to be anywhere near this wing of the palazzo."

When Veronica arrived in Florence two months earlier, she spent most of her time for the first week alone in her quarters in supplication and reflection. This allowed the rest of the family to resume their routines as before, much to Celeste's relief. That all changed after the first time Veronica heard Savonarola preach. As Celeste had predicted to Marco, their sister had become a devoted disciple of the Prior. Veronica began joining the family at meals to admonish them and call them to repent of their pride and sinfulness.

Celeste and Luciano had tolerated her lecturing in the beginning, but as Celeste feared, Veronica had grown more fanatical by the day. This created more than mere annoyance for the family. Veronica's sermonizing was having an increasing effect on Elena and Cristina. Angela and the boys paid their aunt little attention, but the sensitive and impressionable girls were bewildered by Veronica's actions. Celeste and Luciano eventually had to insist Veronica not spend unsupervised time with her nieces. This only stoked her fire of righteous indignation, but she realized she had to bow to their wishes.

A more serious complication had arisen from Veronica's discipleship to the Prior. Luciano was heavily involved with the Arrabbiati in plotting against Savonarola and couldn't risk his activities being discovered. The strain of continuing to run the workshop, deliver his commissions on time, and secretly collude with the Arrabbiati had taken a toll on Luciano. He wasn't sleeping well, he'd lost weight, and he rarely smiled or laughed with the children. Celeste had done her best to ease his burden, but if he insisted on involving himself in political intrigues, there was little she could do. Veronica's disrupting influence had complicated the picture even more. They'd discussed petitioning the Gabriele's in Venice to take Veronica in, but hadn't yet reached that point of desperation. Discovering her sister in Elena's chamber might provoke her into acting once and for all.

Celeste rushed into the room and found Veronica poised to toss an armful of Elena's gowns into the fire. She froze for an instant when she saw Celeste, then stepped away from the fireplace. Little Elena stood near the bed, watching her mother with eyes wide as saucers.

"What is happening here?" Celeste hissed at Veronica through clenched teeth.

Veronica held the gowns closer to her chest and straightened her shoulders. "I'm ridding your daughter of these extravagant garments. It's time someone took charge and taught her Our Father's holy and humble ways."

Celeste stepped toward her with clenched fists, struggling to control her rage. "You cannot be serious. Drop those gowns on the bed and wait for me in my chambers. Livia, escort her to my room and ensure she doesn't run off. Send Lapa to find Violetta and have her report to me here."

Livia curtsied hurriedly and snatched the gowns from Veronica's grasp. After laying them on the bed, Livia gripped her by the arm and practically dragged her from the room. Celeste calmly closed the door before sinking onto the bed. She patted the spot beside her for Elena to sit. She noted the slight hesitation before the girl obeyed her request. *My poor girl must be so confused*, Celeste thought.

Holding Elena's hand in hers, Celeste softly said, "I want you to understand, sweetheart, I'm not angry or upset. You've done nothing wrong, but I need you to tell me what was happening when I came in."

Elena looked up at her with tears forming in her eyes. "Yes, Mamma. I was with Violetta in the study when Aunt Veronica came in and sat beside me. When Violetta asked what she wanted, my aunt said she only wanted to hear my lesson."

"What were you and Violetta studying?"

"The history of Florence."

Celeste was relieved to hear they hadn't been studying the Greek poets or pagans. Veronica wouldn't have tolerated that for a moment, but she couldn't have had reason to object to Florentine history. "What did your aunt say to that?" Without answering, Elena gently pulled her hand free of Celeste's and fidgeted with a loose thread on her sleeve. "Elena, tell me what happened."

Keeping her eyes lowered, she said, "Aunt Veronica dismissed Violetta and said she would teach me. She told me about Prior Savonarola's sermon on the evils of avarice and covetousness. She said wearing expensive clothes is a sin and that we should destroy our gowns. She brought me here to burn them."

Celeste held her breath, struggling to conceal her fury. Until that moment, she couldn't have imagined that Veronica would do anything so outrageous. This was irrefutable proof of Veronica's mental instability and fanaticism.

Celeste tenderly placed her fingers under Elena's chin and tilted her head back until their eyes met. "Do you believe wearing these gowns is sinful? Do you wish to burn them?"

Elena shook her head emphatically, then collapsed against Celeste and sobbed on her shoulder. Celeste gently stroked her hair and considered how best to deal with Veronica. What she wished to do was push her into the River Arno.

The door slowly opened, and Violetta sheepishly shuffled into the room. She sank into a deep curtsy and held it until Celeste told her to rise. Elena sat up and stared at her governess as she wiped her tears on her sleeve. Violetta frowned at her unladylike behavior, which made Elena smile.

Shifting her gaze to Celeste, she said, "Please, forgive me, mistress. I didn't want to leave Elena alone with your sister, but I didn't dare defy her."

Celeste stood and smoothed her skirts, and Elena hopped onto her feet and stood beside Celeste. As Celeste put her arm around her daughter's dainty waist, she said, "Violetta, you've done nothing that requires my forgiveness. The fault is solely Signora Veronica's. I must go speak to her immediately. Please, help Elena compose herself before coming down to dinner."

She gestured at Elena's dresses lying on the bed. "I'll send Mirella in to hang her gowns." Violetta glanced at the bed before looking at Celeste in confusion. "Elena will explain." She gave Elena a warm hug and kissed both her cheeks. "I must go but I'll see you at dinner."

Elena appeared to have recovered her composure and she gave Celeste a lighthearted wave as she left the room. Celeste wished she could say the same for herself.

$\sim$

VERONICA JUMPED to her feet when Celeste burst into the room.

When Livia moved toward her antechamber, Celeste held a hand up to stop her. "Stay. Help me dress for dinner, Livia." Her maid gave her a surprised look, then shrugged and began untying her laces. Veronica stood stone still, waiting for Celeste to speak.

"Have you nothing to say to me, sister?"

Veronica locked her emotionless eyes on Celeste as she said, "Nothing."

Celeste held Veronica's gaze while she shrugged out of her painting smock and let it fall to the floor. While Livia helped remove her undergarments, she said, "I've never gone to hear your prior preach. I hear he's quite charismatic and convincing."

"Don't use that disparaging tone when you speak of Prior Savonarola. He's God's Holy representative in this depraved region of the world."

Celeste's furious glare silenced Veronica mid-sentence. "I did not give you permission to speak." Veronica backed away from the force of her words. "But you are sadly mistaken, Veronica. Archbishop Orsini is God's representative in Florence. Rumors have reached His Eminence that the Holy

Father has sufficient evidence to excommunicate your beloved prior. So, who should we choose to follow?"

"Pope Alexander is corrupt and anything but *holy*. He's turned Rome into a cesspool of evil. I will never bow to that man."

Livia gasped, and Celeste raised her hand to strike her sister. She froze with her hand poised in midair before slowly lowering her arm.

Struggling to control her anger, she said, "That's blasphemy. Do you wish to be excommunicated along with Savonarola?"

Veronica straightened to her full height and raised her chin. "I would consider it an honor."

The fire in her sister's eyes disturbed Celeste, making her more convinced than ever that she had to get Veronica out of their home, for Luciano's safety and the children's.

"In that case, sister, you are a fool. I'm an even bigger fool for letting you out of that convent. I will be writing to Cousin Cesare tonight to petition the Venice Gabrieles to take responsibility for you, as you are no longer welcome under this roof."

"You wouldn't dare do that to me," Veronica stammered. "I refuse to leave and abandon Prior Savonarola."

Livia reached for a pin to fasten Celeste's last lock of loose hair into place but ducked out of the way when Celeste stepped closer to Veronica. Leaning her face within two inches of her sister's, she said, "What will you do? Run away? We all remember how well that worked out for you last time, don't we?"

As Celeste turned on her heel to go, she saw Veronica's lip tremble.

"I only strive to follow God and his anointed servants," she whispered.

"Savonarola is *not* God's anointed. You are the disciple of a ravening wolf." Celeste no longer felt compassion for her lost sister, only pity. Veronica was a poisonous presence that had to be removed.

"I had better not find you anywhere near my children from this moment on. You are not to leave your quarters without my permission. Livia, escort Veronica to her room."

Veronica's voice wavered as she said, "So, I am to be a prisoner in my own home?"

Celeste paused in the doorway with her back to Veronica. "You are mistaken, sister. This is no longer your home."

Celeste moved into the hallway, then stepped aside to allow Livia and Veronica to pass. When they rounded the corner, Celeste slumped against the wall and covered her face with her trembling hands. In the past, Celeste would have blamed herself for failing her sister, but no longer. Veronica had always been emotionally unstable and easily led, but this was not entirely her fault. Celeste blamed the duplicitous and cunning Savonarola for turning her weak-willed sister into a fanatic.

CHAPTER FOUR

FLORENCE 1497

CELESTE APPROACHED a window overlooking the gardens on her way to the studio after a delightful lunch with her children. It was an unseasonably warm winter's day, and she wanted to bask in the sun's comforting rays while she could. Since her bitter confrontation with Veronica two weeks earlier, the weather had been cold and gloomy to match the mood of the household. Feeling the sun's warmth gave her hope they might yet find a peaceful way out of their stressful situation.

When Celeste later recounted the incident with her sister to Luciano, he'd wanted to toss Veronica onto the street that very night, but Celeste refused to let him. She had suffered that same dreadful experience many years earlier and wouldn't wish it on anyone, not even her wayward sister. She told Luciano that Veronica had brought shame to the family before and there was no telling what might happen if she were put out on the street. She persuaded Luciano to allow Veronica to stay so long as she kept to her rooms while they waited for word from Cousin Cesare. Luciano had wanted to place a houseboy at her door to stand guard, but Celeste felt that was a bit drastic.

As a compromise, Celeste instructed the housekeeper to

have the servants keep an eye on Veronica. The only other concession Celeste granted was to allow Veronica to attend Savonarola's sermons, but only after her tantrums became unbearable. Celeste's one ironclad condition was that her sister always be accompanied by two male servants when she left the palazzo.

Allowing Veronica to attend the sermons had sparked an argument with Luciano, but Celeste reminded him that it would only be until they received word from Cesare. Celeste feared that if they refused to permit Veronica to go hear Savonarola, she'd spend every waking moment looking for ways to escape. Celeste didn't have the time or energy to spend dealing with that.

Celeste expected a letter from Cesare any day but was doubtful she would receive a positive answer. The Gabriele clan had never forgiven Veronica for tarnishing the family's reputation. In truth, few people in Venice knew of Veronica's scandalous behavior and the ones who did were either friends or relations and would never dare divulge their secret. After ten long years, most of Venice had forgotten Veronica even existed. If by some miracle Cesare took her in, Celeste had no doubt he would keep her sequestered in his palazzo, which was no less than she deserved.

As Celeste gazed over the gardens, she detected a movement in the corner of her eye which caught her attention. She turned her head in time to see a woman in a plain brown hooded cloak slip through the gate at the rear of the estate. She realized in an instant that it was Veronica, and she was alone. Celeste hurried back toward the sala, calling for Livia.

"Bring our cloaks and hurry. We're going out." Livia opened her mouth to question her, but Celeste shooed her away before she could.

While she waited, she sent her houseboy to prepare the carriage. Veronica was on foot, but Celeste had no doubt of her destination, the piazza in front of the Duomo where Savonarola preached his sermons. If they were lucky, they'd arrive before she reached the plaza. The carriage was ready and waiting in the drive by the time Livia returned with Celeste's cloak. She pulled it over her shoulders as they raced down the front steps to the carriage.

"Where are we going, mistress?" Livia asked as they settled into their seats.

"To hear the Prior preach, and to bring my sister home. I saw her leaving without her escorts through the garden gate."

Livia put her hand to her mouth. "How did she get away?"

"I'll look into that when we return home. Veronica is cunning and determined, and the maids were busy with other chores. I predict she was biding her time, waiting for the perfect time to make her escape. I wonder how many times she has done this. It was foolish to trust her."

Livia laid her hand on Celeste's arm. "What will my Master do when he learns about this?"

Celeste turned to look out the carriage window and did not answer. She knew what would happen, but she pushed it from her mind. There would be time to deal with Luciano later. Her first consideration was to find Veronica and bring her home. Nothing beyond that mattered.

As they descended the hill into town, they had a clear view of teeming crowds of the Prior's devotees making their way toward the piazza. Celeste instructed the driver to park two blocks away. She climbed out of the carriage the instant it came to a stop, with Livia close behind.

As they headed toward the piazza, Celeste said, "Keep your hood low around your face. Speak with no one."

Livia nodded as she tugged on her hood. Celeste wrapped a scarf around her face so all that was visible were her eyes. She was much more likely to be recognized in her fine clothes than Livia was in her servant attire. As she moved among the throng, she was fearful she would be recognized and wrongly identified as a supporter of the Prior. There would be terrible repercussions for Luciano if that happened. As they inched closer to the basilica, she began to question her sanity at rushing off after Veronica. The act was impetuous, and Luciano would be furious when he found out. It would have been just as easy to send some of the servants to bring her sister home or wait for her to return.

As Celeste was about to return to the carriage, Savonarola exited the basilica with his entourage. To her immense dismay, Veronica stepped up behind him, surrounded by ten nuns, about twenty feet from the Prior. It would be impossible to get anywhere near her without coming to the attention of the crowd. Celeste quickly deduced what was happening.

"Why is your sister with the Prior?" Livia whispered. "Why should she matter to him?"

Celeste moved her lips close to Livia's ear. "Because she's related to a prominent Florentine family. She gives the movement credibility. This is worse than I feared. We should go and wait for Veronica at home."

Gripping Celeste's arm, she said, "That would be most sensible, mistress. We must hurry."

When Celeste turned to go, she was met with a solid wall of worshippers. If she and Livia attempted to push their way through the throng, it might arouse suspicion. They were trapped. She glanced at Livia, whose eyes were wide in fear. Linking arms with her maid in a show of feigned confidence, she took a breath and turned back toward the dreaded Prior with her head bowed. They were only twenty feet from where Savonarola stood and would be forced to stay for the entire sermon.

"I'm sorry, Livia," she whispered. "Courage."

Livia gave a weak smile and patted Celeste's arm. "It's just a sermon, madam. How dangerous can that be?"

Worse than you could imagine, Celeste thought as she turned her attention to Savonarola. He stepped towards the front of the throng and raised his arms to silence the crowd. They quieted and held their collective breath as they waited for their beloved prophet to speak. He took advantage of their anticipation and dramatically waited several moments before addressing his eager disciples.

"My devoted flock," he began, keeping his voice gentle and inviting. "This morning I received a courier from the Vatican with a communication from Pope Alexander." He paused as a murmur of alarm arose in the crowd, then raised the message for them to see. "He threatens me with excommunication if I do not cease the preaching of God's truth."

The chattering of the crowd stopped abruptly. Celeste dared to raise her head ever so slightly and glanced at the people pressing around her. She wasn't surprised to see them staring at their friar in stunned silence.

"How dare he claim himself God's mouthpiece on earth? I am Christ's true prophet. He has shown me my calling in glorious visions. Have I not long prophesied of this moment? Have I not predicted that Rome would burn, and Florence will become the New Jerusalem, God's golden city? That time is now upon us. We must cleanse and purify ourselves in preparation."

As the passion rose in his voice, many of the listeners seemed to grow more frenzied. But there were others who appeared to be uncomfortable with the Prior's denunciation of the Holy Father. It was truly daring and dangerous to blatantly criticize the Pope in such a way. As Celeste scanned the crowd, she recognized some who were pushing their way out of the throng toward nearby streets. While Celeste considered if she should follow them, Savonarola raised his voice above the hum of the crowd.

"Four weeks from today," he continued, "we will baptize

this city in fire. Bring your implements of vanity and sin to the Piazza della Signoria. Rid yourselves of ostentation, lasciviousness, drunkenness, and gambling. Bring your blasphemous books. Discard your works of art inspired by the devil to become free of his power. Thrust them into the fires and be sanctified. I will send my young followers house to house to collect your vanities. We must rid Florence of filth if we are to be God's chosen people."

Celeste reached for Livia's hand. "Come, we're going. Don't let go of me."

Before turning to go, Celeste took one last glance at Savonarola and was surprised to find Veronica staring directly at her. She held her sister's gaze, sensing a change in her. It appeared her piety and self-righteous judgement had been replaced with fear and foreboding.

Celeste took a firm hold of Livia's arm, and keeping her head bowed, lowered her shoulder to push her way through the chaotic throng toward their carriage. When they broke free, they ran to the carriage, and Celeste ordered the driver to put the lash to the horses to get them out of the city and far away from the streaming crowds. She closed the curtains, embraced Livia, and prayed they would reach home without incident. She only relaxed when the carriage was safely on the road leading to the palazzo.

Livia crossed herself, and said, "Did you hear what that man said? He blasphemed against the Holy Father and called himself God's prophet. How can he dare utter such things? He's said he's going to burn Florence. What will the Master do?"

Celeste put her arm around Livia and pulled her close. "I heard. As for what Luciano will do, I can't say. Savonarola's puppets have threatened Luciano's artwork before this. What will they do now?"

"And what of your sister? How can she be his disciple?"

"The friar has twisted and manipulated her mind, turning her into his fanatical follower. I must get her away from that poisonous snake. I hope the letter from my cousin Cesare will be waiting for us at home. Sending her to Venice would be the best thing for her."

Celeste's swirling thoughts became a knotted mess. She'd cautioned Luciano against becoming more entrenched with the Arrabbiati, but he hadn't listened. He'd been angry with her when she told him of allowing Veronica to continue hearing Savonarola's sermons and had tried to change her mind. How she wished she'd listened. The Prior truly was an enemy to all they stood for and believed, just as Luciano had tried to make her understand. His attacks against the Holy Father and promise to purge Florence of all iniquity threatened everything they held dear and could lead to bloodshed and reprisals.

She wasted no time exiting the carriage when they reached the palazzo. The page bowed as she rushed into the foyer and said, "Are there any letters from Venice, Bardo?"

"None, mistress."

Celeste's heart sank. Cousin Cesare was the answer to their troubles with Veronica. She couldn't imagine why he'd delayed in responding to her request. Even if the answer were no, he wouldn't have hesitated to write and inform her of it.

"Is your Master in the workshop?" she asked as Livia removed her cloak.

Bardo shook his head. "He hasn't returned since leaving this morning."

"Please, inform me the moment he returns, and Signora Veronica as well." Bardo bowed again as Celeste and Livia headed up the stairs to her chambers. "Livia, please leave me. I need to rest and consider what may be done. I'll join my daughters in the sitting room before dinner. Please ask them to join me there in two hours."

Livia nodded before going to the antechamber. Celeste

climbed onto the bed and took a few deep breaths to quiet her mind before closing her eyes. She had no doubt the coming week would be a challenging one, and she needed to remain strong and collected. She replayed Savonarola's unsettling sermon over in her mind. She shivered at the memory of the crowd's frenzied reaction, and Veronica's role in the entire mess. They'd weathered far worse in the past. She would do all in her power to make sure they conquered this trial too.

Luciano grew increasingly alarmed as he listened to the informant's report. He wasn't the only one. He could see the same reaction in the disturbed faces of the other members of the Arrabbiati in attendance. Savonarola's puppet government lackeys were stepping up their reprisals against the Florentine nobles and patricians who refused to fall into line behind the deranged friar. It was only a manner of time before they were targeted.

When the informant completed his report, Messer Mancini rose to address the men assembled in the tightly packed sala of Mancini's palazzo. The group had been forced to abandon their previous meetinghouse for security concerns. Mancini had doubled his house guard, and, so far, the Frateschi, Florence's ruling government body, hadn't dared target opposition members directly in their homes. Luciano secretly prayed that would never change.

"This is troubling news, indeed," Mancini began. "This friar has deluded himself and many commoners into believing that he is God's representative on earth. He believes he is unfettered by the laws of the Church or the Republic."

The nobleman Graziano Galli, a friend of Luciano's, stood and pounded his fist on the table. "There's nothing more dangerous than a religious fanatic who attempts to usurp political power in the name of God. Such a man is the most dangerous type of creature. He must be stopped and soon. We can no longer wait for Rome or Milan to come to our aid."

Mancini gestured for Galli to return to his seat. "We all agree Savonarola must be stopped immediately, but we're not ready to take such action without the aid of Rome. We can't rush to battle against our own citizens. If we eliminate the friar and those closest to him, I don't believe the rest would cause trouble. We must be patient a little longer." As Mancini was addressing the group, his chief guard rushed in, followed by a young man Luciano didn't recognize. "What is it, Angelo? I've ordered you not to disturb us when we're in session."

Angelo gave a low bow, and said, "Forgive me, master, but Danilo here has just come from the friar's latest sermon. You will want to hear what he has to say."

Mancini waved for Danilo to step forward. "Go ahead. Tell us what you heard."

The man stepped beside Mancini, facing the group. He was of average height, but strong as a plow horse with no neck to speak of. He looked to be no more than twenty.

He gave a slight bow before solemnly turning his dark eyes on the men seated before him. "I have just come from witnessing a most disturbing spectacle. Prior Savonarola said the Holy Father is preparing to excommunicate him." Exclamations of surprise and approval erupted from the men. Danilo waited for them to quiet before continuing. "The friar speaks as if he is declaring war on Rome, and he has thousands of loyal followers here in Florence. I saw them with my own eyes. He publicly stated that he will be holding a bonfire in the Piazza della Signoria four weeks hence, for the people to rid themselves of their sins and vanities. He declares he is going to baptize Florence by fire to cleanse the city. He also says he will send his most loyal followers from house to house collecting sinful articles that should be consumed in flames."

"Outrageous!" one of the men cried. "If the people stand by and do nothing, we must be the ones to put a stop to this."

"Thank you, Danilo," Mancini said, ignoring the man's outburst. "You've done well."

Danilo leaned closer to Mancini and whispered something to him before following the guard out. Mancini turned his gaze on Luciano ever so briefly but said nothing before getting back to the matter at hand.

"I appreciate your zeal, Signore D'Amico, but we're going to do nothing to stop this. Let the citizens of Florence see this crazed cleric for who he truly is, and they will turn against him. Once the Holy Father goes through with the excommunication, Savonarola's flock will shrink from thousands to dozens. Trust me on this."

"How can you be so certain?" D'Amico asked. "The Florentines seem to have lost their minds over this fool."

"Don't mistake him for a fool," Luciano said. "He's cunning and manipulative. He lulls the people into believing he's a saintly follower of Christ. They will soon discover he cares for nothing more than his hold on power."

"Vicente's right," Mancini said. "Return to your homes. Protect your families and watch your words. We'll bide our time until the most opportune moment. I will write to the Holy Father tonight and wait for his word. Then we'll know when to act. We are adjourned."

As the men stood to leave, Mancini headed straight for Luciano. "May I speak with you privately?"

"Of course, friend. What is it?"

Without answering, Mancini motioned for Luciano to follow him to his office. Once they were seated, Mancini said, "Your wife was spotted in the congregation with her maidservant today, Luci, and her sister was seen at Savonarola's side."

Luciano shot to his feet. "Your man must be mistaken.

Celeste would never go anywhere near the friar. As for my sister-in-law, I informed you that she's a disciple of our enemy."

Mancini studied him for a moment before saying, "It's hard to mistake your elegant wife. If she was there, there will be others who noticed her presence no doubt. Speak with Signora Gabriele. Hear her side of the story, but you must warn her to be more cautious. If word spreads that she's become a follower of Savonarola, people will believe that your family has fallen under the spell of that madman, including you. This could weaken our efforts and standing in Florence if you are not careful."

Luciano stood and leaned on the desktop. "I assure you without any doubt that my wife is no follower of the friar. There must be a sensible explanation. Look for word from me no later than tomorrow morning."

Luciano gave a slight bow, then strode out without another word. As he rode home, he struggled to make sense of what Mancini had told him. All he could hope was that Celeste had a good explanation for why she was at that sermon. He pushed his horse to speed up as he hoped he'd find his wife safe at home.

CELESTE NERVOUSLY PACED in the sala waiting for Luciano to return when Bardo came in and handed her a letter.

"The courier just delivered this for you, madam," he said.

"Is he waiting for a response?"

He shook his head and bowed before exiting, leaving her alone with her worries. Celeste turned the letter over and was relieved to see it was from Cesare. She tore it open and skimmed the contents. Celeste's heart sank at what she read.

My dearest cousin Celeste,

When I read your most recent letter, I was deeply saddened but not surprised to learn of your troubles with Veronica. We all hoped that her years in the convent would have led her to repent of her reckless ways. I for one expected the maturity which comes with growing older and wiser in the company of the good sisters would have changed her. It's greatly disappointing to learn that wasn't the case.

After much discussion with the various Gabriele heads of households, we have unanimously agreed that allowing Veronica to come live with us would be most unwise. We cannot risk the scandal that would inevitably result. We pray that you will be able to provide her the guidance and correction she needs at this time. Our best advice is that you find a convent in Florence and beg them to admit your sister and be shed of her forever. She will only bring your family more shame.

We earnestly look forward to your next visit to your home country and pray it will be under brighter circumstances. Please convey our heartfelt wishes to your aunt Portia.

With deepest affection,

Cesare Gabriele

Celeste crumpled the letter in her fist as she lowered her hand to her side. Cesare's answer was what she expected, but that did nothing to soften the blow. Cesare strong words about Veronica made her again regret bringing her sister back into her household. It was made worse coming on the heels of the incident at Savonarola's sermon. Veronica still hadn't returned, and Celeste was beginning to fear she'd looked on her sister for the last time.

The hour was growing late, and she had no way of knowing when Luciano would return. Just as she started for the dining room where the children were waiting for her to begin their meal, an angry Luciano burst into the sala. She rushed forward and embraced him, but his arms remained limp at his sides.

She pulled away and looked up at him in confusion. "What is it, my love? Where have you been?"

He led her to a set of chairs and waited for her to sit before saying, "I've just come from a meeting with the Arrabbiati. Messer Mancini has received word that you and Livia attended Savonarola's sermon today. Is this true?"

She stared at him in alarm. "What do you mean he received word? Is he having me followed?"

Luciano placed his hands on the arms of her chair and leaned his face close to hers. "You haven't answered my question."

She lowered her head, and whispered, "Yes, Luciano, we were there."

He straightened and turned his back to her. "What possibly could have compelled you to set foot in that place, especially without any protection? You know the risk. You could have been harmed, or worse. And do you realize the precarious position you've put me in?"

Celeste explained about Veronica escaping and what she'd witnessed at the sermon. "I'm deeply sorry, my love. I realized my error the moment I stepped onto the piazza, but by then it was too late to get away. Livia and I became hemmed in by the surging crowd."

Luciano sank into the chair beside her and rubbed his face. "You must give me your solemn word that you will never again do anything so rash."

"I understand your anger, Luciano, but I've already said I've realized my mistake. It was a harrowing experience that I have no intension of repeating. Livia still hasn't recovered, poor thing. Now tell me how Mancini found out I was in the crowd at Savonarola's sermon."

He hesitated for a moment before saying, "His men weren't following you. They were there to report on the Prior and happened to spot you in the crowd. You're well known in Florence, my dear. Did you really expect you would not be recognized? He recognized Veronica as well."

"I did my best to keep my face covered. I wonder who else recognized me there?"

"We'll know soon enough, once gossip begins to spread." He glanced at her and saw the letter in her hand. "From Cesare?" When she gave a quick nod, he said, "Not the answer we hoped for, then?"

"My family wants nothing to do with Veronica, but the problem may have been resolved for us. Veronica still hasn't returned, and I'm terribly worried. Should we send out a search party?"

"There's no need, sister," Veronica said as she strode into the room as if she were Mistress of the palazzo returning from a routine day in the marketplace.

Luciano shot out of his chair. Celeste held her breath and wondered if her husband might strike her, though he'd never even come close to doing such a thing. Veronica's haughtiness wilted slightly under Luciano's fierce glare.

"I'm shocked you would dare set foot under my roof," he said through his clenched teeth.

"Where else would I go, brother?" she stammered. "This is my home."

"No longer, *sister,*" he said, practically spitting the words. "You have violated every condition I've set for allowing you to remain here. My patience is now exhausted. Pack your belongings and go."

Veronica began to tremble. "Tonight? In the dark?"

"Yes. Now. It's no less than you deserve."

Celeste got to her feet and stepped between him and Veronica. "I won't plead for leniency for my sister, Luciano, but please let her stay until dawn. I'll guard her door all night if need be."

He kept his eyes on Veronica as he shook his head. "Not this time, my love. She leaves tonight."

Celeste moved closer to him and laid her hand on his arm. "But where will she go?"

"Wherever she wishes. That's no longer my concern."

Celeste turned toward Veronica as she said, "Take me to the convent at San Marco's. They'd be honored to have me there."

Luciano barked a laugh. "With no one to pay your support or vouch for you? I wouldn't be so certain of that."

"The Prior will gladly arrange for my support. It will only serve to prove you are the proud and heartless man he claims you to be."

"I care nothing for that wretched man's opinion. Get out of my house and never show your face to me again."

As he turned to go, Celeste said, "Please, Luciano. Don't treat Veronica the way your cousin Maria Foscari treated me all those years ago. Have you forgotten what happened when she threw me out on the streets of Venice in the dead of night?"

Luciano spun around to face her. "How can you ask me that? I'm nothing like Maria. What my cousin did to you was cruel and unjustified. You didn't deserve it unlike Veronica. She was perfectly aware of the risk she was taking, and I won't have that treacherous creature in this house a moment longer."

Celeste bowed her head and folded her hands over her skirts. "You're right, my love. Comparing you to Maria was wrong, but at least allow me to take Mateo and Luca to escort her to the convent."

Luciano studied Celeste for a moment, then gave a slight nod. "Whatever it takes to get rid of her," he said as he stormed off.

Celeste turned toward her sister. "Hurry, gather your things before Luciano changes his mind." Veronica opened her mouth to speak, but Celeste held up a hand to stop her. "The time for words has passed. Go before I toss you out myself."

Veronica flashed her an angry look as she brushed past on her way to her chambers. Celeste called for a houseboy and ordered him to summon Mateo and Luca to the sala. As he hurried out, she sank back into her chair and covered her face in her hands. She'd known since receiving Marco's letter informing them Veronica wished to leave the convent that bringing her to Florence was a bad idea. Her sister's actions had done nothing more than prove her right. She was an unstable woman who'd never been capable of governing her emotions or actions. Her last hope was that the nuns of San Marco's would take her off their hands.

Mateo and Luca followed the houseboy into the sala and in unison asked what had happened. She raised her hands to silence them, and said, "There's no cause for alarm. I need you to accompany me to take Aunt Veronica to San Marco's. She's entering the convent."

"Thank God," Mateo said. "It's about time we got rid of that lunatic."

"Watch your mouth around Mamma," Luca said. "And don't speak of our aunt that way."

Mateo turned to face him. "Who are you to give me orders?"

Celeste stood and stepped between them. "The last thing I need is to listen to you two bickering, but Luca's right. You mustn't talk that way in front of me or anyone else, Mateo. Veronica has her eccentricities, but I won't have you speaking ill of her, young man. Call for the carriage. Luca, go to your aunt and help her carry her belongings to the foyer."

As the boys moved quickly to carry out her orders, she called for Livia. When her maid saw the look on her face, she led her to the closest chair and insisted she sit.

"What is the matter, madam?" After Celeste recounted the scene with Veronica, Livia said, "Praise the Good Lord. It's past time the Master sent that viper out of this house."

Celeste gave a weary sigh. "I never thought I'd hear you sound like Mateo. Please fetch our cloaks. This trying day is not over yet. I'd like you to accompany us if you feel up to it. I need to draw on your strength tonight, my friend."

Livia made a deep curtsy. "I live to serve your command, mistress."

She rose and winked at Celeste as she rushed off. Celeste couldn't help but laugh. She could always count on Livia to raise her spirits.

The five of them were on their way twenty minutes later. Mateo and Livia sat across from Veronica, glaring at her. Veronica simply turned toward the window and ignored them. Celeste sat beside her with Luca on her other side. She tried to hold Veronica's hand, but she pulled it away. It didn't surprise Celeste, but it did sadden her. Veronica had caused more than her share of trouble and heartache over the years, but Celeste still loved her, and she wanted her to know.

Celeste's anxiety increased with each turn of the carriage wheels. When they reached the outer gate, she could hardly breathe. Livia squeezed her hand and gave her a knowing look. Celeste was grateful her maid had agreed to come along for support.

"Stay here," she told her sons as she climbed out of the carriage behind Veronica. "Be ready to bring your aunt's bags."

Livia followed her out and they got into step behind Veronica. When her sister reached the gate, she pulled the bell cord and kept her back to them as the three of them waited. It took nearly five minutes before the small viewing door in the gate slid open and a pair of tired brown eyes surrounded by wrinkles stared out at them for a moment. The Sister seemed to recognize Veronica immediately. They heard the locks opening and the bolt sliding aside seconds later. The iron gate swung open, and the Sister motioned for Veronica to enter.

When Celeste stepped forward to follow her, the Sister held up her hand.

"You are forbidden to enter here, Signora Gabriele," she said softly.

"Very well," Celeste said in frustration. She'd entered San Marco's many times to help render aid to the poor and downtrodden. Without explanation, she was now denied entry. Celeste felt outrage, but she restrained herself. Her task was to get rid of Veronica and that was all.

"Will you wait while I retrieve my sister's belongings?"

The Sister shook her head. "There is no need, madam. Donate what she has to the poor. We will provide for all her needs."

She slowly closed the door in their faces and slid the worn metal bolt into place.

Celeste and Livia stared at each other for a moment, baffled by what had just happened.

"I suppose that is that," Livia said with a shrug, then took Celeste's hand to coax her toward the carriage.

Celeste glanced over her shoulder at the imposing black gate. "My sister is now lost to me forever."

As Livia helped her into the carriage, she said, "You said the same ten years ago in Venice. No one but God knows our future, but I say, good riddance."

"I suppose," she whispered as the driver turned the carriage toward home.

CHAPTER FIVE

FLORENCE 1497

CELESTE SLOWLY CHEWED a bite of bread as she pondered how to tell Aunt Portia about the ordeal with Veronica and her return to the convent the previous night. After breakfast, she walked upstairs and peeked inside her aunt's chamber. Portia was propped up in her bed as usual, but upon seeing Celeste, she smiled and waved her in. She patted the blanket beside her encouraging Celeste to take a seat next to her.

Celeste walked in and sat on the edge of the bed, then took Portia's wrinkled hand in hers. "Leaving Veronica in San Marco's was the last thing I expected to happen when I brought her back to Florence. It feels like my sister was here for the briefest moment and is now gone forever."

"Some are incapable of making good choices. She was never able to see beyond herself. Even her search for God's path was misguided. It is not your fault, my dear. You did everything you could to give her a second chance at a good life. You must forget her. We're all better off with her sequestered behind the convent walls. Elena most of all. How is the girl coping with her mother's sudden departure?"

"It's too early to tell. Elena was surprised, but she didn't seem bothered by it. Honestly, she looked relieved. I believe Veronica frightened her. On the other hand, Mateo and Luca are elated to have Veronica out of the house as are the twins." Celeste massaged her temples to soothe her budding headache before continuing. "I wanted you to hear this from me before the palazzo gossip runs rampant."

Portia chuckled at that. "I appreciate it, dear." Portia yawned and sank deeper into the pillows. "I didn't sleep well and need my morning rest. Visit me before dinner if you can manage it. I know you have many demands on your time, but I miss our daily visits. Now that Veronica is gone, I suspect you will have a little more time on your hands."

"True enough. I'll come as soon as I'm able. Thank you for your words of comfort." She paused in the doorway and gave Portia a tender smile. "I love you, aunt. Rest well. Call for me if you need anything."

Her aunt nodded, then closed her eyes as Celeste shut the door. As Celeste walked down the hall, she wondered how many more days her aunt's body could hold out. It wouldn't be long before she entered the next phase of her journey. She was growing frailer by the day, and Celeste was forced to ponder life without her. Losing Portia would leave a terrible void in her life, which she'd never be able to fill.

As was Celeste's custom, she finished each workday sitting in the window seat in her studio to meditate as she gazed over the manicured gardens. On occasion, she'd see the twins near her favorite spot under an enormous oak with Angela painting and Cristina posing as her model. Angela enjoyed those sessions far more than Cristina, but it always warmed Celeste's heart to see them getting along instead of bickering.

On other occasions, she'd catch Luciano and their son's

tutors teaching Mateo and Luca fencing and swordplay. It was a necessary skill Celeste hoped they'd never need, but it was important for young men to be practiced in the arts of war in their volatile society.

On that day, she'd scarcely sat on her cherished marble seat when she caught sight of Luca and Mateo on the far side of the garden with their swords drawn, clearly not engaged in a playful joust. Both were red faced and agitated, shouting hateful words at each other. She jumped up and raced down the back stairs to the garden door. Crossing the lawn as quickly as her legs would carry her, she reached them just as Mateo lunged at the younger and smaller Luca with his sword. Luca, who was more agile than his older brother, evaded Mateo's violent stroke just in time.

As Mateo raised his weapon to strike again, Celeste stepped between the boys. "Mateo, drop that sword this instant!" she ordered.

Without taking his eyes off Luca, who was scrambling to his feet behind Celeste, he said, "I won't. I must settle this once and for all. My honor demands it. Get out of my way, mother."

Instead of stepping aside, she moved closer to him. "How dare you give me orders? I will not retreat, so you will have to go through me to reach your brother." Mateo shifted his gaze from Luca to her as he slowly lowered his sword. For all his bravado, he knew better than to challenge her even though, at twenty he was an athletic, strong young man. "Good choice. Now, the two of you drop those swords and come with me."

They immediately obeyed and got into step behind her as she marched them to the family sitting room. She pointed toward the two chairs near the fireplace and glared at them while they took their seats. She remained standing, scowling down at them.

"It wasn't my fault," Luca said before she could speak.

"Silence," she said. "I will get to you in a moment. Mateo, you're the eldest. Explain to me why I came upon you as you were about to plunge a sword through your brother."

Mateo leaned back in his chair and calmly looked her in the eye. "He questioned my birthright, so I challenged him to a duel."

"A duel? I've never heard anything so outrageous. He's your brother. If you had a disagreement, you should have come to your father or me. We don't settle arguments with sword fights, which is a sentence I never imagined I'd have the need to utter. You're old enough to know better, Mateo." She turned her eyes on Luca. "How did you challenge his birthright?"

"He was boasting that none of Papa's estate will ever be mine. I told him he'd have Papa's title and Venice estate, but Florence is *my* birthright by blood. He swore that the moment our father is in the crypt, he'd claim the entire estate and throw me out into the streets."

Celeste rubbed her forehead and sighed in frustration. "First off, I don't appreciate the two of you planning your father's demise. He's strong and healthy, and will live for many years to come, God willing. Mateo, you understand perfectly well what you said isn't true. Your father has explained his wishes to you. You'll have no grounds to dispute it when the day comes. I'm also deeply distressed that you would ever consider throwing your own brother onto the street. Is that the kind of man you've become? If so, I no longer want you living under this roof. You're old enough to make your own way in the world. Is this what you wish?"

"You'd love that wouldn't you?" Mateo snapped. "Then you'd have your precious Luca all to yourself."

"Mateo! How dare you use that tone with your mother?" Luciano said as he strode into the room. "Apologize this instant. Then explain what's happening here."

Mateo bowed his head, and said, "Yes, Papa. Forgive me, mother."

His apology was utterly devoid of sincerity, but Celeste said, "You're forgiven, but never speak to me that way again or you will be on the street fighting for food with the wild dogs."

"Yes, Mamma," he said, still keeping his eyes averted.

"As for what's going on," Celeste said to Luciano, "I caught your sons fighting a duel. I stopped Mateo as he was preparing to strike Luca."

"What!" Luciano said. "Get on your feet and explain yourself." Mateo kept his head bowed as he slowly rose. He repeated the story he'd told Celeste, only in a much humbler tone.

When he finished, Luciano glanced at Luca. "Is your brother's account accurate?" Luca gave a slight nod but said nothing. "It seems I'm raising a pair of fools. Mateo, you and I have discussed your inheritance on multiple occasions. You will receive my title and the lion's share of my estate. How dare you begrudge your younger brother his entitlement? Are you so selfish and greedy? You never learned that from me. It's not too late for me to change the bequest. I must admit, at this moment, I'm tempted to do so. Would you prefer I disowned you and tossed you out as you threatened to do to your brother?"

Celeste knew Luciano would never consider disowning Mateo. Even so, she enjoyed the pleasure of hearing him say it.

Mateo sank to his knees and raised his clasped hands to his father. "No, Papa. Please, I beg you to forgive me. I became angry and lost my head. I never would have harmed Luca. You must believe me. I'll never do such a thing again. You have my solemn word."

"Get up," Luciano ordered. "What a pathetic display. You beg my forgiveness when your inheritance is on the line. Would you have done so out of remorse or regret?"

Mateo got up and looked Luciano in the eye. "Of course, Papa. I see how wrong I was. You know my temper."

"Yes, unfortunately I do. We've talked about you learning to control your emotions, but I've seen little improvement. Make sure that changes at once."

Luciano turned his sons to face each other. "It is not only your mother and I that need an apology. What do you have to say to Luca, Mateo?"

Celeste caught Mateo's slight hesitation before saying, "Forgive me, dear brother. What I did was unconscionable and undeserved. It will never happen again. Forget the hurtful things I said and know I meant none of it."

Luca eyed him for a moment before smiling and gripping Mateo's forearm. "Of course, I forgive you. We're both fools who acted in error. Let's be friends and loving brothers once more."

Mateo dipped his head in agreement, then quickly pulled his arm free. "Done."

"Both of you go to your chambers until dinner and reflect on what happened here today. Let us never speak of it again."

"Yes, Papa," they said in unison as they left the room.

When they were out of earshot, Celeste said, "That's all you're going to do to Mateo? No repercussions? No punishment? He would have killed Luca if I hadn't reached them in time."

Luciano smiled and shook his head. "You heard what Mateo said. He never would have injured Luca. He was just trying to prove his superiority over his little brother. You know he's always been jealous of Luca, believing you love him more because he's your blood son."

"Mateo only says what you want to hear. Have you forgotten he nearly killed Luca out of jealousy when he was a baby? What's to stop him now?"

"You can't seriously compare what happened then to this

incident. Mateo was an eight-year-old boy in turmoil after being torn from the only life he'd ever known. He never has harmed Luca deliberately since that day. The two of them squabble like all brothers, nothing more."

"This was no squabble, Luciano. You didn't see Mateo's eyes. He would have killed Luca."

Luciano pulled her close and kissed the top of her head. "It may have appeared that way in the moment. Mateo would have come to his senses before he acted. Our son is no murderer."

"I pray you're right, but all the same, please keep a closer eye on him. He's becoming more arrogant and restless by the day. You see how strong he has become. He could easily hurt Luca."

"I will. These are delicate and turbulent times. We can't have Mateo lashing out at his unruly friends in the heat of a drunken moment, adding to our trouble. I've been planning to turn some of the more menial tasks of running the estate over to him. Perhaps now is the time."

"Without question. Mateo needs to be kept occupied. Teach him that being a Duca is about more than power and wealth. It's about responsibility, leadership, and service. The sooner he understands this, the safer we'll all be."

"Very well, my love. We'll begin tomorrow, but let's put this from our minds for now and change for dinner. I'm starved from working through lunch." As they ascended the stairs, he said, "What's the progress on the commission for Messer Ardinghelli?"

"I completed it today. Come to the studio after dinner and I'll show you."

He smiled and kissed her cheek. "With pleasure."

They walked the rest of the way to their chambers in silence, each lost in thought. As much as Luciano had told Celeste to put the incident with Luca and Mateo from her mind, she couldn't forget the look in Mateo's eyes. Recalling the disturbing image made her quiver with fear. She wondered what thoughts lurked in Mateo's heart. She resolved to be on her guard and would tell Luca to give his brother a wide berth. She was certain he wouldn't need much encouragement.

"AM I never to know a moment's peace with my children?" Celeste said when she came upon Angela and Cristina during an argument in their chamber the next day. "As if your brothers don't give me trouble enough. What is it this time?" When they both started talking at once, she held up her hands to silence them. "One at a time. Angela, you are first."

"Angela always gets to go first just because she's two minutes older than I." Cristina whined.

Celeste nodded, realizing Cristina was right. "Very well, sweetheart. Why are you arguing with your sister?"

Cristina frowned at Angela, then said, "She said Papa loves her more because she's a talented painter, and I'm not good at anything."

"Angela," Celeste snapped. "What a cruel thing to say. That's not like you. Apologize to your sister."

Angela pointed at Cristina. "She said I think I'm better than everyone else, but I'll never be as good a painter as you or Papa. Admit it, Cristina."

Celeste was surprised. Cristina was usually a docile peacemaker, and she wondered if Angela had struck a soft spot. "Is this true?" Cristina nodded and looked away. "What brought this on? You're usually the best of friends and have your bond as twins."

Angela stole a peek at Cristina but held her tongue.

Cristina dropped into a chair and crossed her arms. "She wanted me to go into the garden and pose for her, but it's too cold for me to stand outside for hours on end, and I have better things to do with my time."

Angela huffed at that. "What do you have to do that's more important than helping me finish my painting?"

Cristina stuck her lip out in a pout. "Plenty, not that it's any of your concern."

Celeste sank into the chair beside Cristina with a sigh. She'd reached the end of her patience with all the bickering between her offspring. "Is there no way you can work this out? You're not the only ones with pressing matters to attend to."

"Sorry, Mamma," they said in unison.

She smiled as she studied her beautiful daughters. "You're both lovely and accomplished young women. Your father and I adore you equally, more than you can imagine. It pains me to see this animosity between you. Angela, you know as well as I do that Cristina has many talents and interests. Cristina, never let another, even your beloved sister, make you believe you are inferior to anyone. Papa and I couldn't be prouder of the young woman you're becoming. We're not disappointed in the slightest that you've chosen a different path for your life. In fact, I admire you for it. You must follow your heart, no matter what others think."

"But what is her chosen path, Mamma?" Angela asked. "All she speaks of is embroidery and managing her own household someday. Isn't there more to life than just being some man's wife?"

Celeste gestured for her to sit on the arm of her chair. Putting her arm around her, she said, "Marriage is about so much more than just being a wife. It's an honorable state that requires much more than embroidery and childbearing. Just because I'm also an artist doesn't mean my family isn't my highest priority. I strive to manage our home and take care of you to the best of my abilities. I'm prouder of what I've accomplished as the mother of my children than of my career as an artist."

"But will you be disappointed if I don't want to marry and manage a palazzo? All I wish to do is paint."

"I'll never be disappointed in what you choose to do as long as it's your decision. But you'll feel differently when you're a little older."

"No, I won't, Mamma," she said emphatically. "I'll never be a mere piece of property to any man."

Celeste frowned at her. "Is that what you think I am to your papa, a piece of property?"

"No, Mamma," the twins cried in unison.

Angela took her hand and said, "Papa isn't like other men and treats you better than most husbands. Most men treat their wives harshly. Some even lock their wives away and never give them a second thought."

"Listen to me, sweetheart. Your father is different from most men, but not all. Unfortunately, some husbands treat their wives abominably, but most are considerate and fair to their wives, even if you don't see it. When the time comes for Papa to find matches for you, he'll listen and take your feelings into account."

Angela glanced at her, and said, "Will he force me to marry if I don't wish to?"

"Never, but that day will never come. One day, you'll meet the man of your dreams and realize you can't live without him. Then, you'll be begging your father to arrange the match."

Cristina tucked her clasped hands under her chin. "That sounds wonderful, Mamma, and I can't wait for that day."

Angela rolled her eyes, then giggled at her sister. "You'll have to be happy enough for both of us."

Celeste stood and helped her daughters to their feet. Taking hold of each of their hands, she said, "I just pray it doesn't happen too soon. I'm nowhere near ready to part with either of you. Now, please make up, and no more bickering."

The twins embraced and tearfully apologized to each other. *If only I could get Luca and Mateo to do the same,* she thought as she left them, but some things were just too impossible to hope for.

CELESTE COULDN'T HIDE her excitement when she asked Livia to find Filippo and have him bring Luciano to her studio.

Livia grinned at her enthusiastically. "Has the Master's gift finally arrived?"

Celeste held up the ornately carved wooden box wrapped in a lovely red satin bow. "It was delivered an hour ago. I've hardly been able to contain myself while I waited for Luciano to return from town."

Livia clasped her hands in delight. "May I stay while you present it to him?"

Celeste shook her head. "I'm surprised you'd ask. I wish to give it to him when we're alone."

Livia leaned closer and peered at the box. "May I see it now?"

"Go, go," Celeste said, laughing as she shooed Livia away.

She didn't blame her for being as excited as she was. She'd told Livia of her plan months earlier. It had been a long wait for the special gift to arrive. Celeste cleaned the paint from her hands and removed her smock before carrying the box to the window. She fidgeted as she watched the doorway, waiting for Luciano. She prayed he'd be as pleased with the gift as she was.

When she was about to go searching for him on her own, he strode in with a look of concern. As he approached, he said, "What's wrong, Celeste? Filippo said it was urgent. I came as fast as I could."

Celeste gave him a warm smile as she ushered him to the

seat beside her. When he dropped down next to her, she said, "I'm sorry, my love. I didn't mean to alarm you. All is well. I just have a gift I've waited a long time to give you."

Luciano's face brightened. "A gift for me? Is there an important occasion I've forgotten? It's not my birthday, or the anniversary of our marriage. We've only just celebrated Christmas a month past."

Celeste turned and reached for the box sitting on the other side of her. "No particular occasion, my dearest. This gift is an expression of my profound love for you. I still shudder to think how my dear family and I would have ended up if you hadn't rescued me from my previous life."

When she slowly lifted the wooden box, his eyes widened as he took it and studied the carvings. "This is magnificent, my love. Is that the work of young Michelangelo Buonarroti? I thought he'd left Florence."

She couldn't help laughing as she said, "Yes, it's Messer Buonarroti's work. He carved it before moving to Rome, and I purchased it from a local merchant. The box is only part of the gift. Open it."

Luciano untied the satin ribbon and eagerly lifted the lid. He reminded her of watching Luca opening Christmas gifts as a child. Luciano peered into the box and stared in stunned silence. It was just the reaction Celeste hoped for. He withdrew the gold reliquary pendant with a crucifix in the center surrounded by inlaid gems. The Vicente Coat of Arms was engraved on the back, and the pendant was attached to a heavy chain woven in gold.

Tears glistened in Luciano's eyes when he looked up at her. "This is magnificent, my darling. I've never seen anything so exquisite. This is a gift meant for a king."

Celeste took the pendant and chain from him and hung it around his neck, then gave him a lingering kiss. "You are my king. You deserve this and so much more."

He lovingly stroked her cheek, as he said, "How can I ever repay such a gift?"

"You already have many times over, but there is something I want from you in return. I want to paint your portrait wearing the pendant. I've long wanted you to sit for me. I have no commissions at the moment, so now is the perfect time."

He looked down and fingered the pendant. "I would be honored to have my portrait painted by the famous Maestra Celeste Gabriele. Only you could paint me in a way that I won't come out looking like a scruffy ox."

She laughed as she got up and closed the studio door, making sure to lock the latch. "You are the most handsome man in the world to me." She gave him an alluring look and began unlacing her painting frock. "I can think of the perfect way for you to show me your appreciation right now."

He stood and removed his tunic. "It would be my greatest pleasure."

CHAPTER SIX

FLORENCE 1497

CELESTE RUSHED toward the physician as he exited Aunt Portia's chambers. "How is she, Messer Morelli?"

He wiped his face with a handkerchief before answering. "It grieves me to tell you it's time to gather the family. Signora Gabriele hasn't much time."

Though Celeste thought she was prepared for the inevitable event, the news still hit her like a blow. "Is there nothing more you can do?"

"I've exhausted all the known treatments, Signora. Your aunt has always been a favorite of mine. If I had it in my power to prolong her life, I would do it in an instant."

"We have no doubt of that, but there must be something. I don't know how I'll get on without my Portia."

Messer Morelli gave a deep bow and told Celeste he was very sorry he could do no more. Celeste sent Bardo to summon the family and servants. She quietly slipped into Portia's room and sank into the chair beside her bed. She watched her aunt's chest slowly rise and fall and wondered how many more breaths she had left in her. Celeste reached into her sleeve and withdrew the handkerchief Portia had embroidered for her wedding. After wiping her eyes, she laid her hand over her aunt's as she struggled to control her emotions.

"Is that you, my darling girl?" Portia said weakly without opening her eyes.

"I'm here, aunt," Celeste whispered. "The physician has just gone. He's instructed me to gather the family. Are you up for other visitors?"

"That silly old coot. There's life in me yet. Has my darling son Tomaso arrived from Lucca?"

"Not two hours ago. He's anxious to see you but waited for the doctor to go. Should I bring him in?"

Portia pulled her hand free and patted the bed beside her. As Celeste moved to the bed, she said, "In a moment. I have some things I wish to say to you alone first."

"Of course, Aunt Portia. What is it?"

"Prop me up." When Celeste gently arranged the pillows behind her head, she said, "I must make you understand how much joy you have brought to my life. I was a miserable creature and expected to remain one for the rest of my life until Luciano asked me to take you to Lucca. That year we spent together training you to be Duchessa was one of the happiest of my life. It led to me marrying my beloved Paolo when I thought I would be one of those sad spinsters for the remainder of my life. Then my precious Tomaso made his surprise appearance. How greatly blessed I've been."

Celeste's voice caught in her throat before she said, "We both have, and I cherish those times as well."

"Then there was that glorious year of traveling through Italy on your art tour. I'd never expected such a great adventure in my life. Thank you for inviting Paolo and me as your chaperons."

"I was honored to have you at my side, and you know I literally wouldn't have survived the ordeal without you."

Portia closed her eyes and smiled. "Let's not speak of the

trying moments. Only the joy."

"Agreed."

"Enough reminiscing. Down to business for I fear there is not much time. My Tomaso tells me he isn't content with Luciano's plans for him to become manager of the Lucca estate. He's deeply grateful to Luciano for affording him the opportunity, but it's not the life he wishes to lead. He envisions himself off on the high seas, following the trade routes to the East to seek his own fortune. He's young and adventurous with no wife or family to hold him back. I suggest Luciano replace him, and I have the perfect man for the job, your youngest brother, Sandro. He knows that estate better than any living person. He is an honorable, industrious man. I believe he would be the perfect one to handle the estate."

Celeste clutched her aunt's hands in delight. "Such a marvelous idea! I'll have Luciano speak with Tomaso tonight and get a letter off to Sandro in the morning."

"No, not a letter, niece. Luciano must speak to Sandro in person, which brings me to my last request. I wish to be interred beside my Paolo overlooking the lush fields of Lucca. This is my dying request."

Celeste reached over and embraced her aunt. "Consider it done. You have my word."

"Then, I will rest content, my dear." She managed to open her eyes and gaze lovingly at Celeste. "You are the most amazing person I've ever known. You must stay good and kind and strong for the family's sake." Celeste buried her head in her Aunt's breast and sobbed uncontrollably. Portia quietly stroked her hair until her tears were spent, then said, "Don't mourn for me, dearest, but be joyful. I'm going to be reunited with my Paolo. How I've missed him all these years. I'm ready to see Tomaso now. Please, bring him to me."

Celeste reluctantly left her aunt's side, knowing she'd spoken with her for the last time. Her grief weighed on her like a cloak of stone. She patiently waited as each family member took a turn saying goodbye before escaping to the gardens to pour out her grief and gratitude alone in the peace of the cold night.

~

(LUCCA 1497, Ten Days Later)

"There you are, my love," Luciano said, as he stepped onto the terrace and joined Celeste at the railing. "The entire household has been searching for you."

Celeste raised an eyebrow as she turned to face him. "How is it this wasn't the first place you looked?"

He swept his gaze over the picturesque view of the Lucca countryside and nodded. "I see my mistake. In my defense, Livia told me you were resting. How did you manage to sneak out here without her knowing?"

"I wasn't able to sleep. It's been such a heart-wrenching day, so I slipped out here to enjoy a moment of solitude in my favorite place."

Luciano stepped behind her and wrapped his arms around her waist. "It has been rough, but the Mass was lovely. I've never seen such a large turnout for a memorial service."

Celeste closed her eyes as she recalled the endless line of grieving friends, family, and servants who followed the processional through the main street of Lucca to the cathedral. Mourners journeyed from the local villages and from as far away as Venice. Even most of the Gabriele clan came to pay their respects. Only a fraction fit inside the church to hear the funeral mass. The rest patiently waited outside to offer their condolences when the family exited. Celeste had been deeply touched by the show of love and respect shown to Aunt Portia. She had been a remarkable woman who was loved by all who knew her.

Celeste's voice caught as she said, "How will I manage without her? She was my closest confidant, my mother, my friend."

Luciano gave her a squeeze. "Do I count for nothing?"

Celeste laughed and rested her head against his chest. "You know what you mean to me, my darling, but you're a man. There are things you'll never understand. Portia could read my most inner thoughts."

"I felt that on occasion as well. It could be quite disconcerting." He gently turned her to face him. "Though no one could replace Portia, you'll have to find a new confidant. You've always shared a special bond with my sister, Angelica."

Celeste gave a slight smile at the thought of her sweet sister-in-law. Angelica was aptly named. Celeste had never doubted Angelica loved her and appreciated how she overlooked her many shortcomings. She felt the same for her and considered her the sister Veronica could never be.

"Yes, I'll have to learn to rely on Angelica now that Portia's gone," she said softly. "She'd been a tremendous help in managing the unexpected horde that descended upon us for the funeral. I couldn't have managed this day without her."

"It's always been Angelica's talent to gracefully take charge in the most difficult circumstances."

Celeste grew quiet for a moment before looking up at Luciano. "Have you spoken with Sandro about management of the estate?"

He shook his head. "Not yet. I thought it best to get the funeral behind us first. I've asked him to meet me here tomorrow afternoon. I'm sure he has an idea of what I wish to discuss. He is aware Tomaso is not happy. Sandro becoming Master of the estate will be a drastic change for his life. He will need guidance, and he will not be comfortable playing the role of a nobleman. Sandro is a good administrator and an accomplished farmer. His vineyards and orchards are some of the most productive in the region."

Celeste kissed him, then said, "If I could rise from being a lowly nanny to Florentine Duchessa, I'm sure Sandro can handle managing your country estate."

He nodded and returned her kiss. "I agree wholeheartedly." He paused for a moment, then said, "There's the bell to change for dinner. Are you up to facing the crowd or should I tell the housekeeper you'll take your dinner in our chambers?"

She took a breath and raised her chin. "Angelica would never forgive me if I abandoned her now after all the work she's done supervising the dinner. Portia wouldn't have backed down from such a challenge. Nor shall I, as long as you promise not to leave my side until this farewell meal is behind us."

"I wouldn't dare."

"Then, lead the way, my darling."

Celeste rose and gave Sandro a warm embrace when he joined Luciano and her in the sala the following afternoon. His hair had remained as golden as it was when he was a child, and his face still looked younger than his twenty-six years. Her brothers were all handsome, but he was the only one with light features, almost Nordic in appearance. Celeste found his appearance quite striking and was sure the local maidens did as well.

She grinned and took his hands as she said, "You never change, brother. I still see you as the boy hiding behind Masina's skirts the first time you saw me in Lucca."

Sandro laughed as he took the chair across from Celeste when she returned to her seat. "You were like a luminous specter appearing out of the mist. I hardly remembered you as my sister since we parted when I was only two."

"Yes, it broke my heart to leave you with a stranger when I went to work for Maria Foscari. It was an unexpected blessing we were reunited in time, and I get to see the fine man you've become."

Luciano said, "I've asked you here with a particular purpose in mind. With the sad passing of Aunt Portia, your cousin Tomaso has decided to leave Lucca and strike out on his own. That leaves me without an estate manager here. Your sister and I would like to offer you the position."

Sandro jumped to his feet and stared in shock. "Me? You can't be serious. I'm just a farmer. I could never run the estate. The noblemen will not respect me."

"Just how I predicted he'd react," Celeste told Luciano with a laugh.

Luciano motioned toward his chair, and said, "Sit down, man. I am perfectly serious. You're far more than a farmer. My steward tells me you manage the entire farming operation for him. My crops have never yielded as much as when you've been in charge, and my tenants are content. That is no small feat. I have complete confidence in your ability to manage my concerns here."

"As do I," Celeste added. "Marco manages Luciano's Venice estates, which are far larger. Why shouldn't you do the same here? If Aunt Portia were here, she'd say, 'You are a Gabriele, after all. It's in your blood.'"

"Ah, yes, dear Aunt Portia. I can almost hear her in your voice." Sandro leaned back in the chair and blew out his breath. "I never could have imagined this. I'm honored, Luciano, and truly grateful. Of course, I accept your offer. I'd be a fool to refuse."

Luciano rose and extended his hand. "Splendid! We'll meet with my solicitor in the morning. Tonight, we celebrate."

Sandro stood and beamed as he ignored Luciano's offered hand and pulled him into a hug. "I will honor your name and Aunt Portia's memory by making it the most productive estate in the land. You will not regret this decision. You've made me happier than I could have thought possible, brother."

Celeste struggled to control her emotions as she watched the scene unfolding in front of her. Her hopes for her youngest sibling had finally been realized. It was a welcome blessing of comfort in her time of grief.

"Thank you, as well, sister," he said as he hugged her.

Celeste furtively wiped her eyes, and said, "We have one more thing to discuss. Since you have no wife to manage the household, we wondered if you'd be willing to invite our sister Bianca and her family to live here with you. She's more than capable of taking on that responsibility. There is plenty of room, and I would love for Bianca and her five children to have a decent place to live." Celeste noticed his smile fade slightly. "Is that a problem, brother?"

He shook his head. "None with Bianca. She's a fine, responsible woman, and a wonderful mother to her children. She'd do a remarkable job with the manor. It's her husband, Enrico, who concerns me."

Luciano frowned as he nodded at Sandro. "I remember Aunt Portia mentioned there had been some sort of trouble with Enrico but never shared much detail. What's the problem with the man?"

"He enjoys his wine and strong drink a bit too much. Bianca tells me it feels like she's living with Papa at times, though Enrico has never been violent to her or the children. He neglects his crops at times, preferring to spend his days in the public house. I've spoken with him more than once on the matter. He'll mend his ways for a time, but it never lasts long. I feel for our poor sister. She insists he's a good-hearted man otherwise, but I have my concerns."

Luciano stroked his beard thoughtfully for a moment. "Celeste and I will visit them tomorrow and extend the invitation to move into the manor. I'll make sure he understands the offer is on the condition that he abstains from overindulging in drink and is conscientious about his responsibilities. Send me regular reports and inform me if he violates those conditions."

Sandro nodded thoughtfully. "Certainly. Those requirements are more than fair, but it has been my experience, brother, asking a drinker to abstain is like asking a fish not to swim. Maybe he will be different."

"We will make the offer and go from there," Luciano said, nodding. "Perhaps the lightening of his financial responsibility and greater expectations will be enough motivation for him to mend his ways."

"On the subject of you having no wife," Celeste said, interrupting them, "do you have any future prospects in mind?"

Sandro's cheeks reddened as he said, "There is one maiden in the town I've admired for some time. Her name is Rachele Marita Gardella. She's the beautiful daughter of a prosperous oil merchant who thinks I'm too far below his status to consider me a viable suitor."

Celeste crossed her arms and frowned. "How dare he? Does he know who your family is?"

"He recognizes the name but isn't aware I'm related to you or Luciano, which is as I wish it. I want him to accept me on my own merit."

Luciano gave a hearty laugh. "I know this man. He can be an officious prig. Wait until he finds out who's running the manor. I'm sure he'll be singing a new tune."

Sandro gave a half grin. "I would love to see his face when word reaches him of my new position."

"We will waste no time informing him that your status has

changed and that you are a more than suitable match for his Raquel," Celeste said.

Sandro smiled for a moment before growing serious. The color drained from his face as he said, "I'll be Master of the Manor. Everything about my life is going to change, isn't it?"

"Yes, brother," Luciano said, "it will take time to adjust. Tomaso will teach you. He's agreed to say in Lucca until you're ready to take over for him."

"That's a relief, and I'll have Bianca here learning right alongside me."

"You will," Celeste said. "I'll tell her to write if she needs encouragement or advice. I'll only be a few days' ride away."

"I don't want to wait until tomorrow to tell her," Sandro said. "Let's send for Bianca and Enrico now to share the good news. Hope she doesn't faint from the shock."

"We'll have to break it to her gently," Celeste said, smiling as she rang for the page.

Within an hour of receiving the summons, Bianca and Enrico arrived at the manor looking confused and more than a little worried. Celeste got up and embraced her sister, then held out her hand to Enrico. She felt his hand tremble slightly when he kissed it.

Enrico then turned to Luciano and gave a solemn bow. "I'm deeply humbled to be invited into your presence, Signore Vicente. To what do my wife and I owe this grand honor?"

"Stand up, man," Luciano said with a laugh. "I've asked you to stop bowing to me. I'm your brother-in-law, not the Holy Father."

"Yes, sir. Forgive me, sir."

Bianca laughed at him and threw her arms around Luciano. "It does take some getting used to. I always felt more at ease with you when Aunt Portia and Paolo were here."

"Me, too," Sandro said, as he walked into the room followed by Tomaso. "Good afternoon, sister. You look well."

"You saw me yesterday at the funeral," she said, then kissed his cheek.

Sandro's smile faded. "I was distracted by the circumstances of the day."

Bianca squeezed his arm and gave him a sad smile. "The world will never be the same without dear Aunt Portia." She then turned to Tomaso and squeezed his hand. "How are you holding up, cousin?"

Tomaso put his arms around her and Enrico. "I'd never seen so many Gabrieles in one place as I did yesterday. Not even on my trips to Venice."

"We're like locusts," Celeste said, then pointed to four chairs across from her and Luciano. "Please, sit. You must all be weary."

Once they were seated, Bianca said, "I suspect you've asked us here for more than just a casual visit."

Luciano gestured at Sandro for him to answer.

"You're right, sister. We have something rather momentous to discuss with you."

Celeste had to bite her cheek to keep from laughing at the looks on their faces.

When Enrico had recovered enough to speak, he said, "Momentous? What can you mean? Does this have to do with Aunt Portia's bequest?"

"No," Tomaso said. "We'll gather the family for the reading next week. This is regarding an entirely different matter." He turned back to Sandro and nodded. "Tell them, cousin."

"Tomaso has decided to find fame and fortune plying the trade routes. He will leave Lucca, so he won't become manager of the estate when he's of age. Luciano has graciously offered the position to me. I am to be Master of the estate."

"Congratulations, Sandro!" Enrico said. "There's no one more deserving."

"I appreciate that, but I'm not finished. I'll be living here, but since I'm unmarried, I'll need someone to manage the household. We've all agreed that Bianca is the best person to fill that role."

Sandro's prediction that Bianca would faint at the news had nearly been on target. Her face went so white that Celeste got up and put an arm around her shoulder. "Call for Livia to bring wine," she ordered the page.

Bianca took a breath and shrugged Celeste's arm off. "I'm fine, sister. Sandro just caught me off guard." She stared at Sandro. "Do I understand correctly that you're asking us to move into the Master's house and have me serve as Mistress of the manor?" Bianca looked to Enrico in anticipation. "The decision is yours, husband."

"Need you ask, my dear?" He got up and enthusiastically shook Luciano's hand. "How can I begin to express my gratitude?"

Luciano gave him a quick nod. "I appreciate you accepting on your wife's behalf, and I'm grateful. You and I have a few matters to discuss in private, Enrico. When that's completed, we'll sign the contracts."

Enrico released Luciano's hand and bowed. "Done, sir. I'm at your disposal."

"I couldn't be more pleased for all of you," Celeste said. "This has been *my* lifelong dream and it softens the sting of losing our dear Portia. I can live the rest of my life content knowing you and your family are comfortably situated."

After a round of hugs and congratulations, Celeste stood back watching her family, grateful beyond measure to see their lives coming full circle. "We made it, my dearest aunt," she whispered. "I credit all of it to you and my good husband." She kissed her fingers and raised them to the heavens before rejoining the others. She raised her goblet, and the family joined her. "To Portia Gabriele!"

CHAPTER SEVEN

FLORENCE, 7 FEBRUARY 1497

FOR THE FIRST time Celeste could remember, she wasn't relieved to see the Duomo come into view on returning from a journey. She rested her head on Luciano's shoulder, and said, "Let's make Lucca our home. I've grown weary of Florence with all this Savonarola business."

Luciano sighed as he stared out the window. "How I wish we could, my love, but I'm needed in Florence now more than ever. And I'm sure my apprentices wouldn't appreciate relocating to Lucca."

Luca wrinkled his nose in distaste. "Neither would I, Papa. Who wants to live in the boring countryside."

"I agree," Angela said. "Life in Lucca is too quiet. Florence is bustling and vibrant."

Cristina squeezed Celeste's hand. "I'll move to Lucca with you, Mamma. I enjoy the serene countryside. Florence is too busy and noisy for my tastes."

"Someday, sweetheart. For now, we'll store that as a future dream," Celeste said.

As the carriage neared the Piazza della Signoria on their way through Florence to the southern hills, Luciano abruptly sat forward and pounded on the top of the carriage for the driver to stop.

"What's wrong, Papa?" Elena asked in alarm.

Luciano pointed toward the massive throng of people gathered in front of the cathedral, spilling onto the roadway.

Celeste felt a pang of panic when she looked where her husband was pointing. A crowd of that size was never a good sign. She knew an unruly mob could turn violent in an instant. "What are we going to do, Luci? We shouldn't take our children through the middle of that mob."

Luciano stuck his head out the side window, and said, "Vico, take us around the outskirts of the city to get home." He turned and whistled to the driver of the wagon behind them who carried the servants and luggage. "Follow Vico. Don't attempt to cross the piazza." The driver touched the rim of his cap in acknowledgment and got behind Vico as he turned the carriage. Luciano signaled to Mateo who was riding on horseback beside them. "You too, son. Turn around and follow us."

Mateo wheeled his horse around and galloped off in the opposite direction.

"I fear that's the last we'll see of him until tomorrow," Celeste mumbled.

Luca groaned as he fell back against the seat and crossed his arms. "Why can't we go straight through, Papa? Detouring will add at least an hour to the trip. They're just the Prior's followers listening to one of his endless sermons."

Luciano shot him a look to silence him. "As I've told you, those crowds are becoming increasingly unpredictable and unruly, and should be avoided. We can't risk getting trapped."

His words reminded Celeste of her ordeal in the piazza with Livia, and a thought sprang to her mind. "This is the day of the bonfire. Savonarola said it would be held four weeks from the day Livia and I followed Veronica to the piazza.

That's today, Luciano. Portia's death and funeral had driven it from my mind."

Luciano put his head back through the window. "Quick as you can, Vico." As the driver urged the horses to quicken their pace, Luciano reached for Celeste's hand. "Don't worry, my love. We're probably overreacting, and we'll be tucked away at home soon."

Celeste gave him and the children a reassuring smile, but she was far from convinced. More than once in her life she'd seen such gatherings spiral out of control at the drop of a pin. In that moment, all that mattered was getting her family safely behind the palazzo's imposing walls.

Luca had been right. The detour added nearly an hour to their trip. She let out her breath in relief when they pulled into the drive to find all well. She hurried her brood inside and instructed the servants to get them settled and fed while she and Luciano went to their chambers.

The instant they were behind their closed door, she said, "Did you have any messages with plans from the Arrabbiati waiting for you?"

He shook his head, then stroked his chin as he paced the room. "I should get out there and assess the situation."

She laid her hand on his arm to stop his pacing. "Are you mad? The sun is setting, and the situation will only escalate after dark. Can't you wait until morning?"

He laid his hands on her shoulders and looked her in the eye. "It may be too late by then. This could be our opportunity to get Savonarola out of the way. I give you my word I'll be on my guard and won't take any unnecessary risks. I'll take three of the house guards with me."

"I won't sleep until I see you walk through that door." He gave her a final kiss before turning to go. When he reached the door, she said, "Has Mateo returned? He should have arrived long before we did."

Luciano looked at her over his shoulder. "I'll ask Bardo on my way out and tell him to report to you. I hope Mateo has enough sense not to venture into the unrest."

Celeste folded her arms. "Enough sense? You mean like his papa?"

"That's not the same and you know it. Keep the family inside and make sure the doors are bolted. Make sure the house captain arms the servants," he said as he rushed out of the room.

Celeste rang for Livia to help her off with her dusty traveling clothes. While she washed and dressed for dinner, she tried not to dwell on thoughts of Luciano rushing headlong into that crowd. She prayed he'd been right that they were overreacting, but instinct told her otherwise.

As Celeste descended the stairs towards the dining room, a frightened Bardo rushed toward her. When she reached the bottom step, she said, "What is it? Is it the Master?"

Bardo shook his head and took a moment to catch his breath before answering. "The guard, Guido, who my Master left at the main gate says four young disciples from Prior Savonarola are here collecting vanities for the bonfire. They are demanding entrance in the name of the Prior. What should I tell Guido, mistress?"

"Ask Guido to wait for me before acting. Go to Messer Rinaldi and Master Luca in the dining room and ask them to meet me in the foyer. Has Master Mateo returned yet?"

Bardo bowed his head. "No, mistress."

It wasn't the answer she'd hoped to hear. "Inform me the instant he does. Now go and do as I asked and tell my daughters not to leave the dining room."

She tried to ignore her growing uneasiness as she watched

him rush off to carry out her orders. She hurried to the foyer where Guido was waiting for her.

He gave a quick bow, and said, "Forgive me for disturbing you when you've only just returned home, Signora."

"You've done right in coming to me with this. You may speak freely. Do you fear these disciples of the Prior are a threat to us?"

He struggled to stifle a laugh as he said, "A threat, madam? They're barely older than Master Luca. They've put on airs to appear imposing, but they're no danger to us. They carry no weapons."

Celeste let out her breath in relief. "Bardo had me imagining all sorts of dangers."

Guido laughed. "Bardo fears his own shadow. These youths merely wish to collect vanities, as they call them, to add to their Master's fires. I suggest you hand them a few trinkets and send them on their way."

"Thank you for setting my mind at ease. You may let them enter, Guido."

Luca and his tutor, Messer Rinaldi, entered the foyer with Bardo on their heels.

Luca came forward and reached for her hand. "Are we under attack, Mamma? Bardo said we must come at once."

Celeste laughed as she gave his hand a squeeze. "Guido assures me we're in no danger. It's just some young followers of Prior Savonarola seeking vanities. He's gone to fetch them. Wait here to greet them while I find some baubles for their collection."

Messer Rinaldi bowed as she passed, and said, "We will, madam. I'll not leave Master Luca's side just in case."

"Very well and thank you. I won't be long."

Celeste headed for the dining room where her daughters waited for her. When she entered, she was glad to see them eating and merrily chatting. They each looked up and smiled warmly when they noticed her.

"What was Bardo going on about, Mamma?" Angela asked through a mouthful of food.

Celeste put her hands on her hips and scowled at her. "Darling, that's very unladylike. I've asked you to please swallow your food before speaking."

She gulped her food down and took a sip of wine. "Fine, if it means that much to you. You haven't answered my question."

Celeste explained to them about the youths' collecting vanities. "I'd like each of you to search your rooms for hair ornaments, baubles, embroideries, and other such items of a nonspiritual nature that you don't mind parting with. Take what you can easily gather, then bring them to the sala to donate to the young men."

The girls got up and raced to their rooms as if it were a game, while Celeste headed to her chambers to find her own donations. When she'd gathered an amount of items sufficient to appease the disciples, she carried them downstairs to the sala. The girls were already there, suspiciously eying their uninvited guests. The young men were dressed in homespun hooded cowls over their plain robes. Their heads were bare, with their hair cropped in the manner of monks, but Celeste recognized two of them as sons of local merchants. She assumed the dress and hair styles were merely symbolic to designate them as members of Savonarola's community.

Guido, Bardo, Luca, and Rinaldo stood behind the youths, doing their best to look imposing. When Celeste approached the boys, they bowed respectfully, then raised their eyes to hers as equals.

She nodded to acknowledge them, and said, "Welcome to the home of Signore Vicente. How may I be of service to you?"

The eldest and most formidable of the boys stepped forward, and said, "It is we who have come in service to you, Signora Gabriele. We are here to cleanse this house of iniquity and rededicate it to our Lord Jesus."

"How dare you speak to the Signora in such a way, you insolent whelp?" Guido said as he stepped forward with his hand raised to strike.

Celeste held up her hand to stop him. "There is no need for violence here, Guido. I am not offended."

"But, Signora," he started, but she signaled for him to move behind her. He glanced at her before doing as she wished.

Turning to the young disciple, she said, "And how is it you intend to cleanse our home?"

"We will search for articles our Master has deemed unworthy of belonging to the faithful followers of Christ and remove them."

Celeste feared Guido would suffer a fit as he restrained himself from striking the young man. She gestured with her hands for him to remain calm. He relaxed his fists and took a breath before backing down. The last thing they needed was for him to cause one of the boys an injury.

"It is unnecessary to search our home," she said calmly. "In anticipation of your purpose for coming here, we have collected items fit to feed the cleansing fires of your Master." She handed him the bag holding the items she'd collected and gestured toward the table behind her.

He untied the bag and peered inside while the other boys gathered the items on the table the girls had piled there. "This is a promising start, madam, but we're aware you possess a myriad of articles of a sinful and wicked nature which displease God."

Celeste heard a collective gasp behind her as Luca lunged

forward and grabbed the boy by the collar of his cowl before Guido or Rinaldi could stop him.

"Are you calling my saintly mother a sinner?" Luca hissed.

Celeste saw a look of fear mixed with righteous indignation as he freed himself from Luca's grip.

While arranging his cowl, he said, "I know nothing of your mother's spiritual standing, Master Vicente. Only the Father can see into her heart. I merely repeat what the Prior has learned from reports by a close member of your own family, Sister Veronica."

Celeste felt the strength drain from her legs and grabbed onto Luca for support. He put an arm around her waist and helped her to the closest chair. She'd had no misgivings about Veronica's religious fanaticism but never could have imagined she'd betray her family so ruthlessly. And after all they had done for her. The thought of Veronica's treachery sickened her.

"What has my sister told Savonarola?" she asked, struggling to control the tremor in her voice.

In answer, he withdrew a scroll from his robe and deliberately unrolled it. "I have an inventory here of items we've been commanded by our most reverent and humble leader to remove from Signore Vicente's palazzo."

Luca grabbed it from him and handed it to Celeste. She quickly scanned the list, hardly able to comprehend what she was reading. The inventory contained lists of antique family jewels, ancient tapestries, valuable silver plate, one-of-a-kind books of philosophy and history, and worst of all, priceless, irreplaceable works of art.

Celeste strength returned with a fury as a fire of indignation ignited in her soul. Savonarola was using his bonfire of vanities to rob the ruling class of Florence of their valuables to fund his campaign of religious warfare and to amass political power. He was nothing more than a common thief hiding behind God's word. Poor Veronica had been duped by this malevolent devil to destroy her family.

Celeste rose to her feet and boldly walked to the fireplace, then tossed the scroll into the flames. Turning to face the young men with her chin raised in defiance, she calmly said, "You have no right to barge into my home demanding I turn over precious and valuable family possessions. Guido, throw them out this instant."

The leader raised his hands in surrender as Guido moved toward him, and said, "If you resist us and force us out, many others will come in our place."

Celeste gave him a dismissive wave. "Your threat does not frighten me. We will simply refuse them entrance, as we should have done with you. We've done nothing to violate God's laws and have nothing to fear."

He crossed his arms over her chest, arrogantly eying her. "You're wrong, madam. Under the authority of the Frateschi, endorsed by our righteous prophet, we have every right to remove whatever we deem impure."

Celeste's thoughts swirled as she struggled to decide what to do. She knew next to nothing of Florentine law under the Frateschi. She needed to find Luciano for advice of what to do with the interlopers.

She quickly pulled Luca away from the others. "Luca, we must lock these men up so they cannot ransack our home or report to their masters. Tell them we will accede to their wishes and direct them to the storage room where several of my old paintings are stored. Once they are inside, shut them in and lock the door. It will buy us some time."

Luca smiled, "Yes, Mother. Leave this to me."

Celeste followed Luca as he returned to the room to address the men. "As you are on errand for God, we will allow you to inspect our humble home. You will see our paintings depict holy scenes from the Sacred Scriptures, which can in no way be offensive to God. I will show you."

Celeste watched as Luca escorted the three men toward the storage room and invited them to examine the paintings that were shrouded in cloth coverings along the way. As the men began to busy themselves with removing the coverings and examining the paintings, Luca slowly moved out of the storage room and abruptly slammed the door on the unsuspecting youths. The last thing he heard as he returned to his mother was the pounding of their fists on the locked four-inch oak door.

"Stay where you are until I return," she ordered the young men. "Angela, Cristina, take Elena to your chambers and remain there until you hear from me. Guido, you, and Luca must escort me into the city to find Signore Vicente. Call for the carriage. Messer Rinaldi, find Bardo, and help him guard the storage room door. Do what you must to ensure they stay locked in until my return."

"Yes, Signora," he said, then gave a bow and turned to do her bidding.

"Is it safe to go into the city, Mamma?" Luca asked. "Papa ordered me not to set foot out of the palazzo tonight."

Celeste cupped his chin in her hand. "You'll be with me, and I'll have you and Guido to protect me. You performed brilliantly with those boys, my son. I didn't know you were such a good actor."

Luca stood taller, straightened his shoulders, and looked her in the eyes. "Thank you, Mamma. I'd die before letting anything happen to you."

"I've never doubted that for one moment, my brave darling, but I pray it doesn't come to that." Guido came in to tell them the carriage was waiting. "Off we go, son, into the night on our daring mission."

CHAPTER EIGHT

FLORENCE, 7 FEBRUARY 1497

CELESTE SAT beside Luca in the carriage, gripping his hand as they headed into the city. Guido rode next to the driver, scanning his eagle-eyes around the carriage and what lay ahead down the road. He needn't have bothered. The route they traveled was empty and the crowd below in the center of town had grown by magnitudes since earlier in the day on the family's trip back from Lucca. It appeared the entire citizenry of Florence had turned out to take part in the extraordinary event and were packed into the piazza and surrounding streets. Tall sheets of light from the bonfire's flames dotted the center of the city, but the one in the central piazza outshone them all.

Luca turned to her in alarm. "How will we ever find Papa in that mass of people?"

"I wish I knew," Celeste mumbled, unable to tear her gaze from the vivid scenes below. "Guido will know where to look."

As the carriage descended into the valley, Celeste seriously questioned the wisdom of rushing headlong into the melee and dragging her dutiful son along with her. Luciano had warned them to stay behind the bolted doors of the palazzo. It would have been safer to send Guido on this errand alone. No one would have dared bother with him.

When they were a mile from the edge of the city, the driver reined the horses to a stop. Guido jumped down and came to her window.

"I'm afraid we'll have to walk from here, mistress. The streets are too congested to get closer, and we don't want to spook the horses. It might be better for you and Master Luca to wait here."

She knew he'd given sound advice, but her curiosity won out over her fear and common sense. "That's not necessary," she said, giving him a smile far more confident than she felt. "I'm in the mood for an evening walk. Tell the driver to wait for us here."

After informing the driver, he helped her and Luca exit the carriage, and said, "I suggest the two of you not leave my side until we're safely back to the carriage. If either of you were to be harmed, my Master would have my head."

Celeste linked her arm in Luca's as they got into step behind their faithful servant. "No worries on that score, Guido. We promise to stay close."

Celeste struggled to keep pace with Luca and Guido as they started for the Piazza della Signoria, but they were slowed by the thickening crowd half a mile before they reached their destination. Guido did his best to clear the way for them, but Celeste was jostled and shoved as she moved forward. She'd never witnessed such a spectacle in all her days, not even in Venice during Carnival. She clung to Luca with all her strength as the last thing she wanted was to get separated in the chaos.

The mass of people began to thin as they neared the blinding light and the searing heat of the enormous pyre burning in the square. Celeste stood near the front of the clearing around the bonfire, staring wide-eyed as Florentines continued feeding the flames. A giant caricature of the devil danced around the fire as if taunting and encouraging the crowd while the people flung books, clothing, jewelry, sculptures, and paintings into the roaring flames. Tears streamed down Celeste's cheeks as she watched the priceless, irreplaceable artifacts and heirlooms burning out of existence and turning into nothing more than vaporous smoke.

As she turned to pull Luca away from the tragic scene, the crowd beside her parted as renowned painter, Sandro Botticelli, stepped toward the fire carrying rolled canvases in his arms. When he got as close as he dared, he dropped all the canvases but one at his feet. He lifted the canvas he still held above his head to cheers from the crowd, and prepared to toss it in. Celeste lunged at him, grabbing for his arm to stop him. When he turned his eyes on her, she hardly recognized him for the good-natured, kind, supremely talented artist she'd known for years.

"Sandro, no," she cried. "I beg you not to do this. Savonarola has poisoned your mind. If you want to rid yourself of these paintings, give them to me. Let God strike me down for possessing these works if that's His will, but please don't destroy them."

Sandro stared at her, seemingly uncomprehending for a moment, then suddenly recognized her. "The Prior hasn't poisoned my mind, Maestra Gabriele, he has opened my mind and heart to the will of God. These paintings are an abomination and must be destroyed. I refuse to taint your purity by passing them to you. Please, release my arm and permit me to do God's work."

Luca stepped behind Celeste and removed her hand from Botticelli's arm. "Come away, Mamma. There's nothing you can do to stop him. We must find Papa."

Celeste released Botticelli, but instead of turning away, she sank to her knees and openly wept as the genius painter voluntarily tossed his brilliant works of art into the hungry flames. When the last was gone, Botticelli stared down at her for a moment, then sadly shook his head as he turned and faded back into the crowd.

Luca helped Celeste to her feet and led her toward the rear of the throng. As they moved along, Celeste's heart broke further as she looked into the eyes of Savonarola's deluded disciples. Instead of reverent followers of Christ, they appeared fanatical and frenzied. The bizarre scene strengthened her resolve to resist the plans of the misguided youths to rob her family of their possessions. They would have to pry her precious belongings and artwork from her cold, dead fingers to get them for Savonarola.

As she raised her chin and straightened her shoulders, Guido came pushing through the crowd with Luciano on his heels. "I've found the Master, Signora!"

She rushed forward and threw an arm around Luciano while she held tightly to Luca with her other hand.

"What possessed you to venture out into this madness?" Luciano asked as he freed himself from her embrace and put his arm around Luca's shoulders. "Let's get you two home. The crowd is already spiraling out of control."

"You'll get no argument from me," she said as she took his other arm. "I have much to tell you."

Luciano increased his pace as he guided them out of the piazza. "I'll ride in the carriage with you and Luca. Guido, my horse, Zeus, is tethered outside the Palazzo Medici. Will you recognize him?"

"Of course, sir," he said as he bowed. "I'll get him and catch up to escort you home."

Luciano gave him a nod. "Good man. We'll look out for you."

The three of them practically ran once the chaos of the piazza was behind them. Celeste jumped into the carriage when they reached it. She relaxed for just a moment when Luciano and Luca climbed in behind her and closed the door.

Luciano pounded on the roof of the carriage three times as a signal for Vico to get moving. When he'd caught his breath, he said, "Tell me what made you come for me."

Celeste told him of the young men locked in the storage room at the palazzo and said their sudden appearance made more sense to her after what she'd witnessed in the piazza. She recounted the heart wrenching scene of Botticelli destroying his priceless masterpieces. "Has all of Florence gone mad? I hardly know what to make of what's happening."

"Madness is a fitting word, my love," Luciano said. He removed his cap and combed his fingers through his hair as she'd seen him do so many times before. "Now you understand the urgency of ridding Florence of Savonarola."

"Without question, Luci."

"What about those boys at the palazzo, Papa?" Luca asked. "What to do you plan to do with them?"

"I'll toss those whelps onto the street the instant I return home. They have no authority to rob us, regardless of what the Frateschi told them. Trust me, the Signoria will hear of this outrage."

"You understand why I came in search of you," Celeste said. "They never would have left by my command."

"They will by my father's command, or they will suffer the consequences," Luca said with quiet determination. "We will see to it."

Celeste gazed proudly at her brave son, who was becoming like his father. With them at her defense, she had nothing to fear.

The instant they pulled into the front drive, Luciano bounded from the carriage, followed by Luca and Guido. Celeste took her time going inside, knowing she had no role to play in the drama. As Luciano said he would, he made quick work of removing the intruders from the premises. The boys made threats of reporting him to Savonarola, but they knew better than to disobey the command of a powerful Duca. Once the gate was locked behind them, peace returned to the palazzo, but Celeste feared their troubles were far from over.

AFTER TOSSING in their bed for hours, Luciano gave up all hope of sleep and went to brood in the sitting room. As he stared into the fire, his thoughts turned to the growing threat encircling him and his loved ones. How he longed for those busy, pleasant days of painting and managing his workshop without the risk of religious interference or political reprisals. Members of the Arrabbiati were growing more anxious over the increasingly bold actions of Savonarola. The truth was that even with opposition from Rome, the Prior's power had continued to strengthen. The Vatican had been slow to act against him. Luciano feared that when the pope finally did act, it would be too late for Florence.

As he continued to mull over his precarious situation, Filippo came in and bowed. "Yes, what is it?" Luciano asked without taking his eyes from the fire.

"You asked me to tell you when Master Mateo returned, sir. Your son's manservant just informed me he came in not ten minutes ago."

"Tell Mateo to wait for me in his quarters. I'll join him shortly."

"Yes, sir," Filippo said as he hurried out.

Luciano rubbed his face before rising to his feet to go deal with Mateo. It was the last task he wished to carry out at such a moment, but it had to be done. He'd stumbled across Mateo at the bonfire and had ordered him to go straight home. Mateo had tried to argue, but Luciano had grabbed him by the collar in a fit of rage and told him to do his bidding immediately. He'd had enough on his mind without having to worry about his son running wild on the dangerous streets of Florence.

That had been six hours earlier and yet he'd only just returned. It was a blatant act of disobedience. Luciano knew he couldn't let such behavior go unpunished. His feet dragged as he shuffled to his son's room, feeling every one of his fifty-one years. All he wanted was to get the unpleasant business behind him and give sleep another try.

Mateo rose from his chair and bowed when Luciano entered the room. Showing such reverence was something he rarely did anymore. Luciano took the display as a hopeful sign. Mateo had recently told Luciano he still honored him as his father and Lord of the estate, but since reaching manhood, he considered himself equal to his father. Luciano had explained to him that he had to earn the right to be called his equal. He'd raised Mateo to be confident and self-assured, but he had instead grown proud and self-entitled, both characteristics Luciano found troubling.

He was preparing Mateo to inherit the title of Duca one day, and taking ownership of the Venice estate, but Mateo showed little interest in these future responsibilities. He preferred wasting his days and nights running with other noblemen's sons who were indolent, arrogant, and reckless. Luciano had once blamed Mateo's friends for negatively influencing him. He'd since been forced to admit that the reverse was likely true.

That night, Mateo stood humbly before Luciano with his head bowed. He'd removed his cap, revealing the crown of blond curls that adorned his head. Luciano had to resist shivering at the sight. He'd always hoped the boy's hair would darken as he aged, as his dead mother's, Isabella, had. Instead, Mateo's locks remained as golden as the man who'd sired him. Mateo's complexion and features favored Isabella, but there was no denying he was Marcello Viari's blood son. This frequently provoked questions of his true paternity from others. To most of the world, Mateo was Luciano's eldest son from his first wife, Isabella, who had died in childbirth. Few remained alive who knew the truth that Mateo was the son of Isabella and that dead scoundrel, Marcello.

Mateo wasn't responsible for his parentage but had unfortunately inherited more than his appearance from Marcello and Isabella. He had his mother's recklessness and love of flaunting his material wealth. From Marcello, he'd inherited his hardheartedness and depravity. His son wasn't completely devoid of favorable character traits, but they tended to be overwhelmed by the negative ones.

The way Mateo treated women as no more than playthings for his own amusement greatly disturbed Luciano. He and Celeste tried their best to instill a sense of decorum and a love of God in Mateo, but he often seemed incapable of overcoming his genetic inheritance. Luciano hadn't given up on his adopted son, but it was becoming increasingly apparent Mateo might not become the man Luciano wanted him to be.

"You may sit," Luciano said, when he felt Mateo had demonstrated sufficient remorse.

He was about to say more, but Mateo interrupted him. "I beg your forgiveness, Papa. I am terribly sorry. I deserve whatever punishment you consider just."

Luciano had no delusions about his sincerity. Mateo was skilled at saying exactly what he believed Luciano wished to hear. "This matter isn't solely about disobedience and punishment, son. You put yourself and other family members in unnecessary danger. I'm disappointed by your lack of regard for anyone but yourself."

The color rose in Mateo's cheeks. "You know I am loath to disappoint you, but I struggle to resist the lure of excitement and adventure. My friends are skilled at persuading me to join in with their exploits. I meant it as no slight to you, Papa."

Luciano frowned at his son. "I accept your apologies, but not your excuses. You say you're unable to control yourself. Those are the words of a child. A true man has the power to govern his actions. We all sin and make mistakes, but we must own up to those actions, not blame them on others. You must learn to harness your behavior and take full responsibility when you act wrongly. Do you understand me?"

Luciano was pleased that Mateo held his gaze and didn't look away. "I do, Papa, and I agree. I vow to do better. I wish nothing more than to be like you are."

"No, Mateo, you must aspire to be a man better than I am. This is my greatest desire for you."

"Yes, Papa. I will do my best."

"Very well. As way of punishment, you will remain in the palazzo and be at your studies for the next two weeks. I'll assess your progress at that time. You have much to learn, and you've greatly neglected your studies."

Mateo did his best to mask his disappointment, but it didn't escape Luciano. "Yes, Papa," he said quietly.

After giving Mateo a hearty embrace, Luciano said, "I love you, son, and I haven't lost faith in you. Listen closely to what I am about to say." He laid his hand on Mateo's shoulder as he looked him in the eye. "You should have been here in my absence last night when those young men came to the palazzo. We were fortunate they were so easily dispatched, but this may not always be the case."

"What young men do you speak of, Papa?"

"I'll explain later. For now, let me finish. If anything dire were to happen to me, God forbid, I want your assurances that I can trust you to watch after your mother and sisters. You would be responsible for their welfare in every respect. I believe you're capable of handling that responsibility, but I want to hear from your own mouth that you understand and are willing to take on such a solemn duty. I pray God grants me life for years to come, but our fates are not ours to command. I expect you to leave your childish ways behind and become a man of virtue, son."

Mateo gave a formal bow. "I understand you, sir, and give my solemn vow to care for and protect Mamma and my sisters when that fateful day comes. May it be many years in the future."

"Well said, son. I believe you. Now get to bed. I need you ready to face the day."

He gave Mateo a nod and walked to the door hoping that for once, his son had taken his words to heart. He decided to go to his private chambers instead of returning to the room he shared with Celeste, so as not to disturb her. As he reached for the door handle, Bardo came hurrying down the hallway toward him and handed him a letter.

"This just arrived from Messer Mancini's page. He says it is urgent."

Luciano gave a weary sigh. "Is the page awaiting a reply?" he asked as he broke the letter's seal.

"No, sir. He's already gone."

"Thank you, Bardo. You may go. Get some sleep." Luciano tore open the letter and scanned the contents as the boy hurried away. Before he reached the end of the hallway, Luciano said, "Bardo wait. Find your Mistress and bring her to me in the sitting room. And hurry!"

CELESTE SLEPT FITFULLY, plagued by disturbing dreams of the Bonfire of Vanities, as the Florentines called the event. She rose at dawn and walked to the terrace where she had a clear view of the city. She pulled her robe tighter against the frigid wind as she stared down at the still smoking embers of the various pyres. The crowds had cleared the piazza, but the scars of what had taken place the previous night remained. Celeste was coping with scars of her own from what she'd witnessed. She knew Florence, and the world at large, had suffered a great loss and would never be the same.

When the February chill became too much for Celeste, she ventured back inside and wandered toward her studio. The recently started portrait of Luciano rested on the easel. The work had been put on hold after Portia's passing. Celeste now wondered if she even wanted to finish the painting. *What is the point*, she thought as she stood before the easel. *Savonarola will probably burn it.*

She went to the window seat and rested her chin in her hands on the windowsill, trying to shake a feeling of foreboding. She hoped her mood was because of Portia's passing combined with her deep sadness from the bonfire, but her heart told her it was something more. Luciano warned her of the grave threat Savonarola posed to their existence, but she hadn't truly understood until she witnessed in the diabolical scenes in the piazza. If one friar could so easily persuade an entire city to destroy their precious possessions, he wielded far more power than she'd ever imagined. Veronica's strange obsession with the man should have been enough to make her understand the danger Savonarola posed.

"Signora," Bardo said from the doorway, "the Master sent me to bring you to him. He says it's urgent."

"What now?" she mumbled, as she got to her feet and followed the page to the sitting room where Luciano was waiting.

"Where were you so early," he asked as he kissed her cheek. "I've had the whole household looking for you. I thought you'd sleep in after our eventful night."

She led him by the hand to a pair of chairs near the fire.

"Bardo knew right where to find me. I was in my studio. What is it, my love?"

Instead of taking the chair beside her, he paced in small circles around the room. "I've just received word from Mancini. The Frateschi called an emergency session this morning. The Prior's boys apparently went directly to their leader last night and informed on us. Mancini's inside spy says they've declared members of the Arrabbiati, including me, as blasphemers and traitors. They're planning to freeze our accounts and force Arrabbiati members into exile or arrest them."

Celeste rose out of her chair and stepped in front of him to stop his pacing. "I can't believe it. You're a nobleman and honorable Florentine citizen. How can they possibly do any of this according to the law?"

"Mancini says they're within their rights. They make the laws now. We knew my joining the Arrabbiati was a risk, Celeste." He rubbed his forehead, then raised his eyes to hers. "There's more, my dear."

She laid her hand on his arm as she felt her anxiety growing. "What is it, Luci? It's too late to keep anything from me now."

He took a deep breath before saying, "It was Veronica who betrayed me to the Frateschi. Your sister is the one who informed them I'm a member of the Arrabbiati."

Her eyes widened in alarm. "I understand why she'd report us to her beloved Prior, but I couldn't imagine she'd betray us in this way. She must know it puts me and the entire family in grievous danger."

"Savonarola has used her as a pawn against us. The evil man twisted her mind to make her believe she was doing God's will."

Celeste felt she'd been stabbed in the gut and after everything she had done for Veronica, it was too much to bear.

The events of the past two weeks had left Celeste exhausted and depressed. Her world was spinning out of control, but despite her swirling emotions, she knew they had to act swiftly. "We have to get out of Florence before they come for us. We should return to Lucca," she told Luciano.

"Agreed. Rouse the children. Get the servants packing the trunks. Let's be on the move within the hour."

CHAPTER NINE

FLORENCE, 8 FEBRUARY 1497

CELESTE COULDN'T RELAX until the family reached the western edge of Florence. She'd expected to be overtaken by the Frateschi's condottiere forces at any moment. When no one paid them the least attention, her spirits lifted, and she thought it possible they'd reach Lucca before the Frateschi had time to act. It was impossible to know how long they would have to hide out in Lucca. Luciano feared it could be months, maybe longer. Escaping Florence under threat of arrest wasn't how she'd wished to return to her beloved safe haven, but she was grateful just the same.

She was in the carriage with their three daughters while Luciano, Mateo, and Luca rode on horseback beside them. She'd noticed Mateo nodding off as he rode. Luciano had told her of Mateo sneaking home in the early hours before dawn, and of their conversation afterwards. Celeste was glad to hear that Mateo had shown some contrition. She hoped a prolonged separation from his feckless friends would do Mateo good.

"I'm so looking forward to spending more time with Aunt Bianca and Uncle Sandro," Cristina said, drawing Celeste from her thoughts. "Aunt Bianca's children are so darling."

"Cousin Tomaso promised to teach me falconry next time I was in Lucca," Angela said.

"Aren't you afraid of those birds?" Elena asked. "They frighten me."

Angela laughed. "I'm not at all afraid of them. Tomaso says they're gentle creatures when properly trained."

"I'm afraid Tomaso won't remain in Lucca for long after we arrive, Angela," Celeste said. "Since your papa can now oversee your Uncle Sandro's training, Tomaso will wish to leave for Venice as soon as possible."

Just as Angela frowned at that news, the carriage jerked to a halt, nearly throwing her off the seat.

"What's wrong, Mamma?" Elena asked as she reached for her hand.

Celeste drew the carriage curtain aside and peered out to see for herself. Her gut tightened when she saw the line of ten armored condottiere mercenaries on horseback, blocking the road before them. Luciano's house guards positioned their horses in front of their master to shield him, but they were too few in number and no match for the condottiere.

Luciano moved his horse between two of his guards, and Celeste heard him say, "What is this? Do you know who I am?"

The imposing leader of the mercenaries raised his chin as he said, "Yes, Signore Vicente. It is because of who you are that we're here. We're under orders from the Frateschi to bring you before the Signoria to answer for your crimes. We're to arrest you if you resist."

"You'll not take our Master," Guido shouted. "Not as long as we draw breath."

In a flash, one of the condottieri raised his crossbow and let loose an arrow. The arrow struck Guido's throat. He slumped dead over his saddle before sliding off his horse and landing with a thud.

Celeste watched in horror when Luca began to dismount, as he cried out, "Guido, no!"

"Stay on that horse, son," Luciano ordered without turning to face him. "Mateo, take your brother back to the carriage."

"But Papa, I should stay to help you protect the women," Mateo said in protest.

Luciano held up his hand to silence him. "Don't argue. Do as I say."

Mateo locked eyes with his father for a moment before his shoulders slumped, and he signaled for Luca to follow. They silently positioned their horses on either side of the carriage, then waited along with Celeste and the girls for what would happen next. Celeste had never been so frightened, but she maintained a calm demeanor to reassure the children.

The mercenary who'd first spoken to Luciano said, "I would prefer to avoid any more bloodshed, sir, so I advise you to keep your men quiet and surrender peacefully."

Luciano turned toward the carriage and looked to Celeste. With pleading eyes, she slowly shook her head and mouthed the word *no*.

He hesitated for a moment before turning back to the mercenary. "I will surrender if you give your word that my family will be allowed to pass unharmed."

"No, master, you mustn't!" one of Luciano's loyal guards cried as he wheeled his horse between him and the mercenaries.

Another of the condottiere fired his bow, striking the guard's horse in the chest. The animal reared back, throwing his rider before falling to the side as his life drained from him. He struck Luciano's horse on the way down, knocking both horse and rider to the ground. Luciano's horse landed across his torso and legs, crushing him against the uneven, rocky ground.

Celeste screamed as she flew from the carriage to get to

Luciano. His guards quickly dismounted and rushed to get the horse on his feet to free their Master. The condottiere calmly looked on but offered no help. Once up on his legs, the distraught horse fidgeted on his hooves as he eyed his dead companion lying beside Luciano.

Celeste sank to her knees and cradled her beloved's head in her lap as he struggled to draw breath. He opened his mouth to speak, but only managed a quiet gasp. The force of the horse's body had smashed Luciano against the jagged rocks where he now lay.

"Hush, my darling. No need to speak," she said tenderly. "You are my love and my life." He nodded and gave her the faintest smile. "Rest now, my love. Your work is finished. Be at peace." She leaned down and pressed her lips to his as he breathed his last.

As the others surrounded her in stunned silence, she raised her tear-streaked face to the mercenary who shot the horse. "Without just cause, you've killed one of the best men who ever lived. I will make you pay. If it takes the rest of my life, I will see that you pay for this crime."

The head condottiere gave her a half grin, then shrugged as he wheeled his horse in the opposite direction and rode off without a word. The other mercenaries followed at a gallop and were out of sight in moments. Celeste climbed to her feet and looked at the guards who stood frozen.

After tenderly covering Luciano's face with her scarf, she said, "Get a litter. We must carry our Master home." As they jumped into action, she became lightheaded and felt her legs give out. "Mateo, Luca, help me to the carriage. Hurry."

Her sons quickly dismounted, and each took an arm. As she struggled to make her way up the carriage steps, a sob escaped her lips at the sight of her daughters' pale faces staring at her in shock. It struck her that these children had lost their dear papa. She longed to comfort them but hadn't the strength.

She collapsed onto the seat and surrendered to her grief. Her greatest champion was dead. The men working in Savonarola's service had robbed her of all that mattered and destroyed her life. She raised her eyes to the heavens and pleaded with God to pour out His vengeance upon all their heads.

CELESTE HEARD someone calling her name from a great distance. She forced her eyelids open, then squinted in pain from the fire that burned her eyes. Taking a moment to recover her wits, she gazed around her chamber in confusion. She had no memory of how she'd ended up in her bed. She felt under the blankets for Luciano, but his side of the bed was empty. Memories of the nightmare from the previous day crashed over her like a tidal wave.

"Celeste," the voice said again, closer this time. Through the fog in her mind, she recognized it as Livia's.

Celeste rolled onto her back and threw her arm over her eyes to block the blinding light streaming in through the open curtains. "What's the meaning of this? I ordered you not to disturb me."

"Forgive me, Celeste," she said softly.

She moved her arm slightly and peeked at Livia with one eye. The sight of her friend's red, blotchy face and swollen eyes gave Celeste a stab of guilt for being harsh with her.

She sat up and swung her feet over the edge of the bed, and a thunderstorm exploded in her head. Putting her fingers to her temples, she said, "Please tell me you brought something for this pain?"

Livia walked to a tray resting on the small table near the fire. "I have your favorite spiced wine." She filled a goblet and carried it back to the bed. "Drink this. It will help."

Celeste swallowed a few sips before setting the goblet on

her bedside table, then sank back against the pillows. "I hope that wine is laced with poison. You'd be doing me a favor."

Livia put her hands on her hips and stomped her foot. "If you weren't my Mistress, I'd slap you for uttering such evil words."

Celeste turned her back to Livia and pulled the quilt over her head. "Then, thank goodness I am your Mistress. What are you doing here, Livia?"

"You've suffered the worst tragedy imaginable and should be allowed your time to grieve, but three members of the Frateschi have arrived with their guards. They're in the sala insisting to see you. They said if you refuse to come to them, they will come to you."

Celeste threw off the quilt and sat up. "Such insolence! How dare they come armed into my home at such a time? Will my troubles never end? Send Bardo to tell them I'll be there shortly. Have Filippo call the house guards, then return to help me dress."

"Yes, madam," Livia said, then gave a formal curtsy before hurrying out.

Celeste grabbed the goblet off the table and downed the rest of the wine in one gulp. She was incensed that less then twenty-four hours after Luciano's murder, the men responsible were under her roof demanding she appear before them. Did their cruelty know no bounds? Only her fury at their heartless invasion into her private misery could raise her from the darkness threatening to consume her.

With each passing moment, her heart grew colder and harder. Soon it would be replaced by nothing but icy stone. No one understood the depth of her suffering. Not Livia. Not Luciano's sisters. Not even the children. The bond she and Luciano had shared was stronger than any of them could fathom. He'd been the other half of her being, but he was gone, and she would never be whole for as long as she drew breath.

She retrieved the wine decanter and took a long draught of the magical elixir, numbing herself to what she was about to face. Livia raised an eyebrow at her as she came into the room, but for once, she said nothing. Contrary to their usual custom, neither spoke while Livia dressed her.

Half an hour later, Celeste descended the staircase in a haze, but strode into the sala like a queen. She refused to give her enemies the satisfaction of intimidating her. The men bowed in unison and remained standing as she took her seat. Her house guards marched from the opposite end of the room and stood at attention in a semicircle behind her chair.

The ranking member of the Frateschi stepped forward, and said, "Forgive us for disturbing you in your time of grief, Signora Gabriele."

Celeste barked a laugh and gave him a backhanded wave. "Messer Rossi, you dare ask me to forgive you for disturbing me? You should be on your knees begging my forgiveness for ordering the murder of my husband, a greatly respected Florentine nobleman and renowned Maestro." He winced when she said, "And where is your pious puppet master, Savonarola? I know it's he who pulls your strings."

Messer Rossi bowed his head before saying, "You have our deepest sympathies for the tragic, but accidental, death of your most excellent husband. The parties responsible have been severely punished."

Celeste sat forward, struggling to control her rage. "Your words are meaningless. Will they restore Luciano to me? There was nothing accidental about my husband's death, and nothing short of executing the men who killed him will satisfy me."

Messer Rossi raised his head and met her eyes. "Do not forget, Signora, that the Frateschi, governing body of Florence, had earlier that morning declared your husband a blasphemer and a traitor. We sent the condottiere to bring him before us for questioning. We wouldn't have considered ordering his execution for one moment without a proper hearing."

Celeste raised an eyebrow. "You admit you would have considered ordering his execution?"

He hesitated before giving a quick nod. "If the evidence had warranted it. The penalty for treason and conspiracy is death, madam." He paused and raised his hands. "This hypothetical discussion is pointless. Your husband's death was an accident."

Celeste crossed her arms and looked away. "So, you say."

One of the men standing behind Messer Rossi stepped forward, and said, "Enough of this. You have our condolences, Signora, but we have not come to discuss your husband's death. We're here to inform his intended heir that as of this morning, the Vicente title is temporarily suspended, and all your deceased husband's Florentine holdings and assets are frozen pending a thorough investigation. We would also wish to inform you that your husband's intended heir, Mateo Vicente will stand for questioning in his father's place after a proper period of bereavement. We would not want you to think us heartless."

Celeste pushed herself to her feet, then grabbed the arm of the chair for support. "What are you saying? I don't understand you."

He pulled a scroll from inside his tunic and held it out to her. "Have your husband's solicitor, pardon me, I mean your son's solicitor, read this, and explain it to Master Mateo. Now if you'll please excuse us, we'll take our leave." He bowed once more, then motioned for the others to follow him out of the sala.

Celeste gripped the scroll to her chest as she stood staring after them in shock. When she regained her senses, she turned to her guards, and said, "Find Filippo and Bardo, and have them report to me at once. Make haste." While the guards hurried off to do her bidding, she called for Livia as she sank back into her chair. When her maid appeared, she said, "Have you unpacked all our belongings we were taking to Lucca?"

"Not all, but we've made a start. It's been a difficult morning."

"Once I've explained our situation to the family and staff, we'll begin preparations for travel to Venice. We're leaving Florence at dawn, permanently. You'll need to repack the trunks you emptied. Tell the housekeeper to have the maids gather as much as we can carry in the carriages and wagons. We'll send for the rest later."

Livia stepped closer and laid her hand on Celeste's arm. "But you haven't yet buried the Master. How can we go at dawn?"

"I'm taking Luciano to Venice to bury him in his mother's family tomb. I won't abandon him in this city that betrayed and killed him."

Livia stared at her as if she'd gone mad. "It's a six-day journey to Venice. Then you must arrange the funeral, and he will have been dead two days by the time we leave tomorrow. Forgive my indelicacy, but won't his body have decayed by the time he's buried?"

"The weather has been particularly cold of late. That will preserve my beloved's body. No more questions, Livia. Bring me paper, ink, and quill. I must send word to Luciano's sisters."

Livia pressed her palm to her forehead. "Curse my feeble brain. In all the turmoil, I forgot to tell you that Luciano's sisters sent word they'll arrive this morning after breakfast."

"Very well. Gather the maids. I want the entire household here within the next ten minutes."

"Yes, madam."

As Livia went out, Bardo and Filippo rushed into the sala. She ordered Bardo to summon Luciano's solicitor and told

Filippo to gather every member of the staff he could find. He started to offer his condolences, but she silenced him, and said, "There will be time to grieve later. We have more pressing matters to attend to." He gave her a look so forlorn that she immediately regretted her sharpness. He'd been Luciano's loyal and hardworking servant for decades. He would have been suffering from the loss of his master and position. "Please forgive me, Filippo. All will soon be made clear. Just gather the staff."

Filippo did as she ordered, and fifteen minutes later, anyone associated with the estate was assembled in the sala, including Luciano's solicitor and his steward. The sight of her distraught children looking to her for comfort nearly broke her resolve, but she clamped down her feelings and got on with the business at hand.

Climbing onto a step stool Bardo had found for her, she raised her arms to silence the murmurs. Once the room was quiet, she said, "This family has suffered a horrific tragedy. I understand that many of you are grief-stricken, as am I, but our situation is worse than you know. I was visited by three members of the Frateschi not an hour ago to inform me they have suspended my dear deceased husband's title and taken hold of all his Florentine estates and holdings pending an investigation."

Exclamations of shock and disbelief erupted from the group.

Mateo stepped from behind her chair, and said, "What are you telling us, Mamma? The Frateschi have seized my title and inheritance?" She dipped her head in acknowledgment. "Then, we must fight it!"

"Messers Bianco and Vitali, please come forward," Celeste said.

Luciano's solicitor and steward pushed their way to the front, eying her in confusion. She handed Messer Bianco the scroll that the Frateschi had left with her. He unrolled it and scanned it before handing it to Messer Vitali.

After giving it a cursory read, he raised his eyes to Celeste. "This is utterly outrageous," he stammered.

"It is," Celeste said.

"But is it legal?" Mateo demanded. "Can we fight it?" Messer Bianco leaned closer to Messer Vitali and pointed to something written on the scroll. When he'd read it, they both raised their eyes to Mateo. "What is it? Answer me."

Messer Vitali glanced at the scroll, then said, "The Frateschi intend to question you in place of your father for his alleged crimes."

Mateo crossed his arms and raised his chin. "How dare they? I am now Duca Mateo Vicente, and I won't stand for such insolence. I will refuse to answer their summons."

"That won't be necessary, son," Celeste said quietly. "We're leaving Florence in the morning for good. We'll return to Venice where the Frateschi have no power over us."

As a cacophony arose from the crowd, Mateo said, "You're just going to run like a coward, Mamma?"

Celeste glared at him with eyes like flint. "I am no coward," she hissed, and Mateo backed away at the force of her words. "I refuse to live in a city run by murderers and thieves who turn on you at the drop of a pin. They can feast on each other's corpses for all I care."

"I refuse to go," Mateo said.

Celeste looked on him with pity and slowly shook her head. "And how do you propose to live, son? You'll have no access to your father's money, horses, or goods. I'm not even sure you can remain in the palazzo. You'd have to go live with one of your aunts, if they'll take you."

"I will fight the Frateschi and find a way to survive. I'm not a child. I'm a Florentine Duca."

Celeste was growing weary and had no strength to argue

with her obstinate son. He could live in a ditch for all she cared, but she climbed off the stool and laid her hand on his shoulder. "Have you forgotten that you're also now Lord and Master of the Venetian estates? Come to Venice with us and take up your rightful place."

Her words had hit the mark. He held her gaze for a moment, then gave a nod. "I'll go with you, but I won't abandon my title to these Florentine curs."

"I'm pleased to hear that, and nor should you." Turning to Messers Bianco and Vitali, she said, "I'm counting on the two of you to remain here and fight our cause in our place. Are you willing to carry the Vicente banner?"

The men bowed in unison, and Messer Bianco said, "I have long served Signore Vicente, and I will not desert his family now. It would be my honor to stay. I will do whatever is in my power to put this right and restore my Master's good name."

"And I will fight right alongside him, Signora," Messer Vitali said.

Celeste felt tears prick at her eyes but refused to give in to them. "I have complete faith and confidence in both of you." She turned and swept her gaze over the assembled group. "I will prepare a list for those of you who will travel with us. The rest will stay to maintain the palazzo and estate. I will make sure you are housed and fed, so don't concern yourselves on that point. In your Master's name, I thank you all for your years of loyal and committed service. Now, let's all get to work and prepare for our journey."

"THIS IS MADNESS," Elisabetta said an hour later when Celeste explained her plan to bury Luciano in Venice. She put her arm around Celeste's shoulders in a show of sympathy. "I know you've suffered a tragedy. We all have." She lifted a handkerchief to her cheek to wipe a nonexistent tear. "I still can't believe our dear brother is gone, my own flesh and blood. Who are you to decide his burial place?"

It was no more than Celeste had expected from her overbearing sister-in-law, but she was still determined to get her way. There was a time when Luciano's eldest sister intimidated and frightened her, but those days were long past. In her state of emotional turmoil, Celeste cared even less than usual for Elisabetta's theatrics.

"I know this is unorthodox, and I understand your misgivings, sister," she said, "but as far as I'm concerned, the matter is decided."

Elisabetta turned to her younger sisters with a look daring them not to take her side. "Angelica, Diana, what do you two have to say?"

In answer, Diana broke into a fit of tears. "Our brother is dead for only a day, and you're already arguing over him. Who cares where he's buried? All that matters is that he's gone."

Celeste caught Elisabetta struggling not to roll her eyes at her, but Angelica wrapped her arms around her youngest sister and whispered comforting words to her. When Diana had composed herself, Angelica guided her towards her husband, Umberto, standing across from them, then turned to Celeste.

"You couldn't be more a sister to me than if you shared our blood, Celeste, but I'm afraid I agree with Elisabetta."

Celeste wouldn't have been more surprised if Angelica had struck her. She was unable to recall a time when she'd ever agreed with her older sister. Celeste wrapped her arms around herself and turned her back to them. "I thought I could rely on you of all people to support me in this."

Angelica said, "Our mother's family mausoleum may reside in Venice, but our mother does not. She is laid to rest beside my father in the Vicente family crypt, as are our ancestors going back countless generations. This is where Luciano belongs." A sob escaped her lips, so she stopped and took a deep breath before continuing. "Aside from that, Celeste, your plan just isn't how these things are done among our people. Luciano's processional and funeral should take place no later than tomorrow or the following day."

Celeste understood the logic of her words, but they tore at her heart. She needed her beloved close to her in Venice and loathed the thought of him lying in a city she never planned to set foot in again for the rest of her life.

She sighed and turned to face them. "A compromise, then. We hold a quiet funeral at dawn. No processional with a mile of mourners. No inviting the whole of Florence. I will say goodbye to my love and be on my way."

She, Diana, and Angelica turned their eyes to Elisabetta, anticipating her opposition. Instead, to their shock, she said, "I consent to your compromise. In light of our brother's status and circumstances surrounding his death, I think it best we keep his service quiet. We'll hold a proper memorial when the time is more favorable."

Celeste let out her breath as she embraced Elisabetta. When she released her, she said, "I have one more favor to ask. Would you be willing to make the funeral arrangements? I'm overwhelmed preparing for our departure, which will be immediately after the burial."

Angelica put her arm around Celeste's waist and answered for her sister. "You needn't even ask. He was our beloved brother. Go now. See to your children and travel preparations. We have everything in hand."

She embraced Angelica and held her tightly for several moments. "How will I survive without you? Portia's gone. Luciano's gone. Now, I'm losing you. I am alone."

Angelica pulled away and tenderly pressed her hands to Celeste's cheeks. "I promise to write every day. The Gabrieles in Venice will be waiting to support and comfort you. You have your children to surround you. They loved their father and have suffered a tragic loss. They will need your strength."

Celeste gave her a sad smile. "Sadly, my sweet sister, I have none to give. Please excuse me. I have much to do."

She curtsied to her brothers and sisters-in-law, then hurried from the room, leaving them staring after her. Unable to take another instant of their pitying looks, no matter how genuine, she climbed the stairs to her studio. It was the one room in the palazzo that always granted her peaceful sanctuary. As she entered, the face of her beloved stared back at her from his half-finished portrait. She removed the canvas from the easel and lovingly rolled it before carrying it to the window. Holding it to her breast, she curled up on the window seat and released her raging storm of tears.

She wasn't sure how long she'd laid there crying out her anguish, but in time, her sobs quieted. She pushed herself off the window seat, and climbed to her feet, drained from her crippling despair, lack of food and water, and the overwhelming weight of responsibility. She had no one to share her burden. The survival of her family once again rested squarely on her shoulders, just as it had when she was young. This time, there would be no Aunt Portia or Luciano to rescue her.

She carried the canvas to her worktable and tied it with string before placing it into a trunk with her other unfinished paintings. Her other art supplies were still locked in the trunks where Luciano's apprentices had packed them for the trip to Lucca. Now, she'd carry them home to Venice, where they belonged.

When she'd prepared her supplies for the journey, she stopped and took a final look around her studio. Memories of the day Luciano first showed it to her twenty years earlier forced their way to the surface of her mind. The kindness of his loving, generous gift had overwhelmed her. In time, she'd learn that generosity was at the core of who he was.

She closed her eyes, recalling the feel of his lips pressed against hers as he'd passionately kissed her that day. It took all her strength not to allow him to take her completely in that very moment, but they were not yet married. In all their years of marriage since, that passion had never cooled. Now, she'd never again know the feel of his lips or the warmth of his arms enveloping her.

She shook her head to clear it. It was no time for such thoughts. As she started for the door, Angela burst in and threw her arms around her, nearly knocking her over.

"Here you are, Mamma. I've been searching for you everywhere."

Celeste broke free of her embrace and led her by the hand to the window seat. "Why is it no one ever checks the studio first? I'm always here."

"You never will be again," Angela said as she laid her head in Celeste's lap.

As her daughter quietly cried, Celeste stroked her hair, and whispered. "No, I never will."

Through her tears, Angela said, "Is Papa truly gone? How can I go on without him? I wish I had died instead of him."

Celeste shared her feelings, but she sat Angela up and looked her in the eye. "Never let me hear you say such a thing again. My heart is shattered just like yours, but we must find a way to go on with our lives. We'll do it together."

She gave her a sad smile and wiped her face with her sleeve. "Yes, Mamma. We have each other. Papa always said we could overcome anything together."

As Celeste stood and helped Angela to her feet, Luca and Cristina walked in, with Elena behind them. Elena ran to her and wrapped her arms around her waist. Cristina and Luca each followed, and soon, the five of them clung to each other in desperation. Celeste loved her children so very much, but as she'd told Angelica, she had no strength or comfort to offer them.

Celeste gently freed herself, and said, "I wish I could make you understand how much I would like to take your pain away, but I haven't found a way to do that for myself. For now, we must focus our energies on getting to Venice. Once there, we'll seek that elusive peace we so desperately crave. I love you, my darlings, and wouldn't survive this without you. For now, come with me. Let's try to move on and close the door on this tragic chapter of our lives."

The four of them nodded, then took each other's hands as they walked out, leaving their beloved husband, father, and Florence behind.

PART II

VENICE, ROME & MILAN: 1497-1498

CHAPTER TEN

VENICE 1497

Six Weeks Later

Celeste lay on the floor of her studio, unable to summon the strength to stand. She couldn't recall how long it had been since she'd eaten or slept. Days? A week? Her joints and muscles throbbed, likely from a lack of nutrients. Trays of food appeared at the studio door on a regular schedule, but she left them mostly untouched. She had no appetite and had found it nearly impossible to swallow through her painfully constricted throat for the past few days. The only substance she could get down was the spiced wine Livia left outside her door. With her stomach empty, the wine left her brain in a dense fog, but it provided the minimum amount of sustenance to keep her alive. She doubted she would survive much longer in such a state but hadn't decided if that alarmed her or not.

Since arriving in Venice, she'd rarely left the studio despite Livia's and the family's concerted efforts to coax her out. She managed to keep her crippling sorrow at bay long enough to see the family settled in the palazzo before retreating to her sanctuary where she succumbed to her unbearable grief. Matters of ordinary life had ceased to have any significance.

All that mattered in her cocoon was the portrait of her beloved Luciano resting on the easel.

She shifted her head slightly to get a clearer view of the painting. She had worked in an impassioned frenzy from the moment she'd set foot in the Venice studio. The work was three-quarters of the way finished, but before she could add the final brushstrokes, her legs had failed her, and she collapsed. If she died on that hard, dusty floor, her one regret would be not completing the most important work of her life.

Gathering what little strength remained, she rolled onto her side and pushed up onto her hands and knees. As she panted to catch her breath from the herculean effort, someone pounded on the door, which startled her so much that she nearly dropped back onto the floor.

"Mistress, open this door now!" Livia shouted. "If you don't, I'll make Carlo break it down."

Celeste crawled to her cot and heaved herself up. As her head dropped onto the pillows, she said in a trembling voice, "I'm too weak to reach the door, but there's no reason to break it down. A spare key hangs by the bookshelf in my old closet room next-door. You remember the one?"

"Don't move, madam. I'm coming to help. Hold on," Livia called as Celeste heard her footsteps retreating down the hallway.

Less than a minute later, the key rattled in the lock before the door swung open. Celeste almost cried for joy when the door opened. To her it was a sign she was destined to live since she had meant to bolt the studio door.

"Good Lord," Livia exclaimed as she rushed toward her. Celeste closed her eyes as Livia slid her arms under her shoulders to raise her enough to slide pillows under her back and head. "What have you done to yourself? I curse myself for not coming sooner." She turned toward the door and said, "Hey, you there, boy." A houseboy Celeste didn't recognize poked his head in through the doorway. "Find Signore Gabriele and tell him to come at once. Then run to the kitchens and tell Cook to prepare a tray of broth and bread. Take it to the Mistress' chambers. If Cook grumbles, tell her your Mistress demands it."

The boy's eyes widened when he peeked at the emaciated Celeste before running off.

Celeste tried to laugh, but it came out as a croak. "He'll have nightmares after seeing me in this appalling condition."

Livia stared at her for a moment. "You do look a horror. It reminds me of the first time I saw you in this very room. Your father had beaten you nearly to death. You look worse now and don't smell so pleasant, either." She quickly poured wine into the goblet and made Celeste drink. "So much has happened while you've been entombed in your studio feeling sorry for yourself. We must get you to your chambers. Can you walk?"

Marco rushed in before she could answer. He dropped to his knees beside the cot and took Celeste's hand. "My poor sister. What's happened? Why wasn't I told you were ill?"

"She's only sick of heart, Master Marco," Livia said, answering for her. "Come, help me get her upstairs."

A wave of dizziness overcame her, and bile rose in her throat as Marco and Livia carefully lifted her to her feet. She closed her eyes and whispered, "Please, stop. Give me a moment."

As she took deep breaths to calm her queasiness, she heard Livia and Marco gasp in unison. She slowly opened her eyes to see what had caused the reaction and found them staring at Luciano's portrait. They seemed to have forgotten about her standing between them, wilting from weakness.

"Astounding," Marco said reverently as Livia turned and stared at her.

"What's wrong?" Celeste stammered. "Do you not approve, brother?"

Tears welled in Marco's eyes as he shook his head. "That is the most exquisite painting I've ever seen. I've long known you were one of the most gifted artists of our age, but this is sublime, sister. I can't tear my eyes away from it."

Celeste's legs gave way, and she started slipping through their arms. As they got a tighter hold on her, Livia said, "We'll have plenty of time to gush over her painting. We must move her now."

After a slow, steady struggle that nearly ended in disaster more than once, they managed to get Celeste up the two flights of stairs to her chambers. Before attempting to bathe or change her, Livia spoon-fed her bone broth and soft bread with olive oil and restorative herbs. Celeste didn't resist and felt strength flowing back into her with each bite.

On her last sip of broth, she wrapped her fingers around Livia's hand before the spoon reached her mouth. "I also remember you doing this as you nursed me back to health after my father beat me. Thank you, dear friend. You've saved my life yet again."

Livia finished giving her the spoonful of broth, then laid the spoon in the bowl and firmly grasped Celeste's paint-stained hands. "It's been my great honor to serve you and call you dearest friend, but I've reached my limit. I beg you to stop giving me reason to save your life."

Celeste laughed weakly, and said, "You have my word. From here on, I'll do all in my power to take care of myself."

Livia flashed her a warm smile. "Most appreciated."

Growing serious, Celeste said, "I've been in such a dark place these past weeks. I wasn't trying to end my life, but there were many moments when I pleaded for the end to come. I am grateful God chose not to listen to His foolish daughter."

"As are we all. You haven't been alone in navigating through the darkness, but we must put these things behind us. There will be difficult days, but we'll overcome them as we always have. Now, before I faint from your foul odor, let's get you bathed."

~

THREE HOURS LATER, Celeste's children, except for Mateo, surrounded her bed, talking at her all at once. She raised her hands to quiet them and said, "We all have much to share, but I don't have the strength now. I must rest. I just needed to see my darlings and express my regret for neglecting you these past weeks. I'm deeply sorry. I know you've been mourning your papa as I have. It was unforgivable of me to shut you out."

Cristina reached for her hand and said, "There is no need to apologize. We understand. We've had Uncle Marco, papa's Venetian family, and the Gabrieles to comfort us. Uncle Marco told us to respect the time you needed and that you'd return to us when ready."

Tears glistened in Celeste's eyes as she said, "I'll make a point to thank him for that. Sounds like you've had more than your share of visitors."

"A never-ending stream of them," Angela said. "It was a challenge at times when we just wished to be left to mourn in peace."

She put her hand to Angela's cheek. "One thing you'll soon learn is Venetians don't understand the meaning of being left in peace. I'm sure tongues are already wagging about my not coming out to greet them. But our relatives here have good hearts and mean well."

"We know, Mamma," Luca said. "We're enjoying getting to know them better and hearing stories of Papa when he was young. Just yesterday, cousin Federigo told me about having you as his nanny."

Elena looked at her in surprise. "You were once a nanny, Mamma?"

Celeste laughed and nodded. "Shocking, I know, but that is a long story for another time." "Where is Mateo? Is he not home? I'd like to speak with him."

She noticed Luca averting his eyes when the girls glanced at him.

"Our *brother* is in his office," Angela said. "He wishes me to inform you that he will attend you later. He says he has more pressing matters to attend to at the moment."

"I see," she said, baffled by her use of such formal speech. When Luca and Cristina avoided her eyes, Celeste had no doubt they were keeping secrets from her. Once she was recovered, there would be time to get to the truth. She yawned and sank against the pillows. "I must rest now but seeing your lovely faces has been the balm I needed. I'll do my best to join you at breakfast. You know I love all of you with my whole heart."

They each got up and expressed their love before kissing her cheek on their way out of the room.

Livia came in from the antechamber a moment later. As she fluffed Celeste's pillows, she said, "They're such wonderful children. They've weathered this difficult time like champions. You must be extraordinarily proud of them."

"As always. What's happening with Mateo?" When her maid didn't answer but continued to fuss with the blankets, Celeste said, "Livia, I demand an answer."

Livia straightened and put her hands on her hips. "Forgive me, Signora, but now is not the time. Once you've rested, I promise to tell you all but not until then."

Celeste raised her eyebrows, trying not to laugh at her maid's disobedience. "Not good news, then?"

"Can I get you anything for the night, madam?"

Celeste waved her hand to shoo Livia out, then closed her eyes, trying to ignore the anxiety rising in her gut. *Will I ever know peace again?* she asked herself as she drifted into a deep, dreamless sleep.

AFTER SLEEPING for more than a day, then eating a hearty lunch, Celeste excused herself from the table, promising to join the family for dinner. She reluctantly made her way to the studio, fearing she might sink back into the abyss, but she couldn't avoid that room forever. She was pleased to find early spring sunshine and fresh air flowing through the open shutters in the studio. The housemaids had scrubbed and tidied the room, so the grime and darkness of the past weeks had vanished.

She crossed the room and sank onto the cot, which gave her a direct view of Luciano's portrait. Folding her hands in her lap, she silently studied her work as she recalled Marco and Livia's words from the previous day. Though she was content with what she'd accomplished and appreciated their praise, she didn't judge the painting from an artistic perspective. Her aim was to bring her beloved back to life on the canvas. If she couldn't have Luciano alive, she could gaze at his image every day and pretend he was still with her.

The portrait still needed work, but the energy and desire to apply them seemed to have drained out of her. The unfinished image stared back, begging to be made whole, but she couldn't summon the will to comply. She'd sat for an hour without coaxing herself off the cot when Livia burst into the studio.

"You must come with me this instant, madam!" she cried. "Master Mateo has lost his mind. He's forcing Marco and his family out of the palazzo at the point of his sword. He says they have no right or reason to live here since he's now Lord of the estate. You must come before he kills your brother."

Celeste jumped to her feet and made for the door, surprised her weak legs so easily supported her weight. When she reached the sala, Celeste was horrorstruck to find Marco on his knees at Mateo's feet with Mateo holding the point of his sword inches from Marco's chest. Mateo was a fully grown man, but his immaturity and fiery temper made him act more like a dangerous ten-year-old. Though seemingly incapable of controlling his emotions, he could wield his sword masterfully, and seemed about to drive the sword through the heart of Celeste's unarmed brother.

"What is the meaning of this?" Celeste bellowed with renewed strength fueled by her fury. "Mateo, lower that sword at once, or I shall summon the guards to wrest it from you."

Mateo raised his eyebrows at her. "Summon all you'd like. The guards answer to me, Mamma. I am Lord of the palazzo."

"Are you willing to test that theory?" He wavered for an instant but held his ground. "Drop that weapon, or I'll take it from you myself."

He eyed her for a moment before slowly lowering his sword. "I do this not because you ordered me but out of respect for you and to show how magnanimous I am."

Marco jumped to his feet and ran to console Adrianna along with her parents who stood watching the scene in horror. As he embraced Adrianna, he turned to Celeste and mouthed, *thank you, sister.*

With a wave of her hand, Celeste said, "Please leave us, Marco, and take your family and the servants with you."

"Stop!" Mateo shouted. "I'm your Master here. I say when you're dismissed."

The family and servants stood still as the statues in the palazzo garden, looking from Celeste to Mateo, unsure who they should obey. Celeste kept her eyes locked on Mateo as she gave a small wave. In unison, the spectators made a rush for the doors. All except Livia, who stepped beside Celeste and crossed her arms, refusing to budge.

"You too, Livia," Celeste said without taking her eyes off Mateo.

Her maid emphatically shook her head. "No, madam. I don't dare leave you alone with this fiend."

Marco leaned closer to Livia and said, "You allow a servant to speak to you with such insolence? Outrageous."

Ignoring him, Celeste turned to Livia and patted her arm. "He's no danger to me. Please go ask Cook to prepare me a plate and take it to my chambers. I'm famished." Livia glanced at Mateo before curtsying and leaving without another word.

As soon as she was out of earshot, Celeste rushed at Mateo and grabbed the sword from him before he had time to strike. After flinging it across the room, she calmly raised her hand and summoning all her strength, slapped him across the cheek.

He stared at her in shock before raising his hand to the reddening palm print on his face. "How dare you strike me?"

Without answering him, she turned and lowered herself into the closest chair. After calmly resting her hands on the intricately carved arms, she said, "Your papa and Nonna Francesca would be utterly ashamed if they were here. Your uncle Marco is the best, most kindhearted man I've ever known. He's been nothing but supportive and loving to you. I should be the one asking, how dare you?"

As her words hit their mark, Mateo's shoulders slumped, and he dropped into the chair beside her. "Uncle Marco had the nerve to question my authority over him."

He cringed when Celeste burst into laughter. "Who are you, the Doge? Marco is a well-respected master artist and a Gabriele. You may be Lord of this estate, but your uncle Marco never should have been threatened and humiliated in such a way. You have offended his honor and that of my entire clan."

Mateo raised his chin and scowled at her. "My uncle doesn't hold a title as I do."

"No one in Venice cares a fig for your *suspended* Florentine title and owning this estate does not make you Marco's superior. In fact, he is your superior in every way. Is this how your father taught you to settle disagreements? Is this the way a noble Vicente acts? You've learned nothing. In this moment, I am ashamed to call you son."

Tears dripped from his cheeks as he bowed his head and stared into his lap. "I don't know what comes over me, Mamma," he said quietly. "I feel incapable of controlling my anger as Papa, and other men do."

Celeste felt little sympathy for him as he sat there, quietly crying like a pathetic child. "Don't make excuses to me. Yes, you are young and need time to grow into your role, but the best men learn to control their passions. It doesn't happen without effort. You will have to work harder than most. You should be looking to your uncle Marco and others for guidance, not threatening them at the point of a sword. What is it you ordered Marco to do?"

He raised his eyes to hers. "The palazzo is too crowded with all of us living here. I've ordered Marco to take his family and leave, but he ignores me."

She slowly shook her head. "This palazzo is big enough to house half of Venice, Mateo. And you're perfectly aware your papa promised Marco and his family they could live here for as long as they wished."

"Papa's not here now, is he? I had my steward and solicitor scour Papa's papers. They found no contract stating Marco and his family may reside here indefinitely."

Celeste felt her anger rising yet again, so she took a few deep breaths before continuing. "It's disturbing to see you would go to such lengths to evict your own uncle when he's done nothing to deserve it. Your father gave Marco verbal permission. I heard him say it. Or is my word not good enough for you either? Where is your sense of honor?"

"I am not disputing that Papa invited them in, but he's dead, and I'm Lord here now. I have the final say over what happens under this roof. I don't require your permission. Marco and his family must go."

Celeste pushed herself to her feet, then crossed the sala to where the sword lay. After picking it up, she pointed it at Mateo's heart. "You disappoint me, *son*. I will abide by your heartless decision, but you will allow Marco sufficient time to find suitable lodgings for his family. He will be allowed to continue operating his business in your Papa's workshop downstairs. If you interfere with this in any way, you will have to deal with me."

She spun on her heel and marched out, carrying the sword, and leaving him staring after her. The instant she reached the landing, she slumped against the wall and dropped the sword. Since she'd left the studio only two days earlier, she was still physically and emotionally drained. After the disturbing and frightening confrontation with Mateo, she longed to retreat to her sanctuary and forget the world once more. Only her overly heightened sense of obligation prevented her from succumbing to the temptation.

When Carlo bounded up the stairs a few moments later, she straightened and smoothed the folds in her skirt. He came to an abrupt stop and glanced down at the sword.

With a raised eyebrow, he said, "I heard the sword clattering on the tile and came to see if you needed my assistance. This isn't what I expected to find." He glanced at the sword before looking back up at her. "It seems you've managed quite well without me. What happened, madam?"

"I'm sure you'll hear once the gossip spreads through the palazzo like wildfire." Pointing to the sword, she said, "Please tuck that away in the guardhouse, then come to my studio in thirty minutes. I have a matter I wish to discuss privately with you."

"Yes, madam," he said as he bent to retrieve the sword. Before heading toward the stairwell, he turned and looked at her with obvious concern. "Take care, mistress. The palazzo isn't the haven it once was."

He rushed down the stairs before she could ask what he meant. *What else has happened here while I was lost in the darkness?* she asked herself as she went in search of Marco.

CELESTE STOOD outside Luciano's old workshop door, trying to coax her hand into lifting the handle. She hadn't been able to set foot inside the busy workshop since returning to Venice, fearing her cherished memories of times spent there with Luciano would overwhelm her. Reminding herself she was there for her brother, she reached for the latch.

When she stepped inside, the apprentices stopped their work and stared at her in a respectful silence. She gazed around the room with fondness, remembering when she would have given nearly anything to be allowed inside the wondrous place. Then, the idea of her working alongside those apprentices would have been ludicrous, even sinful. That Luciano would have risked so much then to help her achieve such heights despite her sex still puzzled and amazed her.

She was pleased to see the room filled with so many budding artists. When Marco reached the level of master artist, he left the Bellini brothers' employment to build his own establishment. Luciano's workshop had stood empty in the years since he'd left for Florence, which left Marco with the perfect location to set up his business with no extra costs. With Luciano's favorable reputation in Venice and Marco's promising one, he had no trouble attracting new apprentices. In no time, he had a bustling and profitable workshop.

The young man Celeste guessed to be the chief apprentice, stepped forward and gave her a respectful bow. "Welcome Maestra Gabriele. We're honored to have you here."

She smiled and gave a slight nod. "Thank you. It is my honor to be here. I have an urgent matter to discuss with your Maestro. Is he in his office?"

The young man nodded and gestured toward the rear of the workshop. "Would you like me to escort you?"

Celeste shook her head. "Thank you, but I know the way."

"Of course, Maestra," he said, then stepped aside with his head bowed to let her pass.

She felt several pairs of eyes following her as she headed to Marco's office and was glad when she reached his door. She found him inside, dropping an armful of rolled sketches into a trunk. The rest of the room was in varying stages of disarray from packing up his workshop supplies.

"I knew I'd find you here," she said as he straightened and turned to face her. "Put those drawings back where they belong." When he raised an eyebrow, she said, "Mateo may be forcing you out of your house, but the workshop is still yours."

He dropped into his desk chair and covered his face with his hands. After a few moments, he wiped his damp brow with a paint-stained cloth before looking up at her. "Thank you, sister. I'm greatly relieved. Finding a new home is a simple matter. Locating and moving to a new workshop is another thing entirely. I was at a complete loss for what to do." He gestured with his thumb toward the door. "That roomful of young men out there depends entirely on me. If I were to fail them, my career and reputation would be finished."

"There's no need to worry on that account, brother." She sat opposite him and watched him pour a generous helping of wine into his goblet. She couldn't help but notice his hand trembling as he held the bottle up to offer her some. She shook her head and said, "How are you and your family coping after the nightmarish encounter with Mateo?"

"I'm managing, and Adrianna and her parents were recovering in the sitting room when I left them." He took a gulp of wine, then closed his eyes and sighed. "What a humiliating and frightening ordeal. I'm not sure what would have happened if you hadn't come in when you did. You are the only one Mateo listens to now that we don't have Luciano to keep him in line. He seemed intent on running me through with that sword, the little mongrel. I've been forced to swallow my pride since you all arrived because he is the Master, but what will happen to me when he stops obeying even you?"

Raising her eyebrows, she said, "The important thing to focus on now is that I arrived in time to prevent a tragedy, and Mateo still trusts and listens to me for some reason. I regret that I couldn't persuade Mateo to let you stay, but he reluctantly agreed to allow you the time you need to find new lodgings. I'll ensure he keeps his word. Do you know where you and the family will go?"

He shook his head as he walked to the window and peered over the canal. "Not yet, but with Luciano's bequest, I'll have no trouble finding more than adequate accommodations for our family."

"Will Alfonso and Florina stay with you, or will they return to live in their son's quarters at the silk mill?"

He turned and leaned against the wall with his arms folded. "They'll come with us. I promised them a roof over their heads when I married Adri. We all assumed that would be here at the palazzo. Wherever we go, it will be a step down from this. Adrianna is devastated. She fears she'll be ostracized by her patrician friends and excluded from the social events she enjoys so much."

Celeste looked sullenly at her dear brother and said, "This

entire situation is outrageous, and I'm powerless to stop it. And all because of my cruel, arrogant son. Luciano would be deeply grieved if he witnessed this outrage. I always said he was too lenient with Mateo." She got to her feet and went to face him. "I promise you I won't stop until I see this rectified. I will see Mateo pays for this insult to you and your family, even if he is my adopted son."

Marco laid his hand on her shoulder. "Celeste, you deserve none of the blame or responsibility for this. Mateo is in his rights, no matter how heartless they are. We'll be fine. In fact, better off than most. I have the bequest and earnings for my artwork. Don't concern yourself with this trifle. You have more pressing matters to worry about."

Celeste gave him a quick hug and kissed his cheek. "I'll assist you in any way I can." As Marco opened the door for her, she paused in the doorway and said, "Marco, what else has happened in my…absence?"

Marco's smile faded. "You've only just rejoined us, sister. Now is a time for healing. Let other weighty matters rest for a while."

His eyes told her that he was keeping unpleasant secrets from her. She squeezed his hand, then stepped into the workshop before rushing back upstairs. Carlo was waiting for her in the studio, standing before Luciano's portrait, studying it intently.

When he heard her enter, he wiped a tear from his cheek in embarrassment and said, "It's a magnificent likeness, Signora. Stunning, in fact. I've never seen its equal. Your husband was the best of men, Signora. He was taken from us too soon."

Celeste nodded her thanks before gesturing toward a small table in the corner. When he remained standing as she took one of the chairs, she said, "I insist that you sit." He hesitated for an instant before lowering himself onto the chair. As he watched her, waiting for her to speak, she said, "I remember a time when you picked me up by my waist and practically tossed me into a gondola in the dark of night." He looked away as the color rose in his cheeks. "Don't be ashamed, Carlo. You and I were equals then. I would even say you outranked me. I'm that same woman. I may hold a title now, but nothing has changed inside."

Carlo chuckled and said, "Yes, I recall that night. Your feet were bare, and you wore only a nightdress under your cloak. You were attempting to disobey your maestro by not attending your lesson. He made me vow not to let you. You were nothing but a wisp of a girl." He raised his eyes to meet hers. "How far you've come, Duchessa Gabriele. Would I be impertinent to say I'm proud of you?"

She shook her head and grinned at him. "Not at all. You flatter me. Luciano once told me he hired you to carry out what he called *delicate assignments*. I have one such task for you. I'll compensate you more than fairly."

He eyed her curiously before saying, "What is it you need from me, mistress?"

"I wish you to secretly keep a close watch on my son and give me regular reports of his activities."

He raised an eyebrow but kept his face guarded so she couldn't read his reaction. "Do I understand you to mean Master Mateo? Forgive me. I meant Signore Vicente."

"Yes, Carlo. I understand he's your Master, and you could lose your position if your actions were discovered. If that were to happen, I would protect you and personally arrange a favorable situation for you. But we will be ever so discreet, so it won't come to that."

Carlo stroked his beard for a moment as he considered her proposal. "To be clear, you're asking me to spy on your son?" She felt her cheeks redden as she gave a quick nod. He gave her a wry smile and said, "I would be delighted to take on this most intriguing assignment, madam."

"Excellent," Celeste said with a laugh. "Arrange with Livia to make your reports. She will be our intermediary. She'll know the best times for us to meet without arousing suspicion."

She thought she caught a wink when he said, "With pleasure, madam. I will begin at once." He executed a flourishing bow, then grew serious. "All of Venice mourns your esteemed husband, Signora. I pledge my life to you in honor of him and will gladly serve you expecting nothing but your esteem in return."

CHAPTER ELEVEN

VENICE 1497

Four Weeks Later

"Mamma, where is Papa's portrait?" Angela asked as she breezed into Celeste's studio.

Celeste gestured to a trunk in the corner. "Locked away until I'm prepared to finish it."

Angela looked to the spot where the easel had stood. "But I look forward to seeing it every day when I come in. It helps me miss him less."

Celeste leaned against the worktable and folded her arms. "I felt the same, but to heal, I need time away from painting. I'll know when I'm ready to work on it again."

Angela kissed her cheek, then said, "Take whatever time you need. Why did you ask me here? You said you had something important to tell me."

"I do, sweetheart. Come, let's sit." She took hold of Angela's hand and led her to the small table. Once seated, she said, "Marco told me you asked to apprentice in his workshop."

She crossed her arms and pouted. "I did. He said no." An instant later, her face brightened as she leaned closer to Celeste across the table. "Did you persuade him to change his mind? Is that why you asked me here?"

Celeste shook her head. "No. I'm not going to try to change your uncle's mind. I know you worked alongside your father in his Florence workshop, but those apprentices were accustomed to your presence. Your father started taking you to work with him when you were a very young girl. Uncle Marco's situation is far different."

Angela slumped back with a sigh. "I was afraid you'd say that. So, why *did* you call me to your studio?"

Celeste covered Angela's hands with hers. "I asked you here to tell you I'm turning my studio over to you."

Angela stared at her in confusion. "But where will you paint? The studio is too cramped for both of us to work here."

"I'm not going to paint."

Celeste rose and silently studied every inch of the small room. It was the magical place where she sprang to life as an artist. She closed her eyes and recalled when Luciano discovered a scrap of her drawing that fluttered to the floor during Federigo's art lesson. Luciano picked it up and looked into her eyes as if seeing her for the first time. Her life's joys and successes could all be traced to that singular moment in that little studio.

Celeste opened her eyes and found Angela quietly watching her. "It's not just Papa's portrait locked in the trunk. I'm putting down my brushes as well."

"You can't do that. You're in the prime of your career, and your work is becoming more masterful by the day. You had more commissions than you had time to paint before Papa..." She paused and glanced up at her mother. "Yes, I understand, Mamma."

Celeste nodded. "You know the fire that burns inside you, driving you to paint? Those flames inside me have died." She turned her back to her daughter. "It's as if when I lost your father, I lost all desire to paint. It's faded away like the early morning mists of Venice, Angela," she whispered.

Angela stood and rushed to Celeste's side. Throwing her arms around her, she said, "It won't be forever, Mamma. It will return. Just give it time."

Celeste pulled her closer and rested her head on Angela's shoulder. "I pray it will, my darling, but until then, you must paint for both of us." With tears in her eyes, she said, "The studio is yours, and Uncle Marco will give you lessons when he can spare the time. Maybe someday, I will work with you, too." She released Angela and gazed around her beloved sanctuary. "For the time being, I must step away from the canvas."

"I have faith that you will find your fire someday, Mamma," Angela said softly behind her.

Celeste wiped her cheeks, then turned to face her. "Enough tears. This is a happy day. Bring your supplies from your chambers, and I'll help you set up."

Mateo's manservant, Alfredo, tapped on the open door as Angela started to go. "Forgive the interruption, madam, but my Master wishes to see you in his office."

"That can't be good," Angela whispered.

Celeste shook her head and motioned for the servant to lead the way. When they reached Mateo's office door, Alfredo gave her a quick bow and hurried off before she could open it. She took a moment to gather her wits before entering her son's holy sanctum.

Her relationship with Mateo had become more strained with each passing day, and the mood in the palazzo had gone from mournful to unpleasant to intolerably tense. Her worst fears about Mateo had been confirmed by Carlo's frequent reports. Mateo oppressed the household staff and alienated half the local merchants because of his arrogance and short temper. Even the extended family had begun keeping their distance, including his mother's sisters, who had taken him in for a time following his grandmother's death.

In the first weeks after leaving the studio, Celeste had done her best to guide him, but he'd never forgiven her for threatening him after the recent confrontation with Marco. He'd even told her he didn't need to listen to her since she was a mere woman. After coming close to striking him more than once, she decided it was best to keep her distance. She'd appealed to her male Gabriele relatives for help, but they wanted nothing to do with him. She'd next tried his mother's family. His uncles attempted to help, but Mateo ignored their advice since they weren't noblemen.

With nowhere else to turn, Celeste's only recourse had been to give Mateo a wide berth and shield her children from him as best she could. As she stood outside his door, she knew Angela had been right. Whatever the reason he'd summoned her, it couldn't be good. She pasted on a warm smile before reaching for the door, hoping it would be enough to disarm him.

"Welcome, Mamma," he said without getting up to greet her with a kiss.

He sprawled in his chair, behaving like he owned the world. Celeste's anger rose at the sight of him, so she took a slow, deep breath to tamp down her anger. There was no call to lose her composure before she knew the purpose of the meeting.

Mateo pointed to the chair across from his, and as she lowered herself into it, she said, "How are you, son? I haven't seen you for days."

He gave a backhanded wave. "You'd see me if you bothered to join me for dinner instead of hiding in your quarters. But since you ask, I'm doing quite well."

She gave him a look that made him sit up and straighten his tunic. She was relieved to see she still wielded a modicum of power over him.

"I'm pleased to hear you're well, but you're mistaken in believing I've been *hiding* in my quarters. Adjusting to life without your father has been extremely difficult. I miss him at dinnertime most of all. I'm sure you understand since you must be mourning him as much as the rest of us."

He bowed his head, feigning a sadness she wondered if he actually felt. She wasn't entirely sure he ever experienced any real emotion beyond anger. The thought disturbed her more than she cared to admit.

"Yes, of course, I miss Papa every day," he said without raising his eyes.

Hoping but doubting that was true, she said, "Why is it you've asked to see me, Mateo?"

His feigned grief evaporated in an instant. He raised his head and studied her with his expressionless eyes. "I've just learned that you refused an invitation to a gala at the Doge's palace. Why he sent the invitation to you instead of me is a mystery. Please, Mamma, explain why you responded to the invitation without informing me."

Struggling to maintain her composure, she said, "Informing you? The invitation, as you say, was addressed to me. I saw no reason whatsoever to involve you in my decision. Frankly, the matter was none of your business, son. How did you even hear of this?"

In a flash, his eyes transformed from cold and empty to being filled with a ferocity that gave her chills. She fought the urge to back away from him, not wanting him to sense her fear or yield ground to him in their contest of wills.

"I have my ways. Did you truly believe I wouldn't find out you've had Carlo watching me?" He stood and walked around the desk, then leaned down and rested his hands on the arms of her chair. "You've never seen me as more than an incompetent child, but it's time you learn I'm a force to be reckoned with. Your little spy has been dealt with, so don't expect any more reports from him, and don't dare try to replace him."

Celeste jumped to her feet, shoving Mateo out of her way as she did. She grabbed the fire poker and pressed it to his chest. "Dealt with? How?" she said between clenched teeth. "What have you done to Carlo?"

Mateo glanced down at the poker, then gave her an eerie grin as he yanked it out of her hand and laid it on the desk. "He's alive, if that's what you're wondering. I've had him clad in irons until I decide what to do with him. Don't bother trying to free him. I've ordered my guards to bring you directly to me if you interfere with my commands."

Celeste climbed onto the footstool beside her chair, so she equaled him in height. Harnessing her fury, she grabbed the collar of his tunic. "You think yourself so mighty, son, but I have allies more powerful than you can imagine. Don't toy with me. Trust me when I say you will live to regret it."

His imposing facade faltered for the first time since she entered the room, and she thought she saw a momentary flash of concern in his eyes. She hopped off the stool and swept out of the room before he had a chance to speak. After ordering Ivo, Mateo's head footman, to have the gondolier prepare a boat, she told him he would escort her on an errand. He hesitated for a moment, then bowed and left to carry out her orders. She then went in search of Livia and found her in her antechamber.

"Bring our cloaks. We're going out," Celeste said as Livia got to her feet.

She eyed her Mistress for a moment before saying, "I recognize that look, Celeste. I'm not going to like this, am I?"

"Definitely not, friend. Hurry, we have little time to lose."

～

LIVIA PEPPERED her with questions as the gondola took them to Cousin Cesare's palazzo. Celeste told her in a whispered rush about Carlo and Mateo to keep Ivo from overhearing. Finally losing her patience, she said, "I promise to tell you all in time, Livia. For now, I need to gather my thoughts before we arrive."

Livia nodded, then folded her arms and leaned into the plush cushions. Celeste knew she had to present her case to Cesare delicately as her cousin wouldn't be eager to jump into the middle of Vicente family squabbles. Her clan had never approved of Luciano's adopting Mateo, believing he should have been left in the hands of his mother's family.

When Mateo's behavior grew more disturbing over time, Celeste agreed with them, but the situation had been out of her control. Luciano had always defended his adopted son out of regret for how he'd treated Isabella, and for the trauma he'd suffered in watching her die giving birth to Mateo. It was a testament to Luciano's good heart, which had left Celeste to deal with the aftermath of decisions made years earlier. All that mattered for the present was that she rescue Carlo and protect her family.

When Cesare's palazzo came into view, Celeste's thoughts raced back to the day years earlier when she'd gone there, desperately seeking aid, broken in body and spirit, but had been denied entrance. She smiled as she thought about the course her life had taken that day despite the Gabriele clan's uncaring refusal to help her.

When the gondolier pulled to the landing, Ivo got out and helped Livia and her from the boat. "Wait here for us," she told him. "We may be gone for some time."

He gave a slight bow, then climbed out to tie the gondola to the post. Celeste raced up the steps with Livia and the footman struggling to keep up with her. She rang the bell, then paced impatiently, waiting for someone to answer. When the door finally swung open, she swept past Cesare's startled footman into the foyer.

When she stopped, he bowed and said, "Welcome, Signore Gabriele. Forgive me. I was not told to expect you."

"This is a surprise visit, Gino," she said as he took her cloak. "Is my cousin Cesare at home? I have an urgent matter to discuss with him."

"I'm sorry to say he is not, but his brother, Master Francesco, is available, madam. Please follow me to the sala, and I will inform him you're here."

Celeste preferred to speak to Cesare, but Francesco would have to do. Fortunately, he had the authority to order Cesare's guards to come to her aid if he consented to her plea.

"Very well, Gino." Turning to Ivo and Livia, she said, "Wait for me here. Be prepared to leave the instant I return."

Ivo bowed, then leaned against the wall while Livia caught her eye and gave her an encouraging look. "All will be well, mistress. You'll see."

Celeste followed Gino to the sala. She was too agitated to sit and began to pace but fortunately didn't have to wait long before Francesco appeared. He came straight for her, smiling as he took her hands in his and kissed her cheeks.

"This is a lovely surprise, cousin. Gino says you have an urgent matter to discuss."

He led her to a pair of chairs near the fire and motioned for her to sit. She ignored it and remained standing. "Forgive me, Francesco. I am in a desperate situation and have no time for pleasantries." She rapidly explained conditions in the palazzo under Mateo's rule and recounted the situation with Carlo. "I'm responsible for Carlo and promised him my protection. He's been one of Luciano's most loyal servants since I met my husband, and he's been of great service to me. I honestly fear Mateo capable of executing him, and I'm begging for your help to prevent that."

"I'm deeply grieved to hear of your situation, especially since the recent passing of your honorable husband." He quickly crossed himself, then gave her a warm smile. "Put your fears to rest, cousin. It would be my greatest pleasure to put that bastard, Mateo, in his place. I have no doubt Cesare would feel the same. We have twice the number of house guards as those of Mateo's. Let me gather them and follow you back to the palazzo."

Celeste sighed in relief as she reached for Francesco's hand and kissed it while she curtsied. "You have set my mind at rest. I cannot repay this great kindness."

"Nonsense, Celeste." He gave her a mischievous grin as he raised her out of the curtsy. "We're family, and this is what we do. Besides, I'm looking forward to this. It will be the greatest fun I've had in some time."

Celeste nodded her thanks but secretly wasn't as confident as her cousin. Mateo had been right about one thing. He was a force to be reckoned with. "You must hurry. I'll wait for you in my gondola," she said as she headed for the door. "I won't rest until Carlo is free and released from Mateo's clutches."

WITHIN TWENTY MINUTES, Francesco was beside Celeste in her gondola, with ten of his house guards following in two more gondolas close behind. Celeste twice ordered the gondolier to pick up the pace.

When she asked a third time, Francesco put his hand on her arm to stop her. "He's paddling as quickly as possible, Celeste. Let the man do his job."

Celeste grinned sheepishly at the gondolier. He raised his brow as he tried to stifle a smile. She shrugged, then switched seats, facing forward in the direction they were headed. When she caught sight of the palazzo as they rounded the corner, she wished she could get out of the boat and race across the water to get there quicker. The best she could do was be on her feet, ready to climb out the instant the gondola reached the landing.

When she, Francesco, and her servants were heading past the courtyard toward the guardhouse, followed by Francesco's guards, he pulled her to a stop. "This is no place for you, cousin. Take Livia and go inside to await word from me."

Celeste stretched to her full height and stared intently towards the palazzo as she crossed her arms.

"Here it comes," Livia whispered loud enough for them to hear.

Celeste frowned at her before saying, "Francesco, I will stay out of the fray if it comes to that, but I am going with you. Livia, I release you and Ivo to go inside if you wish."

Ivo didn't hesitate to run off in the opposite direction, but Livia didn't budge. "How dare you even consider I would leave your side for one moment? You offend me, mistress."

When Francesco looked at her in surprise, Celeste glanced at him and shook her head. "And you think *I'm* stubborn? Come, we're wasting time."

Francesco led the way and stopped just out of sight of the guardhouse. He ordered his guards to wait until they called for them. Turning to his guard commander, he said. "I will only take one of you for now. We don't want to give the impression this is an unprovoked attack. Listen for my whistle."

The commander bowed, then called his troops to attention. Celeste and Livia stood behind Francesco and his guard as he pounded on the guardhouse door. When one of Mateo's guards answered, Celeste peeked around Francesco and was relieved to see it was one of the youngest, most inexperienced men.

Francesco donned an air of authority and said, "Tell your commander I'm here and bring him to me at once."

The guard bowed and left to do his bidding without a

word. While they waited, Celeste wondered how it must feel to have men obey you without question the way the guard had done. It wasn't that men didn't respect her, but in such a situation, she wielded no authority. Few women had ever set foot in such a place and hadn't the first inkling of the workings of men. She was unique in that respect, but it only took her so far. She again prayed for a day when women stood as equals to their male counterparts. She had no expectations of it occurring in her lifetime.

The guard returned with his commander, then faded into the darkness beyond the doorway. The commander bowed, then looked at Francesco in confusion. "How can I be of service, Signore Gabriele?"

"I am here to order Carlo Riva's immediate release. I will accompany you to his cell," Francesco said nonchalantly, as if he were asking for a crust of bread.

He hesitated for a moment before shaking his head. "Under who's authority, sir? I received no order from my Master to release the prisoner to anyone, especially you."

Francesco leaned closer to the commander, who didn't back away. "You will receive no order from your Master, but I am taking the prisoner, nonetheless."

The commander looked at Francesco and his guard and then raised his eyebrows when he spotted Celeste for the first time. Unintimidated by their presence, he emitted a loud, shrill whistle. Five guards, including the one who'd opened the door, immediately appeared, marching in double-time and formed a semicircle behind their commander.

The commander gave Francesco a half-grin. "I refuse to release the prisoner or allow you entry into his cell, sir. I suggest you take your boys and women and depart before we force you to do so."

Francesco yawned and stretched before giving an even louder whistle than the commander. Celeste and Livia stepped aside as his ten guards appeared at a double march and formed two lines behind him. Celeste and Livia smiled at each other, enjoying the theatrics.

Casually leaning against a stone wall with his arms crossed, Francesco said, "Care to reconsider your threat?"

The commander shot him an angry look before turning to his closest guard. "Get the Master, now," he barked.

The guard glanced at Celeste as he brushed past her before taking off at a full run.

"I'm not waiting for that whelp Vicente to get here," Francesco said as he and his guards stepped closer to the doorway. "Out of my way."

Celeste held her breath as she watched the commander debating in his mind who he feared more, Francesco and his guards or Mateo. She was greatly relieved when he stepped aside and handed Francesco a ring of keys. Her cousin stepped through the doorway with half his men while the others held their place to guard his back.

Celeste glared at Mateo's guards as she and Livia stepped around the men and followed Francesco's forces inside. In truth, Mateo's men were duty-bound to protect her, and she never should have needed to call on Francesco to help her free her own servant. Her world had flipped upside down, but she hoped freeing Carlo and putting Mateo in his place would set it right.

She'd only seen the dungeon once in the years since she'd known Luciano. She'd wandered down there one day when Luciano told her if she were to be Mistress of the palazzo, she needed to become familiar with every inch of it. The guard had given her a quizzical look when she'd told him to give her a tour, but he'd obeyed.

According to family records, no one had been incarcerated there for years. Unlike dungeons in Florence and other cities, Venetian ones were built at ground level since the city rested on top of the ocean. That didn't prevent them from being dark and dank, and Celeste had been relieved when the tour ended. When she recounted her dungeon visit to Luciano that night, he laughed and told her she had taken his advice to get familiar with the estate a little too literally. She assured Luciano she would never again visit those horrible cells.

As Celeste followed the guards' torches that day, she was devastated to see that things had changed since her last visit. Carlo wasn't the only prisoner. She counted at least five others. Celeste was powerless to free them that day but vowed to do whatever it took to see them released as soon as possible. When they reached Carlo's cell, she pushed her way to the front and leaned against the bars to get a better look. Carlo lay on his side on the straw-strewn floor, resting his head on his arm. In the flickering torchlight, she could see the bloodied cuts and bruises on his face, arms, and legs.

"Carlo, what has that demon done to you?" Livia gasped when she saw him lying there. "Please, unlock the door," she pleaded to Francesco. "We must get him out of this hellish place."

After unlocking the door, Francesco signaled for two of his guards to follow him into the cell. Francesco roused Carlo, and Celeste cried out in relief when he raised his head and looked around. Francesco quickly explained who he was and what was happening as his guards helped Carlo to his feet. As they practically dragged him from the cell, he raised his eyes to Celeste and tried to smile through his cracked and swollen lips.

He put his full weight on is legs when he reached her, and with the guards holding his arms to support him, he gave her a deep bow. "How can I thank you, mistress?" he said in a weak, raspy voice. "I doubt I'd have survived another day in this place."

"Don't thank me, Carlo," Celeste said, struggling to control her emotions. "It's my fault you ended up here."

He grimaced in pain as he tried to shake his head. "No, madam. You bear no responsibility. That rests squarely on the shoulders of your son."

Francesco glanced around as he stepped closer to Celeste and whispered, "Can you debate this later? We should go now."

She gestured for the guards holding Carlo to get moving toward the guardhouse. When the group had moved no more than twenty feet, the slap of approaching footsteps echoed against the stone walls. A moment later, Mateo's enraged face was illuminated in the torchlight. *Livia's right,* she thought as she peered at him through the darkness. *He is a demon.*

Mateo stepped in front of the guards holding Carlo, blocking their path. "Drop that dog this instant!" he shouted.

Francesco gestured for them not to move as he stepped around them to get to Mateo. They were of a similar height and build, but for reasons Celeste couldn't fathom, Francesco appeared to tower over him.

"Out of our way, cousin," Francesco said calmly. "This is a battle you won't win."

Mateo's eyes narrowed as he leaned closer to him. "Who are you to give me orders on my own property. You're the intruder here, and I will see that you pay. Drop my prisoner."

Celeste saw Francesco's hand move to his sheathed knife, so she pushed in front of him and faced Mateo with her hands on her hips. "Son, stop making a fool of yourself this instant. Have you forgotten this is my property, too, and Carlo is my servant? Move aside and let us pass. You and I will discuss this matter later in private."

Mateo gestured with his arm at their surroundings. "Not one of these stones belongs to you, Mamma. It's all mine, and I order you to tell these men to put my prisoner back at once."

In a flash, Francesco backhanded Mateo across the face. The blow sent him sprawling across the floor. He raised his head and stared at them with dazed eyes as blood dripped from his mouth.

Francesco squatted down and lifted him by the back of his collar. Holding the point of his knife pressed to his throat, he said, "Don't you ever speak to your mother that way again, you worthless rat. She is worth at least a thousand of you. And just so you know, cousin, you have incurred the wrath of the entire Gabriele clan. Cross us again, and you'll get more than the back of my hand."

He released Mateo's collar, and his forehead dropped to the stone with a thud. Francesco stepped over him and waved for the rest to follow. Celeste felt the slightest twinge of pity as he gazed up at her when she passed, but it immediately faded.

When they were all back at the boat landing, she said, "Can you take Carlo back to your palazzo and have your servants tend to his injuries, Francesco? It's too dangerous for him here."

Francesco laid his hand on her shoulder. "Gladly, cousin, but what about your safety? It won't take Mateo long to recover. We humiliated him in front of his own people. He won't let that pass without retaliation."

She gave him a weak smile. "I appreciate your concern, but Mateo would never harm me. Despite his show of bravado down there, he still respects and fears me just enough to hold him at bay. I'll be fine."

He turned and watched his guards loading Carlo into one of the gondolas. "If you insist, but I am not convinced of that. Don't hesitate to send for help if you need me. I would relish showing that young man his place."

"Go. Get Carlo home so he can recuperate. Tell Cesare to look for me immediately after breakfast. I wish to speak with both of you on another matter. And Francesco, thank you. You saved a servant's life today without any thought to your own safety. I'll not forget this."

He gave her a formal bow, then climbed into the boat without another word.

"That was one of the most selfless and heroic things I've ever seen," Livia said behind her. "It's comforting to know there are still such goodhearted men in the world."

Celeste nodded but remained silent as she watched the boats until they were out of sight, knowing her life was about to change once more.

CHAPTER TWELVE

VENICE 1497

CELESTE FELT the mood had changed the moment she stepped into the palazzo. She wasn't sure if the situation had shifted in her favor or against. Either way, she knew it was finally time to act. She sent Livia to inform her children, Marco, and servants still loyal to her to gather in her studio. When everyone was gathered in the cramped room, she bolted the door and climbed onto a chair so they could all see her.

"I'm certain most of you have heard what transpired in the dungeons. Carlo is free and safe at the Gabriele palazzo. I'm deeply indebted to my cousin, Francesco Gabriele, for coming to Carlo's aid. I've gathered you to announce that we're moving on once again. Rome will be our new home." She waited for the murmurs of surprise to subside before continuing. "It's no longer safe to remain under this roof. I've contemplated this decision for some time but can no longer wait. We leave in two days. Those who wish to stay may do so. Anyone wishing to go, be prepared to leave at first light two days hence."

Marco and the children rushed at her as she climbed off

the chair. Cristina and Elena grinned as they threw their arms around her.

"I'm so glad we're going, Mamma," Cristina said. "I haven't been able to sleep or feel at ease for days, and there are too many memories of Papa here. We'll make a fresh start in Rome."

Elena emphatically nodded her agreement. "I've never been to Rome," she said. "What's it like?"

Celeste smiled at her. "Very different but wonderful. Cristina, take your sister and tell her about it while you help her start packing."

Marco stepped beside her as she watched them go. "I'm heartbroken that you have to go. I've just grown used to having you back in my life, but your decision is right. Mateo is out of control. I've begun looking for a new workshop since I'm sure he'll toss me out the moment you leave Venice."

She raised her eyebrows as she turned to face him. "Luciano left the workshop to you, brother. Mateo has no right to evict you. You could fight him if he tried."

He gave her a warm smile. "Don't worry yourself, sister. I intend to make Mateo buy the workshop from me, so I won't have lost anything. I don't wish to fight any more battles, and I won't stay in a place I'm not wanted."

"I see you've thought this through."

"I've thought of little else for weeks but enough about me." He folded his arms and leaned against the worktable. "You'll be so far away in Rome, and I thought it was a chore to travel to Florence."

"It is far, but I'll visit when the time is right, and you'll come to us in Rome. I need this change, Marco. My time in Venice hasn't been a happy one. Cristina was right. There are too many memories of Luciano, hindering me from moving forward, and Mateo has made our lives unbearable here, as you well know. I've felt a tremendous weight lifted off my shoulders since I decided to go."

Marco gave her a warm embrace before pulling away. "I'm glad for you then. The day will come when you may return to Florence and visit here with a cheerful heart." He kissed her cheek before heading out. "I must get back to the workshop. Promise not to leave without saying goodbye."

"I wouldn't dream of it." Celeste closed the door behind him and turned to Angela, who had been standing quietly in the corner. "What is it, sweetheart?"

She came out of the shadows and ran her fingers along the worktable as she walked to Celeste. "I know why we can't stay, Mamma, but it breaks my heart to go. Uncle Marco and I were just getting started with my lessons. I have this amazing studio all to myself. What will happen in Rome? Who will be my mentor? We have no family or friends there. It all feels overwhelming and lonely."

Celeste brushed a hair from her forehead and looked into her eyes. "I feared this would be how you'd feel, and I understand. I don't want to uproot you again, but I see no other way. I wish it could be different for you. Better for you." She looked around her beloved room. "There's a lovely studio waiting for you in the Roman palazzo. Much better than this dark, cramped space. We will find the most excellent maestros in Rome for you, so you can learn your craft properly."

Angela wrapped her arm around Celeste's waist as they started for the door. "Then, what more could I possibly wish for?"

～

CELESTE SAW nothing of Mateo that night or the following morning. After a hurried breakfast, she dressed and took Luca to escort her to the Gabriele palazzo. She asked Luca to find his cousin, Giovanni, who was his age, and stay with him until she came for him. She then followed Cesare's footman to his master's office. When she entered, her cousins stood, and each kissed her cheek in welcome.

"My brother told me of your ordeal in the dungeons," Cesare said once they were seated. "Why is it you perpetually surprise us, Celeste?"

"Why would you expect otherwise? I'm a Gabriele," she said with a smile before growing serious. "How is Carlo?"

"He'll recover in a week or so. Mateo's guards gave him quite the beating," Francesco said. "Just to think of it infuriates me."

Celeste let out her breath in relief. "I'm greatly relieved to hear he'll recover. I hold myself responsible for the entire debacle."

Cesare got up and moved to the fireplace. Holding his hands over the flames to warm them, he said, "You shouldn't. The fault belongs squarely with your ruthless, cold-hearted son." He paused for a moment and studied her intently. "Surely, your servant's welfare isn't all that brings you here this morning, cousin."

She shook her head. "It's not. I come with news and two favors to ask. I wanted both of you to know I'm leaving Venice for good tomorrow. I'm taking my family to settle in Rome."

"Rome?" Francesco said, raising his eyebrows. "That's an awfully long way to go just to put distance between you and Mateo."

"And where else will I go? Florence is closed to us. Sandro and Bianca live in the Lucca manor, and the children and I aren't quite ready to retire to the country. Rome is the only other place where Luciano had an estate. The palazzo there is nothing compared to Florence or Venice, but it's more than adequate for our needs." She stood and joined Cesare by the fire. "The house has sat empty for some time. We've spent little time there since Luciano purchased it nine years ago." Turning to face them, she said, "There are no ghosts. It will be a new beginning, and I shall be my own Mistress."

Cesare stroked his beard as he studied her. "The property belongs to Luca now, doesn't it?"

"Yes, legally it does, but he's fourteen," she said with a laugh. "I don't see him lording that over me anytime soon."

Francesco stood and took her hands. "Then, we wish you all our best. We will miss you, cousin. Our sister, Alexandria, most of all. We were just getting reacquainted."

"I'll miss you and Alexandria, as well. She's always been more of a sister to me than a cousin. I'll make a point to bid her farewell before I go."

When Francesco returned to his seat, Cesare said, "You told us you had two favors to ask."

"Yes. You've done so much already, but I was wondering if you'd allow Carlo to stay until he's recovered, then send him to me in Rome if he wishes to join us there."

Cesare gave a slight wave. "That's no trouble."

"And if he doesn't wish to leave Venice?" Francesco asked. "He's lived here his entire life."

Celeste gave them a sheepish look. "I was hoping you could find a position for him here. You won't find a better worker or more loyal servant."

"Done," Francesco said. "We can always use another guard."

"I'm deeply grateful. I'm hoping he'll come to Rome. I'll need a trusted ally there. But if not, I'll rest easier knowing he's settled here."

Cesare gave her a quick nod. "Of course. You said you had two favors to ask?"

She lowered her eyes and said, "The second is more difficult to ask, and I have no right to."

"You wish us to keep our eyes on Mateo," Francesco said.

She raised her eyes to his and nodded. "Not just Mateo, but Luciano's estate as well. I've spoken with Marco and Isabella's brothers-in-law as well. Despite his myriad of character defects, Mateo is a boy thrust into a man's role far too soon, and I'm afraid to say he was spoiled by his father. You own me nothing in this matter, but it would put my mind at ease knowing you were looking out for him."

"We'll do what we can, Celeste," Cesare said, "but our hands are tied. We'll keep you apprised of the situation, though."

Francesco leaned forward and looked her in the eye. "Mateo's youth isn't the only concern here, cousin. His behavior yesterday disturbed me greatly. He seems incapable of controlling his emotions and lust for power. Is there no one he respects who can help guide and restrain him?"

"No one. Luciano was the only person who could truly manage Mateo, but he's gone. I've considered Luciano's sisters' husbands in Florence. They're the only family he considers his equals and not competitors, but it would be impossible to persuade him to leave Venice now. He's drunk with power and wealth. This is why I fear for him and the estate. One day, he'll anger the wrong person, or they'll anger him, and he'll lose control. That could be disastrous."

"We'll do whatever we can to prevent that for your and Luciano's sake." Cesare got up and kissed her cheek. "I'm sorry to go, but I have business to attend to. Take care, cousin, and safe journey."

As Francesco walked her out, he said, "Put Mateo and Venice out of your mind. Look to your new future, Celeste. The rest will happen according to God's will."

She embraced him before climbing into the gondola. "Thank you, dear Francesco. Please send word of Carlo once you've spoken to him. May our paths cross again soon."

Francesco remained on the landing, waving until the boat

was out of sight. Though Celeste was eager to put Venice behind her, it saddened her to leave her family so soon after reuniting with them.

As she reflected on memories in the city of her birth, she felt Luca watching her. Looking up at him, she said, "What is it, son?"

He hesitated briefly before saying, "Giovanni told me what happened in the dungeons yesterday. I wish I'd heard it from you, Mamma."

Celeste studied him for a moment, feeling both proud and sad at how quickly he was becoming a man. A part of her wished he'd stay a boy forever. "I'm sorry, Luca. The news should have come from me, but I hadn't had a chance to tell you yet. I planned to tell you and your sisters tonight after dinner. How do you feel about what Giovanni told you?"

Looking her in the eye, he said, "I feel like I want to hurt Mateo just like he did Carlo."

"You're entitled to those feelings, son, and I understand. As your papa taught you, we only use violence as a last resort in defense of our family, our honor, and our reputation. What Mateo did was appalling, and he deserves punishment, but not from you or me. Besides, we both know you're not like your brother."

He lowered his eyes and fiddled with a cushion tassel. "No, I could never be so cruel, but that doesn't mean I didn't want to wreak vengeance on him. I hate that Mateo will get away with this outrage like he always does."

"I don't like it either, but life isn't always fair. A day will come when Mateo answers for his actions." Desperate to change the subject, she said, "How are you feeling about going to Rome?" She was relieved to see his face brighten.

"I'm excited to go even if I'll miss my cousins and new friends here. Giovanni said I'll be Lord of the estate in Rome. Is that true?"

She smiled as she said, "It is, Master Vicente."

He sat straighter and crossed his arms. "I like the sound of that."

"Being Master comes with a great deal of responsibility. It requires good judgement, kindness, and prudence. Are you prepared?"

His eyes widened as he sat forward. "What will I have to do?"

"Don't fret," she said, laughing. "Until you come of age, the estate manager will train you, and you'll continue your lessons with Messer Rinaldi. I'll be there to advise you, as well. When the time comes, you'll make an excellent Lord of the estate."

"Thank you. I want to be just like Papa. He taught me well and was the best man who ever lived."

Celeste felt that familiar emptiness in her heart and stinging behind her eyes at the mention of her beloved. "Yes, he was, my dear. I look forward to watching you step into his place one day."

Luca sank back into the cushions with his hands tucked behind his head. As he smiled at the sky, daydreaming of future possibilities, Celeste longed to build a shield around her son and protect him from all the evil and disappointment in the world. He'd seen enough of that already.

She thought back to herself at his age. Nothing in her life had turned out as she'd imagined it then. Some things had exceeded her wildest dreams. Some experiences had been far more painful than she thought possible. Standing on the edge of the unknown, preparing to put the shadows behind her, she prayed she would discover nothing but light, peace, and joy.

∾

As CELESTE WATCHED two servants carry the last of her trunks from her chambers, she struggled to contain her emotions, knowing she would never again set foot in that beloved room. *No time for nostalgia now*, she thought after shaking her head to clear it. The children were already waiting for her in the gondola. It was time to go. She started for the door but froze when Mateo burst into the room. It was the first she'd seen of him since the scene in the dungeons.

He stepped two feet from her with his hands on his hips. "So, the rumors are true. You're running away from home like a spoiled child who's favorite toy has been taken away."

She would have broken into laughter at the simile if the situation had been less traumatic. If anyone was the petulant child, it was Mateo. Doing her best to hide her fear, she looked him in the eye and grinned.

"Who says I am running away? I'm merely taking my family to live in a home not ruled by a childish tyrant. My children deserve peace and happiness. There is none to be found under your roof."

His look softened, and he clasped his hands behind his back. "And are you not also *my* mother?"

"What proper son treats his mother in such a way? From the moment we arrived in Venice, you've made us feel unwelcome and miserable at a time when we were mourning your father's death. Then, there was your barbaric treatment of Carlo and Marco. No son of mine or your dear, deceased papa would have committed such heartless acts. You sicken me, and I cannot bear to remain under this roof for one moment more."

As Celeste raised her chin and stormed toward the door, she was pleased to see Mateo's haughty demeanor fade under the force of her scathing rebuke. But in the end, she knew it would not matter.

Before she reached the door, he caught hold of her wrist to

stop her. "You're just going to abandon me here all alone?" he cried.

She yanked her arm free and rubbed the spot where he'd gripped it. "I'm doing exactly that. You've made it abundantly clear that you loathe my very presence under your roof and have treated me with distain, at best. You don't believe me capable of providing loving support or offering useful advice. I see no other option but to go."

She rushed out of the room before he could stop her and hurried toward the staircase. She didn't dare pause when she passed the studio on her way down but kept her gaze forward. When she realized he hadn't followed her, she stopped in the foyer and raised her eyes to the heavens. "Please don't leave that poor, desolate boy alone, my beloved, Luciano," she whispered. "Protect and watch over him. I can do nothing more."

With that, she gave the palazzo a final look, then pushed her way through the doors, never to return.

CHAPTER THIRTEEN

ROME 1497

THREE MONTHS Later

As Celeste sat on her terrace overlooking the ancient city surrounded by a crown of hills, her gaze repeatedly wandered to a familiar and cherished spot. Her thoughts drifted back to the year she spent in Rome more than a decade earlier. After a year-long art exhibition tour that ended there, she achieved such great success that she decided to stay put for a time. Her patron assisted her in establishing her own workshop. He hired a kindly minor painter and his wife to manage it so she could avoid the scandal of a woman owning a shop. But it had been hers and most of the artistic community understood and approved. After years of sacrifice and rejection, Celeste finally achieved the recognition and respect she so richly deserved.

She had neglected her children during that period in search of artistic fame, and her relationship with Luciano became strained to the breaking point. He'd written incessantly, pleading for her to come home. She loved him dearly but wasn't prepared to abandon her dreams of success to return to being nothing more than a wife and mother. But another entanglement also kept her in Rome.

She had developed a close friendship with a wealthy, handsome widower named Piero Leoni. Though their platonic relationship never crossed the line of friendship, that didn't prevent the gossips from wagging their tongues. Rumors of an affair soon swirled around Rome and word of it eventually reached Luciano in Florence. The truth was, Celeste had remained faithful to her husband in body, but the same couldn't be said of her heart.

When Portia heard of these rumors, she rushed to Rome to be with Celeste. Portia convinced her she was risking her family and all she held dear was not worth the price for fame and a love affair. Celeste took her wise aunt's advice to heart and returned to Luciano and her children in Florence. Her aunt's words touched Celeste profoundly and made her realize there was much more to life than her flourishing art career in Rome. Her work was important, but her family was everything. It had been wrong to become emotionally intimate with Piero, and she realized a future with Luciano and their children was the only path to true happiness and fulfillment.

Looking back, she regretted her earlier behavior and how she handled the situation. She had feared returning to Florence would mean the end of her career. In truth, her career only flourished and grew after she went home. She and Luciano, working side-by-side, had risen to become two of the most recognized and revered painters in Europe. It had been a golden time, traveling the continent together, doing what they both loved.

Since then, they'd only traveled to Rome on rare occasions. The last time had been more than two years earlier. Luciano had even once suggested they sell the Roman estate. Celeste persuaded him to hold on to it, reminding him one or more of the children might require it one day. She couldn't have envisioned at the time how accurate that prediction would come to be.

"Mamma!" Cristina said, making Celeste jump and prick her finger with her embroidery needle. "Sorry, I didn't mean to startle you. I called you three times, but you were far away. What were you thinking of?"

Celeste laid her embroidery on the table and dabbed her bleeding finger on a scrap of cloth. "Nothing important, dear. Just memories. I seem to be doing that more lately. Must be getting old."

Cristina smiled and shook her head. "You're only forty-one, but you'll never be old to me. Were you thinking of Papa?"

"I'm always thinking of Papa, but I also remembered living here years ago. I missed you so terribly then, but I have fond memories, too. I haven't asked how you're enjoying living in our new home. Are you happy here?"

Cristina shifted her gaze toward the city as she considered her answer. "It's too soon to tell. I still think of myself as a Florentine, and I even long for Venice at times. Romans are…different."

"I understand exactly what you mean," Celeste said with a laugh. "I was miserable when I arrived her on my initial visit, feeling as if I were constantly being judged and found wanting. In time, I understood the Romans and came to admire them. They're warmhearted people with a zest for life. Once they allow you into their circle, you become family."

Cristina considered her words for a moment. "That sounds wonderful. I've missed being surrounded by friends and family. It's lonely sometimes with only the five of us for company, and I feel so far away from everything familiar. Angela has her painting. Luca has his training, and Elena has Violetta. What do I have?"

Celeste reached over and squeezed her hand. "You have me. I know that isn't much of a substitute for your cousins and friends."

"I'm grateful for the times we spend together, Mamma, but

I sometimes miss young girls my age. Would it be possible to invite some of your Roman friends to visit?"

As lonely as Cristina was, Celeste was content. Life was uncomplicated and tranquil for the first time in longer than she could remember. The past three months had been just what Celeste had needed to have time to grieve in peace and recover from the stressful weeks with Mateo. Since she and Luciano had spent so little time in Rome, she wasn't haunted by the ghosts of memories that had plagued her in Venice. Her life in Rome was so different from anything she'd experienced. It truly felt like a new, but also strangely familiar, fresh start. It had been quiet so far and that was exactly what she needed. It helped that she had kept a low profile since arriving.

She felt a pang of guilt for not paying attention to how lonely Cristina felt. She should have expected it. The twins were no longer children and should have been surrounded by young women their age. If Luciano were alive, he'd be arranging matches for his daughters. Sixteen was young, but the twins were definitely of marriageable age. Celeste had no male family in Rome to help her search for appropriate suitors for the girls. She would have to write to her brothers-in-law in Florence and ask their advice on the matter. In the meantime, she promised to make more of an effort to become involved in Roman social life for the sake of her children.

"I'll write to a few of my friends I've kept in touch with who have daughters your age," she told Cristina.

Her face brightened at the prospect. "That sounds lovely, Mamma. Will you write to them today? Maybe they'll invite us to galas and dinners. I'm old enough to attend with you now."

Celeste gave her a sad smile, reluctant to dampen her enthusiasm. "Luncheons are one thing, sweetheart. Galas are another. With no male relatives in the city to act as escorts, it will be difficult for us to enter society in a properly accepted manner, and Luca is too young to fill that role."

Cristina leaned forward with excitement still glowing in her eyes. "But you're the famous Maestra Gabriele. Everyone knows who you are. You've even had an audience with the Holy Father."

"Being well known only opens a limited number of doors, and it doesn't change the fact that I'm just an unchaperoned widow."

Cristina slumped in her chair and crossed her arms. "It isn't fair. Why do men get to do whatever they want?"

"Because they make the rules. Don't fret, my darling. I'll figure out another way to unlock those doors."

When Celeste picked up her embroidery, Cristina said, "Do you ever miss painting? Angela speaks of it as if it's as important as food."

Celeste looked up from her stitching and raised an eyebrow. "You're in a talkative mood this evening. I usually struggle to get a full sentence out of you."

Cristina grinned at her. "It must be the warm summer air. You didn't answer me."

Celeste nodded. "I miss painting occasionally, but surprisingly, not often enough to make me wish to pick it up again. I once felt as Angela does, but those days are long past. For now, I'm content to pass my days with you. For a time, I placed too much importance on becoming a respected master painter. It feels right for me to put away my brushes and canvases." Eager to avoid more questions, Celeste stood and straightened her skirts as the sun slipped below the horizon. "Come, it's time to dress for dinner."

Cristina continued chatting as they made their way to the family quarters, but Celeste hardly heard her. While Livia helped her dress for dinner, Celeste allowed her thoughts to wander into territory she'd been avoiding since her conversation with Cristina. There was one person she could think of who could escort them into society, but the idea of contacting her made Celeste uneasy.

Piero Leoni had a married sister named Rosa, who had become her dearest friend in Rome. After returning to Florence, Celeste broke off contact with her, fearing that even writing to Piero's sister would divide her feelings for Luciano. Besides, she had promised Luciano she would cease all communications with her friends in Rome. Two years later, on a trip there, Celeste learned in passing that Piero had remarried, and his wife had borne him a son. It would have been safe to renew her friendship with Rosa at that point, but she decided it best to let the matter lie.

Celeste hated admitting that Piero had been on her mind from the moment her carriage rolled into Rome. She was happy that he had found happiness with another woman, but she recognized that deep inside she still harbored affection for the man. If she wanted to avoid dredging up old feelings, she would have to seek out someone else to provide companionship for Cristina.

CELESTE SMILED in excited anticipation as the carriage neared the Vatican walls. Her old friend, Cardinal Orsini, had arranged a private tour of the Sistine Chapel for her and the children. Her most cherished memories of her year in Rome were the time she spent in the Chapel. Not only was it one of the holiest places in all Christendom, but the chapel walls contained the most exquisite works of art ever created.

Her earlier conversation with Cristina reminded her that the children had seen very little of Rome. The few times they'd traveled there with Luciano and her, they'd been too young to tour the city. Since that was no longer the case, it was time they became familiar with their majestic new home.

"I can hardly contain myself," Angela said as they approached the Vatican gate. "Thank you for arranging this, Mamma."

"Yes, thank you, Mamma," Cristina and Luca said in unison.

"Rome is full of treasure, but none compares to what we're about to see. The Chapel is one of my most sacred and cherished places in the world."

The carriage pulled to a stop where Cardinal Orsini was waiting to meet them. They each took their turn bowing or curtsying before kissing his ring. When the formalities were out of the way, he offered Celeste his arm as he led them toward the Chapel.

"I can't thank you enough for arranging this, Your Eminence," Celeste said as they walked. "The children have been beside themselves since I told them."

"I was delighted to receive your letter requesting the tour. I wasn't even aware you were back in Rome."

Celeste nodded. "We've kept to ourselves since we arrived. It's been a difficult year for all of us, and we needed time to settle in and heal."

He stopped and turned to face her. "You have my deepest sympathies, Signora. I was devastated to hear of the tragic death of your honored husband. I only met him a few times, but Lorenzo de' Medici spoke highly of him."

Celeste bowed her head. "Thank you, Your Eminence."

The Cardinal nodded, then resumed walking. "Are you aware the Holy Father excommunicated that blasphemer, Savonarola? He was more deserving of execution."

"Yes, Luciano's sister wrote to me with the news, and I was greatly relieved to hear it. I will forever hold him responsible for my dear husband's death."

"As do many others. He continues to preach his blasphemous sermons without authority and continues to

defame the Holy Father. I hear his flock is rapidly dwindling."
When Celeste didn't respond, he said, "I'm sure you have no
wish to speak of such unpleasant things. Please, forgive my
thoughtlessness, Signora."

Celeste smiled up at him. "Put your mind at ease,
Eminence. I am not offended but changing to a cheerier
subject would be most welcome."

The Cardinal chuckled and patted her hand. "Of course."

He updated her on the doings of their mutual
acquaintances and developments in the Church, but she hardly
heard him. Speaking of Savonarola had rekindled her lust for
revenge against her husband's murderers with an
overwhelming ferocity. She was relieved when her intense
emotions instantly dissipated as the Cardinal opened the door
to the Sistine Chapel and beckoned them to enter. It took her
eyes a moment to adjust after coming in from the sunlight. The
moment they did, her heart soared at seeing the sublime
beauty surrounding her. It was impossible to harbor evil
thoughts and feelings in such a place.

She and Cardinal Orsini gave the children an hour-long
tour of the Chapel. When they announced it was time to go as
the next Mass would soon begin, the children begged to be
able to stay and attend.

"I'm afraid you must receive a special invitation to attend
the Papal Mass," the Cardinal told them. "I'll do my best to
arrange it for another time, but in the meantime, there's still
much to see."

He escorted them from the Chapel, then pointed out
various sights as they wandered the piazza and Basilica San
Pedro. In a quiet moment when the others were occupied,
Celeste stepped away for a moment of prayer and reflection.
As she moved toward one of the smaller chapels, she heard
men conversing, clearly not in worship. She peeked into the
chapel and was stunned to find the young Florentine sculptor,

Michelangelo Buonarroti, precariously perched on an enormous block of grayish-white marble. He was surrounded by about fifteen apprentices, who looked on with intense interest as Michelangelo ran his hands gracefully along the face of the stone and described his vision for the marble's future.

As she attempted to tiptoe away without disturbing them, Michelangelo glanced over his shoulder and caught her eye. He immediately recognized her and appeared as surprised to see her as she'd been to find him there. She had met him on a few occasions in Florence and had heard a rumor he'd left the city to avoid Savonarola.

He jumped down and strode toward her with a broad smile. He was covered in dust and paint and looked like he hadn't bathed for several days, which, according to gossip, was his normal state of grooming. The young sculptor bowed energetically and kissed the back of her outstretched hand. "Maestra Gabriele, this is an unexpected honor. What brings you to Rome?"

"I'm residing here now. Florence's religious and political climate is no longer to my liking."

He grew serious as he said, "Of course. My reasons for leaving that city as well. I was distraught when I heard the tragic news of your excellent husband. You have my deepest sympathies. Maestro Vicente was always kind and encouraging to me."

"Thank you. I'm pleased to hear it. My late husband once told me your genius is unrivaled."

"I'm flattered. Maestro Vicente was a genius in his own right."

She nodded toward the marble. "What is that glorious piece of stone for?"

He glanced at it over his shoulder. "Cardinal Jean de Bilhères-Lagraulas, French ambassador to the Vatican, has commissioned me to sculpt a *pietà* for his funeral monument. The stone I'll sculpt has just arrived from Carrara, as you see."

"Truly?" When Michelangelo nodded, she said, "That is an extraordinary accomplishment for one so young. Congratulations. I look forward to seeing the finished work."

"I'll see to it you're invited to the unveiling, Signora, but that won't be for at least two years."

She gave him a warm smile. "Naturally. I may stop in occasionally to view your progress"

"I'd be delighted and honored to have your opinion. And what of your work, madam? I haven't heard of any new paintings from you in some time." When she hesitated, he said, "Forgive me. That was thoughtless of me. You've been engaged with other matters."

Shaking her head, she said, "Don't apologize, Michelangelo. My husband's passing profoundly altered the course of my life, so I've retired my brushes. My primary focus now is to support my children. They need a mother, not a painter."

"Then the world has lost two of her greatest artists. I understand, but I'm deeply saddened to hear it." His eyes brightened as he said, "I don't suppose I could persuade you to change your mind?"

She gave a quiet laugh. "I'm afraid not. That part of my life is behind me. I had started a portrait of my dear Luciano shortly before his death. I worked on it day and night, neglecting my grieving children and my own health. Then, just as suddenly, my creative fire inexplicably died. I locked the painting away and haven't touched my brushes since."

He eyed her for a moment before saying, "I most fervently pray your fire will rekindle in time."

"Thank you, maestro. I appreciate your prayers." She saw him watching something over her shoulder and turned to find Cristina waving to her. "I must return to my family, but it was a pleasure to see you and hear of your success." She lifted her hand toward the marble block. "I'll be awaiting that invitation to the unveiling."

He gave another bow before hurrying back to his curious apprentices. As the carriage rolled toward home, some part of her wondered if her artistic passion was gone for good or only dormant. Seeing the enthusiasm in the young sculptor's eyes made her miss that yearning drive to create.

Three Months Later

Celeste pressed her forehead to the damp window and sighed as she stared over the gloomy city. It was the tenth day of drenching rains, and Celeste was starting to despair of ever seeing blue skies and sunlight again. She left the window and sank into a chair beside the fireplace. It wasn't the rain alone that had brought on her dreary mood. Though she'd done her best to arrange outings and visits for the children, the truth was, she longed for something more.

The only times she'd known idleness in the past was when she was recovering from illness or injury. Even then, she'd always had something to keep her mind occupied. Before she met Luciano and began painting, she'd been responsible for caring for her younger siblings, which consumed all her time and energy. When she became a nanny, then a maid, she could hardly manage to stay on her feet by the end of her day.

Eventually, Luciano rescued her from a life of servitude. He sent her to Lucca with Portia to learn the art of being a Mistress and Duchessa in preparation for her marriage. In time, she added mother and artist to her responsibilities. Motherhood was all she had left on her list. Her children were a constant source of joy in her life, but as they grew older, they needed her less and showed diminishing interest in their mother. Celeste felt aimless and was growing restless and lonely.

Livia bustled in and said, "Time to dress for the day. The children are already at the table waiting for you."

"Send Marissa to tell them to eat without me," Celeste said without taking her eyes from the fire. "I'll take my tray in my chambers,"

Livia clapped once to get her attention, then reached over to get Celeste out of the chair. "Not if I have a say. Your mood's been darker than the clouds these past two days. You're going to get up and join your lovely children for breakfast. It will cheer you. It always does."

Celeste knew better than to argue with Livia when she was determined, so she climbed to her feet and removed her robe. "If you insist, *madam*," she said.

"None of your sarcasm, mistress," Livia said, emphasizing the word *mistress* as she lifted Celeste's gown over her head.

"Why? It makes me feel better," Celeste mumbled. Instead of answering, Livia pulled Celeste's laces tighter than usual. "Are you trying to suffocate me? I won't be able to eat with my dress so tight."

"Forgive me," Livia said as she loosened the laces slightly. When she'd finished, Celeste sank onto the bed instead of heading for the door. "What is the matter with you this morning? It must be more than the weather making you behave this way."

Celeste's shoulders slumped as she stared at the floor. "What is my purpose, Livia? The children no longer need me. My career is finished. I've been exiled to a strange city with no friends, family, or even a man to protect or love me. I utterly feel like an ornate, but pointless piece of furniture. What kind of life is that?"

Livia sat beside her and reached for her hand. "Your life has been unique in most respects, and you're feeling the loss of your husband. And it's ridiculous to say the children don't need you. You're an important part of their lives, and no matter how old they get, they will always need you."

"I wish I could believe that. Other than my children, I'm finding it difficult to care about anything in my life. I'd donate all I own to the poor and return to my hovel in Venice in exchange for having Luciano back."

"So would every person who's lost a loved one. Your husband is gone. It's time to do what you always have, search for your purpose. You have so much to offer the world. Don't underestimate that. Start by acknowledging your blessings. You have much to be thankful for, so stop pitying yourself, and get off this bed."

Celeste gave her a tight hug, then got to her feet. "What would I do without you, Livia? Be patient with me. It may take time to find my way out of this wilderness."

Livia linked her arm with Celeste's as they walked to the door. "Nonsense. You'll be back to your old self in no time."

Celeste smiled and gave her a peck on the cheek before heading into the hallway. She'd only left her chambers to please her friend, but she had little faith in her ability to find the thing that was eluding her. She shook off her gloomy thoughts as she hurried down the stairs. When she reached the sala, Bardo came toward her carrying a letter.

"This message just arrived for you, mistress," he said as he handed it to her.

She nodded her thanks, then turned it over to read the address. She smiled when she recognized Maestro Leonardo's handwriting. She unfolded it and read as she continued to the dining room.

"What is that, Mamma?" Elena asked before taking an enormous bite of cheese.

Celeste shook her head. "Angela is a bad influence on you. It's a letter from Maestro da Vinci, inviting me to Milan."

Angela jumped to her feet and came to read over Celeste's shoulder. "Are we going?" she asked, hardly able to breathe.

Celeste turned and looked up at her. "We? The invitation is only for me, and no, I'm not going."

"Why not?" Angela asked, looking shocked that Celeste would say such a thing. "He's the most famous artist in all of Europe, and not just anyone gets invitations from Maestro da Vinci."

"Because I'm an old widow who no longer paints. A visit to Milan would be pointless. I don't have anyone to travel with me as a chaperone, and Milan is in a state of political uproar, as usual. It's a great distance to travel, and I don't like the idea of leaving all of you alone and unprotected here."

Angela slumped onto her chair in a huff. "Those are just excuses."

"She's right, Mamma," Luca said. "You're always telling us not to give you excuses."

"This is different, son. I see absolutely no reason to make a journey that takes three-weeks one-way, just to visit an old friend."

"Does he give a reason why he's suddenly invited you to visit him?" Cristina asked.

Celeste finished reading the letter. "He doesn't, but it is a bit odd. He sent a brief condolence letter when he heard the news of your dear father, but I haven't heard from him since." She stopped and did a quick calculation. "He may have written to me in Florence, and the letter didn't reach me before we left Venice. I have no idea how he found me in Rome."

Cristina daintily wiped her mouth before saying, "He wouldn't have bothered to invite you without good reason. You've seemed so forlorn lately, Mamma. A nice, long journey to visit a friend might be just what you need. He wouldn't have asked you to come if it would put you in danger."

Celeste carefully folded the letter and laid it on the table.

"True, sweetheart, but you forget my two other major objections. I refuse to leave the four of you here alone, and I have no chaperon to travel with me."

Angela gave her a mischievous smile. "If you took all of us along and brought Carlo with a few of the house guards, no one would question the propriety of you traveling without a male relative. Plus, Carlo and the guards would protect."

Luca sat forward and leaned his elbows on the table. "Angela's right, and we could all use an adventure. I've always wanted to see Milan."

His enthusiasm was infectious, and Celeste started to waver. She loved Milan and had longed to see it.

"What of your objections now, Mamma?" Angela said smugly.

"There's one more. None of you are invited. Where would we stay?"

"Write to Maestro da Vinci and ask him to arrange lodging for us," Cristina said.

"Yes, Messer Rinaldi says the Maestro lives with Duca Sforza," Luca said. "He must know someone willing to house us for a few weeks."

Celeste looked at her children, staring up at her expectantly, and couldn't help but laugh. "Give me time to weigh this before I reply to Maestro da Vinci. We're not talking about a little visit to Lucca. A journey such as this requires a great deal of planning. If I go, that is."

"You will," Angela said, grinning as she took a bite of bread.

Celeste winked at her. "Know me so well, do you?"

When they finished eating, Celeste sent the children off to their various activities while she took Leonardo's letter to her chambers. She was relieved to find her room empty. Livia would have been more than willing to give her opinion as soon as she learned of da Vinci's invitation. Celeste wasn't in the mood to hear it.

The very idea of traveling to Milan filled her with excitement and dread. As she paced the room, she contemplated the situation from all angles. The children had given reasoned arguments against her objections, and the thought of making the journey with her family was enticing. She'd never once entertained such a notion since Luciano's death. She was an experienced traveler and didn't doubt she would manage the trip well.

The biggest mystery was why Leonardo wished to see her. Besides his letter after Luciano's passing, she'd had little contact with him since she'd spent time in his workshop in Milan a decade earlier. She'd never forget his impassioned letter in her favor when the *Arte dei Medici e Speziali* Guild in Florence voted on admitting her as a guild member. His support of her carried the day with the guild members. He'd always been so kind and encouraging to her, though he existed in an artistic and intellectual class of his own. No matter the reason he wished to see her, she probably owed it to him to go.

She finally had to admit that planning the trip would give her the purpose Livia spoke of, at least in the short term, and it would cheer her considerably. Getting out of Rome would also go a long way to lift her spirits. Despite the recent deluge, she had no objection to living in the city, but a change of scenery might just be the boost she needed.

"This is one of the more outlandish things you've done," Celeste told herself as she headed to her desk to reply to Leonardo.

Livia just happened to choose that moment to enter. She looked around in confusion before saying, "Who were you speaking to?"

Celeste felt her cheeks redden as she said, "Me, if you must know."

Livia raised an eyebrow at her. "Should I be concerned?" When Celeste shook her head, she said, "What outlandish thing are you planning?"

Celeste read the letter to her, then said, "How would you like another trip to Milan?"

"You're truly going? Who will chaperon?" After Celeste recounted her conversation with the children, she clasped her hands and said, "I'm so delighted. It's not outlandish at all but just the curative you need."

"That is yet to be seen," Celeste mumbled, then began her reply to Leonardo.

CHAPTER FOURTEEN

MILAN 1497

Eight Weeks Later

Celeste stood in the doorway of Maestro da Vinci's workshop, quietly watching the genius at work. His workshop was as crowded and disorganized as she remembered it. The Maestro was furiously sketching what looked like a mechanical bird. She'd never seen anything like it and could think of no other way to describe it. He seemed to have forgotten they had an appointment scheduled, which wasn't unusual for him. They shared the habit of becoming so absorbed in their work that the rest of the world ceased to exist.

After several minutes, one of his apprentices noticed her and tapped Leonardo on the shoulder. He jumped and swung his arms, which sent brushes, chisels, charcoal, and scraps of wood flying in all directions.

"What is it, Renzo?" the Maestro bellowed. "One day, you'll frighten me to death."

Renzo didn't seem intimidated by his maestro's outburst, which made Celeste wonder if it was a frequent occurrence. The boy rolled his eyes in Celeste's direction, and Leonardo spun around to face her. It took a moment for him to recognize her, but when he did, he crossed the workshop to reach her in just a few strides. Celeste had forgotten how Leonardo did everything with hurried enthusiasm.

"Celeste," he said, smiling as he took her hands and kissed her cheeks. "Forgive me for ignoring you. It's delightful to see you. Come, I must show you my latest project."

He released one of her hands and pulled her by the other toward his worktable. He moved so quickly that she struggled to keep up with him. She was flattered to see his apprentices bowing reverently as she passed. When they reached the worktable, he stood to the side and motioned proudly for her to examine his sketch.

She studied it for several moments before saying, "It's a masterful sketch, Leonardo, but what is it?"

He beamed at her like a child with a magical new toy. "It's my design for a flying machine."

She couldn't have been more perplexed by the sketch. "You mean for a kite?"

He shook his head impatiently as if he were speaking to a child. "No, no. I mean a machine for men to use to fly like birds. Let me explain."

Using that sketch and several others spread on the worktable, he pointed out the aspects of his design and how it would work. He used mathematical equations and scientific words she'd never heard. She nodded and smiled in the right places, making him believe she knew what he was talking about. Celeste had never received a formal education and it would have been generous to say she understood a quarter of what he'd said. Leonardo's mind was always bursting with innovative ideas no one had ever thought of before, and the flying machine certainly fell into that category.

When he finished, she stared at him, speechless for a moment, feeling like a mere monkey in his presence. She had seen some of his other inventions, which were far more practical. This was something else altogether. "You intend to build this, Maestro?"

He nodded enthusiastically. "I've already built a few models, but they weren't quite right. I have further calculations to make. Of course, most who see this say I've gone mad, but the science is correct. If not, how would birds, bats, or kites be able to fly?"

She gave him a warm smile and kissed his cheek. "You never cease to amaze me. I'm glad to see you haven't changed."

He linked his arm in hers and led her toward the door. "It's a lovely day. Let's walk the castle grounds and get reacquainted. I didn't invite you all this way to babble about my silly musings."

"Nothing you do is silly, friend."

"There are many who would disagree with that statement. How are you finding your lodgings?"

"They're lovely. I appreciate you going out of your way to arrange them for us given how busy you are."

He gave a backhanded wave. "It was nothing at all. I simply wrote to our mutual friend Piero to ask if his guest quarters were available. He was delighted to hear you were coming to Milan and to make his manor available for you and your children."

She stopped and stared up at him. "You're speaking of Signore Piero Leoni?"

Leonardo gave a quick nod. "Of course, Celeste. What other Piero do we share in common?"

"I assumed he was in Rome all this time. When did he come to Milan?"

"Then you haven't heard?"

She shook her head. "Of what, Leonardo?"

"He brought his children here when he lost his dear Simona nearly a year ago. Wet lungs. It was a slow, painful death. Poor man to have lost two wives. At least he has his son and daughter to cheer him."

She bowed her head and fought back her tears, remembering how devastated Piero had been after losing his first wife and child not long before she met him. "I see. Yes, poor Piero," she said softly. "I understand that kind of heartbreaking loss."

He patted her hand. "You certainly do. He asked me to send his deepest condolences."

"How kind of him."

Leonardo turned and nudged her to start walking again. "Enough of gloom and despair. Our Piero has rallied like a champion and wishes to meet with you."

Celeste's heartbeat quickened, and she felt the color rise in her cheeks. Seeing Piero was the last thing she expected, and she had intensely mixed feelings. It would be awkward to refuse to see him, especially since he had offered them his guest manor. She would agree to one brief meeting and let that suffice.

"Since my schedule is entirely open, tell Piero I'll see him at his convenience."

"Done," Leonardo said cheerfully.

When they were out of earshot of the apprentices, she said, "Speaking of my schedule, I've waited more than a week to ask why you asked me to Milan. You must have had a pressing reason to invite me to travel so far to see you."

"I apologize for that. I would have traveled to you, but my duties wouldn't allow it at present." He glanced at her out of the corner of his eye. "Perhaps time away from Rome will be good for you."

"Perhaps," she said, trying to hide her smile.

"As for why I wrote to you. Roughly three months ago, I received a most curious letter from an art collector friend in Rome. He's acquainted with that young upstart, Michelangelo.

In conversation one day, Michelangelo mentioned being dismayed to have learned that the renowned Maestra Gabriele had locked away her brushes forever. My friend recalled that you and I are closely acquainted, so he conveyed this troubling news to me." He stopped and turned to face her with his arms crossed. "Is this unthinkable rumor true?"

She straightened her shoulders and looked him in the eye. "You invited me to travel hundreds of miles to ask if I retired from painting? I could have answered that question in a letter."

"I needed to hear from your lips and talk you out of it in person. Well, Celeste, is it true? Have you given up the brush?"

She lowered her shoulders and sighed. "Yes, Leonardo. I'm no longer painting, but don't try to talk me out of it. I am content with my choice."

He led her to a stone bench beneath an enormous oak tree and gestured for her to sit before joining her. "Do you remember our conversation a decade ago when we met?"

She looked out over the garden and softly said, "I do."

"You were considering giving up your career just as it was beginning for the sake of Luciano and your children. The Guild refused to reinstate your husband to membership as long as you continued to paint and sell your artworks. What did I tell you then?"

Tears welled in her eyes, and her voice caught as she said, "You told me I had a rare genius and not to give up. You said depriving the world of what I have to share was selfish. I didn't give up, Maestro, and I've shared my gift. My time is past, and we must make way for the young Michelangelos of the world."

He waved off her comment. "Nonsense. You're only forty. I intend to keep working until I can no longer stand, and maybe not even then. What brought this on? Losing Luciano?"

She took a breath and told him of painting Luciano's portrait in Venice, then losing her desire to paint. "That part of me died with my beloved."

He got off the bench and knelt at her feet. "Listen to me. I've been painting since I was a child, and I've known hundreds of artists. It's not uncommon for this to happen after a tragedy, but it's seldom permanent. Do me this favor. Vow to me that you'll finish Luciano's portrait once you return home. Your passion for painting will return like a torrent and you won't be able to stop until your eyes have failed and you're too old to see the canvas. Celeste, this is the most important work of your life. Don't leave it unfinished." She eyed him for a moment before nodding. "I want to hear you say the words."

She couldn't help but smile. "Leonardo, I vow to finish Luciano's portrait."

He jumped to his feet and gave a clap. "Excellent. I shall hold you to your promise. Write to me of your progress and notify me when the work is completed."

As he helped her to her feet, she said, "You have my word, Maestro."

"You have made the right decision. Now, I must get back to the workshop. I'll speak with Piero about joining us for lunch. We'll dine with you at the manor to avoid scandal if that's agreeable."

"It sounds lovely." She kissed his cheek before motioning for Carlo to escort her back to the carriage. "I look forward to seeing you soon."

CELESTE STRUGGLED to hide her trembling hands from the children as they waited for Bardo to escort their guests into the parlor. Her anxiety escalated when she heard their voices before Bardo walked in and stepped to the side to let them enter. Piero came through the doorway looking as resplendent and handsome as Celeste remembered him. He wore his typical midnight blue tunic trimmed in silver, in striking

contrast to his full dark curls. Only a few strands of gray
streaked his hair. Piero met her eyes and gave her a smile that
brought back a flood of memories. Celeste felt like a young
maiden and blushed a deep red and hoped Piero would not
notice. Piero was followed by a boy and girl who looked a few
years younger than Elena that stood shyly peeking around their
father.

Piero bowed and said, "Signora Gabriele, how wonderful
to see you again after so long. Please, let me introduce my son,
Master Giuseppe, and my daughter, Signorina Serena."

Celeste curtsied, then extended her hand to him. Just the
feel of Piero's warm breath on her skin as he kissed it sent a
shiver up her arm. Doing her best to ignore her reaction, she
coaxed his children forward and said, "It's an honor to meet
both of you. I would say welcome to our home, but this manor
belongs to your papa. We're merely boarders here, but it is a
great pleasure to meet you." She looked over her shoulder and
waved for Elena to come closer. "Please, take Giuseppe and
Serena to Violetta in the sitting room. Tell her I said you may
take your lunch there."

Celeste was glad when Elena's face brightened, pleased to
have visitors her own age to share her meal with. She took
Piero's children by their hands and chatted cheerfully as she led
them from the sala.

With the children taken care of, she faced Piero and said,
"Where is Maestro Leonardo? I expected you to arrive in the
same carriage."

"He sends his apologies, but an urgent matter arose that he
couldn't ignore. I considered writing to postpone, but the
children were so eager for our outing."

Celeste caught his emphasis on the word children and had
no doubt he was making a veiled reference to himself.

Angela stepped beside Celeste and said, "It's only you,
Signore? Maestro da Vinci isn't coming? How disappointing.

I've been so looking forward to meeting him." When Celeste glared at her, Angela dropped into a curtsy and bowed her head. "Forgive my rudeness, sir. Of course, we're delighted to have you and your children joining us for a luncheon."

Piero gave a quiet laugh. "Please, rise, Signorina. There's no need for apologies." He gave a warm smile when Angela rose and glanced at him. "I'm aware that I'm no substitute for Leonardo da Vinci. He promised to reschedule as soon as his time allows."

Celeste shook her head slightly at Angela before saying, "That's gracious of the Maestro. Come, let us sit and get reacquainted until lunch is ready."

"Before we do," Piero said. "Would it be rude of me to ask which of your lovely daughters is which. Their appearance truly is identical, and so like their enchanting mother."

Celeste felt the color rise in her cheeks as Cristina curtsied and said, "I am Cristina, Signore Leoni." She motioned for Angela to move closer, then linked arms with her. "And this is Angela, the eldest by mere minutes. To help you remember, I wear green ribbon, and Angela wears rose. These are colors of the Vicente family crest."

Celeste was stunned to see Cristina explaining how to tell the twins apart. She typically stayed in the background, quietly observing while Angela commanded the attention. She couldn't help but wonder if her daughter was as captivated by Piero as she was.

Piero nodded in thanks. "Immensely helpful, Signorina Cristina." She smiled shyly, though she was clearly pleased with herself. Turning and extending his hand to Luca, he said, "And you must be the future Duca Vicente."

Luca beamed at him and said, "That will be my *brother*, Mateo, but I come of age in three years. Until then, you may call me Luca."

Piero raised an eyebrow at Celeste, but said, "Good man. Thank you, Luca."

Celeste stood back, marveling at how Piero broke down barriers with her children in moments to become their friend. She'd forgotten what a commanding man he was and yet so courteous and attentive to others, even children. Adult men generally ignored children and left them to the servants. In contrast, Piero seemed genuinely interested in getting to know them. His children were fortunate to have such a father.

"I want to offer all of you my deepest condolences on the loss of your honored husband and father," Piero said as they settled into their chairs. "I only met him on two occasions but could easily see what a goodhearted and honorable man he was. I'm sure you miss him greatly."

"We do. I imagine you understand exactly how much. We offer our sympathies on the loss of your wife as well. I'm sorry we never had the chance to meet her."

Looking her in the eye, he said, "You and my Simona would have gotten on well, I believe. It's been a difficult year for us, but the children have adjusted. That's one of the reasons I brought them here. They've always enjoyed their time in Milan, and there are fewer memories of their mother to grieve us here."

"That's one of the reasons we left Venice," Cristina said.

Angela leaned back in her chair and lowered her eyes. "That, and our wicked brother, Mateo."

Piero glanced at Celeste in question. She shook her head and was relieved when he let the comment pass.

Taking her hint, Piero abruptly changed the subject. "How are you all enjoying your visit so far?" he asked cheerfully. "Is the manor comfortable enough for you?"

Angela's face brightened, and she sat up straighter. "We haven't had time to do much touring, but Mamma has promised to ask Maestro da Vinci if I may visit his workshop.

Did she tell you I am a painter too? We were hoping to ask today, but I suppose that will have to wait. We're also planning to visit some of the sights Mamma remembers from past trips here. I'm looking forward to touring the cathedral."

"I don't doubt you are a highly skilled painter like your mother. I was her guide for her first visit to the cathedral. We enjoyed a lovely afternoon with her patron, aunt, and uncle. Do you recall that day, Signora?"

How could I forget? she thought, but said, "It was a memorable day. I thought my feet would never recover after all the walking we did, though. It makes me think of my dear Aunt Portia. She passed just two weeks before Luciano. I miss her every day."

Piero gave a sad smile. "She was a unique and remarkable woman. I'm grateful to have known her."

"It's strange to think you know so much of our family, but we've never met you," Luca said. "Why is that?"

"Distance, I suppose," Piero said without hesitation. "I break up my time between Rome and Milan, so I have spent very little time in Florence or Venice. The opposite is true of your family. When we return to Rome, we'll be able to see much of each other." He grew quiet for a moment, then gave Celeste a look she couldn't decipher. "Speaking of your family, there's another member I'm well acquainted with. Your uncle, Jacopo."

Angela's eyes widened as she said, "You know Uncle Jacopo?"

"I do," Piero said simply.

Celeste sat forward and stared at him in shock and felt the children watching her. "I wasn't aware you still had contact with my brother."

Piero stroked his chin for a moment before saying, "I never lost contact with him. He's been working for me for the past ten years."

The housekeeper came in to announce lunch before Celeste could get any more information out of him about his shocking announcement. As they rose to head for the dining room, he offered her his arm and allowed the children to go in front of them.

As they followed at a slower pace, Celeste whispered, "Why have you never told me?"

Keeping his voice lowered, he said, "Jacopo swore me to silence. I couldn't betray his confidence, but this breach between you has lasted long enough. And Celeste, you made it clear you were not interested in maintaining a correspondence with me. Do you not remember? I'll explain in more detail later when we have a moment alone."

Celeste nodded as she attempted to make sense of his startling revelation. She couldn't count the times she lay awake, wondering where Jacopo was or if he was even alive. Between seeing Piero again and wanting to know more about her brother, she struggled to focus on the conversation during their meal. The instant they finished eating, Celeste asked the twins to entertain the other children and sent Luca back to Messer Rinaldi.

Once they were alone, she rose and said, "Let's take wine on the terrace." It was a chilly autumn day, so she sent Livia for her heavy cloak while she and Piero made their way outside. She immediately began interrogating Piero as they stepped onto the terrace. "Tell me everything, Piero. I can't wait another moment."

Before he could respond, Livia came out carrying her cloak. She gave Celeste a furtive glance before laying it over her shoulders. "Would you like me to stay in case you need anything else?"

Instead of answering, Celeste waved her hands to shoo her away. *I'll get an earful for that tonight*, she thought as she lowered herself into the closest chair.

Piero took the chair beside her and turned it to face her. "Are you angry with me, Celeste?"

"Not at all. You must believe me. I'm disheartened that Jacopo forced you to keep his whereabouts from me all these years. The last I heard of him was when your sister Rosa wrote to tell me the two of you had nursed Jacopo back to help and given him work until he was strong enough to return to Florence or Venice. Then, not another word. None of this makes sense. Why would he prevent you from telling me the truth?"

"Patience, Celeste, so I can explain. Rosa was right that I initially planned on Jacopo's stay to be temporary. Honestly, I had little faith in his ability or desire to change his appalling behavior. But as the weeks passed, a new man began to emerge. He abstained from drink and worked harder than anyone I'd ever seen to mend his ways. He truly was contrite and ashamed of what he had become. He even started attending mass and confession regularly. I kept him on and continued to mentor him. Jacopo has become an indispensable asset to me." She turned away, struggling to stave off the tears stinging her eyes. "Does this upset you, Celeste?"

She pulled her handkerchief from her sleeve and wiped her tears as she turned to face him. "You couldn't have told me anything about Jacopo that would have astonished or pleased me more. This is wonderful news, Piero! But why not contact his family after all these years?"

"One word; shame. After a time, he became so embarrassed by his abominable behavior at your gala he couldn't bear to face you. Jacopo believed you and Luciano would never accept an apology. I tried to convince him otherwise, but he was adamant. As the years passed, I stopped trying."

She leaned closer and said, "Is my brother with you in Milan? May I see him?"

He shook his head. "I'm sorry to disappoint you, but I left him in Rome to manage my affairs. I never expected to see you here. If only I'd known you were coming to Milan."

His words trailed off, so she said, "The trip was unexpected, but don't concern yourself. I still live in Rome and will contact Jacopo the instant I arrive home."

"I'm pleased to hear that. I'll write Jacopo today and let him know of our conversation. He'll be relieved to know you're willing to see him. Your last reunion with him wasn't exactly congenial."

"No, it wasn't," she replied, recalling the scene ten years earlier during the gala in Piero's palazzo. She'd come upon a drunken Jacopo in a compromising situation with another woman in the garden while his pregnant wife waited inside. As Celeste and Piero worked to diffuse the resulting confrontation with his in-laws, Jacopo blamed Celeste and attempted to run her through with a sword. Piero stepped in and disarmed Jacopo. Celeste hadn't heard a word about Jacopo since Rosa's letter a few months later. She felt Piero watching her, so she smiled to reassure him.

"I assure you, Celeste, Jacopo isn't the same man from that horrible night."

"This is the best news I've received in ages. You are a kind man for taking my brother in. I'm deeply indebted to you."

"You owe me no debt, and Jacopo has repaid me, thousands of times over." He paused and studied her face until she grew uncomfortable under his scrutiny. "How is it you haven't aged? You're as exquisite as ever despite the sadness I sense in you. Leonardo told me of the events surrounding Luciano's death. I was incensed when I heard how he died. Losing another wife was heartbreaking, so I understand the intensity of your suffering."

"The passage of time is softening the blow somewhat, but

the pain will never heal entirely. I fear the scar will always remain."

"You collected your fair share of scars in your forty years of life. I'm pleased I could lighten your burden with happy news of Jacopo."

"You've given me a much-needed gift today and raised my spirits." She rose and rubbed her hands together. "I'm becoming chilled. We should go inside to the children."

He stood and offered her his arm. As they crossed the terrace, he said, "I would like to host a small dinner to welcome you back to Milan. Is it too soon for you to attend such a gathering?"

Smiling up at him, she said, "It's not too soon. Luca and the twins will be thrilled for an evening out. Thank you for the invitation."

"It will give me something to look forward to as well. Bring Elena, too. She can spend the evening with my children."

Celeste nodded but was quiet as they made their way inside. Nothing about their visit had gone as she'd expected, but she couldn't remember feeling so content since Luciano's death.

ONE MONTH later

"It's late, and I must depart," Maestro da Vinci told Celeste as they pushed their way through the throng in the foyer of Piero's palazzo. "When will our good host learn the meaning of a *small* family gathering?"

"That's a mystery never to be solved," she laughed. "My mother-in-law was the same. Her intimate family dinners included half of Venice."

Leonardo stopped and turned to face her. "It was a fitting farewell to honor you. I shall miss your company, Maestra."

"And I yours, Maestro," Celeste said. "When will you come to us in Rome?"

"I seldom travel to that city, but perhaps we'll meet in Florence one day."

Celeste crossed herself. "God willing."

"Don't forget your vow to me. I expect a letter with news of your finished portrait soon."

"You have my word, Maestro. I'll begin work as soon as I reach Rome."

"And continue to encourage your Angela. She's a bright and talented girl, and I expect great things from her."

Celeste gave a small laugh. "I couldn't stop my daughter from painting even if I wanted to. I wish more people in Rome shared your attitude. All I hear is, 'When will we hear news of your daughters' weddings?'"

Leonardo patted her hand. "We were born before our time, you and me. This is our burden and our curse."

She kissed his cheek and gave him a quick hug. "Truer words were never spoken, especially in your case."

He gave a slight bow and turned toward the door. "Blessed journey to you, friend. May our paths cross again soon."

She watched him until he was out of sight, wishing he lived in Rome. What a treasure it would be to learn at his side every day.

She sighed heavily and spied Angela hurrying towards her. "Has the Maestro gone? I wanted to wish him farewell."

"I'm sorry to say you just missed him." She linked her arm in Angela's and walked with her back to the sala. "He paid you a great compliment." She recounted Leonardo's words, then said, "I happen to agree with the great man."

Her daughter stared up at her in shock. "The Maestro said that about me? If I were a man, I would have begged you to let me stay and apprentice to him. The world isn't fair. Why couldn't I have been born male?"

"A question I've asked myself many times. I must speak with someone before we return to the manor. Please, gather your brother and sisters, and wait for me here."

"Must we go so early, Mamma?"

"Early? It's past midnight. Off with you."

Angela reluctantly sauntered off to do her mother's bidding. Celeste took the opportunity to sneak out to the deserted terrace. As she stood at the railing, she closed her eyes and breathed in the fragrant air. Though it was late autumn, the weather had warmed the previous few days, allowing them to spend more time outdoors. She knew it wouldn't last and wanted to enjoy the lingering final moments before they headed home in three days. It was hard to believe their time in Milan was ending. It felt like they had just arrived. She was reluctant to go, but it was imperative to begin their journey before the weather turned and the roads became impassable. The children had begged her to change her mind and let them winter in Milan, but she was eager to get home and reunite with Jacopo. If not for that, it wouldn't have taken much for the children to persuade her to stay.

She heard a sound behind her and turned to find Piero watching her from the doorway. "It was no surprise I'd find you here," he said as he approached her.

She turned back toward the snowcapped mountains in the distance. "This is one of my favorite views in the world. After much cajoling over the years, I convinced Luciano we needed a summer residence in Milan, but he never had the chance. If we ever manage to liberate Luciano's assets in Florence, perhaps I'll advise Luca to purchase an estate here when he comes of age. I don't think it would take much encouragement. My children adore Milan."

He leaned against the railing facing her and folded his arms. "There's no need to go to that trouble or expense. You and you're family are welcome to stay on my estate whenever you'd like. My palazzo is big enough to house half of Milan. Most of it goes empty, even with all the aunts, uncles, and cousins. I wish I'd been able to persuade you to move here from the manor on this visit. It seems a waste to travel across Milan whenever you leave."

"It was simpler to stay where we are, but I'll consider your generous invitation on our next trip."

She felt a pang of guilt for lying to him, but she couldn't tell him the real reason she'd stayed at the manor. Her passionate feelings for Piero made her feel she was violating Luciano's memory, and she didn't wish him to know. She and Piero had grown closer as the weeks passed, as if the intervening years hadn't existed.

Even though they no longer had marital commitments separating them, she couldn't do that to Luciano. She'd tried to avoid physical intimacy, but it was becoming more difficult each time they were together. She was falling in love, and she was sure Piero felt the same, but the time wasn't right. One of the reasons she'd gone onto the terrace was to clear her head and calm her heart. Yet there he was, standing within arm's reach, tempting her.

She heard his feet shift as he moved closer, so she glanced up at him. He was grinning mischievously. "Why have you been avoiding me all night?"

She took a deep breath to stall before answering. "Need you ask?"

He reached up and brushed a stray lock of hair from her cheek. "Yes. You share my feelings, Celeste. There are no impediments between us, so why do you resist?"

She stared down at her slippers to avoid the intensity of his gaze. "Simple. Time. I don't deny my feelings for you, Piero, but this is all happening too soon. More time has passed since you lost your wife, and her death came on gradually, giving you time to prepare. My Luciano was gone in a flash like lightning, right before my eyes. That tragedy was followed immediately by our family having to flee Florence, only to face the ordeal with Mateo in Venice. We had just gotten settled when I had to uproot my children once more and take them to an unfamiliar city. You were right that first day when you spoke of my scars. They're healing but not healed yet. I can't predict the future, but I beg your patience."

He leaned down and gave her a tender kiss. "You have whatever time you need, my love. I will wait no matter how long it takes. I loved my sweet Simona. I'm thankful for the years I shared with her and the children she bore me, but no woman has compared to you from the first instant I saw you on this very lawn. None ever will."

Her eyes glistened as she gazed up at him. "When the time comes, I vow to give myself wholly to you."

CHAPTER FIFTEEN

ROME 1497

FOUR WEEKS Later

The journey home seemed endless between the muddy roads and her sullen children. She'd been as reluctant to leave Milan as the children but was overjoyed when their palazzo came into view.

"If I never set foot in this carriage again, it will be too soon," Luca said as he leaped out and raced up the front steps.

"Amen," Angela said, massaging her back. "I never thought I'd be so happy to be back in Rome."

Cristina climbed out and linked arms with her sister. "But it'll never be Milan," she said with a sigh.

"That's because you left Messer Vespucci behind." When Cristina scowled at her, she said, "I saw how you gazed at him with dreamy eyes."

When Angela imitated her, Celeste couldn't help but laugh. "You did do a poor job of masking your feelings for the man."

Cristina put her hand to her mouth as the color rose in her cheeks. "He's so handsome and charming. I couldn't help myself, but he hardly seemed aware I existed."

Angela shook her head. "Not true. He couldn't take his

eyes off you that last night at Signore Leoni's dinner. Maybe he'll ask for your hand."

"No hope of that," Celeste said as she shooed them inside. "He's betrothed to another, and I would never consent to a husband for you so far away. How would I live without my Cristina nearby?"

"We would all just have to move to Milan," Elena said. "I could be happy with that."

Celeste reached for Elena's hand as they climbed the steps. "As could I, sweetheart, but we're home, and Rome is where we'll stay."

"And Uncle Jacopo lives here," Angela said. "It's a comfort knowing we have family in the city."

Celeste couldn't help but feel a surge of emotion whenever the topic of her lost brother Jacopo came up. She felt tears well up in her eyes as she said, "That discovery was so unexpected. He truly sounds like a changed man. I'm so thrilled for all of you to meet him. I'll write as soon as we're unpacked."

Angela dropped her cloak in a chair the instant they were inside. Celeste frowned at her, but she pretended not to notice. "Does Uncle Jacopo have a wife or children?"

Celeste was unsure how to explain her brother's complicated situation to her children. Piero told her that Jacopo's father-in-law still refused to let him anywhere near his wife, Gisella, or twelve-year-old daughter, Bella, who he'd never even seen. Piero had attempted to sway the man in Jacopo's favor multiple times, explaining that his son-in-law was a reformed man, but he'd gotten nowhere.

Since their marriage was still binding, neither was free to marry and both had been in a purgatory of sorts for the past decade. Even after ten years, Jacopo harbored no desire to be with another woman. He only wanted to reconcile with his wife, who he had treated so shamefully.

There was no denying Jacopo had once been a cad, a

drunkard, and a womanizer. For those reasons, his father-in-law denied him an opportunity to reunite with his wife and daughter.

Despite ample evidence that Jacopo had repented of his old life and taken full responsibility for his actions, Bernardo Carbone, still stubbornly refused to give his son-in-law another chance. Jacopo vowed to spend the rest of his life putting things right, and Celeste prayed that his father-in-law's heart would be softened.

Celeste gave Angela a brief version of the story, then said, "Your uncle had a troubled past and made some grievous mistakes. His wife and daughter live with her parents, and Jacopo isn't allowed to see or speak with them. He hopes to be reconciled with them one day, but it may never happen."

"That's so sad. Poor Uncle Jacopo," Cristina said. "If he has confessed his sins and repented of his old ways, they should forgive him as God has done."

Celeste cupped her daughter's chin in her hand. "You're right, my tenderhearted Cristina. If only it were that simple. We must pray for your uncle, but it's probably best we don't mention his family when we see him. For now, let's get unpacked."

As she headed for the stairs to her chambers, a footman came toward her carrying a stack of letters.

After handing them to her, he said, "These came while you were gone, mistress. I thought you'd wish to see them right away."

"Thank you, Luigi. Please put them in my sitting room. I'll go through them tomorrow. Have Maria tell Cook we'd like dinner early in our chambers. We've had a long, tiring journey." He gave a quick bow, then rushed off to fulfill her orders. Celeste kissed each of her children, then said, "I'm exhausted and will see you at breakfast. Thank you for joining me on our journey."

After the children wished her goodnight and headed off to unpack, Celeste dragged herself to her rooms. Livia was already there heating her wash water. Celeste tossed the letters on her desk before she lowered herself onto the bed. "Blessed silence," she whispered.

Livia eyed her before saying, "You look as if you pulled the carriage instead of the horses."

She threw her arm over her eyes and groaned. "How is it we're the same age, you do all the hard work, and yet you look as fresh as if you just climbed from bed after a full night's sleep?"

Livia massaged her neck for a moment before answering. "I just hide it better than you do, and I don't have the weight of the world on my shoulders. That can be more exhausting than a long day of manual labor."

"Why is that do you suppose?" Celeste asked without opening her eyes.

"One of life's unsolvable mysteries. You may also feel the weight more after having someone to share the burden in Milan."

Celeste shifted her arm and peeked at her with one eye. "What are you babbling about, Livia?"

Livia raised an eyebrow at her. "How are you feeling after leaving Signore Leoni behind? That can't have been easy."

Celeste sat up and pulled her knees to her chest. "Nothing escapes your notice, does it? I'm missing Piero terribly if you must know." She rested her chin on her knees and stared into the fire. "He wanted me to stay but I wasn't ready to make such a life-altering commitment. My heart is still too raw. I've wondered a thousand times since we left Milan if I made the right choice. Do you believe my leaving Piero was a mistake?"

Livia sat beside her and took her hand. "The children were content in Milan and begged you to stay. You had Piero offering you his heart and a life with him, yet you chose to return to Rome. There is your answer. If you believed it right to be in Milan, that is where we would be. Your intuition is right often enough to be trusted."

Celeste laid her head on Livia's shoulder. "I can always count on you to strike at the heart of the matter, my friend. Where would I be without you?"

"You would probably be asleep by now."

Celeste raised her head and grinned at her. "True enough."

Livia chuckled and said, "Piero aside, I can't believe Master Jacopo is alive and well here in Rome. To be honest, I was certain your brother had gotten himself killed by now. I was truly overjoyed to hear he has mended his ways with the aid of your champion, Piero."

"It is quite miraculous, though Piero takes little credit for Jacopo's transformation," Celeste said, then grew quiet. "I confess I still harbor doubts about my brother. Ten years is a long time, and I trust Piero's judgment, but I've known Jacopo all my life. Mamma used to say he came from the womb making trouble. He's caused more than his fair share of heartache, and I fear being betrayed by him again. I've had enough of that from Veronica and Mateo."

Livia considered her words while she poured water into the basin. "It's reasonable to be cautious, but the only way to know for certain is to meet him."

Celeste climbed off the bed and stretched. "I'll write him in the morning, but my brain is too muddled to tackle the task tonight. Thank you for hearing me out, Livia. I'm feeling more confident in my choice to leave Milan, and truth be told, it feels good to be in Rome again."

As THE CARRIAGE pulled up to the gates of the Colosseum ruins, Celeste questioned her choice of location to meet

Jacopo. She'd chosen the spot as a not-to-subtle reminder of the last time she met Jacopo there ten years earlier. She had been touring Rome that day with Piero and Rosa when she got separated from them inside the ruins. Jacopo had secretly followed her to a secluded area where the ancient seats once stood. They had an ugly confrontation, which ended with her saying she never wanted to lay eyes on Jacopo again. She'd only seen him once since, on the night he threatened her at the point of his sword. If what Piero told her about Jacopo's transformation was true, asking her brother to meet her at the ruins bordered on cruelty.

"What have I done?" she whispered as she reached for Livia's hand. "I should have asked Jacopo to meet me at the palazzo or some peaceful garden. Being here will only dredge up ugly memories for both of us. What was I thinking, Livia?"

Livia shook her head. "Maybe those memories must come to light for the two of you to truly reconcile. Regardless, it's too late for second thoughts. Jacopo is likely waiting for you already."

The carriage pulled to a stop. Carlo had followed on horseback with two house guards. After dismounting the carriage, she ordered Carlo to keep himself and his men out of Jacopo's sight, where they had a clear view of her. As they moved into position, she clung to Livia's hand and insisted she not leave her side.

Livia chuckled at her as she freed her hand from Celeste's iron grip. "Don't be ridiculous, mistress," she whispered. "You were less nervous when you met the Holy Father."

As they crossed the last few yards to the spot where her brother waited, Livia fell a few steps behind Celeste, giving her privacy for her first encounter with Jacopo in more than ten years.

When Jacopo spotted Celeste, he stepped toward her and prostrated himself at her feet with his face pressed to the dusty stone. When Celeste recovered from the shock, images sprang into her mind of Veronica doing the same thing when she and Marco retrieved her from the convent. She'd recognized her sister's behavior for the charade it was, but instinct told her Jacopo was sincere.

She squatted beside him and reached for his hand. "What in the world are you doing, Jacopo? I won't have a brother of mine groveling on the filthy ground. Get up this instant."

Jacopo climbed to his feet but immediately bowed so low that his cap nearly touched the stones. When he straightened, he kept his eyes lowered and said, "I was humbled to receive your kind invitation. I have longed for years to offer my humble apologies for my abysmal behavior the last time we were together when I threatened to run you through with a sword."

Celeste saw Carlo peek around a column and raise his eyebrows at her. She waved him off before putting her hands on Jacopo's shoulders.

"Fine, you've given your apology. Please, quit bowing and speaking to me like I'm the queen and let me embrace you."

Jacopo glanced at her and couldn't help but smile. "If you insist, your majesty. I guess my performance was slightly over dramatic. It made more sense in my head when I concocted the idea."

She couldn't help but laugh as she threw her arms around him and held him close for several moments. When she stepped away, she took a moment to look him over. His appearance to Marco was so similar that it could have been him, except for a few subtle but telling differences. Jacopo was a few inches taller than their brother and had a more dashing air about him and was more gregarious. Both were handsome men, but Jacopo was aware of his attractiveness, which had contributed to his downfall. Like Marco, he strongly resembled their worthless, but handsome papa. Celeste prayed

Jacopo had finally found his way from under their father's shadow.

She took hold of his hand and led him to the stone seats where they'd once spoken as enemies. When he sat beside her, she wiped her cheeks and raised her eyes to his. "When I unexpectedly ran into Piero in Milan, he told me of your transformation, but I struggled to believe it was real. Livia and I feared you were dead, yet here you are as if risen from the grave. I never expected to see you again after that terrible night at the gala."

Jacopo turned and faced Livia, standing ten feet away watching them. Jacopo waved her closer and, as she approached, said, "Hello, Livia. It's refreshing to see some things never change. Are you still woefully insubordinate to your Mistress?"

Livia winked at him as she curtsied. "Only when necessary. You're charming as ever, I see, Master Jacopo."

Celeste gave her a backhanded wave and said, "You may wait for me in the carriage. I'll send Carlo for you if you're needed."

Livia smiled mischievously at Jacopo before scurrying off.

He gave a hearty laugh. "That woman is incorrigible. I don't know why you still tolerate her after all these years."

"You just sounded like Aunt Portia. Livia's my dearest friend in the world, and I literally wouldn't be alive without her."

He sat forward and looked at her expectantly. "Is our aunt with you in Rome? I hoped to reconcile with her if such a thing is possible."

Celeste shook her head. "Poor Aunt Portia passed nearly a year ago, just weeks before Luciano. When our tragedy struck, we had just returned from her funeral in Lucca."

"Two tragedies, then. Poor sister." Jacopo reached for her hand and tenderly held it in his. "Piero told me of Luciano's death. I will regret for the rest of my days that I will never be able to offer my apologies for betraying him. He was a patient, generous maestro, and mentor to me. I didn't deserve all he did for me."

"At first, he blamed himself for failing you, but when I told him of our confrontations here and at the gala, he no longer took responsibility. He'd said you were a grown man making your own choices."

He lowered his eyes and nodded. "He was right, and I'm glad he stopped taking the blame for my failings." He stared over the massive ruins for a moment before turning back to face her. "How are you coping, sister, and what are you doing in Rome? I'd heard you relocated to Venice after the turmoil in Florence following Luciano's death."

She recounted the details of the nightmare in Florence and the ordeal with Mateo in Venice. "This was our last port of call, I'm afraid. We had nowhere else to go. Not that I'm complaining, but it's been lonely without friends or family here." She gave him a warm smile. "But now, we have you."

"Why did you never attempt to contact Piero when you arrived in the city? He's always spoken so highly of you. Truth be told, sister, that man loves you. He never told me in so many words, but I think he helped me initially out of his affection for you."

Not wanting to reveal the real reason behind her reluctance to reach out to Piero, she said, "We've mostly kept to ourselves, needing time to heal. I assumed Piero was living in Rome with his family and hadn't heard of his wife's passing. Piero's been a true friend to me. I'm glad we had the chance to see each other in Milan, and I give Maestro da Vinci full credit for that."

Jacopo studied her for a moment. "I sense there's more you aren't telling me."

She shook her head. "Allow me my secrets, brother. What have you heard of the rest of the family?"

"Nothing. Marco and I kept in contact at first, but I'm ashamed to admit I'm the one who broke off correspondence. It's been several years since I've had any word of the family."

Celeste spent the next half hour updating him on the Gabriele and Vicente clan's doings. He was especially delighted to hear of Bianca and Sandro.

When she finished, he said, "And what of Veronica? You haven't mentioned her."

Her smile faded. She'd purposefully left out mention of Veronica, hoping he wouldn't ask. Since he had, she was forced to tell him the truth.

After hearing her tale, he gave a quiet whistle. "Marco had written of her entering the convent, so I figured she would live there for the rest of her life. Forgive me for dragging up such a painful subject."

She patted his hand. "You couldn't have known, but we'll likely never learn of her fate. It truly is disheartening when she had all she needed for a stable, happy life."

"She sounds like a lost soul, but people can change, right? And Elena? Does she know Veronica is her mother?"

"She does, and I love her as if she were my own daughter. Elena is a well-adjusted, lovely child. You'll see when you meet her."

He smiled and said, "I'm pleased to hear you and Luciano took her in." He grew quiet and leaned against the stone behind him. "So much loss and heartache since we've been separated. I regret not being there to support you when you so desperately needed it, but I was too afraid to reach out because I was so ashamed of what I had done to you, sister."

"I had the help I needed, but it's not all been doom and sadness. We've known our share of joy and success. I would have loved to share it with you, but the past is gone, and we'll leave it buried starting today."

"Sadly, I can't bury all of my past."

She watched him for a moment, seeing the sadness in his eyes. "You speak of your wife and daughter?" He gave a slight nod. "If there's anything in my power I can do to help you, I promise I will."

He hung his head as he rested his elbows on his knees. "I appreciate your kind offer, but there's nothing to be done. I will pay for my sins against my family for the rest of my life, as I deserve to do."

"You cannot predict the future," she said emphatically. "I never could have envisioned a path to being reconciled with you, yet here we are. Perhaps in time, your desires will be fulfilled."

Tears shone in his eyes as he looked up at her. "I'm grateful for your love and forgiveness, sister. After all the pain I've caused you and the loss and heartache you've suffered, you still have a brightness of hope for the future. You truly are remarkable."

When she rose, he joined her. After embracing him, she stepped away and said, "Thank you, brother. I'm just beyond elated to have you back in my life. If your transformation and our reunion are possible, I have hope in an answer to any prayer."

"Your faith is contagious. You almost persuade me to believe in miracles."

"My work is finished, then, brother," she said laughing. "Are you free to return to the palazzo with me and join us for lunch? The children are eager to meet you."

He bowed and offered his arm to escort her back to the carriage. "I would be honored."

CHAPTER SIXTEEN

ROME 1498

AFTER TWO WEEKS of settling back into Roman life, Celeste decided it was time to face her demons. She had consented to be her daughter's Maestra and was setting foot in the studio for the first time since moving to Rome. The trunk containing Luciano's portrait sat locked in the corner, mocking her and daring her to act. She'd made her vow to Leonardo and fully intended to fulfill it but hadn't yet summoned the courage to open the trunk just yet. *Perhaps I just need more time,* she told herself as Angela swept in, eager to get to work.

They spent an enjoyable and productive day together, and Celeste was pleased with Angela's progress. Livia came in and curtsied just as she was removing her smock at sunset.

"Two visitors are waiting for you in the sala, madam, a Messer Fasciano and Maestro Michelangelo. They apologize for arriving without an invitation and ask you to forgive the interruption. They're waiting to speak with you in the sala."

"Michelangelo, here to see me?" Celeste said, raising her eyebrows. "And Messer Fasciano? I don't recall that name."

Livia slapped her palm to her forehead before reaching

into her bodice and pulling out a letter. "My feeble brain. Messer Fasciano asked me to give you this as an introduction."

As Angela watched over her shoulder, she unfolded the letter and began to read.

Most honorable Maestra Gabriele,

You won't remember me, but I was present at your first art exhibition in Florence and was acquainted with your most excellent husband, God rest his soul. Please forgive me for arriving without a proper introduction. I am an art collector and patron who has dealings with Maestro Michelangelo. He mentioned you in a conversation recently and insisted I needed to meet with you to discuss your current situation. Maestro Michelangelo tells me Maestro Vicente served as your patron and manager before his tragic and untimely death and that you've had no patron since. I pray you will give me a moment so we may schedule a more appropriate meeting time.

Most sincerely,

Messer Salvatore Fasciano

"Astonishing," Celeste mumbled as she lowered the letter. "Why would Leonardo tell this stranger about me? He's perfectly aware I no longer paint and have no need of a patron."

"Michelangelo here?" Angela said excitedly. "How thrilling. May I join you to speak with them, Mamma?"

"Certainly not. I would be wasting Fasciano's time and mine. Livia, please thank the gentlemen and tell them I do not wish to arrange a meeting. Bid them farewell on my behalf."

Livia stayed where she was when Angela said, "But why, Mamma? You can't just treat them so rudely, and perhaps they will persuade you to change your mind."

Celeste turned to face her daughter and put her hands on her shoulders. "I'm aware you wish for me to begin painting again, but I have no desire to do so. That part of my life is behind me. I'm sorry if that disappoints you, but my answer is final. I have no wish to meet with these gentlemen, no matter how well-respected they are."

Angela pointed to the trunk. "What about your promise to Maestro da Vinci? You haven't even lifted a brush since we returned to Rome, and you must finish Papa's portrait."

"One painting hardly makes for a career. I'll finish the portrait in my own time, but I could never sell it. Messer Fasciano would have no work to show or sell." Angela frowned at her and crossed her arms as she marched out of the room. Celeste felt Livia staring at her and said, "Didn't I give you an order?" When Livia didn't budge, Celeste turned and glared at her. "My brother is right, you are insubordinate. Well, spit it out. What's wrong?"

She kept her eyes on Celeste as she stepped closer. "I agree with Angela. Your decision is final? You won't reconsider?"

Celeste sighed and rubbed her temples. "I spent the first several years of my career persuading men to allow me to paint and to take me seriously. Now, I seem unable to persuade them to allow me to stop. Shouldn't I be the one to decide when I'm ready to retire?"

"You should. But you must make such a momentous decision for the right reasons."

"Trust me, I am, Livia. Please, do as I ask, then wait for me in my chambers. I'll join you momentarily."

Livia gave her one more disapproving glance before leaving. Celeste stared after her for a full minute before forcing her feet to walk to the trunk. She removed the key for the lock from a hook on the wall above it. After turning it in the lock, she stepped back as it fell open, unable to bring herself to lift the lid. *Too soon,* she thought as she reached up to rehang the key without bothering to close the lock.

"And what is hiding inside that box that frightens you so? A demon?" a voice said behind her.

She spun around to find Michelangelo framed in the doorway, watching her with a mischievous grin. A man she vaguely recognized, who must have been Messer Fasciano, stepped beside him and made a formal bow. She curtsied, then motioned for them to enter.

"Did my maid not give you my message?" she asked as they approached.

"She did, Signora Gabriele, but my friend here chose to ignore her," Messer Fasciano said.

"He's right. The fault is all mine, Maestra." Celeste couldn't help but smile as she extended her hand for Michelangelo to kiss. After he did, he said, "Allow me to properly introduce Messer Fasciano, renowned art patron. Messer Fasciano, meet Maestra Celeste Gabriele."

When Celeste extended her hand to him, he said, "The Maestra requires no introduction. We have met before, though I'm certain she doesn't remember me. I'm honored to see you again."

Celeste led them to a pair of chairs and lowered herself onto the closest one. Messer Fasciano took the other, but Michelangelo remained standing.

"Of course, I remember you, sir, now that I see your face, but I'm afraid you have wasted your time coming here, gentlemen. As you're aware, Maestro, I'm retired and have no need of a patron."

Michelangelo shook his head. "So, you say. Word has reached me that da Vinci is bragging all over Milan that he persuaded you to pick up your brushes. He swears you gave him your solemn vow."

Celeste felt the color rise in her cheeks. She'd hoped her promise would have remained private between Maestro da Vinci and her, but if news of it had reached Rome, even the art guilds must have been aware of it.

"Maestro da Vinci has greatly exaggerated my promise. I merely told him I would complete a portrait of my husband, which I had started before his death. I made it clear to da Vinci that I had no intention of painting anything else. I'm sorry if you misunderstood our informal and private agreement."

Messer Fasciano stroked his beard as he considered her words before saying, "And have you finished the portrait?"

Celeste stood and walked to the trunk. After taking a deep breath, she removed the lock and opened the lid. "To answer your first question, Maestro Michelangelo, there is no demon here. It's only the unfinished portrait in question, and I haven't yet had time to complete it."

"Or maybe you fear painting more than a demon," Michelangelo said.

Celeste gave him a weak smile. "Perhaps."

Fasciano got to his feet and stepped beside her. "May we see what you've completed so far?"

"Messer Fasciano, I'm flattered by your interest, but I will never sell this painting, so showing it to you would be pointless. The work is of a personal nature and will remain with my family."

Fasciano gave a quick bow. "I understand fully, but may I ask to be allowed to view the finished work merely to satisfy my curiosity? I give my word I won't pressure you to sell it."

She gave him a warm smile. "In that case, I would be delighted to show it to both of you when the time comes."

"Don't let that be too long," Michelangelo said. "I agree with da Vinci on this one matter. If you pick up your brushes, the creative forces within you will reignite, and the world will have Maestra Gabriele once more."

Celeste dipped her head in thanks, not wishing to argue the point any further.

Messer Fasciano turned and headed for the door. "Come, Michelangelo, we've intruded on the Signora far too long." Before leaving, he faced Celeste and said, "It's been a pleasure to see you, madam, and I look forward to your invitation to view the portrait."

Michelangelo moved aside for Fasciano to pass but didn't immediately follow him out. Instead, he looked at Celeste with eyes that penetrated her soul. She held his gaze for a moment before lowering her eyes to escape his piercing scrutiny. He gave a slight nod when she dared glance up at him, then hurried out. The silent exchange with Michelangelo left her feeling vulnerable and exposed.

"That man will become a force to be reckoned with," she whispered to the empty room, then left to dress for dinner.

CELESTE SPENT the night tossing fitfully in her bed, disappointed that da Vinci has shared her private commitment, and she couldn't get the searing image of Michelangelo's stare out of her head. As the first rays filtered through her chamber curtains, she quietly put on her robe and slippers, then made her way to the studio. The still-opened trunk greeted her when she entered the room. Before talking herself out of it, she approached the box and retrieved the canvas bearing Luciano's portrait. Once she had unrolled and mounted the painting on the easel, she stepped away to study her work.

Once again, her throat constricted, and her breath caught at the sight of Luciano's lifelike eyes staring out her from the canvas. Fighting the urge to lock the painting away forever, she took three deep breaths and did her best to examine the work with a calm, dispassionate eye. As she did, Marco's words sprang into her mind that it was the most exquisite work he'd ever seen. She thought he was exaggerating then to lift her spirits, but viewing the painting after so long, she was forced to admit his critique may have been accurate. She had painted many portraits but had to admit there was almost something mystical about this work.

Luciano had perpetually scolded her for undervaluing her

skills. Celeste tended to see nothing but flaws when she looked at her paintings. She still saw where the portrait needed corrections and improvements but knew in her heart it was her most accomplished work. She felt a twinge of sadness that it would be her last.

After lovingly preparing her materials, her hand trembled slightly as she picked up her brush and touched the bristles to the paint. The motion gave her an unexpected, almost sensual, pleasure. After checking to ensure she was alone, she closed her eyes and breathed deeply of the comforting smells of oils and pigments and let the familiar sensations of being in the studio wash over her. She granted herself sufficient time to savor the moment, then opened her eyes and stepped up to the canvas.

Before adding the first strokes of new paint, she tenderly ran her fingertips over her recreation of Luciano's cheek. "I do this in your honor, my darling and beloved Maestro," she whispered.

Nothing existed for Celeste but the swish of the brush as she guided the bristles over the canvas. She was oblivious to the passage of time or the buzz in the palazzo as it stirred to life. Curling wisps of hair clung to the perspiration on her forehead. Breathing was a distraction. Ignoring her cramping fingers, she brought the image of Luciano to life on the canvas.

"Mamma, it's magnificent," Angela whispered behind her, making her jump. Celeste spun around and found her daughter gazing at the painting with her hands clasped under her chin. "It's as if Papa were here."

Celeste laid the palette and brush on the table, then massaged her aching fingers as she smiled at her. "I'm so pleased you approve, sweetheart." Celeste took her hand and led her closer to the easel. As they stood side by side studying the painting, she said, "It still needs finishing touches, but I'm quite pleased with it so far."

Angela's eyes widened as she stared at Celeste. "Those are

not words I ever expected to hear from your lips. You've never been satisfied with your work."

Celeste gave a quiet chuckle. "This will be the one and only time."

FOR THE FIRST time Celeste could remember, she wasn't nervous about revealing a finished work. She had invited Maestro Michelangelo and Messer Fasciano to see the portrait as a courtesy, but their opinions mattered little to her. She was content with the quality and knowledge that this was the last painting created by her own hand. She had no intention of selling the portrait and was determined that it would never leave her home.

She sat surrounded by Jacopo and her three eldest children in the sala, patiently embroidering as they waited for the men to arrive. The framed portrait rested on an easel in an area with the most favorable light, making her feel as if her beloved was there with them. Once her visitors had gone, she would have the servants hang the painting in her sitting room, where she could view it each day. The children tried to persuade her to hang it in the sala, but that room was too large and impersonal. She wanted Luciano where the two of them had once sat in the quiet evenings when they'd traveled to Rome.

Bardo came in and bowed before saying, "Your visitors have arrived, mistress."

Celeste calmly laid her embroidery on the side table and said, "We're ready to receive them. Bring them here to the sala."

Angela got to her feet and smoothed her skirts. "I can't believe I get to meet Maestro Michelangelo. What's he like, Mamma?"

Celeste considered her question for a moment before

saying, "Serious and intense, but quite friendly. You will like him."

Bardo led the two gentlemen into the sala just as she finished speaking. Celeste felt her cheeks redden, fearing the Maestro had heard them talking about him. As Bardo presented their visitors, he seemed relaxed and supremely confident.

After kissing Celeste's hand, Messer Fasciano said, "I've looked forward to this day since our last meeting."

Celeste gave him a demure smile. "I hope not to disappoint you."

She introduced her brother and children, struggling not to laugh when Angela stammered while greeting Michelangelo. It was rare for her confident daughter to become flustered.

With introductions out of the way, Celeste said, "Shall we move on to the unveiling?"

She led them to the ideal viewing spot, then asked Luca to remove the covering cloth. He pulled it off with a dramatic flourish before stepping back. Michelangelo and Messer Fasciano gasped as they stared at the painting. Celeste stood behind them, grinning as she quietly watched them. It was the reaction she'd hoped for but hadn't dared expect. As Messer Fasciano leaned closer to the painting, he lifted a round glass hanging from a chain around his neck and held it to his eye. As he scrutinized her work, Michelangelo stood with his arms crossed, intently eying the painting. Celeste was accustomed to rigorous examinations of her artwork, but she began fidgeting when Michelangelo didn't speak for several minutes.

Messer Fasciano finally straightened and turned to face her. "Are you still determined to retire your brushes, Signora?" Celeste gave a slight nod and almost laughed to see the disappointment on his face. "I unequivocally declare that decision a tragedy. You are robbing the world of one of the greatest artists it has ever known. You are healthy and young enough to paint for many years to come. How dare you deprive us of your extraordinary gifts?"

Celeste calmly watched him for a moment before saying, "As I recall, Messer Fasciano, you gave your word not to pressure me. I invited you here in good faith, expecting you to honor your promise."

"She's right, sir," Michelangelo said with a grin. "You did promise."

"I thought you, of all people, would support me on this, Maestro." Fasciano held up his index finger and said, "But you're both only partially correct. As I remember, I said I wouldn't pressure you to sell this portrait. I never said I wouldn't encourage you to keep painting."

Celeste and Michelangelo glanced at each other, and Celeste shrugged. "This is true."

He turned and faced the portrait. "After seeing this, I may be forced to break my word. I could find a buyer in a day." He glanced at Michelangelo over his shoulder. "Come, Maestro, you haven't shared your impression of Maestra Gabriele's work."

The Maestro grew serious as he lifted his gaze back to the portrait. "I can honestly say I've rarely seen this painting's equal. You've given me great heights to aspire to, madam."

The Maestro was young and just beginning his career, but it was obvious he was already a master at his young age. To receive such a compliment from him was profoundly touching.

She nodded and said, "I'm deeply grateful, Maestro. Your words honor me."

Michelangelo turned his intense gaze on her once again. "My statement was not meant as flattery. I agree with Fasciano. To waste such talent is selfish. God blessed you with a magnificent gift for a purpose. You owe it to Him to continue your work. Who knows what sublime works of art you have yet to produce."

She was about to protest when Fasciano interrupted. "Allow me to arrange a small private showing for the portrait. Perhaps some of my collectors will persuade you to continue painting."

Jacopo moved closer to Fasciano and put a hand on his shoulder. "Please, sir, my sister has given her answer. Can we not leave it at that?"

Celeste nodded. "My brother is right. I appreciate what you are trying to do, but I must end this now. The painting is not for public view. It will never leave my possession. Never. The decision to retire is final and is mine alone." She turned her eyes to Michelangelo. "And it is not an affront to God. I have shifted my efforts to training my daughter, Angela, a gifted painter in her own right. I will notify you when the time comes for her first exhibition, Messer Fasciano. Until then, I beg you to respect my wishes."

Fasciano gave her a formal bow. "You have my apologies, madam. Forgive my boldness."

"Most certainly," she said, giving him a warm smile. "Now, we would be honored if you would stay and dine with us."

"Gladly," Michelangelo said as Fasciano nodded his assent.

"Lovely," Celeste said to the Maestro as she took hold of Messer Fasciano's arm. "I'm eager to hear of progress on your Pietà, Maestro."

While they walked toward the dining room, Celeste glanced at Jacopo and smiled. Having her brother back in her life was proving to be a blessing in more ways than she could have hoped.

CHAPTER SEVENTEEN

ROME 1498

One Month Later

Celeste's heartbeat quickened as the carriage approached the palazzo belonging to Piero's brother-in-law, Romeo D'Amico. Signore D'Amico was the husband of Piero's sister, Rosa, who had once been a dear friend. When Rosa had written to invite her to dinner three days earlier, Jacopo had encouraged her to accept, and he gladly agreed to escort her. She replied to Rosa that she would be delighted to attend. She looked forward to seeing her friend after so many years, so her feelings of apprehension baffled her. She and Jacopo had chatted comfortably as they rode along, but she tensed and grew quiet when the palazzo came into view.

Noticing the change in her demeanor, Jacopo said, "What is it? Your face has gone pale. Are you ill?"

Celeste tried to appear casual as she waved off his questions. "I'm perfectly well, only anxious at being in society again, especially with people I haven't met."

Jacopo gave a quiet chuckle. "I've never known you to be nervous about attending a social gathering, and this is just dinner with Rosa's family. If I remember correctly, sister, you're typically the most commanding presence in any room you enter."

She frowned at him. "Are you saying I seek attention and praise?"

"No, Celeste. I'm stating that you have an attractive quality, which makes it difficult for people to resist being near you. I used to be jealous of that."

She gave his arm a playful slap. "What utter nonsense, brother. If anyone possesses that quality, it's you."

"But mine comes from a place of arrogance. I crave attention while you shy from it. I'm a vain and impulsive person, just like our worthless papa and Veronica. You have no idea why people flock to you."

She considered his words for a moment before saying, "I won't disagree about Papa or Veronica, but what you're saying about me is an exaggeration. And let's not forget how much you have changed for the better, my brother."

Jacopo shrugged. "I have changed, but the old me is ever ready to rear his head. It's a constant struggle to keep him buried. Your attractiveness and kindheartedness come naturally, which I envy and now strive to emulate." The carriage stopped, and he said, "Here we are."

After Jacopo climbed out, he extended his hand to Celeste. As she reached for it, she said, "Now you've made me self-conscious and anxious. Thank you very much for that, brother. And please keep the old you under wraps. You remember what happened the last time we attended a party together?"

Jacopo gave a hearty laugh. "Touché. I deserved that. Anyway, you'll forget our entire conversation the instant you greet Rosa. Nothing compares to reuniting with an old friend."

She took his arm and gave it a squeeze. "Or a brother."

He gave a quick nod and patted her hand as they mounted the palazzo steps.

A footman stood in the open doorway and bowed as

Celeste and Jacopo approached. After taking their cloaks, he said, "Please follow me to the sala."

Her conversation with Jacopo distracted Celeste for a moment, but as they followed the footman to the sala, her anxiety roared back to life. She chided herself for being so silly. Rosa and her husband were gracious, kind people. She reminded herself that she had nothing to fear from them. She relaxed somewhat until she stepped into the sala and found it crowded with at least fifty people.

When the footman announced their arrival, the crowd parted as Rosa hurried toward her. She'd always been a beautiful woman with her straight ebony hair, shimmering dark eyes, and brilliant smile, but maturity had made her even more stunning.

She embraced Celeste when she reached her and held her tightly for several moments. When she finally stepped away, she brushed tears from her cheeks and said, "How I've missed you, dear friend. May we never be parted again."

Celeste took her hands and gave her a warm smile. "That is my wish as well. It's wonderful to see you. Thank you for inviting us."

After greeting Jacopo, she took Celeste's hand and led her toward the waiting crowd. "I would have done so sooner, but Piero told me of the loss of your excellent husband and the ordeal afterward. I thought it best to give you your time to recover. The other day at lunch, he assured me I had allowed you enough time."

Celeste stopped and stared at her wide-eyed. "Your brother is in Rome?"

Rosa raised her eyebrows. "Yes, he showed up unannounced on my doorstep last week. Didn't I mention that in my invitation?"

Celeste shook her head, wondering if the omission had been deliberate rather than accidental. Rosa had told her on

more than one occasion that she wished she'd met Piero before
Luciano so they could have been sisters. She could feel Rosa
studying her before bluntly asking, "Are you not pleased to see
Piero?"

Celeste gave her the warmest smile she could manage. "Of
course, I am. You caught me off guard, is all. I assumed your
brother was still in Milan."

Rosa appeared greatly relieved at her comment, and
Celeste began to suspect more was behind the invitation than a
family dinner. Rosa presented Celeste and Jacopo to her
husband, Romeo, then left Jacopo to chat with him while she
took Celeste to find Piero. He was engaged in an animated
conversation with one of his uncles, but he froze when he
spotted her across the room. After several moments, he gave a
slight nod, then broke into a smile as he headed toward Celeste
and Rosa.

When he reached them, he gave a formal bow, then kissed
both her blushing cheeks. "I'm delighted as always to see you,
Signora Gabriele."

"Why so formal, brother?" Rosa asked as she released
Celeste's hand. "I need to check on dinner with the cook. I'll
see you at the table."

Rosa strode off, leaving Celeste alone with Piero. She gave
him a shy smile as she reminded herself to breathe. "I'm
pleased to see you, Piero, but greatly surprised. Why didn't you
tell anyone you were coming?"

Piero offered her his arm before answering, then led her to
a quiet corner. As they walked, he said, "It was a last-minute
decision brought on by something Maestro da Vinci told me."

"What could the Maestro possibly have to do with you
traveling to Rome?"

Before he could answer, dinner was announced. Piero
escorted her to the table and took his seat across from hers,
near Rosa and Romeo. A cousin of theirs peppered Celeste

with questions throughout the entire meal. She and Piero exchanged occasional glances or smiles but had little chance to speak. After dinner, they danced and mingled before Piero whispered for her to meet him on the terrace. She went out first and had to wait several minutes for him to join her.

He waited for her to sit before saying, "What were we saying before we were interrupted?"

"You were going to tell me of something Leonardo told you."

He nodded slowly. "I'll explain in a moment, but you should know I've done more than travel here for a visit. I've left Milan and relocated to my Roman palazzo."

Celeste's heart pounded so hard she feared Piero could hear it. "The surprises keep coming tonight," she said when she'd recovered enough to speak. "Please, tell me what's prompted this. I got the impression you intended to remain in Milan permanently."

Piero moved the second chair closer to hers before sitting. He was near enough that she could feel the warmth of his body and smell his sweet, wine-scented breath.

"I crossed paths with da Vinci at a festival gala, and he mentioned he'd recently received a letter from you. He said you'd finish Luciano's portrait but were still refusing to pick up your brushes. Shortly afterward, he ran into a patron and collector colleague who told him of a most remarkable painting by Maestra Gabriele. He went on and on about what an extraordinary masterpiece it is. Da Vinci hopes to see it for himself one day." He stopped and lowered his eyes. "Since the day of that conversation, I have thought of nothing but you. I know you well enough to predict that you've discovered my subterfuge with my sister in luring you here."

Celeste couldn't help but smile as she nodded. "Your prediction is correct. It wasn't difficult to figure out, Piero. Was Jacopo involved as well? He never let on that you'd returned."

"I swore him to secrecy and shared my intentions toward you. You should know he approves and is very happy for us."

She gave a quiet laugh. "I'm pleased to hear that, but I will need to have words with that scoundrel for keeping secrets. No wonder he was so insistent that I accept Rosa's invitation."

"Please, don't think ill of my sister. Rosa was eager to see you. She's never cherished a friendship as much as yours, but she invited you at my request. I've also informed her of our marital plans."

"I see, but why not just tell me you were back in Rome and would be here tonight?"

Looking her in the eye, he said, "Because I feared you'd refuse to come. I have never been able to predict your actions with any degree of certainty."

As she looked into his face, the memory of his lips pressed to hers when they last met rose in her mind. Her voice was thick as she whispered. "I wouldn't have refused."

He let out his breath in relief. "At our last parting, you said you would tell me when you were ready to become my wife. I've had no word from you in all these months."

She looked down at her hands clasped in her lap. "Piero, I'm not yet ready to take that step, but that doesn't mean I'm not delighted to see you." She glanced up at him and felt a pang of guilt at seeing the disappointment on his face.

"Those are not the words I've longed to hear. I returned to Rome for one reason only, to be near you. While I decided without notifying you first, I believed I'd kept my distance long enough. Luciano has been gone for nearly a year. How much longer will you need?"

She stood and began pacing. "How could I possibly answer that question? My situation is too complicated to set a time limit. The day will come when I'm prepared to give my whole heart and body to you. Until then, I beg you not to pressure me."

He got to his feet and stepped into her path. "As I told you in Milan, I will wait no matter how long it takes. I give you my word that I'll not pressure you, but I must also beg that you do not take too long." He tenderly wrapped her in his arms. "I'm not sure I can survive much longer without you."

When she gazed up at him, he pulled her closer and kissed her passionately. She gave in to her desires briefly, but summoning all her strength, she pressed her hands to his chest and pushed herself free of his embrace.

Between gasps for air, she said, "Piero, I think it best we keep our distance from each other for now."

He reached up and tucked a stray curl under her cap. "As much as I hate to say this, I agree. I can no longer trust myself in your presence."

She reached for his hands and gave him one small kiss. "I think that would be wise. I'll do my best not to keep you waiting too long. For now, it's late. I'd better go. Please take me to find my rascal of a brother."

CELESTE FOUND Jacopo playing an animated game of Primero and resisted her insistence that it was time to leave. With one look from Piero, he immediately got up from the table and bid his farewells. He and Celeste were in the carriage fifteen minutes later. As they rode home, Celeste recounted her exchange with Piero.

When she'd finished, Jacopo said, "I was surprised when Piero told me of your intention to marry. I suspected he loved you, but I had no idea about your feelings on the matter. I'm truly happy for you, Celeste."

"Piero wasn't thrilled when I asked him to wait a bit longer, but I'm not ready to commit to him just yet. I'll know when the time is right."

Jacopo studied her for a moment, then nodded. "I trust you, as I'm sure Piero does."

"I appreciate that." She gave him a mischievous grin. "I should be angry with you for keeping Piero's presence in Rome a secret."

"I could say the same. You never let on about your relationship with Piero."

She turned and looked out the window. "It was a difficult time for me when we met. I'm not sure you're aware that Luciano and I were separated for a brief time."

Jacopo raised an eyebrow. "I never knew. When?"

Celeste let out a weary sigh as she recalled those weeks and months she was parted from Luciano. "When I went on my first art exhibition tour, eleven years ago. Luciano and I had quarreled, and he stormed off to Lucca. I left on the tour before he returned. He regretted his rashness and rushed back to Florence but missed us by hours. We didn't see each other for a year, though we'd reconciled by letter long before the year was up. It was while we were estranged that I met Piero. And found you."

He gave a low whistle. "I had no idea. That must have been so difficult if you were attracted to Piero. I shudder to think how I made your situation even more complicated and stressful."

"It was long ago, Jacopo. Luciano and I reconciled and shared another ten blissful years together. Piero never would have met his Simona, who gave him two wonderful children. It all happened as it was meant to."

"But the story hasn't ended, Celeste. You and Piero have the chance to know happiness once more. What's the real reason you're resisting his proposal?"

She was quiet for several moments before saying, "It used to be because I didn't want to abandon my dear Luciano and his memory out of a prolonged sense of duty to him. But now, fear has taken over. I suppose I fear giving my heart to Piero and losing him as I did Luciano. I'm only now able to speak and think of my beloved without it tearing at my heart. I couldn't bear to suffer through that a second time."

"Do you think Luciano wants you to be happy?"

"Yes, of course, he would desire my happiness and want me to remarry if that is what I wished."

He stroked his beard as he studied her for a moment, and said, "Do you regret your years with Luciano, then?"

She shook her head. "Not for one instant. You know that."

"And if you were to have twenty glorious years with Piero, even if it meant you'd lose him one day, would that not be worth the risk?"

Celeste hadn't ever considered that question. She had only envisioned the pain she'd suffer if she lost Piero the way she did Luciano.

"Well, you'd better hurry and decide. Piero will be unbearable to work for until the marriage contracts are signed," he said with a chuckle.

She gave him a half grin. "Which is no more than you deserve."

～

(ROME 1498, Three Weeks Later)

Celeste was finishing breakfast in her chambers when Cristina came in and handed her a letter. "This just arrived from Aunt Angelica."

Celeste quickly opened the letter, delighted to be hearing from Luciano's sister. Angelica hadn't written in the five weeks since Easter. Celeste generally received letters roughly every two weeks, so she'd begun worrying that something was wrong. "Finally. I hope all is well with our Florentine clan."

Cristina sat beside her and said, "Will you read it out loud so I can hear her news?"

Celeste gave her a warm smile. "Of course, darling. Angelica's letters are always so uplifting." She held the pages up to the firelight and began to read.

My dearest Celeste, I write with most astonishing news. Prior Girolamo Savonarola is dead! He and two of his most devoted followers were hung and burned in the Piazza della Signoria on Papal orders not three days ago.

Celeste stopped and lowered the letter when Cristina gasped.

"Can it be true, Mamma?" she whispered. "Our prayers are answered."

Too overcome to answer immediately, she closed her eyes and took a deep breath before facing Cristina. "Angelica wouldn't have written if it weren't true, but I'm still afraid to let myself hope."

Cristina gestured at the letter in Celeste's lap. "Keep reading, Mamma."

Celeste lifted the letter and went on.

My own dear Silvio witnessed the event. I won't sicken you with the disturbing details, but many, including children, danced in the streets while Savonarola's body burned. Celebrations have been ongoing in our beloved city since that day, and our leaders are busy forming a new republic under the wise guidance of Signore Piero Soderini. There is even talk of electing him leader of the Republic for life.

When Celeste paused, Cristina said, "Do you know Signore Soderini? Is he a good man who will help us redress the wrongs done against Papa?"

Celeste nodded. "He was a friend and supporter of your father and the Medici. I believe we will be able to rely on him."

"What else does my aunt say?"

Celeste scanned the letter for a moment before saying, "Angelica urges us to make haste in returning to Florence. Your uncles Silvio and Giulio have already visited your papa's solicitor and are confident they have a solid case." She finished the letter, then laid it on the side table before rising to her feet. "I must write to your Uncle Jacopo to have him ask Signore Leoni to allow him to accompany us to Florence. I will write to notify your other uncles as well. The letter was dated two and a half weeks ago, and much may have happened in that time."

Cristina stood and took Celeste's hands. "Oh, Mamma, I'm so happy I could burst. Our long exile may soon be over, and Luca can take his rightful place as Duca."

Celeste froze at hearing her words. "No, Cristina. The property belongs to Luca, but the title is Mateo's."

"I'd forgotten. Do you suppose Mateo has heard of Savonarola's death?"

"I imagine most of Italy has heard before us. We must get to Florence and reclaim your brother's estate before Mateo has the chance." She handed the letter to Cristina. "Show this to Angela and Luca and tell them to be ready to travel to Florence come daylight." As Cristina hurried out, Celeste called for Livia and recounted Angelica's letter when she came in from the antechamber.

"Organize the packing. Tell Violetta that she and Elena will join us as well."

Livia's face glowed with excitement. "Are we going home to stay, Celeste?"

Celeste slowly shook her head. "Not yet, I'm afraid. We can't return permanently, but we'll stay in Florence as long as it takes to restore Luciano's estate and repair his good name. Go now. There is much to do."

After spending a hectic day of letter writing and preparations to leave for Florence, Celeste was weary as she descended the stairs on her way to the dining room for dinner. She was concerned that she hadn't heard back from Jacopo. She would make the journey without him, if necessary, but she much preferred to have him at her side for support. Celeste wouldn't blame Piero if he refused to let Jacopo go, but she would be greatly disappointed.

As she crossed the sala, there was a commotion in the foyer. Her stomach tightened as she changed course to find out what was happening. They rarely had visitors, and she wasn't expecting anyone. When she rounded the corner to the foyer, she found Jacopo hurrying toward her with Piero on his heels. Jacopo being there wasn't unexpected, but she was astonished to see Piero. They had only exchanged a few polite letters since the night of Rosa's dinner and hadn't spoken in person.

Jacopo gave her a hearty embrace before kissing her cheeks. "If true, this is miraculous news, sister."

"It is," she said, beaming. "Angelica wrote when Savonarola was excommunicated last year, but never let on that the Florentines had joined the Pope in turning against him."

Piero nudged Jacopo out of the way as he stepped closer to Celeste. He gave her a formal bow and reached for her hand to kiss it. She straightened her shoulders and raised her chin, giving him a welcoming smile.

"This is an unexpected pleasure, Piero. What brings you here?"

He feigned shock at her question as he said, "If you're going to steal my right-hand man away for goodness knows how long, the least you can do is feed me supper."

She couldn't help but laugh. "So, you're saying you'll allow Jacopo to accompany me to Florence."

He gave a slight nod. "Most definitely. I wouldn't hear of you traveling without him."

"Then, we'd be delighted to have you join us for dinner. I'll have the housekeeper send word for Cook to prepare two more plates."

As she turned to go, he reached for her hand to stop her. "Send Livia to do that. I wish to speak with you privately before we dine."

"I'll go to the cook," Jacopo said. "Excuse me."

He rushed off before Celeste could stop him. She had no doubt of what Piero wished to discuss, but she was in no frame of mind for it. All she could think of was getting to Florence, but she had no way to put Piero off without being rude.

She wrapped her hand in the crook of his arm and said, "Let's go to the sitting room where we won't be interrupted."

They walked in awkward silence, and she was relieved when they were seated near each other beside the empty fireplace.

Piero deliberately rested his hands on the arms of the chair and was quiet for several moments before turning to face her. As she grew uncomfortable under his scrutiny, he finally said, "I must know. Were you planning to rush off to Florence without one word to me?"

She sighed, relieved he hadn't repeated his proposal. "Do you truly believe me capable of such a thing, Piero? I planned to send you word the instant I finished dinner."

Seeming unsatisfied with her answer, he said, "So as not to allow me time to bid you farewell in person?"

She leaned closer and laid her hand on his. "That was not my intent. I understand you're growing frustrated waiting for my answer, but it doesn't mean my affection for you has dimmed. My head has been spinning since I received my sister-in-law's momentous news this morning. You understand what this could mean for me, especially my children. It takes enormous work to prepare for such a long journey on short notice, but please, do not assume you haven't been in my thoughts. You always are."

He leaned back and rubbed his face in relief. "I feared you were planning to go home and forget I existed. I even told Jacopo I'd travel with you, but he politely said I would only get in your way."

She gently brushed her thumb over the back of his hand. "I would never consider you to be in my way. It would be difficult to explain your presence, and I'm not yet ready to reveal the nature of our relationship to the world. This is my fight, Piero."

He lifted her hand and pressed it to his lips. "I promised not to pressure you, but every moment away from you is empty and devoid of pleasure. I long to embrace as man and wife. How will I survive this time we're separated? It could be months."

She shook her head. "It won't be. Once Luca is settled in his rightful place, I will return."

"To become my wife?"

Before she could answer, Livia came in and curtsied. "The family is expecting you in the dining room."

Celeste glared at her, then nodded and got to her feet. "Tell them we'll be along in a moment."

Livia looked at Celeste impatiently, then glanced at Piero and back to Celeste before turning to go.

Piero laughed heartily at that and said, "Aunt Portia was right about Livia."

"More than you can imagine," she said, chuckling. "Come, we shouldn't keep the others waiting."

Instead of following her to the door, he pulled her into his arms and gave her a long, passionate kiss. When he pulled away, he said, "I think I should go. You don't need me underfoot distracting you. Safe journey, my love, and may the Lord grant you success and a swift return."

He gave her a final lingering kiss. "What a colossal fool I am," she whispered as she went to join her family.

PART III

FLORENCE, LUCCA & ROME: 1498

CHAPTER EIGHTEEN

FLORENCE 1498

As the carriage crested the hill, the magnificent Duomo came into view. Celeste's heart swelled with joy at seeing her beloved Florence spread out before her.

"On the day we fled to Venice, I never imagined I'd see this city again," she said softly.

"None of us did, Mamma," Luca said as he stared out the window. "It's good to be home, but I'm also uneasy. What if the city leaders reject our petitions?"

"They won't if I have any say in it," Celeste said matter-of-factly.

"As a *mere* woman, you don't have any say," Angela blurted out.

Celeste sighed in frustration. "I can always count on you to confirm my worst fears."

Angela lowered her eyes. "Forgive me, Mamma. I just meant that you'll be barred from the proceedings based solely on your sex."

"How many times must I remind you, daughter? As women, our influence occurs behind the scenes of pivotal events unfolding at the forefront. We possess far greater power to shape the future than you know. You must learn to wield that power for good."

Angela shifted her gaze to Jacopo. "Do you agree with my mother, Uncle?"

Jacopo shrugged. "In Celeste's case, wholeheartedly. I haven't otherwise had the opportunity to witness it in person."

Cristina shook her head. "You diminish our roles as mothers and wives, sister. The influence we have on our children and husbands spans generations. Men wield words and swords. Women shape history."

Celeste gave her a warm smile. "Well said."

Angela just rolled her eyes and looked out the window, unconvinced by her sister's words. Celeste agreed with many of her eldest daughter's opinions, but even she feared they went too far on occasion. "Born before her time," she whispered, recalling the conversation she'd once had with Maestro Leonardo.

"What was that, Celeste?" Jacopo asked after hearing her soft musing.

She shook her head. "Not important. We haven't asked how you feel to be returning to Florence. You haven't been here in how long?"

"Fifteen years," he said and gave a low whistle.

"Hard to believe it's been so long. On the night when I ran away from the city with only the clothes I wore, I had no idea where my path would lead. I hope to make amends for the wretched things I did to my family."

Celeste squeezed his hand. "You paid the penalty years ago. Stop berating yourself. It's a joy to have you with us again."

"How much longer until we're home?" Elena asked. "I can't bear another moment in this wretched carriage."

Luca shifted in his seat and said, "I agree."

"Thirty more minutes," Celeste said, "but we're not going

home, remember? We have to wait until we secure permission to enter the palazzo. We'll be lodging with your Aunt Angelica and Uncle Silvio until then. We're praying it won't be long before we can return home."

"It will be odd to enter our own home as boarders when the time comes," Luca said.

Celeste nodded, "That should be short-lived. Once your papa's holdings are unfrozen, the palazzo will be ours again."

Luca crossed himself. "May they not keep us waiting long."

"Amen," Celeste whispered.

CELESTE SMILED PROUDLY as the family rose simultaneously when she and Luca entered the sala for their first dinner in the palazzo. The customary sign of respect was meant for the Lord of the house, not her. Luciano's holdings hadn't yet officially been conferred upon him, but when he came of age, he would be their Lord with the full rights, privileges, and powers of a nobleman as long as the legal hurdles could be overcome. Celeste fervently hoped the family lawyers would quickly resolve the legal issue imposed by Savonarola and the Frateschi. She couldn't have been happier to see her son taking his rightful place after being denied for so long.

In the week since arriving in Florence, Celeste hadn't felt truly home until she crossed the threshold of the palazzo that morning and saw the servants lined up to welcome them. To mark the long-awaited day, Celeste had invited the entire Vicente clan to join them for dinner. She'd forgotten how many there were until she saw them seated at the tables around the crowded sala. She counted at least forty-five.

As Luca escorted his mother to her seat beside him at the head of the table, he whispered, "Was it necessary to invite all of them, Mamma?"

She smiled as she shook her head. "The family expects this. It's a momentous day, son, and one you rightly deserve, but it's just this once. The servants are here to honor you as well. You must show loyalty and gratitude to them as a just Lord. After tonight, we'll dine quietly with only our immediate family, but you must always be attentive to their needs."

She sat beside Jacopo and nodded at Luca for what came next. It was customary for the Lord of the estate to welcome his guests before the meal began. She'd practiced Luca's speech with him every day since their arrival and hoped he wouldn't be overcome by nerves. She needn't have worried. When he stepped to the head of the table and cleared his throat, their guests quieted, eagerly waiting for him to speak.

Luca held his shoulders straight and raised his chin as he said, "This night has been too long in coming. Since the tragic loss of my revered father, I have longed to stand here to honor him and assume his role as Lord of the household. If Papa were present, he would extend a warm welcome to each of you and thank you all for joining us for this sumptuous feast and raise a glass. I am not as eloquent as my father, but I offer my humble toast." He paused and lifted his goblet. "To the venerable Vicente and Gabriele clans, welcome to our feast, and may you depart with full bellies and hearts."

Celeste scanned the room as they all raised their goblets and drank as one before breaking into loud applause. At that moment, Luca ceased to be her young son and became the man of the house.

As Luca gestured for their guests to resume their seats and begin the feast, Celeste leaned closer to him and whispered, "Masterfully done."

He took a gulp of wine, then wiped his arm on his sleeve and gave her a lopsided grin. "Glad that's over."

She couldn't help but laugh, realizing that in some ways he was still a boy.

As LIVIA HELPED CELESTE prepare for bed that night, Celeste said, "I saw you peeking into the sala when Luca made his speech."

"Of course. I feel Luca is almost as much my son as yours, having been there when he drew his first breath."

Celeste's face brightened. "Didn't he do an excellent job? Just as if he were born to it."

Celeste raised her arms as Livia lowered her night shirt over her head. As she tied the laces at her neckline, she said, "I just want this business with the estate resolved, so the palazzo will be our home again. I can't help but feel like a guest here. I'm ready to put this behind us and get on with our lives."

Livia paused on her way to hang Celeste's gown in the wardrobe and turned to face her. "So, you *are* planning to live in Florence once your troubles are resolved?" Celeste hesitated before giving an unconvincing nod. "And where does Piero fit into that plan."

Celeste looked away in embarrassment. "I haven't worked that part of the problem out yet."

Livia put her hands on her hips and glared. "Don't dare tell me you are considering refusing his offer of marriage."

"What else can I do? We have Jacopo in Rome, but I want my children surrounded by family. You saw how overjoyed they were to reunite with their countless cousins tonight. I haven't seen Cristina and Elena smile so much since we were in Milan. How can I deny them that? My children are Florentines, not Romans. I can't expect Piero to uproot his poor children yet again and haul them to a foreign city where they know no one. Besides, Piero has obligations in Rome. There's nothing for him here. We may love each other, but where would we live?"

Livia gave her a wry smile. "That was quite the speech. Come." Livia pulled Celeste by the hand toward the bed and made her sit. After settling beside her, she said, "These are only excuses, and I am weary of this game you are playing. There is no question sacrifices will need to be made, but if your love for Piero is powerful enough, and I know that it is, those sacrifices will be worth the price."

Celeste looked down and shook her head. "The answer to that is what continues to elude me."

"Consider this. Your children are nearly grown. The twins will each marry soon and begin new lives with their husbands. Luca will have the guidance and support he needs from his uncles here. Elena is young enough that she'd not be as attached to Florence as the others, and she adores Piero's Giuseppe and Serena. I believe she'd be content to stay in Rome with you."

"So, I may have my children or Piero, but not both? How can I be expected to make such a choice?"

"It's not as if your children will disappear. Piero would not object to extended visits here, and the children will come to you in Rome."

"But the children are my world." When Livia put her arm around Celeste's waist, she rested her head on her shoulder. "How would I live without seeing them every day?"

"Simple," Livia said, laughing softly. "You'll still have three children to fill your days with Elena and Piero's two children, and Piero to fill your bed at night."

Celeste raised her head, trying to scowl but couldn't help laughing herself. "Now, that is a convincing argument."

~

"I wish you would sit, Celeste," Elisabetta said. "Your pacing makes me anxious, and you'll wear yourself out. You know how the men are. They may not return for hours."

Celeste spun to face her sister-in-law. "It's not just the men.

Have you forgotten Luca is with them? He's only fourteen. This morning, he was riddled with nerves before they left to meet the solicitor."

"He's not the only one," Elisabetta mumbled as she peered at Celeste.

Celeste scowled at her, wishing Elisabetta would just go home and leave her in peace. In the three weeks since Luca's celebration dinner, Celeste's in-laws had insisted on dining with them every night to make up for the time they'd missed while they were in Rome and Venice. Celeste didn't mind Angelica or Diana joining the family with their husbands, but Elisabetta and Giulio were another matter. They did nothing but grate on her nerves. Giulio considered himself the foremost expert on all legal matters, and Elisabetta continually corrected everything Celeste said or did. If the men didn't get the matter of Luciano's estate resolved soon, Celeste feared she'd lose her mind.

The solicitor was confident they had a solid case and that it was just a matter of plowing through the bureaucracy, but it was slow going. Celeste hadn't expected them to walk into the *Signoria* and demand they unfreeze Luciano's estate. Still, she hadn't been prepared for the incessant delays. She was certain that if she'd been allowed to take charge of the case, Luca would be ruling the estate with the help of his uncles, and she'd be on her way back to Rome.

Angelica got up and wrapped her arm in Celeste's to join her as she paced the room. "Elisabetta's right, sister. This constant anxiety isn't healthy. Silvio said Messer Vitali told him it may take several weeks to completely settle the case. You can't work yourself into a state of nerves every time they meet."

Celeste patted her hand with a smile, then returned to her seat to reassure Angelica. "Honestly, I'm fine, just anxious because today is when the *Priori* is announcing their decision on whether they'll unfreeze Luciano's estate. Sorting out the estate between Mateo and Luca will take time, but at least the solicitor will be free to move forward. Poor Luca understands so little of what's happening. I wish I could do more to put his mind at ease."

Diana waved off her comment. "You're an excellent mother. Luca is devoted to you and is a bright boy. His tutor and uncles have instructed him well. Umberto says all this paperwork is nothing but a pointless trifle. The entire ordeal will soon be behind us, and we may return to our normal lives as if it never happened."

Diana was always the dreamer and had been saying the same for days, so Celeste gave her a weak smile. Celeste had done her best to convince the extended family there was no need to sit with her every time the men met the solicitor, but just as had happened with the dinners, they insisted on staying. Celeste would have preferred to join Angela in her studio or embroider with Cristina in the sitting room.

Celeste was about to feign a yawn and excuse herself for a nap when the men burst into the sala. They appeared agitated or sullen, not cheerful, and enthusiastic as she'd expected. Even the usually reserved Silvio seemed angry.

Luca was pale as he moved toward her with Jacopo on his heels.

Celeste got to her feet and reached for Luca's hand. "What is it, son? Did the *Priori* refuse to release the estate?"

Jacopo pulled off his cap and ran his hand through his hair. "They freed the estate, but that may not matter in the end."

Before she could ask him to explain, Luca said, "My wretched brother, Mateo, has struck our case a serious blow."

Celeste stared at him in confusion. "Mateo? What has he done?"

Giulio came forward and handed her a document. She

quickly unrolled the scroll and felt the strength drain from her legs as she read.

"Well, don't keep us in suspense, Celeste," Elisabetta blurted out. "What does it say?"

Celeste was too overcome to form the words, so Silvio answered for her. "Mateo's solicitor has filed a claim for Luciano's entire estate. Not just Venice. Lucca, Rome, and Florence as well."

Elisabetta gave a backhanded wave. "Let that little monster claim all he wishes. Giulio says Luciano's bequest was clear. He only left the title and Venice to that bastard child."

As Jacopo looked at Celeste with raised eyebrows, she said, "Elisabetta's correct. Luciano assured me years ago that since Mateo was born in Venice, he had no claim on the other holdings."

Giulio shook his head. "Vitale says his solicitor claims that once Luciano, as a Florentine citizen, proclaimed Mateo as his son, the boy became a Florentine. By rights, that made him full heir to all Luciano possessed. To strengthen this legal claim, they pointed out that Luciano raised Mateo in Florence, and the boy came of age here. When Luciano died, he was considered a citizen of Florence by name and in the eyes of the law."

Celeste sank into the closest chair, struggling to draw breath. If Mateo was victorious in his claim, she had no doubt he would strip the entire family of any rights to Luciano's property. She and the children would be at Mateo's mercy for every florin and left without a coin or purse to call their own. The very thought made her physically ill.

"Is there a legal basis for their claims?" she asked between gasps for air.

Jacopo rested his hand on her shoulder. "Vitale began a thorough search through the records immediately after receiving Mateo's filing. He fears it will take time, possibly a year, if not more. This is a very complex issue that needs to be untangled. The records in Florence are poorly organized and difficult to access. Our hope was that this nightmare was nearly at an end. Now, it may just be beginning."

Celeste gestured for Luca to help her to her feet. As she straightened and smoothed her skirts, she raised her chin and faced the family. "Don't think me ungrateful, but I believe you all should return to your homes. I need time to weigh this development. Please, notify me when there's news, but otherwise, I'd rather be left alone."

"Of course, sister," Angelica said before embracing her. "We'll go and leave you in peace."

As they began to file out of the sala, Silvio said, "I'll instruct Filippo not to allow anyone entry into the estate without clearing it through you. I'll also have him send any correspondence connected with the case directly to us."

Celeste nodded. "That's thoughtful of you."

Diana came forward and kissed her cheeks. "Is there anything else we can do?"

"Pray," was all Celeste could think to say.

CHAPTER NINETEEN

FLORENCE 1498

CELESTE WAS on her third stroll of the gardens the following afternoon, trying to make sense of the latest crisis when she spotted Bardo running toward her. *What now?* she thought, not sure she could take much more after having her hopes crushed the day before.

When Bardo reached her, he bowed and said, "I'm relieved to have found you, mistress. I've been searching for nearly half an hour."

He pulled a letter from his tunic and handed it to her. "A courier delivered this from Signore Marco Gabriele in Venice. He instructed me to tell you it's an urgent matter."

"Thank you, Bardo," she said as she started for the house. "I'll read it in my chambers. Is the courier waiting for a response?"

Bardo shook his head as he fell into step behind her. "No, madam. He's already gone."

Celeste didn't say more as she hurried up the steps to the terrace. When she reached her chambers moments later, she tore the letter open while dreading what she might find.

My dearest sister,

I hope you're well and that this missive reaches you in time. I'm writing to warn you that Mateo is on his way to Florence. He may have already arrived by the time you receive this. I've learned through a conspirator in his Venetian household that Mateo intends to claim Luciano's entire estate as his own. You must do all in your power to prevent this.

It should be no surprise that Mateo has made a disaster of the Venetian estate, but it's worse than imagined. As soon as he left the city, I persuaded my conspirator to grant me entrance to the palazzo. What I found was shocking. The house was in complete disarray, and most of the guards and servants have deserted the estate.

My contact tells me his accounts are nearly drained. He spends much of his time in public houses and with courtesans. He runs about with a group of reprehensible sons of noble families, who are draining him of all his funds in riotous living. Respectful merchants and fellow Patricians have closed their doors to him, and he's become a pariah wherever he goes. He ignores his creditors and treats anyone beneath him with disdain and threats of violence. Those guards who remain loyal to him are as reckless and depraved as he is.

I regret to alert you to these developments, but you need to understand what has happened to the family legacy in Venice. You must prevent Mateo from winning his claim over the entire Vicente family holdings, which he would strip bare in a matter of months.

I am preparing to join you in Florence and hope to arrive soon after you receive this message. My prayers and hopes are with you, sister. May goodness and honor prevail.

With deepest affection,

Marco

Celeste wasn't surprised by any of what Marco had written, but she was deeply saddened and disturbed by the description of the Venetian residence. Mateo was doing all he could to dismantle the legacy Luciano had built. Celeste silently pledged to do whatever she could to stop Mateo from destroying everything Luciano had left behind for his family.

After reading the letter, she tossed it in the fire and went in search of Carlo to escort her to her brother-in-law, Giulio. Celeste had kept Carlo close since Mateo imprisoned him in Venice. She had known and trusted Carlo since her early days when she was a nanny for the Vincente family. They had a long history and because of his unquestioned loyalty, trustworthiness, and discretion, she had come to admire and respect the man. He was someone she needed in her corner.

When she found him in the guardhouse playing cards, he rose and bowed before saying, "How may I be of service, mistress?"

She gestured with her head for him to follow her outside and led him toward the carriage house. After ensuring no one was listening, she said, "Please, have Vito prepare the carriage for you to accompany my brother, Jacopo, and me to Signore Giulio Ferretti's palazzo."

"Yes, right away, mistress."

"Thank you. I'll meet you at the front entrance. Please, make haste."

Celeste next went to find Livia and tell her Mateo was on his way to Florence.

Livia crossed herself when she heard the news. "Just hearing his name makes my flesh crawl. You are right to inform Signore Ferretti. We'll need his protection and that of the rest of the family."

"We may need all of Florence on our side," Celeste said as she hurried down the stairs to find Jacopo. "Have you seen my brother today?"

Livia slowly shook her head. "I've not seen him since last night."

Celeste gave a backhanded wave and changed directions toward the foyer. "No matter. We don't have time to search for him. We must go at once."

Livia stopped just inside the doorway and said, "Do you believe it's wise to leave the palazzo without him to escort us?"

"I've already enlisted Carlo as our escort."

Celeste couldn't miss how Livia's mood brighten considerably when she found out they would be traveling with Carlo. Celeste made a mental note of Livia's reaction and promised to ask her about Carlo at a more opportune time.

"Excellent thinking," Livia said as she rushed to catch up with Celeste.

Celeste was relieved to see Carlo mounted up and waiting for them as they rushed down the front steps. As she and Livia were climbing into the carriage, a coach pulled into the drive from the opposite direction. Celeste stopped on the carriage step to see who it was and thought she'd be sick when she saw Luciano's Venetian family crest emblazoned on the door.

Mateo sprang from the carriage as she frantically struggled to figure out what to do. Reminding herself he was still her son, she stepped to the ground and attempted to appear pleased her son was paying an unexpected visit. Mateo kept his eyes locked on hers but couldn't hide his surprise to see her smile and spread her arms as if to embrace him.

Mateo stepped toward her but froze when he noticed Carlo on the horse. His eyes narrowed as he moved closer to him. "You traitor," he hissed. "Dismount my horse this instant and get out of my sight."

As Celeste's smile faded, she gestured for Carlo to stay where he was. "Carlo serves me, and you have no right to issue orders to him. And that is my horse from my stables in Rome."

Mateo huffed at that. "Your horse? Your stables? You may be a famous artist who fancies herself equal to men, but you are only a homeless widow. As such, you own nothing. All of Papa's property now belongs to me."

She dropped her arms to her side and stood tall before her unbalanced, violent adopted son. "Not yet, it doesn't, *son*, and

I'll remind you to watch how you address me. As I told you in Venice, I have allies more powerful than you can imagine, and you would do well not to cross me."

His bravado diminished for only a second or two, but he immediately recovered. "The instant Papa's assets are released, you will be the one who should be on her guard."

"Until then, get off Luca's property, and don't let me find you here again."

Mateo breathed heavily with his fists clenched before turning on his heel and heading back to his carriage. As he rode away, Celeste bent over resting her hands on her knees and took a few deep breaths.

Carlo dismounted and moved beside her as Livia climbed out of the carriage.

"Mistress, I beg you not to leave my sight until Signore Mateo has vacated Florence. Only the lowest sort of man would even conceive of harming his own mother. I fear Mateo is just such a man."

Celeste studied the hint of a scar on Carlo's neck from the beating he suffered at the hands of Mateo's guards. "Don't fret on that score. I had already planned to ask you to stick by my side. Come, we must alert Giulio that Mateo has invaded Florence."

THE DAYS that followed were some of the most intense and fearful days Celeste had endured since Luciano's death. True to form, Mateo made life miserable for anyone who dared cross his path. Word of the battle for Luciano's estate became public knowledge, much to the shame of the Vicentes and Gabrieles. Out of loyalty to Luciano and Celeste, most Florentines sided with her and Luca. A much smaller contingent of patricians, who weren't acquainted with the family or their history, felt

Mateo had a valid claim. Either way, the fight would not be decided by public opinion. The verdict lay with the lawyers and judges.

As the case raged on, Mateo became increasingly brazen in confronting the family. Celeste became fearful of leaving the palazzo and insisted the children remain inside its protective walls with her. Luciano's sisters moved in with their families and husbands' guards. Celeste's earlier annoyance at having them underfoot evaporated in light of the threat she faced. She found comfort in having the family rally around her.

On the fifth morning after her confrontation with Mateo, Marco sent word he'd arrive the following evening. The next afternoon, Celeste had asked the housekeeper to have Cook prepare for an additional guest. She'd gathered the children to welcome their uncle and asked the Vicentes to give them their privacy for the reunion with Marco. Her brothers hadn't seen each other for nearly fifteen years, and Celeste was more than excited to be included in their special reunion.

When Jacopo came in dressed in his most elegant attire, Celeste stood to greet him.

"Look at fancy Uncle Jacopo," Elena said, giggling.

Celeste embraced her brother, then stepped back, examining him from head to toe. "Marco will be flattered to see you dressed in such finery to welcome him."

Jacopo bowed with a comical flair. "I can't meet my famous brother in dusty street clothes now, can I?"

His merriment was contagious, and Celeste felt the tension drain out of her. Laughing softly, she said, "I suppose not, but you never dressed up for me."

Jacopo winked at her. "Perhaps next time."

"Marco cares nothing for fancy dress. He's happiest wearing a paint-stained smock. Luciano was always the same."

Jacopo smiled kindly. "I remember, sister."

Celeste returned to her chair, and Jacopo took the one beside her. "When do you suppose he'll arrive?"

Celeste noticed his fidgeting. "I don't recall ever seeing you so anxious, brother. You and Marco reconciled through your letters years ago. He bears you no ill will and is delighted you've traveled with us to Florence."

Jacopo sank back and blew out his breath. "I've always looked up to our brother and wanted to be like him." He huffed and said, "More than that, I wished to be him. I've always admired his even temper and humility."

"You have your admirable qualities to equal our brother. No one expected you to become Marco. As I once told you, Luciano always said you reminded him of himself when he was young and felt an affinity with you. It broke his heart that he never got the chance to see you grow into your potential. Wherever he is now, he must be very happy to see us together again and the changes you have made."

Jacopo nodded. "Thank you for saying so, Celeste."

They both jumped to their feet at the sound of a commotion in the hallway.

"Here he is," Luca said and headed for the hallway.

He stopped cold in the doorway before making it through, then took several steps back. Instead of Marco coming in behind Bardo, Mateo entered, followed by a contingent of five guards all heavily armed with swords, daggers, breastplates, and helmets. Jacopo, who was unarmed, strode across the sala quickly and placed himself between Mateo and Luca.

Jacopo put on a jaunty air and gave a mischievous smile. "You must be the infamous Mateo I've heard so much about."

Mateo studied him for a moment in confusion before saying, "Who are you? You resemble my uncle, Marco."

"More dashing, right," Jacopo said, laughing. "I'm the other brother, Jacopo."

Mateo, who was armed only with a small, sheathed knife, leaned closer to Jacopo. "Mamma told me you were dead."

"My death announcement was clearly premature."

Keeping her eyes locked on Mateo, Celeste said, "Children, go to your rooms."

"But it's just our brother, Mateo," Elena whined. "I want to stay and greet Uncle Marco."

"Uncle Marco's coming here?" Mateo snapped.

Cristina put her arm around Elena to usher her from the room. "Let's do as Mamma says."

Mateo moved aside and signaled his men to allow the girls to pass. Angela held her head high and sneered at Mateo as she walked by him. When Luca started to follow her, Mateo blocked his path.

"Not you, brother," he growled softly. "You're the person I've come to see."

"You don't give orders here," Celeste said. "Jacopo, please call Luca's guards."

When Jacopo started for the door, Mateo held up a hand to stop him. He swayed sightly, and Celeste could smell the stench of cheap wine on his breath.

"Stay where you are, *Uncle*. My mother is mistaken. Luca has no guards, or perhaps you haven't yet heard the news. The judges ruled in my favor on the estate this very evening. All my father possessed is mine. I am now your Lord and Master. I've just come from celebrating my glorious victory."

"No, this can't be true," she gasped.

Jacopo and Luca rushed to her side and tried to get her to sit, but she brushed them off. The very idea of Mateo wresting Luciano's legacy away from Luca infuriated Celeste. She moved within inches of Mateo. "Why should we believe your lies? What proof can you produce to back your words?"

He raised his palm, and one of his guards placed a scroll in his hand. He held it out for Celeste, but she refused to look at it. Mateo shrugged and unrolled the parchment. "I don't mind reading it if you prefer."

Jacopo snatched it from him and read it silently before turning to Celeste. The color drained from his face, and he shook his head as he handed the scroll to Luca.

"No," Luca whispered. "What he says is true, Mamma."

Carlo marched into the room with four armed guards and signaled for his men to shove Mateo's guards out of the way. The men faced each other with their hands on their hilts, each awaiting the command to strike.

After weeks, months, and years of suffering abuse and torment from Mateo, Celeste unleashed the terrible secret that had lain buried in her for twenty years. "There's something you should know, Mateo. Luciano was never your father. You are the illegitimate product of a liaison between your impure mother and a lecherous man named Marcello Viari. You are a bastard, Mateo."

The room fell silent. The guards on both sides stared at Celeste in stunned silence, probably more from shock at hearing a refined lady speak such words with unfettered ferocity.

Mateo's face turned cherry red, and his breath quickened. "You lie," he hissed. "You would say anything to keep my father's wealth for your *real* son."

"What my sister says is true," Marco said calmly as he entered the room behind Mateo.

"Brother!" Jacopo cried as he strode toward Marco with open arms. They slapped each other's backs and clung together for several moments before pulling apart. "This wasn't the welcome we had planned for you."

Marco clasped Jacopo's shoulder. "It certainly isn't what I expected, but it's wonderful to see you again, brother." He went to Celeste and embraced her before facing Mateo. "I heard what you said as I walked down the hall. Luciano told me with his own lips years ago. He was not your blood father. Your mother, may she rest in peace, confessed the truth to Luciano shortly before you were born."

Mateo's face turned gray, and he looked like he was about to be sick. Celeste continued her attack. "I once caught your mother and Marcello Viari in his sister's garden in the very act of intimate relations. At that time, your mother and Luciano hadn't shared their bed for over a year. He couldn't have been your father. Others can and will testify to your parentage. Not one drop of Vicente blood flows through your veins. You must have wondered why you bear no resemblance to anyone in the Vicente family."

Mateo bent over and vomited on the sparkling clean marble tiles, then straightened and wiped his mouth with his sleeve. Looking at Celeste with pleading eyes, he said, "Then why? Tell me. Why did Luciano ever claim me as his son?"

"There were two reasons. His father died the same day as your mother, and Luciano was called to Florence to arrange his father's funeral and assume his title. He was distraught at losing your mother, even after the disgraceful way she treated him. Your fine grandmother, Francesca Niccolo, pleaded with him to declare you his blood son to avoid a scandal. You were baptized mere hours before he left Venice."

Mateo still eyed Celeste with suspicion. "And the other reason?"

"Your father knew you weren't responsible for your parentage. He adopted you to spare your nonna the shame of your mother's depravity creating a scandal. Luciano loved and respected your Nonna Francesca and declared her his mother. He cared for her and treated her as such for the rest of his life. When she died, Luciano could have left you in Venice with your mother's sisters. Instead, he honored his word to Francesca and brought you here. That's why he only bequeathed the Venice estate to you, which was more than generous when he could have left you in an orphanage."

"Mamma, why didn't you or Papa ever tell me the truth?" Luca stammered behind her.

Celeste turned and put her arms around him. "Your papa and I planned to tell you when you were of age. Then, we felt like the truth no longer mattered. You were our son. We acted in the way we thought best."

"Enough!" Mateo shouted. "This is meaningless babble. It changes nothing. By your own admission, Luciano Vicente legally adopted me, named me his heir, and left me the title. And thus, the judges have decided. That is an end to it."

"But he never meant for all of his estates to be yours," Jacopo said. "His bequeath was clear, and Luca was to have everything but the title, and Venice. How can you knowingly steal what Luciano never intended you to have?"

"Easily, Uncle," Mateo said. "It's done. The ground you stand on is now mine!"

Luca rushed him, but Mateo's guards raised their swords. Marco and Jacopo grabbed him by the arms to stop him.

Giulio strode into the sala at that moment, leading the rest of the Vicentes. He came to an abrupt stop when he noticed Mateo and his guards. He stared Mateo down for a moment, then skirted past the guards to get to Celeste.

"We were dining at the Vespucci palazzo when we heard about the judgement and rushed straight here. Are you all safe?"

Celeste gave a slight nod.

"We'll fight this, Uncle," Luca said as he pulled his arms free of Marco and Jacopo. "I refuse to concede my inheritance to this heartless bastard."

Mateo grabbed the drawn sword of his nearest guard before any of them realized what was happening. He aimed the point at Luca's chest and said, "Hold your tongue, whelp!" Keeping the sword on Luca, he swept his gaze around the room. "You have defamed my honor, belittled me, and denied my rights long enough. I'm putting an end to this dispute now. Master Luca Vicente, I hereby challenge you to a public duel to the death at eleven, four days hence in the Piazza della Signoria."

Celeste uttered an anguished cry and sank to her knees as one of Carlo's guards handed Luca his sword. The boy stared at it for a moment before straightening his shoulders and raising the blade toward Mateo.

"I accept your challenge, sir. I will face you on the designated dueling field, four mornings from today."

Mateo nodded slightly, then tossed the sword back to his guard. "I return to my quarters to prepare the proper documents with my solicitor. I expect to see your acceptance posted in public view by morning. Choose our weapons well, *brother*."

Mateo stepped over his vomit, then, with a swish of his cloak, led his guards from the room to the sound of Celeste's anguished sobs.

WHEN JACOPO and Marco came to their senses, they helped Celeste to her feet and guided her to a nearby chair.

"Luca, do you realize what you have done?" she cried.

Luca raised his chin. "Yes, Mamma. I've stepped up to defend the family's honor from that mongrel."

Jacopo laid a hand on Luca's shoulder. "You understand that accepting the challenge of a duel is a binding contract? You are obligated to fight, and there is no turning back."

Luca shrugged. "I'm not a child, Uncle. I know precisely what I've consented to. I would do so again, given a chance."

Celeste's heart was filled with a paralyzing dread, but she knew she was powerless to prevent the dual from going forth.

"Luca, you are not a child, but Mateo towers over you," Marco said. "He's an expert swordsman and is also very skilled with a dagger. I'm sorry to say I see no way to victory for you."

Carlo stepped forward and bowed. "I offer my life and sword to fight in Master Luca's place as his second. He is not yet of age, so there should be no question of violating dueling regulations. No man has greater desire or justification for fighting Signore Vicente to the death than I."

"No, Carlo," Luca said. "Mateo challenged me. I can't allow you to risk your life in my place."

"Think Luca," Giulio said. "Your day for defending your honor will come. We need you alive now to take your place as Duca and Lord of the Vicente estates. You were right to accept the challenge. You will also be right to allow Carlo to take your place. No one will think any less of you."

Celeste rose and went to her son. "Your uncle is right. Your papa would have been extremely proud to see you defend the Vicente honor, but he would not let you fight an expert swordsman at your age. You have a long promising life ahead of you, son. Don't be so quick to discard it. When Carlo prevails, all your father had will be yours, including his title, but even more importantly, I could not bear to lose you."

Luca looked her in the eye as he considered her words, then turned to Carlo. Extending his right arm, he said, "Carlo Riva, I'm honored to name you my second."

Carlo clasped his forearm and gave him a hearty pat on the back. "Done, Master. This is the choice of a wise man, not a boy. Come, let us choose our weapons."

As Carlo dismissed the guards and headed for the door with Luca, Celeste called out for them to wait. They turned to face her as she approached. When she reached them, she lowered into a curtsy before Carlo. "You have saved my son's life and defended our family's good name. We can never repay your noble sacrifice and are indebted to you."

Carlo shook his head. "I am the one who owes my life to you since through your efforts I was rescued from the dungeons in Venice. Without your swift and thoughtful action, I wouldn't be here today. When I prevail over Mateo, our debts to each other will be paid, and we will begin anew with a clean slate."

"Agreed. But for now, I wish to issue my final command before you leave to prepare for battle. I order you to survive and emerge victorious, for all our sakes, including Livia's. I will never hear the end of it if anything happens to you."

Carlo laughed heartily and said, "I will fulfill your command to the best of my ability. Please, tell Livia I promise not to die, and I owe her a kiss after the duel."

Celeste's smile faded as she watched Carlo and her brave son go to prepare for battle. She saw the irony of pitting her two sons against each other in a duel. Though Mateo was her adopted son, who she'd raised as her own flesh and blood, and while it pained her admit it, she knew he must be conquered. She had faith in Carlo, but he was twice Mateo's age and already carried battle scars from many fights. If he died at Mateo's hand, their lives would change drastically. Not only would she and the children be forced to rely on the mercy of relatives, but all who depended on them would be subjected to Mateo's tyrannical rule.

She crossed herself and uttered a silent prayer before whispering, "Please, be with us in this direst time of need. Direct Carlo's hand and guide him to victory."

CHAPTER TWENTY

FLORENCE 1498

CELESTE SQUINTED in the morning sunlight, wondering why she'd expected the weather on the day of the duel to dawn gray and ominous. The cloudless azure sky felt mockingly out of place for the event about to take place. Though it was still early, the mid-summer temperature was already rising. She was relieved Mateo had chosen late morning for the duel and not the afternoon. Her anxiety was heightened enough, and she didn't need to fear fainting from the heat in front of all Florence.

After raising her parasol above her head, she swept her gaze over the piazza. She had arrived thirty minutes early with Giulio, Silvio, and Umberto and was shocked to see the piazza already packed. The crowd reminded her of when she and Livia followed Veronica to the piazza on the day of Savonarola's sermon. That day felt like another lifetime.

Celeste had hoped attendees for the duel would be limited to family, friends, and required officials. She should have known such a spectacle would draw hundreds of curious onlookers. Most surprising was the sight of Signore Piero Soderini seated on a dais surrounded by other officials she recognized. If those corrupt officials had applied their time and influence to make the correct ruling in their case, the entire ordeal may have been avoided.

Her children and brothers-in-law used their combined powers of persuasion to discourage Celeste from attending the duel, but she refused to miss the event that would determine her family's future. At least a quarter of the crowd was composed of women who seemed to think it was all a lark. She couldn't imagine witnessing such a gory event without good reason. Celeste thought the entire notion of dueling was a foolish way for men to preserve their so-called honor.

The crowd parted for Giulio and the rest of the Vincente entourage as they pushed their way to the front in preparation for the duel. Jacopo and Marco had ridden to the piazza an hour earlier with Carlo and Luca. They would join Celeste before the proceedings began. As Celeste searched the crowd, she feared her brothers would be unable to find her. But only moments after she took her place beside Giulio, she spotted Jacopo coming toward her in his deep red tunic. Marco followed, wearing the red and indigo colors of the Gabriele crest.

She embraced her brothers, then reached for their hands as they stepped to her sides.

Jacopo put his lips close to her ear and said, "How are you holding up, sister?"

"Need you ask? I couldn't swallow even a bite of breakfast."

Giulio leaned closer and said, "This is no place for a lady. We did our best to persuade your sister to stay home. Behold our failure."

Marco and Jacopo shook their heads. "That was a waste of good effort," Jacopo said. "You should know her stubbornness better than that by now."

Celeste scowled at him, then said, "Why must you men settle your offenses with violence?"

Marco raised his eyebrows as if she'd asked the most ridiculous question he'd ever heard. "How would you have resolved our disputes with Mateo, sister?"

She raised her chin and crossed her arms. "I'd find a civilized way, given enough time."

"Don't forget, this was Mateo's doing, not ours," Jacopo said. "He's the one claiming his honor was violated."

"I haven't forgotten, but that doesn't mean I wish Mateo to die. It seems that is to be the likely outcome. We may never know why he turned out the way he did, but perhaps in time, he may have grown into a fine and honorable man. He's young, rash, undisciplined, and prone to violence, but that doesn't mean he's beyond help."

Marco studied her face briefly before saying, "I'm not convinced you truly believe that, sister. Some people just come into the world with hard hearts. Mateo is such a person. Not surprising, considering who his parents were."

She considered his words before saying, "I seem to recall a young man that many had written off as beyond hope of reform." She looked up at Jacopo. "Including me, yet here he stands, as good a man as we could hope for."

Marco reached behind Celeste to pat Jacopo's shoulder. "Excellent point, sister."

The crowd quieted, which caught their attention. She tightened her grasp on her brothers' hands as Mateo strutted onto the dueling field surrounded by his entourage. A modest round of applause sounded in the crowd. Mateo seemed to take no notice. His face was hard as marble as his men removed his cloak before buckling on his heavy leather armor covered in ornately engraved metal. He had the look of a man who feared nothing. Celeste shivered at the sight of him and wondered if her defense of him to her brothers had been unjustified.

Her attention shifted to the opposite end of the clearing as cheers erupted from the crowd when Luca and Carlo stepped onto the field. Luca was doing a respectable job of concealing his emotions, but as his mother, Celeste understood exactly how terrified he was. She whispered a prayer of thanks that he wouldn't be the one facing Mateo.

In contrast, Carlo appeared as relaxed as if he were about to engage in a friendly game of cards. He was old enough to have experienced combat and death and knew better than to exhibit even the hint of fear to his enemy. Carlo wore similar leather armor but without ornate decoration. All that mattered was that it protected the wearer's vital organs from a mortal blow. Celeste hoped Carlo's would serve its purpose.

The two impartial officials overseeing the duel stepped between the opposing parties.

One of the men raised his arms to quiet the crowd and said, "Signore Mateo Vicente has challenged Master Luca Vicente to a duel to the death, claiming his honor defamed and his name insulted. Master Luca accepted his challenge before witnesses five days previous. The required documents have been submitted and confirmed as valid. The courts declared this matter outside their jurisdiction and have approved this contest. The combatants had selected the customary rapier sword and twelve-inch parrying daggers as their weapons of choice. Both parties have requested that we dispense with the customary speeches and move forward with the dual. Combatants, please step forward."

Luca and Carlo moved closer to the officials as Mateo came forward with his second. Celeste wasn't surprised to see he was one of the guards from that awful day in the Venice dungeons. He was taller than Mateo and had a broader chest and shoulders. The definition of his muscles was visible beneath his sleeves. She prayed he wouldn't be fighting in Mateo's place.

The official signaled to two men standing beside a table behind him. The men lifted the table and carried it to the edge of the dueling field. From across the clearing, Celeste could make out two long rapier swords and two parrying daggers resting on the tabletop.

"Seconds, please inspect the weapons," the other officer called out.

Carlo and Mateo's guard walked to either end of the table and picked up each of the weapons in turn, holding them close to examine them and testing the sharpness of the blades. When they were each satisfied, they replaced the weapons, nodded to the officials, and returned to their places.

"We're ready to begin," the first official said. "Combatants, take your weapons."

Mateo swaggered to the table, retrieved his sword and dagger, then turned to Luca with a smug grin. Celeste was sure he thought the duel would be over in seconds. When Carlo confidently sauntered to the table, taking the sword, and sheathing the dagger, Mateo's smugness changed to one of shock.

To murmurs from the crowd, he stormed over to the officials and, pointing to Carlo, said, "What's the meaning of this? I'm to fight Luca Vicente, not his worthless underling."

The official patiently said, "Master Vicente requested that his second fight in his stead, as is his right. The final documents and announcements stated this quite clearly. If you failed to examine them, the fault is yours."

Mateo glared at Luca as he took a few deep breaths. "No matter," he stammered. "Regardless of who I face, this fight will conclude in my favor."

The official said, "Very well, sir. Please take your position."

Mateo took his place, sneering as he eyed Carlo. "Don't

fool yourself into thinking this noble gesture will save your pet, Luca. When I'm finished with you, I'm going for him."

"If you wish to issue an additional challenge," the second official said, "that will have to wait until this matter is concluded."

"Silence," Mateo snapped at him. "Just give the signal."

Carlo stifled a yawn when Mateo turned back to face him. Celeste understood that his nonchalant demeanor was meant to put Mateo off his guard. Celeste, along with the rest of the spectators, was impressed by Carlo's apparent lack of fear.

When the official signaled for the duel to commence, Carlo and Mateo wasted no time running at each other. Mateo's blows were swift and decisive, but Carlo easily parried them. Mateo appeared both surprised and impressed by Carlo's agility and strength.

When roughly five minutes had passed with neither side landing a blow, Carlo switched from defense to the attack. He lunged at Mateo, aiming for his throat, but Mateo deflected the stroke in the last instant. Carlo's blow went wide and nicked Mateo's unprotected arm. Mateo took a few steps back and glanced at his wound. Finding it superficial, he went on the attack, raining blow after blow down on Carlo. He landed a heavy strike to Carlo's chest, but his armor prevented the sword tip from penetrating. Carlo swiftly fell back to recover, but Mateo came at him relentlessly.

As Mateo gained the advantage, Celeste covered her eyes, but couldn't resist peeking between her fingers. Carlo tripped as he stepped aside to avoid a slash to his arm, throwing him off balance. Mateo took advantage of the opportunity and ran his sword through Carlo's thigh. He dropped his sword as blood poured from the wound, but he uttered not a sound. Carlo raised his arms to protect himself and it looked like he was finished. Mateo paused for only a moment to look at Luca before delivering the mortal blow. In that briefest instant, Carlo was able to unsheathe his dagger and execute a stab to Mateo's abdomen.

It didn't appear to be a mortal wound but was enough to send Mateo into a frenzy. He forgot the incapacitated Carlo and went for Luca, who was standing near the officials. With his rapier upraised, Mateo ran wildly at Luca, who was unarmed. Luca called out to Carlo, who tossed him his sword. Luca, in a feat impossible to replicate, caught the sword at the hilt, and in the same motion, slashed at Mateo's neck below his right ear. With blood pouring from the wound, Mateo crumpled in a heap at Luca's feet. In his dying breaths, Mateo fixed his eyes on Luca and mouthed his name as he faded into oblivion. Luca watched him for a moment, then bent over and vomited up his breakfast. When the crowd realized the duel had ended, they broke into boisterous cheers for Luca and Carlo.

As Celeste started for Luca, Marco and Jacopo grabbed her arms and held her fast.

"That's no place for you, sister," Marco whispered. "If you go to Luca now, you'll embarrass him before all of Florence. Promise me you'll stay here and let us handle this."

When Celeste nodded numbly, her brothers released her and headed for Luca and Carlo. After assuring Luca was fine, the three of them rushed to Carlo. The first official examined Mateo's body and signaled for the physician to join him. The physician checked Mateo for a heartbeat before nodding to the official.

"See to the wounded," he said before addressing the spectators. "Signore Mateo Vicente is dead. I declare Master Luca Vicente the victor."

Luca, kneeling beside the gallant Carlo with Jacopo and Marco, tied off Carlo's wound to staunch the flow of blood.

As an official approach Luca, he shaded his eyes from the sun, and said, "What is it?"

"Sir, as victor, it is your right to declare the disposition of your opponent's body."

Luca rose to his feet and turned to address the crowd. "Mateo Vicente was a troubled man and, taking his life was abhorrent to me, but a peaceful resolution of differences was impossible. He was, however, my brother. I grew up at his side, and he deserves to have his remains interred in the Vicente family crypt beside our father. That is my wish."

At a nod from the official, two men came forward carrying a litter. They lifted Mateo's body onto it and waited for instructions from the official.

"Please transport the corpse to the Vicente palazzo for the family to begin burial proceedings." As the men carried Mateo's body to the waiting funerary wagon, he said, "I declare these proceedings adjourned. Please, clear the piazza."

As the crowd dispersed, Giulio said, "Go home with your brothers and take Luca with you. I'll arrange transport and care for Carlo before I go speak to Vitali with Silvio and Umberto." He gently laid his hand on Celeste's shoulder. "Mateo's death changes everything for us. This isn't the conclusion we envisioned, but the result is the same. Your son is now one of the wealthiest and most powerful men in Florence and beyond."

As Celeste watched Giulio go, her emotions churned within her like a turbulent sea. As she told Marco and Jacopo, Mateo had caused them no end of trouble, but he'd been young and confused. He hadn't deserved to die, but he was gone, and nothing could change that. On the other hand, his passing opened the door for the legacy she had always desired for Luca. Sorting out the meaning would be no simple task for any of them, but Luciano's wishes had been fulfilled in the end.

"THERE YOU ARE," Celeste said as she stepped onto the terrace. Luca stood at the railing gazing out over the gardens in the moonlight. She moved beside him and laid her hand over his. "You were quiet at dinner. I understand why and I thought you might wish to talk about what happened today."

He glanced at her with a slight smile before turning back to the view. "I needed to escape the family's endless toasts and celebrations. They all kept congratulating me. For what? Killing my brother? No one even offered Mateo a memorial toast."

Celeste paused for a moment as she considered how to respond. Finally, she said, "I had the same thoughts when I watched them carting Mateo's body away this morning. He was a deeply disturbed young man, and I'm not sure we could have done anything for him. Mateo was going to kill you and possibly even Carlo. If not for the grace of God, we would be placing your body next to your father instead of Mateo's."

Luca bowed his head as he said, "That occurred to me, but it doesn't lessen my revulsion or guilt at what I did."

"You must give it time, son. Your feelings are natural and only prove you are a kindhearted and moral person. Don't be ashamed. You killed your brother in defense of your own life and bear no guilt."

Putting her arm around him, she said, "How does it feel to be the new Vicente Lord and Master?"

"I hardly know. What will this mean for me, Mamma?"

"I spoke with your uncles when they returned from meeting the solicitor. There are no impediments to your inheritance. Mateo never bothered to declare an heir or rewrite the bequest. By law, you're the next one in line for the title and estates. Your uncles will take you to sign the necessary documents in the morning. If you're agreeable, your uncle Giulio will act as your advisor until you come of age, as we planned."

"Of course, I agree. I wouldn't begin to know how to manage such a vast estate."

"I'm wondering about something else," he said softly.

"I can guess what you're going to ask. What will I do now?"

"Yes, Mamma. I sense you want to be in Rome. You must go where your heart takes you. I know little about these things, but I do know you must find your own happiness. Don't stay here for my sake or the twins. Rome is not so far away."

"It's difficult to part with any of you, but I plan to return to Rome for a time to consider my choices. I'll allow Angela and Cristina to decide where they prefer to live. Elena will come with me, of course. We should go inside. It is getting late."

"Wait, before we do, I must ask how Carlo is. Will he lose his leg?"

"No, thank the Lord. The physician said the sword only pierced the fleshy part of his upper thigh. I have a feeling our brave Carlo has suffered worse. He lost a great deal of blood, but if he avoids infection, he'll recover fully, especially if Livia has anything to do with it. She hasn't left his side since they carted him home. I gave her leave to stay with him until he's stronger."

"I plan to visit Carlo before I go up to bed tonight. It's the least I can do since I owe him my life. I wouldn't have lasted one minute against Mateo. Carlo told me his timely throw of the rapier was sheer luck on his part. Just like him to not take credit."

"Yes, we owe Carlo a great debt, and I will spend the rest of my life doing my utmost to repay it."

"As will I."

CHAPTER TWENTY-ONE

FLORENCE & LUCCA 1498

One Week Later

As the carriage rolled to a stop at the convent gates, unwanted memories crept into Celeste's mind when she, Luca, and Mateo had delivered Veronica there eighteen months earlier. She couldn't have predicted how that event would set off a chain of events which would culminate in Luciano's death, and ultimately, Mateo's. Yet there she was with her brothers, going to enquire after what had become of their sister.

Going to the convent had been Jacopo's idea. He'd heard troubling reports that Savonarola's disciples had been ill-treated, exiled, beaten, and even killed after their leader's execution. Jacopo said he wouldn't rest until he learned of Veronica's fate. Celeste had resisted at first, believing their sister had squandered so many chances and had earned whatever treatment she'd received. On reflection, she'd chided herself for such evil, shallow thoughts. Even if Veronica's actions contributed to Luciano's death, Celeste had to admit her sister hadn't meant for any of that to happen. Veronica was many things but not a malicious killer.

Jacopo followed Marco out of the carriage, then offered Celeste his hand, but she couldn't make her body move.

"What is it, sister?" he asked.

Celeste lowered her eyes and stared at her hands clasped in her lap. "Now that we're here, I can't bring myself to face her. I've harbored anger, resentment, and even hatred, for Veronica for so long. For months after Luciano's death, I spent sleepless hours hating her and wishing her ill-will. Those feelings have softened but have not disappeared entirely. I know Savonarola used Veronica as his pawn and played on her vulnerability, but she allowed it to happen. If only she trusted her family more than people who wish to do her harm. That has always been her way."

Jacopo climbed back up and dropped onto the seat beside her. "You wouldn't be human if you hadn't suffered such feelings. Have you forgotten that I once threatened your life at the point of a sword?"

She gave him a wry smile. "Does one ever forget such an experience, brother?"

Jacopo gave a quiet chuckle. "I suppose not. Veronica betrayed you and the rest of the family. I'm not asking you to forget what she did or even forgive her, but Marco and I are not allowed to enter the convent. Without Savonarola to protect her and to pay her stipend, she's entirely alone and destitute, possibly dead. We must at least find out what's happened to her."

Celeste gave a weary sigh as she rose to her feet. "Very well. I'll do what I can to discover what's become of our pitiful sister."

She climbed out of the carriage and headed for the gate with Marco and Jacopo at her side. After tugging on the bell chain, they waited nearly five minutes before one of the Sisters slid open the peek hole cover. When Celeste briefly explained the reason for her visit, the sister immediately swung the gate open for her to enter. She led Celeste across the central courtyard to the back of the cloister. When they reached a cell in one of the darkest corners, she unlocked the door and gestured for Celeste to enter before scurrying off without another word.

When Celeste stepped inside, the first thing to greet her was the stench of human waste. She pulled a perfumed handkerchief from her sleeve and held it to her nose as she waited for her eyes to adjust to the darkness. When she could make out her surroundings, she noticed a waste bucket nearly filled to the rim in one corner, which explained the odor.

A cot covered with a straw mattress stood in the opposite corner. In the dim light, Celeste could just make out the pathetic creature she hardly recognized as Veronica. She had on the same gown she'd worn the night she entered the convent. The strained fabric was in tatters, composed more of rough patches than the original material. Celeste gasped when her sister pushed herself to a sitting position and stared at her with sunken eyes rimmed by black circles. What hair she had left was knotted in matted tangles. No matter what her wayward sister had done, she didn't deserve such appalling treatment.

"Celeste?" she said with a raspy voice. "Are you real or just another vision?" Before Celeste could answer, Veronica leaned forward and sniffed the air like a dog would. "You must be real because my visions never include perfume."

Celeste's voice caught as she said, "I'm real, sister, and I'm here to take you home."

Veronica slid off the cot and crossed the room to Celeste on her knees. When she reached her, she threw her arms around Celeste's legs and sobbed into her skirts. As Celeste stared at the pathetic sight, she shivered after noticing an army of lice covering her head. She was loath to touch her, but she swallowed her disgust and reached down to stroke her hair.

Fighting back tears, she said, "It's going to be all right now, Veronica. Your nightmare is over, and I'll take you away from this place."

Veronica gazed up at her in disbelief. "No, you must go and never return. I deserve to die here. How can you even bear to be in my presence after what I did to you? I got your beloved Luciano killed. I didn't mean to, but I was ultimately responsible."

"Get up now," Celeste said as she helped her to her feet. "It's not your fault. Those evil men used you. Come, let's leave this place. Can you walk?"

Veronica slowly shook her head. "We'll need help. Sister Vittoria doesn't despise me quite as much as the others. She's in the cell five doors down."

Celeste sat Veronica on the cot and hurried to find Sister Vittoria. She was relieved when the woman opened her door. Celeste quickly explained who she was and what she needed. The Sister nodded and followed her back to Veronica's cell. They carried Veronica to the front of the convent, and it took them nearly twenty minutes to reach the gate. Word of Celeste's sudden appearance must have spread because the Reverend Mother was waiting for her.

She bowed and said, "We're relieved to see our poor Signora Gabriele's family come to claim her, Signora."

Celeste thanked Sister Vittoria, then told Veronica to hold herself up with the gate rungs before turning to face the Reverend Mother. "Why haven't you sent word of my sister's deplorable condition?"

"That is not our place or calling, madam. Why have you not called on her before now?"

Celeste stepped closer to her. "My family and I were driven from Florence after my husband's murder at the hands of Savonarola's puppets. I've only been able to return since the Prior's execution."

"Forgive me. I was unaware of your tragedy, but I must ask if you knew your sister was a fervent disciple of the Prior." Celeste hesitated for an instant before nodding. "Then, how is it you're willing to take her with you now?"

"Because I understand the true meaning of charity and forgiveness. How is it you call yourself a Bride of Christ yet treat another human being as if she were a dog on the street?"

"I have no need to justify myself to you, Signora. Many in our order suffered at the hands of Prior Savonarola and his followers. Some were unwitting puppets, like your sister, but they were his disciples, nonetheless. Your sister never took Holy Orders. She is not a true member of our order, but I permitted her to remain here, and I generously provided her with food, a bed, and a roof to cover her head. Most others would not have been so charitable or forgiving."

If the woman considered Veronica's treatment generous, then Celeste knew it was pointless to argue with her. "If you're expecting my thanks, prepare for disappointment. You may justify your cruelty to my sister however you wish, but don't dare to name it charity. You're no better than Savonarola and will one day answer to God for what you've done."

As she helped Veronica toward the carriage, the Reverend Mother whispered, "One less mouth to feed. Good riddance to you both," then slammed the gate behind them.

Celeste was tempted to turn around and slap her but feared God would strike her dead. As Marco and Jacopo rushed forward to help them, she was forced to admit that she'd entertained similar thoughts, so who was she to judge the Reverend Mother?

As her brothers placed their arms around Veronica, they gaped in shock to see the state she was in.

Veronica stared wide-eyed at Jacopo and whispered, "I thought you were dead, brother."

"That seems to be a common assumption." He warmly

embraced his filthy sister before stepping away to get a better look at her. "You're nothing but a skeleton. Let's get you fed and cleaned up. Marco, help me lift her into the carriage."

As they lowered her onto the seat, Veronica squinted in disbelief. "Have I died and miraculously landed in heaven? Marco, what are you doing in Florence?"

Marco smiled warmly down at her. "That is a long story for another time. Welcome home, sister."

CELESTE STOOD on the steps of the palazzo a week later, bidding Luca and Cristina a tearful goodbye. Angela had decided to return to Rome for a time with Celeste, but Cristina had decided to stay in Florence and to help manage the household for Luca, saying it was her calling. Angela had teased that her decision to stay had more to do with Uncle Silvio's charming nephew, whom she'd met at a dinner party a week earlier. Cristina didn't deny her sister's claim. Celeste mentioned the conversation to Silvio at their farewell dinner the previous night, and he'd eagerly promised to check into the matter.

The rest of Celeste's family, including Veronica and Marco, were on their way to Lucca to visit Sandro and Bianca before Marco returned to Venice, and the rest went on to Rome. When Celeste had written ahead to prepare them for the visit, she realized that she and her five siblings would be gathered in one place for the first time in more than twenty years. Her heart felt like it would burst for joy at the thought of it. As heart wrenching as leaving two of her children behind was, she happily anticipated the family reunion.

"It's time to let him go, sister," Jacopo called from the carriage. "We must get on the road before losing too much daylight."

She reached for Luca and Cristina's hands and said, "Take good care of each other and write to me daily. I'll do the same and I promise to return as soon as possible. Rely on your uncles, Luca, and don't hesitate to ask for help." She gave each a final hug, then dabbed at her eyes with her handkerchief. "I love you both. May God smile kindly upon you until we meet again."

She turned and rushed down the steps before she could change her mind. As the carriages pulled away, she wondered if her heart would ever again be whole.

~

LUCCA, Two Weeks Later

Celeste gazed fondly at her siblings gathered around the dining room table, comfortably chatting and laughing as if the years separating them had never existed. The scene was a long-held dream of Celeste's and one she often feared would never come to pass. Marco and Jacopo hadn't seen Sandro and Bianca since they were young, but to any observer, it would appear they'd only been parted for weeks.

In the days since arriving in Lucca, Celeste had known so much joy and contentment. Despite missing Luca and Cristina, and profoundly feeling the absence of Luciano, she was surrounded by her most cherished loved ones. She longed for the family to remain together, but that wasn't possible. Her one comfort was that they'd be free to visit each other as often as they wished in the future.

After dinner, she slipped out to the terrace unnoticed to have a moment alone to say her goodbyes to Lucca before they left for Rome in the morning.

Marco came up beside her as she was enjoying the warmth of the evening breeze and savoring the picturesque view of the valley. "I thought I'd find you here. Forgive me for interrupting." He grew quiet as he joined her, gazing out over Lucca. "It is a beautiful place. I see why you enjoyed painting it so much."

Without taking her eyes from the view, she said, "This has been my favorite place in the world since I first saw it when Portia and I arrived more than twenty years ago. I was delighted when Luca agreed to sign it over to Sandro. He and Bianca grew up in Lucca. It should be theirs."

"I thought Sandro was going to fall out of his chair when you made the announcement at dinner," Marco said, laughing quietly. "He and the steward are meeting with the solicitor in the morning, then he'll be true Lord of the Manor."

"The estate should be his. He's done a magnificent job managing it, as Portia and Paulo did before him. Luciano would have been pleased." She smiled as she turned to face him. "I'm glad we have this rare moment alone. I have something to discuss with you, and I've been waiting for the right moment. Come, sit with me."

As she led him to an ornately carved stone table with two stone benches, Marco said, "Yes, I have something I wish to tell you as well. Please, allow me to go first." When she nodded, he withdrew a tied leather document pouch and handed it to her. "I'm going to present this to Jacopo but decided you should see it first." He smiled when she raised her eyebrows in question. "Just read it."

Celeste untied the pouch and withdrew the single page of folded parchment. She was both confused and touched by what she read. "What has prompted this, brother?"

"Jacopo told me of your relationship with Piero Leoni. I was stunned by the news, to put it mildly. I hadn't the slightest idea of anything more than friendship between you."

Celeste looked away as the color rose in her cheeks. "No one did until quite recently. I never imagined I'd see him again. Then, we unexpectedly crossed paths in Milan."

Marco tapped the document. "Do you now understand the reason behind that? As your eldest and closest male relative, it fell on me to be the one to engage in marriage negotiations on your behalf and sign the contracts. Until I learned of Leoni, I'd given that obligation little thought. After Jacopo told me your secret, I had Fasciano draw up those documents authorizing Jacopo to act as my proxy should the need arise. Since we live so far from each other, I didn't want you to have to wait for me to travel to Rome. Jacopo says Leoni is the best of men and will make you a fine husband."

She gave him a sheepish glance. "Jacopo wasn't supposed to tell you, but honestly, I'm relieved you know, but don't tell him that. This doesn't mean I've made up my mind. It's a complicated situation, and I have much to consider, but I've put that aside until I reach Rome."

Marco laid his hand over hers. "It's not so complicated. Your predicament seems quite simple to me. Do you love this man, Celeste?" When she slowly nodded, he said, "Then you have your answer. The rest will fall into place. Love between marriage partners is rare in our world. You have a chance to know that twice in one lifetime. Don't let that gift slip through your fingers."

"That's wise advice, little brother." She rose and folded the parchment before sliding it into the pouch and handing it back to Marco. "Let's find Jacopo. I want to see his face when you give that to him, and I have a gift for you. I planned to give it to you in the morning before we parted ways, but this seems a more appropriate time."

Marco followed her inside, and they found Jacopo engaged in a chess game with Bianca's husband in the sala. "We need to steal our brother away for a moment," Marco told Enrico.

Jacopo raised an eyebrow at them. "What is this?"

"Trust me, it'll be worth your time," Celeste said.

Jacopo got up but turned to Enrico as he followed them out

and said, "Keep my place, and no cheating." Enrico shrugged and smiled before turning his concentration back to the board. "I know he'll rearrange the pieces while I'm gone. Where are you two taking me?"

"To Sandro's study," Celeste said over her shoulder.

Once they entered the room, she signaled for Marco to hand Jacopo the pouch.

He quickly read it, then patted Marco on the shoulder. "You honor me, brother. I'll do my utmost to act in a manner that would do you proud. And this will expedite matters if our sister ever decides to put poor Piero out of his misery."

Celeste frowned at him, "I told you not to pester me." When Jacopo held up his hands in surrender, she laughed and said, "It's my turn for gift-giving." She took a scroll from the desktop and handed it to Marco. Tears welled in her eyes when she saw his astonishment as he read. "You have the same look Sandro did at dinner."

"Don't keep me in suspense," Jacopo said as he tried to read over his brother's shoulder.

"I can hardly form the words," Marco said. "Luca has gifted me the Venice estate. He shouldn't do this. The value is at least five times that of the Lucca holdings."

He handed the scroll to Jacopo as Celeste embraced him.

"Luca insisted you have the Venice properties," she said as she stepped away and wiped her eyes. "Luciano would have given it to you if he hadn't been bound to pass it to Mateo. No one can ever evict you and your family or dictate where you live. You are now Lord of your own estate."

"But I've done nothing to deserve this."

Jacopo pounded him on the back. "How dare you claim you don't deserve this, brother? If our worthless father hadn't disgraced himself and gotten disowned by the Gabriele clan, you would have inherited an even bigger Venetian estate."

"Aside from that, you've earned this many times over,

Marco," Celeste added. "The documents are on their way to your solicitor in Venice. Once you sign them, take Adrianna and your children home."

He started for the door, saying, "I must write to Luca at once and thank him, though no words will ever be enough."

"Don't go just yet," she said and turned to Jacopo, smiling mischievously. "Don't think I've forgotten you. When, and if, I marry Piero, the Roman palazzo is yours."

Jacopo chuckled and said, "I understand this is a day for throwing estates around like they're no more than pebbles, and it's a generous gesture, but I'm content where I am."

Celeste shook her head. "But I'm not. We can't have you living in Piero's guest house forever. Besides, I don't want you underfoot when I become Mistress of the Leoni palazzo. Most importantly, when the time comes, you need a fitting home to bring your wife and daughter to."

"*If* that time comes, you meant, but you make sound points, sister. We'll have this conversation again *if and when* you accept Piero's proposal."

She held her hand out to him. When Jacopo shook it, she said, "Fair enough. Now, it's late, and we must make an early start. I'll see you both in the morning."

"Wait, Celeste. You tied all our lives up in a tidy bow, except for Veronica. I understand your reluctance to provide for her, but you can't just ignore her. That would make you no better than Savonarola or the Reverend Mother."

Marco put his arm around Jacopo's shoulder and, as he walked him to the door, said, "Don't fret. Veronica will receive all the care she needs. She'll want for nothing for the rest of her life."

∾

As THE LAST trunks were being loaded, Celeste made her way to Bianca's chambers and was pleased to see Veronica already there. Even after more than three weeks, Celeste hadn't become accustomed to Veronica's shocking appearance. Her lice infestation had been so pervasive that the maids had been forced to shave every bit of hair from her body except her eyebrows and eyelashes. Celeste had spent two hours picking the nits from those areas herself. Livia had fashioned a simple but suitable cap out of silk scarves for her shorn head. The dark circles rimming her eyes had begun to fade, and she'd put on a smidgeon of weight. It would take months to recover her strength. For Celeste, the saddest consequence of her neglect and malnutrition was that she'd lost three front teeth. No amount of time would replace those.

When Celeste entered the room, Bianca came forward and embraced her. "I understand why you must go, but I hope so much time won't pass before we see you. This week has been the happiest I've ever known."

"I'm so pleased to hear it. It has been for me, too. I'll come as soon as I'm able, and you must join us whenever I'm in Florence."

Veronica sat silently, watching them from her chair beside the fire. She seldom spoke and often grew confused about where she was and what was happening around her. Celeste wondered more than once if she'd suffered some hearing loss along with her teeth and hair. Veronica recognized family and staff except for those she'd met since coming home. Celeste prayed her sister's mind would heal in time, along with her body and spirit.

Celeste stepped away from Bianca and knelt at Veronica's feet. "I must leave now, but you're going to stay here with Bianca and Sandro. They'll care for you in my place. Do you understand?"

Veronica nodded, but Celeste saw her confusion. "Will they

feed me whenever I'm hungry? What if they run out of money to buy food?"

Celeste glanced at Bianca, who turned away to hide her tears. "As I told you yesterday, dear, Luca has provided Sandro with enough money to buy all the food, clothes, and whatever else you need for the rest of your life. You will live in this beautiful, serene place, surrounded by people who love you."

"Do you not love me, Celeste? Is that why you're abandoning me here?"

Celeste's throat tightened at the question, and she was unable to answer.

Coming to her rescue, Bianca said, "Of course, she loves you, sweetheart, but Celeste lives in Rome and has many responsibilities. She's not abandoning you. We all decided Lucca was the best place for you to recover. You lived here once and cherished this place. Do you remember?"

Veronica's face brightened, and she nodded enthusiastically.

Celeste let out her breath in relief and got to her feet. "You'll learn to cherish it again. Lucca is my favorite place, so I'll visit as often as possible." She kissed Veronica, then gently pressed her hands to her cheeks. "Be at peace, my darling sister, and may the Lord be with you."

Veronica crossed herself, then fingered the simple but elegant cross pendant Jacopo had given her as a welcome home gift. Celeste squeezed Bianca's hand as she hurried out of the room before bursting into tears. Bianca followed Celeste out and held her as she sobbed onto her shoulder.

When she quieted, Bianca stepped away and dried Celeste's face with her handkerchief. "Put your mind at rest. Veronica will be well looked after."

She shook her head. "I don't have the slightest doubt of that. I'm just riddled with guilt for placing this additional burden on your shoulders when you already have five young children and an enormous household to manage."

"Who declared Veronica your sole responsibility? You've always taken on too much. You were forced to take care of us when Mamma died, but we're all grown now. Sandro and I volunteered to take Veronica, and we all agreed Lucca was the best place for her. I'm even looking forward to having one of my sisters close. So, stop berating yourself, and find your own peace. Lord knows you've had troubles enough for ten women."

Celeste blew her nose before smiling up at her. "I shall. Thank you for putting my mind at ease. I love you, sister. Take good care until we next meet."

CHAPTER TWENTY-TWO

ROME 1498

Two Weeks Later

Celeste frowned as she stared at the enormous pile of letters resting on the table beside her chair in the sitting room. The footman had thrust them at her when she walked through the doorway the previous night. She asked him to deposit them in the sitting room, then promptly ignored them for as long as she could.

As soon as Elena and Angela went their separate ways after lunch, Celeste forced herself to tackle the correspondence. She'd spent the past two months with everyone dearest to her and had told Luca and Cristina not to write until they knew she was back in Rome, so it was unlikely the letters contained anything important.

She picked up the top letter and found it to be a month-old dinner invitation from a new acquaintance. She'd make her way through the stack in half an hour if the other letters were similar. She found nothing of importance until she reached the center of the pile and recognized Angelica's writing on the outside of a letter. She eagerly unfolded it, excited to read news of Florence. She wasn't disappointed.

Silvio had spoken with his brother and confirmed his interest in a match between Cristina and Silvio's nephew, Antonio Barsanti. Celeste was delighted Cristina would have a husband close to her age who she was attracted to. She set Angelica's letter aside and would write to her and Cristina as soon as she finished combing through the rest of the pile.

When she read the writing on the third from the last letter, she immediately recognized the name. It was from Maestro Michelangelo's patron friend, Messer Fasciano. Celeste hesitated before opening it, supposing it was only another attempt to persuade her to sell Luciano's portrait. Deciding she had nothing to lose by seeing what he'd written, she unfolded the letter. It was dated just two days after she'd left for Florence. She skimmed the usual greetings at the beginning, then slowed when she got to his purpose for writing.

I recalled you mention to Maestro Michelangelo and me that you are mentoring your daughter, Signorina Angela Vicente. You spoke of your struggles in obtaining supplies and of how much easier your task would be with access to apprentices. This reminded me of the workshop you had in Rome a decade ago. I wondered if I could assist in arranging a similar situation for your daughter. The workshop would be much smaller and of a different nature since the Signorina is not yet a master artist, but I believe the idea is worth discussing. Maestro Michelangelo agrees. If I cannot persuade you to pick up your brushes, perhaps I may assist in carrying on the Vicente and Gabriele legacies.

If you are interested, please contact me at your earliest convenience to arrange a meeting.

Celeste lowered the letter to her lap, unsure what to make of Messer Fasciano's remarkable offer. Celeste and Marco had discussed sending Angela to Venice to train with him but had agreed to wait until Angela had more experience, and Celeste wasn't quite prepared to part with all her children but one. If she accepted Fasciano's offer, Angela could stay in Rome under

Celeste's watchful eye. Her daughter would be thrilled beyond measure to hear the news.

Celeste gave the last two letters a cursory glance and, finding them unimportant, carried Angelica and Fasciano's letters to her desk to answer them at once. Celeste wouldn't mention Messer Fasciano's letter to Angela until she met him in two days. It was pointless to get her daughter's hopes up before she was sure the arrangement would be satisfactory.

After dashing off a quick reply to Messer Fasciano and writing longer responses to Angelica and Cristina, Celeste got to her feet and stretched. After days in the carriage, her legs needed exercise, and she needed fresh air and time to think. As she turned to leave, she caught sight of Luciano's portrait from the corner of her eye. She'd stared at the painting for several minutes when she'd first entered the room and had even carried on a brief conversation with it, but the second time, she studied the painting with a different eye.

During their journey home, Jacopo pestered her to answer why she hadn't decided to answer Piero's proposal. She'd been quick to remind him of his promise not to pressure her, but he'd brushed that off, saying that had been months earlier, and it was cruel to Piero to continue delaying. She begged him to at least give her time to get unpacked before bringing the matter up once they were home. He'd relented, and she'd been glad to see him mount his horse after breakfast to head back to his guest quarters on Piero's estate.

As reluctant as she was to admit it, Jacopo had been right that it was cruel to keep Piero waiting. There had never been any question in her mind that she'd consent eventually, but she hadn't been able to bring herself to take that step. As Luciano stared down at her from his portrait, the reason slowly dawned on her. She hadn't let go of her past and had created an exact likeness of Luciano, attempting to breathe life back into him.

She wanted him beside her, but he was gone. Her logical mind had accepted that truth months earlier, but her heart hadn't.

Her life had changed drastically since Luciano's death. She had changed, yet she desperately clung to a man who no longer existed. She loved Piero. He was the perfect man for her, and he patiently waited for one word while she continued allowing Luciano to linger between them. She would love Luciano for the rest of her days but had more than enough room in her heart for two.

She stepped closer to the painting and kissed her fingers before tenderly pressing them to the frame. "The time has come. Farewell, my beloved."

"Mamma," Angela said, startling Celeste from her thoughts the following afternoon. "Did you hear what I said?"

Celeste sat forward and rubbed her face. "No, forgive me, sweetheart. My mind was wandering, and this gray weather makes me drowsy." She got to her feet and stretched before going to the window. While pulling the curtain aside, she said, "The rain has stopped. I think I'll walk in the garden to clear my head before dinner."

"The fresh air will revive you, and goodness knows you need it. You've been distracted all morning," Angela said as she crushed a lump of azurite with the pestle. "Are you keeping secrets from me?"

Celeste smiled and shook her head as she headed for the studio door. "I'll check back before dinner."

Angela nodded without stopping her work. Celeste took her time descending the stairs since she had no reason to hurry. She had spent the day with Angela but couldn't take her mind off Piero. She'd decided to give herself time to rest and reacclimate before writing and asking to meet with him. She was daydreaming about their coming reunion when Jacopo came running toward the staircase.

When she reached the bottom step, he quickly kissed her cheek and said, "Here you are. I've searched the palazzo for you and just came from your chambers. Livia said you were in the studio."

"It didn't occur to you to start your search there?" When he glared at her, she said, "Come, let's speak in the sala." As she walked beside him, she said, "What's so urgent? Is there an emergency?"

Once they were seated beside the fire, he said, "I didn't want to waste time writing I was coming. I have good news of a sort that I received just an hour ago. Bernardo Carbone, my father-in-law, is dead."

Celeste sat forward, staring at him in shock. "Are you certain? How? Was he murdered?"

Jacopo shook his head. "I've always assumed Carbone would meet his end at the point of a sword, but he died of an apoplectic fit. That foul man is dead, and my wife is free. After allowing her time to grieve, I will fight to win Gisella and my daughter back."

Celeste stood and took Jacopo's hands. "Is it sinful to be grateful a man is dead?"

Jacopo got to his feet and gave her a quick hug. "If it is, God will have to strike both of us down. I've wished for Carbone's swift demise more often than I can count."

"He was a hateful person that the world is well rid of. Does Gisella have male relatives who will oppose you? Does she have protectors?"

Jacopo's brow furrowed as he considered her question. "Carbone was an only child, and his parents are long dead. Gisella's mother died five years ago. I'm unsure if she had any living relatives. If so, they were never mentioned. Gisella has three sisters, two of whom are married. The third took Holy

Orders when she was young. One of the sisters lives in Florence with her husband's family and the other lives in Rome. I've never met her husband and know nothing of him."

Celeste squeezed his hand, smiling encouragingly. "That sounds promising. I'll do whatever you need to help you reconcile with Gisella."

He nodded his thanks. "Piero has offered his help as well. If the three of us approach her together, we may have a better chance of success."

"Perhaps," Celeste said, "but we don't want to overwhelm her. Send a letter of condolence first. Without Carbone acting as a gatekeeper, there's a greater chance it will reach her. I'll also send one to show your family supports her. Can you stay and dine with us?"

"Yes, Piero isn't expecting me back today."

"Perfect. Let's go to the dining room and start planning our strategy."

As she started for the doorway, Jacopo stopped her and said, "I appreciate this, sister. Once again, I don't deserve your kindness and can never repay you."

"Nonsense. How often must I tell you families don't owe each other debts. Gisella became a member of our clan the moment you married her. It's past time she rejoined our fold."

AFTER GIVING Bardo instructions to bring Messer Fasciano to the sitting room when he arrived, Celeste went ahead to wait for him. When she entered the room, she was pleased to see her servants had placed Luciano's portrait on an ornately carved easel as she'd asked. Not wanting to weaken her resolve, she took a chair facing away from the painting, leaving the other with a perfect view for Messer Fasciano.

She picked up her embroidery to pass the time while she

waited, but her hands were trembling. When she pricked her finger for the third time, she set the stitching aside and searched for a way to distract herself that wasn't quite so painful. As she got up and started for the desk to begin a letter to Cristina, Bardo led Messer Fasciano into the room. Bardo then stepped into the shadowy corner to remain as their chaperon, as Celeste had instructed him to.

Messer Fasciano bowed, then came forward beaming as he kissed Celeste's outstretched hand. "I was thrilled and surprised to receive your letter two days ago, Signora. When I'd had nothing but silence from you for two months, I took that as my answer. I was relieved when you told me you'd been traveling and had just returned to Rome."

She gestured for him to sit, then took her seat opposite him. "I'm sorry for that. Our trip to Florence was unexpected, and we left on short notice without notifying anyone."

"You don't owe apologies or explanations, madam. You could not have anticipated my letter, but better late than never, as they say." He rubbed his hands together enthusiastically as he said, "Shall we move on to the business at hand?"

Celeste held her hand up and said, "Before we do, I have another matter I wish to discuss first. I see you're having difficulty keeping your gaze off Luciano's portrait."

He gave a slight nod, then looked her in the eye. "Forgive me, madam. I don't mean to be rude, but it's such a breathtaking work that I can't tear my eyes away. Thank you for displaying the painting so I could savor it again."

Celeste grinned at him. "I'm pleased you enjoy seeing my work, sir, but it's not on display for your pleasure. I've invited you here to tell you I've decided to sell the portrait. I would like you to serve as an intermediary in finding a buyer."

He stared at her, dumbfounded. "What are you saying, Signora?" he stammered.

She couldn't help but laugh at seeing his shock. "You heard

right, Messer Fasciano. I know I was emphatic about never selling the painting last time we met, but I have changed my mind for personal reasons that I don't wish to share. How long do you estimate it would take to find a buyer?"

He got up without answering and leaned close to the painting, silently studying it for more than a minute. "Today," he finally said, then straightened and turned to face Celeste. "I once described this painting to my best client and told him what a shame it was that you refused to sell. He charged me to secure the painting for him if you ever changed your mind. I can have my men crate it and deliver it to him today."

Celeste slowly rose and moved beside him as they looked at the painting. "So soon?" she said softly. "I wasn't prepared for that."

"And I can likely fetch a greater price than I have for any painting I've ever sold."

Celeste raised her eyebrows as she looked up at him. "And this buyer would pay such a price for a painting he's never seen, on your word alone? Who is he?"

Messer Fasciano wagged his finger at her. "That is his one stipulation. He insists on remaining anonymous. I'm contractually bound to conceal his identity from sellers. Those are his express wishes."

"How mysterious," she whispered, then moved away from the easel. "No matter. Take it away today if you wish." She returned to her seat and folded her hands in her lap. "Now, let's discuss your plans for my daughter."

∽

After seeing Messer Fasciano out, Celeste headed for the studio to give Angela the remarkable news. As she was about to climb the stairs, Bardo caught up with her and handed her a letter that had just arrived. Celeste didn't recognize the writing or seal, and when she asked Bardo who sent it, he just shrugged.

"The courier handed it to me then left without a word, madam."

"Very well," she said as she shooed him away.

Instead of going to the studio, she returned to the sitting room to read the letter. By the time she entered, the portrait and easel were already gone. She felt a stab of regret, knowing the servants had already taken it for packing according to Messer Fasciano's instructions, but she did her best to ignore it. There was no time for second thoughts. Reminding herself of why she was there, she sat in the desk chair and unfolded the mysterious letter.

Dear Signora Gabriele,

I am writing to acknowledge receipt of your letter and thank you for your heartfelt condolences. I must tell you how shocked but grateful I was to receive word from you and your brother, my estranged husband. I have not yet replied to him, believing it better I write to you first.

While I appreciated your words of sympathy on my father's passing, you must understand they were unnecessary. My father was a harsh and even cruel man. Since the death of my dear mother, my daughter, Bella, and I have been little more than slaves in our own home. My father's death has set us free.

I won't deny that Jacopo wounded me deeply by his infidelity those long years ago, but I have wondered many times since if life with him would have been far better than the nightmare I've lived. Signore Leoni sent a touching letter informing me of Jacopo's reformation. He vouches for my husband's character and says he hopes I can see my way to forgive him. Between his words and letters from you and Jacopo, I believe I already have.

Since Bella and I are now alone in the world, my sisters are encouraging me to reconcile with Jacopo. I'm beseeching you to arrange a meeting between us as soon as is convenient for both of you. I must see

Jacopo in person to determine if his transformation is true before I agree to reunite with him.

I eagerly await your reply.

Sincerely,

Gisella Carbone

Celeste reread the letter twice to confirm what it said, unsure if she should cry, shout for joy, or both. "What a day this has been," she whispered to the empty room as she went in search of ink and quill.

CELESTE FEARED her heart would burst through her chest as the carriage pulled up to Piero's palazzo. She'd gone there in secret with only Carlo riding on his horse beside the carriage as an escort. Jacopo was reuniting with Gisella and getting to know Bella, and Celeste hadn't wanted to disturb them. As she climbed from the carriage, she chided herself for not bringing Livia along for moral support.

She'd written to Rosa the previous day, explaining the purpose of her visit, and asking her to make sure Piero would be at home when she arrived. Rosa replied immediately, saying she would be delighted to fulfill Celeste's wishes. Celeste hadn't heard from Rosa since and prayed she'd been successful in making the arrangements. If not, her journey there would have been nothing but wasted time.

It took all her strength of will to force her feet up the stairs at the main entrance. When the footman answered the door, he appeared to have been expecting her, and her fears began to subside. Instead of taking Celeste to the terrace where Rosa told her to wait for Piero, the footman led her toward the sala. Not wanting to correct him and arouse suspicion, she quietly followed, planning to move to the terrace once he was gone. At the doorway, he gestured for her to enter, then bowed and left her alone.

Celeste was familiar with the room, having visited it on many occasions in the past, but this was her first time seeing it since returning to Rome. The room appeared just as she remembered, and she smiled as fond memories of blissful days spent there washed over her. As she swept her gaze over the room before heading to the terrace, something felt out of place. She turned toward the fireplace and froze at what she saw. There, above the mantle, hung two paintings. One was of Piero overlooking his gardens in Milan that she'd painted years earlier. The other was Luciano's portrait.

Before she had time to recover from the shock, Piero came up behind her and said, "You've discovered my surprise, darling."

Unable to tear her eyes from the paintings, she whispered, "How? When?"

"Messer Fasciano is my buyer. One day, he told me of a most exquisite painting by the master painter Maestra Celeste Gabriele. He explained his frustration at failing to persuade you to sell the portrait. When I asked him to describe the painting, I understood in ways he couldn't comprehend. I told him to secure the portrait for me should you ever change your mind, but until then, I urged him to leave you in peace."

As tears flowed down Celeste's cheeks, she said, "Piero, why didn't you tell me?"

Ignoring her question, he said, "Then, just last week, I received the most surprising visit from Messer Fasciano. He appeared on my doorstep with a crate containing the portrait. He offered no explanation but told me the portrait was mine. I gladly had my steward pay him, then ordered my servants to place these two masterful paintings where they now hang. Messer Fasciano had not exaggerated, Celeste. Luciano's portrait is a most extraordinary masterpiece. I've never seen it's equal and never will."

Celeste pulled a handkerchief from her sleeve and dried her tears before turning to face him. "Piero, please send your footman to fetch my brother if he can tear him from the arms of his wife?"

"Your brother? You want *Jacopo* at such a moment?"

"Of course. You need him."

"But why would I possibly need Jacopo now, Celeste?"

"Because you have a marriage contract to negotiate."

He stared at her in confusion before his eyes widened in understanding. He pulled her into his arms and kissed her passionately before calling for the footman.

When the man rushed into the room, Piero said, "Find Signore Gabriele and bring him to me at once, Guido. And fly, my man! Fly!"

PART IV

NEW YORK, NY, USA

EPILOGUE

PRESENT DAY

Luke Vincent raised his coat collar to protect his ears from the frigid air as he ran up the steps of the Metropolitan Museum. Once inside, he stomped the snow from his boots on the marble tiles, and the sound echoed through the nearly deserted museum. It was likely the bitter weather hanging over New York that kept the patrons away, but nothing short of Armageddon could have stopped Luke. He waited his entire life to see the exhibit opening that day.

He navigated his way to the wing of the museum where the new exhibit was housed. He ignored the map he'd grabbed on his way in. He wanted to relish the moment when he discovered the painting. When he spotted the masterpiece hanging majestically on its own wall, he slowed his pace and savored the final few steps. He inched as close to the security rope as possible and gaped at the painting, hardly able to breathe.

He jumped when someone behind him said, "Sublime, isn't it?"

He turned as the curator stepped up beside him. Luke had been too mesmerized by the painting to hear her approach.

"It is magnificent," Luke said as he stared at the work in awe. "I've seen photos of this painting for as long as I can remember, but none of them begin to do it justice."

He and the curator studied the masterpiece for several seconds in silence. Luke wished he had a full day to stay and admire the painting, but he only had an hour before he had to get back to teach his next class. He made a mental note to allow more time in his schedule on his next visit.

"Look at the hands," the curator said, drawing him from his thoughts.

Luke leaned closer and did as the curator asked. Most artists agree that the human hand is one of the most challenging elements to paint, but the hands in the portrait were perfect. It was as if they longed to reach out to touch the observer. An ornate reliquary pendant connected to a heavy gold chain rested in the upturned palm of the subject's left hand. The right hand lay relaxed, palm down, touching the left wrist.

"Have you *ever* seen hands like those?" the curator asked.

Luke turned to her and shook his head. "Never."

"Do you know art?" she asked, still facing the painting. "We've been trying to get this exhibit for years. I consider it the biggest achievement of my career that we finally succeeded."

Luke couldn't help but chuckle at her question. "You could say that I know art pretty well. You have no idea how grateful I'm that you were able to procure this exhibit. I wasn't sure I'd ever have the chance to see the originals."

The curator stepped forward and turned to face Luke with her hands clasped behind her back. Luke guessed the gesture meant she was putting on her curator hat. He bit the inside of his cheek to keep from laughing.

Gesturing to the painting behind her, she cleared her throat and solemnly said, "This painting is entitled *Il Maestro* and was painted by famed female Renaissance artist, Celeste Gabriele. The actual completion date for the work is unknown, but it's estimated to be circa 1515. Maestra Gabriele refused to sell the painting during her lifetime. It passed to her only son, Luca Vicente, upon her death."

"You have the completion date wrong," Luke said, interrupting her. "Celeste Gabriele finished the painting in 1498."

The curator stopped and looked Luke directly in the face for the first time. She leaned within inches of him and studied his features before turning to the portrait. After a minute of studying the painting, she turned back to Luke with her mouth hanging open. He grinned at her, then drew a pendant on a gold chain from his coat pocket. He kissed the pendant, then held it out for the curator to examine. When she recognized it, her eyes grew wider.

She gave Luke a knowing smile. "I see."

"Luciano Vicente and Celeste Gabriele are my direct line grandparents. For as long as I can remember, I've been told how closely I resemble Luciano. That's why I've seen pictures of this painting so many times, especially as I've grown older. Is my family right? Do I resemble him?" Luke turned his head left and right to give her a better look.

"The likeness is astonishing, especially since you're so many generations removed. You could be Luciano's son. It's surprising their genes weren't watered down over time." She held up the pendant. "You're brave to carry this around with you. It should be locked in a vault."

When she handed it back to Luke, he kissed it again and returned it to his pocket. "I took it out of the bank this morning. My father passed it on to me when I graduated with my Master's Degree from Columbia. In painting, of course." The last words caught in his throat, and he looked down, embarrassed by his show of emotion. He quickly wiped his eyes and took a breath. "I brought it to compare to the painting. I'm relieved it's a match. You know how sketchy family lore can be perpetuated over time."

The curator gave a slight nod. "Do you mind if I ask your name?"

"Luke Gabriele Vincent. Our surname was anglicized when my ancestors immigrated to the US in the nineteenth century."

She gave him a slight bow. "Being a direct descendant makes you of noble blood. I'm honored to be in your presence, Mr. Vincent. A Master's Degree in art? Seems your ancestors passed down more than their looks." Luke nodded without responding. "I'm curious why you say the painting was completed in 1498 and not 1515, as is commonly believed? All the sources state it as the estimated year of completion."

"Forgive me for correcting you. I usually don't, not even with my art history professors. Few people outside of family knew of the painting's existence until her death. They included Michelangelo and Leonardo da Vinci, who she swore to secrecy, and her second husband."

She raised her eyebrows in question. "Her second husband?"

"Follow me," Luke said as he led her to a painting hanging on an adjacent wall. The plaque under the work identified the title as *A View of Milan. Subject unknown.* "This man was Signore Piero Leoni, my great-grandmother's second husband. She painted this long before my grandfather's death."

She studied the painting as she had the other, then turned to him with a smile. "It's obvious she had romantic feelings for this man even then. Intriguing. Do you know the story behind this painting as well?"

After texting his assistant, asking him to cover his class for him, he turned to face the curator. "I'm well-versed in every detail behind that painting and much more. Celeste and Luciano's only biological son, Luca, who I'm named for, by the way, kept an account of his parents' histories. We store the journal in the family vault with the pendant, and I've read it many times throughout my life." He gestured toward a nearby bench where they had a clear view of both paintings. Glancing at the portrait of Luciano, Luke took a deep breath. "Let me tell you their true story."

THE END

ACKNOWLEDGMENTS

First, I'd like to thank my talented, award-winning cover designer, Tim Barber, for creating this gorgeous cover. You never cease to amaze.

Thank you to my family and friends, who continue to cheer me on to The End. I feed off your energy, and you strengthen me in times of doubt.

I must thank my husband for patience, endless hours, and sleepless nights he spent helping me bring this project to life. I love you and owe you, big time.

Lastly, thank you to my readers. None of this would have matter without you. I appreciate your continuing kind and enthusiastic support.

ABOUT THE AUTHOR

Eleanor Chance is an award-winning suspense, thriller, and historical women's fiction writer who thrives on crafting tales of everyday superheroes. Her debut novel, Arms of Grace, is a finalist in consideration for production by Wind Dancer Films, a silver medalist in the Readers' Favorite Awards, and a recipient of the B.R.A.G. Medallion.

Eleanor has traveled the world and lived in five different countries. She currently lives in the Williamsburg, Virginia area with her husband, is the proud mother of four grown sons, and Nana to one amazing grand-darling.

She loves hearing from readers! Connect with her at: www.eleanorchance.com or vipclub@eleanorchance.com

Made in the USA
Las Vegas, NV
07 July 2024